In the Kingdom of All Tomorrows

TOR BOOKS BY STEPHEN R. LAWHEAD

In the Region of the Summer Stars
In the Land of the Everliving
In the Kingdom of All Tomorrows

EIRLANDIA · BOOK THREE

IN THE KINGDOM OF ALL TOMORROWS

Stephen R. Lawhead

A TOM DOHERTY ASSOCIATES BOOK

NEW YORK

IN THE KINGDOM OF ALL TOMORROWS

Copyright © 2020 by Stephen R. Lawhead

Edited by Claire Eddy

Map by Jon Lansberg

A Tor Book
Published by Tom Doherty Associates
120 Broadway
New York, NY 10271

www.tor-forge.com

Tor® is a registered trademark of Macmillan Publishing Group, LLC.

The Library of Congress Cataloging-in-Publication Data is available
upon request.

ISBN 978-0-7653-8348-8 (hardcover)
ISBN 978-1-4668-9182-1 (ebook)

Our books may be purchased in bulk for promotional, educational, or
business use. Please contact your local bookseller or the Macmillan Corporate
and Premium Sales Department at 1-800-221-7945, extension 5442,
or by email at MacmillanSpecialMarkets@macmillan.com.

First Edition: 2020

Printed in Canada

0 9 8 7 6 5 4 3 2 1

To the Next Generation
Beginning with
Kit and Gwen

GREAT SEA
NARROW SEA
Robogdi
Venceni
Eridani
Dúnaird
Darini
Concani
Volunti
Nagnati
Cauci
Ulaid
Hill of Tara
Coriondi
Auteini
Brigantes
Laigini
Dead Lands
Breifne
Cruithne
Lands the Scálda Stole

In the Kingdom of All Tomorrows

Aoife

I will remember this day and treasure it always. It began when four young women rushed into the bower we had raised on Tara Hill. In those earliest of days, the hall was only a timber skeleton marked out on the ground and the women's house was still to be planned, much less begun; so I was sleeping in one of the aspen bowers the men had erected for unmarried women and those with infants and small children. In truth, there were so many bowers for so many different folk and families the hilltop looked more like a woodsman's camp than a settlement of any kind.

Still, for all that, it was to me a bright and happy place. I was with my beloved and we were to be married—at long last we were to be married, and this was the day. We had chosen Lughnasadh, at summer's end and autumn's beginning, a time of change and opportunity. Conor's brother, a druid of high rank, had agreed to perform the rite during the celebrations. Unusual, I know, but Rónán was always so kindly toward me. Not so, Liam. To be sure, I always knew Conor's younger brother indulged the hope that I would one day look upon him with more loving eyes. Vexed thing that it was, he kept that poor, sad hope alive and, once he had made certain Conor could never return to Dúnaird and the embrace of his people, he began his assault on my affections. I will forever be in Rónán and Eamon's debt for coming to my rescue when I had fled Dúnaird and Liam's oafish attempt to marry me.

Lughnasadh is much my time of the year—a time-between-times of a sort—for summer has gone and winter has not yet arrived, and the crops are full and ready for the harvest. Among our elders, I have often heard it said that before the Black Ships came, Eirlandia's tribes would gather at Tara for three days of feasting, games, dancing, and music leading to a great fire on Tara Hill on Lughnasadh night. Aye, and there were match-makings and weddings and then, too. Many a maid found her mate, with pledges made and redeemed. My own mother met my father during a Lughnasadh feast. She was dancing in performance of one of the rites and my father, a young warrior of the Menapi tribe, happened to see her. He sought her, wooed her, and wed her the next year. In those far-off, happier times it was common for many tribes to come together for the games and festivities of all kinds.

All this, like so much else, has fallen away in recent years. People hardly dare venture beyond their strong fortress walls, and such festivities as are to be had are poor, thin, shrivelled things indeed.

Ach, but Conor is lord now and he is determined that here at Tara our Lughnasadh would be celebrated with as much of the old flavour as we could command from our mean circumstances. 'We may not be able to make a full return to the old ways all at once,' he said, 'but we can make a start.'

'Will you invite the tribes?' I wondered.

'Some, I think, aye—the Coriondi at least, and maybe one or two others. I would invite the Darini, but Liam would only spurn the invitation and scorn me for it. I will spare him, and myself, that particular humiliation.'

The thought cast him into a gloomy mood, so I said, 'At least Rónán will be here to perform the wedding rite. You can take pleasure in that.'

Conor slipped his arm around my waist and pulled me to him. 'I, for one, mean to take as much pleasure as possible.' He gave me a quick kiss and started away. 'But there is much to be done if we are to feast tomorrow. It won't do to promise an ox and supply a goat.'

'Not if you wish to remain a lord at peace with your people,' I told him as he disappeared. I saw him only fleetingly through the day—now talking to builders and carpenters, now ordering preparations for the feast, now in council with Fergal or Donal about the fianna or some such.

The next morning, I had scarce risen from sleep when the maidens came for me. Four of them, as I say, smirking and giggling and pulling me from my bed. They threw my cloak around me, and led me from the ráth and down to the washing stream—the place where the women bathe themselves and clean their clothes and little ones. Though the sun was new-risen, there were already some of the elder women at the washing stones. They smiled as their younger sisters came twittering down to the water, for they knew well enough what was happening.

The maidens removed my clothes and led me into the cold stream, where I stood shivering while they washed me with soap scented with honeysuckle and meadowsweet. They washed my hair as well, and then drew me from the water to dry me in soft cloths. They bundled me into a clean new cloak, then combed and braided my hair—all the while fluttering around like birds. They plucked flowers from the riverbank and wove them into the elaborate plaits they created.

When my hair was ready, they removed the cloak and dressed me in my wedding mantle—a simple long siarc, but dyed with madder and sewn with tiny shells and pearls and stars made of gold thread. They brought out a fine new green and yellow girdle, and put low-cut, soft leather brócs on my feet.

Then they all stood back and chirped away happily, pleased with their efforts. Each and every one hailed me as a queen of regal aspect, and each one kissed me on the cheek—the last time that familiarity would be permitted them, as I reckon they knew—and then they hugged me and pressed my hands in homage to the friend they had known.

Of course, I knew that it was not merely for myself that they clothed and pampered me so. Nay, it was for themselves and the brides they hoped one day to be that they practiced the age-old preparation rituals of our race. Today, I was all they desired for themselves. Truly, in the deepest part of my heart, I wished them no less.

When I was ready, they led me back up to the ráth, where a simple meal was prepared—the first of several to be served throughout the day. Though it was a festival day, our ráth was so newly begun and so much was yet to be done that the work of the place would continue until later in the day when the invited guests arrived and the festivities began.

And this is the way of the Lughnasadh:

The games are much as you might expect, though very much enjoyed for that. They might vary somewhat one place to another, or so I hear, and change from one year to the next depending on the whim of those taking part. Even so, where a stronghold contains warriors—show me a stronghold that does not, and I will show you a ruin—there will be spear throwing and wrestling and sword skill, and tests of strength of all kinds including the throwing of heavy stones and, sometimes, timber beams. There will sometimes be cammán, though since the games do often descend into brawls and broken heads, many tribes ban them on the day.

There will be racing—both horses and men—and jumping for both.

There will be singing contests and dancing for both men and women and Rónán will tell stories—especially about Lugh Samildánach, the Many-Gifted. Indeed, all the arts fostered and bequeathed by Lugh to the Dé Danann will be indulged and celebrated—or at least as many as can be found among us.

All this will be observed by the lord, who is surrounded by his people. Ordinarily, Conor would take part in the games, but not today and likely not ever again. As lord, it is his place to reward and praise those whose skill or chance grants them victory and it is unseemly for any lord to laud himself in this way.

Then, when all the games and contests are finished and the sun has drifted low, thoughts will turn to the feast, and the oxen, sheep, or pigs that have been roasting all day will be served—along with breads of various kinds and sweet stews of apples and berries. The vats will be brought out and the cups filled with the first fruits of the tuns and the ale poured out. Aye, very much ale. The Dé Danann cannot celebrate anything without a cup or three, to be sure.

The feasting will continue through the evening and into the night until, when the druid has determined that the moon has stretched its full height above the land, he will summon everyone to the meeting place—for some tribes it is a stone circle if there is one nearby, or it might be a cairn, or tomb of a mighty ancestor—and there, his strong voice lifted to the heights, he will tell the old stories and perform the ageless, changeless rites of Danu's proud children.

At a certain time during this ritual, when the moon is heavy and bright with promise, the wedding rite will be performed. Sometimes, only one or two couples might come forward to be married, sometimes more. Once, when I was a little girl, I saw twelve brides married on Lughnasadh night. Tonight, it would be my turn to remove the maiden girdle and exchange it for that of a married woman.

The druid will summon those to be married and will speak the words to bind us in marriage for our time in this worlds-realm. He will ask and we will answer before kin and clan and friends so all will know our hearts and that we are of one mind. When the words have been spoken, the young men of Conor's fianna will bear the groom away. They will pour mead into a jar and they will all share the cup and they will bear him—carrying him bodily, as is usually the custom—to the bridal chamber. For us, this is to be

in our little bower made of cloths and cloaks and such stretched on a frame
of rough timber and thatched with reeds to make for us a sort of lodge.

Once in the bridal chamber, wherever it may be, the young men will
share another cup and they will take their leave of him, first taking his
brócs or his cloak, or some other item of clothing—the laces of his siarc,
perhaps. This, so they say, in preparation for a more complete disrobing
later—making such jokes and jibes as young men do. Or, so I'm told.

The friends will leave the groom then and return to the celebration.
Meanwhile, the young women will have taken the bride to the women's
house where they will remove her fine mantle and dress her in a gown of
new linen. They will anoint her with water scented with herbs and flowers,
and they will unbraid her hair and comb out the tresses and, maybe, tie it
back in a ribbon if there is one. They will put her soft shoes on her feet and
recite a little rune for fertility and the children yet to be born—we all know
it for we have heard it often enough. Then, when all is ready, the young
women will lead the bride to the bridal chamber to meet her groom. They
will pour mead from the jar into the cup and share it with her one last time
as one of their own, and this for the last time as a sister.

Then, smirking and giggling, they will leave the lovers to enjoy their honey
mead and, duty done, return to the feast—hoping, perhaps, to catch the eye
of one of the groom's men whose thoughts have been bent toward marriage by
the rites so observed. It happens more often than you might think!

Conor came to me, looking slightly anxious and flustered by all the
preparations. Even with Dearg and Donal's help, there was yet that much
to do. 'I have heard that long ago a fella might fetch his bride upon his
horse and the two ride away to a woodland bower to begin their marriage,'
he told me, bursting into my chamber and throwing himself onto my bed.
'That seems to me a right worthy and sensible plan.'

'Ach, poor Conor—so sore beset,' I said. Bending low, I gave him a kiss,
then pulled him up by the hand. 'But everything is nearly ready and you'll
not be pinching my wedding from me with a sad tale of hardship and woe.
I've waited too long for this day.'

I pushed him toward the cloth-hung doorway, where he paused and
regarded me with a slightly lopsided grin. 'Did you think this day would
ever come?'

I moved to him and he took me in his strong arms. 'I never doubted,' I
told me, gazing into his clear, hazel eyes. 'Did you?'

'More than once—if truth be told,' he replied.

'More than once! How many more than the once?'

'A hundred times a day at least,' he said blithely. 'Every time I saw you carrying your milk bucket to the cookhouse,' he kissed me lightly on the lips, 'or making butter,' he kissed me again, 'or tending one of your new-born calves,' another kiss, 'or playing your harp in my father's hall.' He kissed me one last time and let it linger. 'My heart, if you only knew how I yearned for this day since I was old enough to desire such a thing.'

Happy tears came to my eyes then and I stood holding him as he brushed them away with this fingertips. 'I love you, Conor mac Ardan. And I will be a good wife to you, you'll see.'

'Now that,' he said, his grin growing wide and handsome, 'I *never* doubted at all.'

'Ach, you'll be having me in tears again,' I said. He kissed me again and I pushed him gently toward the door. 'Take yourself away and do something useful. Rónán will be calling us soon enough.'

To be sure, it is customary for the bride and her beloved to remain aloof from one another before the wedding rite at the stone circle. I do not know where this practice began, or why we hold to it still. My mother always said it was for luck and prosperity, though how this can be, I cannot say. But something in Conor's words recalled a time when a ráth did not always look to its defence in case of attack at every moment of the day and night, a time when, on that solitary day if no other, the couple might take their ease and enjoy the festive rites and share their happiness with their clan and kin. The thought made me a little melancholy—or, perhaps, envious for that time, now long past, when a bride and her beloved could spend the day entire luxuriating in the enjoyment of their wedding.

Then again, maybe those far-off golden times never existed at all.

However it may be, I was determined that my wedding would not be marred by any gloom or shadow of some imagined loss or deprivation. My dear mother, long since in her grave, would have gloried in the match, for she dearly loved Conor, she surely did. And though it chafed me that she would not see her sole surviving daughter wed, I vowed I would enjoy everything the day held for me. And so I did.

After all, when it was over, I was the wife of the Lord of Tara and no other woman alive could say that.

1

Halfway across the wide green oval of the yard, Conor paused to consider the building work on the ráth. He wondered if any of the other lords in Eirlandia had a moment's peace from the relentless beseeching, pleading, and wheedling. He supposed not.

He stood with the sun warm on his back, and drew a deep breath—as if trying to take in all the commotion before him. The air smelled of sawdust and horses, and rang with the sound of axes and hammers. The carpenters and their many helpers were in full cry; their shouts and clamour could be heard from one end of Tara Hill to the other.

In the year and four months since his Lughnasadh wedding, great strides had been made in the work of establishing Tara ráth and settlement. The first of the permanent structures to be erected, the hall, now flaunted its imposing roof above the lesser buildings; the women's house was well begun, and the large stable and pen for the fianna's horses was almost finished—along with two of the four new storehouses. But the first of two planned warriors' houses was still merely wooden stakes pounded into the dirt. A makeshift smith's forge had been set up behind the ancient burial mound a little distance away, and the two existing storehouses on the hilltop had been converted into workshops for the craftsmen.

Constructing an entire ráth from the ground up was an enterprise that would have challenged even the wealthiest and most well-supplied tribe. Having to do everything at once, and having to do it with whatever materials came to hand, made that challenge a veritable ordeal. Even so, the zeal of all those who daily faced that trial somehow made it bearable and, sometimes, even enjoyable. Conor continually marvelled at the fortitude and resilience of his adopted people, and their undimmed determination to make of Tara's fabled hill a genuine home.

He lingered, enjoying the warmth of summer and admiring the work of the thatchers as they hoisted bundles of river reed up onto the steeply pitched roof. This hall, *his* hall, would become the strong beating heart of his realm, and the sight of its fine high roof glowing like gold in the day's early light swelled his heart with unaccustomed pride. Once, Tara Hill had been the crown of Eirlandia's sovereignty—the residence of mighty men, lords of legend and renown, high kings all. It would be so again—at least, it would be if Conor had anything to do with it.

'I am sorry to intrude on your thoughts, lord,' said a voice behind him. He glanced around to see Dearg, his master of the hearth, and two other men striding purposefully toward him. 'Conla, here, would speak to you.'

Conor greeted the men and wished them well, then said, 'What is your pleasure, friends?'

Conla, a short-limbed fellow with a square head bald as a stone hammer, was Lord Cahir's master builder and presently on extended loan from the Coriondi king. Cahir and Conor's father, Lord Ardan, had long been close friends and allies; Conor had inherited that friendship, and now leaned heavily on it. The master builder, along with his two assistants, was overseeing the raising of the ráth. Ordinarily, Conor had only to tell them what he wanted and they worked out how best to go about it. They rarely sought his opinion or advice but, when they did, it usually meant they had encountered some new and seemingly intractable difficulty.

'It's about the wall,' said Conla.

'What about the wall?' wondered Conor.

'Aye, well, it is high time we made a start,' replied the builder. 'There is timber to cut and ditches to be renewed and holes dug to receive the uprights.'

'Not to mention gate fittings to be forged,' put in Partan, the youngest of the two assistants. Realising he had spoken out of turn, he blushed. 'I do beg your pardon, lord.'

'True enough.' Conla gave the youth a reprimanding look, and continued, 'If we hope to be anywhere near finished before winter—'

'Winter!' exclaimed Conor. 'Winter now, is it? We've most of a summer, and an autumn to get through.'

'That is as may be,' replied Conla sagely, 'but a wall will not raise itself.

If we're to be getting the gates hung before the snow flies, we'd better be about making a start. More workers would make the job less of a chore.'

'More men,' repeated Dearg. 'How many do you reckon?'

'Ten at least—fifteen would be better,' answered Conla. 'Strong men who know a thing or two about felling trees and stripping timber, aye—and can go day on day without complaint or injury.'

Conor rubbed his cheek, feeling the old familiar tingle of the strawberry stain—the disfigurement that had shaped so much of his life and set him apart—now awakened to a fresh irritation. More workers . . . where would they put them? How would they feed them?

'Lord?' said Dearg after a moment. 'If you like, I can ask Donal to form a work party to begin with the trees and digging the ditches for the earthworks.'

'Nay, nay,' replied Conor. 'I have been thinking on this very thing and I can save us all a great deal of time and labour.'

'How so?'

'By *not* building a wall.'

'Not building . . .' Dearg and the carpenter exchanged a puzzled look. 'You mean delay construction just now?'

'I mean no offence, my lord, but delaying now will make it very difficult to finish before winter, and if we—'

'I mean to say,' said Conor, 'that my fortress will not have a wall.'

'No wall?' wondered Partan, his voice rising in disbelief. 'None at all?'

Conla frowned. 'What manner of ráth or dún has no wall?'

Conor smiled. 'This one. My friends, we are home to the largest warband Eirlandia has seen in living memory. We are surrounded on all sides by strong and generous kinsmen. If danger comes calling, it will find a rough welcome here. The fianna will be our stout wall.'

The carpenter opened his mouth to object, but Dearg quickly quelled any dissent saying, 'My lord has spoken. You are free to return to your duties.'

Both men made a slight bow of acknowledgement and walked away; after a few steps, Conla could be seen shaking his head while his assistant muttered misgivings.

Conor, watching them, said, 'Tell me, Dearg, what are your thoughts on the matter? Am I making a mistake?'

'It is not for me to say, lord. And we have plenty enough to keep us busy until the snow flies.'

'Ach, well, we shall see.' He turned to his hearth master. 'Was there anything else?'

Dearg, shaking his head, took his leave and hurried off. One of the five original members of the fianna, the redheaded warrior had thrown himself into his new civil duties with the same dedication previously reserved for his weapons and training—so much so that, looking at him now, Conor doubted the young Brigantes would ever wield a spear in battle again. A loss, yes, but his services in his current occupation became more indispensable; for, as the tribe grew, so, too, the duties and responsibilities of the master of the hearth to provide the necessaries of life.

Dearg disappeared among the spread of tents and hastily constructed shelters that had mushroomed across Tara's plateau, and Conor resumed his stroll to the hall, where he was beset by questions and demands from the men thatching its roof before going inside to break his fast with a little bread softened in warm milk into which bits of smoked fish had been flaked and steeped. He was just draining the bowl when Donal appeared. 'Come, join me, brother,' he invited. 'There is more in the pot, I think.'

The dark-haired warrior, Conor's boyhood friend and now head of his ardféne, took a seat on the bench and spooned warm breccbainne from the squat black cauldron into a wooden bowl. 'What do you think of the hall so far? Splendid, is it not? It will be finished soon,' he observed mildly. 'And I have spoken to Conla and he tells me that the women's house will have walls and a roof by Beltaine.'

'Aye, if the weather stays fair,' agreed Conor. 'Perhaps in time for the birth of my son.'

'A boy now, is it?' said Donal, his broad face breaking into an amused smile. 'A few days ago, you were certain the child would be a girl. You were even going to name her Rhiannon, as I recall.'

'What do you expect?' replied Conor. 'All I have is guesses. Unless I can persuade you to cast your inner eye upon that path and tell me one way or the other which it will be, I'll keep on guessing.'

Donal shrugged. 'Speaking of walls, brother,' he said, casually breaking chunks of dry brown bread into his bowl, 'I'm just now hearing that you have decided not to erect a defensive wall around the ráth. Can this be so?'

'I expect you heard it correctly,' replied Conor. 'What do you think?'

'According to your carpenter, that is a misjudgement that invites disaster.'

'Ach, I know what Conla thinks. What do *you* think?'

'I think I would like to hear why you would be saying such a thing before deciding.' Donal took one of the wooden spoons from an empty bowl on the table and began stirring the mixture. He slurped and swallowed, then regarded Conor expectantly. 'I'm listening.'

Conor took up the ladle and dipped into the cauldron, adding a little more of the savoury liquid to his bowl. The voices of the thatchers on the roof above them could be heard, mingling with the sounds of hammering and sawing coming from the yard; somewhere a dog barked and a horse neighed—all sounds of industry, of life, sounds that had not been heard on Tara Hill since the last high king reigned there in time past memory.

'It seems to me that every ráth and dún in Eirlandia has good stout walls and yet that does not keep them safe from the Scálda.'

'Not walls alone,' Donal agreed. 'You need warriors to defend them.'

'Aye, walls are only as good as the warband behind them.' Conor lifted the bowl to his mouth and emptied it again. 'Without a warband to defend the ráth, walls are little more than a hurdle to be climbed over, or a stand of timber to be burned.'

'That is a harsh judgement,' Donal declared, spooning up breccbainne and chewing thoughtfully.

'Harsh, perhaps—but true. Walls are only as good as the warriors behind them. Walls did not save the Gangani, and they did not save the Breifne, or the Velabri, the Uterni, the Osraige, or the Menapi—did they? What use were high walls to *any* of the tribes in the lands the Scálda stole?'

'Ach, but see here,' said Conor, 'with the fianna we are on the way to becoming the greatest warband in Eirlandia—certainly the largest.'

'What so?'

'The fianna will be my fortress wall,' said Conor, his voice taking on an edge of excitement. 'From our high perch here atop this hill, we will command the land as far as we can see. We will be ready to ride out in any direction to defend this island realm. Should the enemy encroach, they will see a ráth that has no need of timber for we possess something far better—a wall of warriors.'

Donal gazed back at him, considering Conor's vision.

'And everyone who visits this place, or merely passes by, will know that we fear no one and stand ready to defend ourselves day or night.' Conor's grin grew expansive. 'Not only that, we will see everything that passes on the plain below and in the wider world—as we do even now. Nothing will escape our notice.'

'Bold words, brother,' concluded Donal. 'Perhaps a little reckless as well.'

'Perhaps,' allowed Conor, growing serious. 'But this throne has been raised on recklessness from the beginning. To pull back now, to hoard our gains—that is a sure sign of weakness.'

'And this is what fortress walls means to you?'

'Aye, that and more.' Conor began pacing as he strained for an explanation. 'See here, Donal. We have begun to fashion a new realm on this hill. Timber walls will make us appear as just another Dé Danann stronghold ruled by a little lord and defended by his little warband. Worse, it would look like we were hiding up here.'

'Hiding?' Donal smiled and shook his head slowly. 'Who would be fool enough to accuse you of a thing like that?' The glancing reference to Mádoc and the hidden bracelet made Conor groan. 'All the same, it is not the lords and lordlings you have to worry about,' continued Donal in a more serious tone, 'it is Balor Evil Eye. I'm thinking he views this hill as a plum worth plucking. He tried once. He might well try again.'

At Donal's words, Conor was instantly back in that terrible storm-torn night of the massacre. In a vicious assault, the Scálda warband had attacked a gathering at Tara and succeeded in decimating the flower of Eirlandia's elite lords and warleaders.

'Let Balor try to pluck us if he dares,' said Conor. 'He will find a plum with a stone to choke him.'

2

Conor and Donal lifted spears and shields from among those hung at the entrance to the hall, and walked out into what was becoming a genuine settlement: as season gave way to season, the clusters of tents and makeshift shelters were slowly giving way to proper dwellings, workshops, and storehouses. Down on Mag Teamhair, the Plain of Tara, the rich earth had been divided into ploughed plots for fields; parts of Mag Coinnem, the Council Plain, had also been cleared and ploughed, and areas marked out for cattle pens, barns, and sheds.

Easy in the soft morning light, the three crossed the wide, green oval of the yard and started down toward the smallest of the plains, Mag Rí, the Royal Plain, which served as the training grounds for both horses and men.

'The crops are coming on well,' Donal observed. 'The weather has been kind to us.'

'An early spring, followed by a fair summer,' replied Conor, 'there is every hope of a fine harvest. But we need the cattle Cahir and Garbha promised so we can begin building our own herd. I do grow weary begging for meat and milk.'

'It is not the begging that makes you weary, brother,' observed Donal.

'What so?' said Conor, catching the edge to his tone.

'I see you running pillar to post all day long. You have a finger in every cup and a stick in every fire.'

'I don't.'

'You do. Ask Fergal if you don't believe me.'

'He's right, Conor,' confirmed Fergal. 'You race about like a man with a hornet in his breecs. But no one can be two places at once—not even you.'

'Is it that you think I'm doing too much? Or that I'm doing it poorly?'

'Ach, nay,' said Donal. 'All I'm saying is that a moment's rest now and then would be no bad thing.'

'You have people now, brother,' Fergal pointed out.

'Aye, people who expect me to make good on the promises I have made.'

'People who stand with you,' corrected Fergal. 'People more than willing to do whatever you ask of them.'

'Only you have to ask,' concluded Donal. 'Promise me you'll ask?'

'I will,' replied Conor, and they moved on, descending the winding pathway to the plain. At the base of the hill was the large pen where most of the horses for the fianna were being kept until the stables atop the hill were finished. Here they paused and Conor whistled for Búrach; the grey stallion pricked up his ears and came trotting over to greet his master. 'Good to see you, old son,' murmured Conor as he stroked the extended neck. 'Did you miss me?' By way of reply, the grey turned his head and gave him a friendly nip on the arm. 'Here now! Behave yourself,' Conor told him, and with a pat sent him away. 'Go and make some colts, why don't you? We need more horses.'

Cáit, the eldest of the stable master's three dark-haired daughters, who served as a groom and stable hand, came running up just then. 'My lord,' she said, a little out of breath, 'will you go riding? I will gladly ready your mount for you.'

Conor, watching the grey jog away, replied, 'Not just now, Cáit.' He glanced around and saw the eagerness on the young lady's face. 'But I have an idea. Why don't *you* take him out? He needs a good run, does Búrach. Get one of your sisters to go with you—or one of the lads.'

The girl's dark eyes grew bigger. 'Truly? You would allow it?'

'I would insist upon it,' Conor told her. 'You will be doing your lord a good service.'

'I hear and obey, lord,' she said, and then raced off to find someone to ride with her.

'Don't let him run away with you,' Conor called after her.

'You just made someone very happy,' Donal chuckled.

'If only everyone was so easily pleased,' said Conor.

Leaving the pen, they moved on to join the warriors and take part in the day's training. As weapons master and chief of battle, Fergal held practice sessions most days. He was an exacting teacher, not to say demanding.

'Our warband is drawn from different tribes, each with their own way of fighting,' he had explained. 'But this is to be *our* warband, and so they will learn to fight *our* way—only then will they be permitted to join the fianna.'

For the most part, the warriors accepted this: the younger ones were glad to learn the old ways and take on new and proven battle skills from so renowned a teacher. The older ones, of which there were more than a few, put up with Fergal's stringent regime for the sake of unity and eventual acceptance into the fianna—though some of these, Conor noticed, were likely to fall back into habits of practice that kept Fergal agitated. But no one complained.

When they were not down on the training field, the warriors were out with the hunters and foragers scouring the woodlands and forest to the south and east in an attempt to satisfy the constant demand for food—a demand that grew as word spread and more people, most of them displaced by enemy raids, arrived to join the nascent tribe. This steady trickle of incomers might have been encouraging if not for the strain it put on their already overburdened resources. To be sure, the new tribe needed people—the industry, skill, and will to succeed the refugees brought were vital if the new realm was to thrive in the future. Conor knew this, but it did not make the day-to-day stresses any less. Indeed, that the settlement had survived the first winter at all was due largely to the generosity of Lord Cahir, who had been the lifelong friend of Conor's father. Cahir had supplied them out of his own stores, and that, as well as smaller gifts from various others who owed debts of honour to Conor and his fianna for saving them on the terrible night of the Tara massacre, had sufficed to see them through the long months of cold wind, rain, and snow.

Now that summer had settled in and, with it, the raiding season, more refugees fleeing enemy attacks could be expected. The arrival of each new family or, sometimes, entire clans, did severely stretch meagre provisions. Many of the newcomers brought welcome supplies—items of food and clothing, tools and weapons saved from the Scálda raids that had driven them from their homes. Others, however, arrived having escaped with little more than the cloaks on their backs. But they came, and Conor was determined to find a place for all of them and welcome them to Tara.

Just now, as Conor and Donal walked down to join Fergal and the warriors, they were discussing the fact that there were not enough horses for each of the warriors to be mounted—a situation which effectively reduced the size and fighting ability of the fianna. Conor looked out onto the plain below them and saw the various groups of men at their weapons practice. Fergal and his second, Médon, had divided the warband into five roughly equal groups, each to work on a separate skill or technique. Over the course of the day's session, the groups would change places so that by the end of practice every warrior would have trained in all five areas. This method was Fergal's innovation, and his pride and confidence in it were absolute.

'We may be able to convince some of the lords with lands along the borders to lend us horses in exchange for protection,' Conor mused aloud.

'It would be easier to capture them from the Scálda,' replied Donal. He paused, then said, 'What is this?'

Conor heard the change in Donal's tone and glanced up. 'Where?'

'Just there.' Donal pointed out across the plain where a company of riders was making its way toward Fergal and the warriors on the training ground.

'Who is that?' wondered Conor. 'Can you see?'

Donal shook his head. 'Not that far.'

'I mean with your—' Conor abandoned the query. 'Never mind. Let's go find out what they want.'

They hurried on to where Fergal had halted the strangers and arrived to see frowns all around. 'These men have come to see you, lord,' Fergal said, without taking his eyes off the lead rider. 'It would seem they have something weighty on their minds, though they will not say what that might be.'

The leader of the group, a lean, flat-nosed chieftain with a silver torc and three gold bands on his bare right arm, looked down from his horse and with a sneer in his voice said, 'Aye, we're looking for the one called Conor who is rumoured to be lurking hereabouts.' He glanced down at Conor and sniffed dismissively.

Conor replied, 'If that is who you seek, your search is at an end. What is it you want?'

'Are *you* Conor mac Ardan?'

'*Lord* Conor mac Ardan to you, friend,' said Donal. 'I suggest you try asking again—and this time let us see some better manners if you have any.'

'Who are you to speak to us this way?' demanded the rider next to the flat-nosed one.

'Only a fella who has your best interest at heart,' answered Donal lightly. 'You will have heard, no doubt, of the terrible temper of our lord. I would spare you the beating you so richly deserve should you persist with your careless insults.'

The warrior's hand went to the sword at his side and Fergal, spear ready, moved to take his place beside Conor and Donal. 'Why not do as our brother has advised?' said Fergal, tapping the spear shaft against the palm of his hand. 'It would save you a deal of pain, I do believe.'

The affronted warrior removed his hand from his sword, and the leader of the group forced a grim smile and said, 'Our apologies if we have bruised your tender feelings. We had no idea the new lord of Tara had such thin and delicate skin.'

'I would not be talking about bruising if I were you,' said Fergal. 'Look around. I think you'll find we can give far better than we get.'

The strangers stole a glance at the ranks of warriors even now forming up behind them.

'Am I right in thinking that this is the vaunted fianna we are hearing so much about?' asked the leader. 'I am impressed. We had heard it was a fair-sized troop, but I did not expect so many—or to meet them all at once like this.'

'Nor would you if you and your companions were not intent on riding through a training ground,' said Conor. He regarded the man. Older than the others by a good few years, his dark hair was streaked with grey and there were wrinkles at the corners of his eyes and mouth; his face was smooth-shaven and set in an insolent expression. 'But I think you did not come here to practice discourtesy or discuss the size of our warband.'

'I did not,' replied the man. 'I am Iollan mac Datho, and I come bearing a message from my lord and others.'

'And who might your lord be?' said Fergal.

'Lord Corgan of the Eridani,' replied Iollan.

'And these others?'

'Lords and kings of northern tribes, let us say.'

'That's not saying much,' said Fergal. He looked to Conor. 'Are we to be tolerating this?'

'Let's hear your message,' Conor said. 'And then you and your friends can be on your way. No doubt your lord is pining for your cheerful presence.'

'What is this? No welcome cup for a king's messenger? My lord will be displeased when I tell him how his men were treated.'

'Had you sent your man on ahead—' began Donal.

'And with a better tongue in his mouth,' added Fergal.

'—you would have been received with a welcome deserving of your rank,' Donal continued. 'But as your errand seems calculated to provoke, you must take us as you find us.'

The chieftain returned an icy smile and shook his head slowly. 'Gracious to the end,' he sniffed. 'I will tell you how we find you, shall I? We find you taking possession of lands that do not belong to you and, unless I am much mistaken, you are even now in the midst of raising a fortress on Tara's hill.'

'You are not mistaken,' Conor told him. 'All the world can see that has become the sole ambition of my heart.'

'And yet,' called the truculent warrior on horseback, in a strident voice, 'this land has been sacred to all Eirlandia. By what authority do you presume to take this place for your own?'

Fergal looked at Donal. 'Did someone speak just now? Or was that a horse fart? Did you hear it, brother?'

'It must have been a fart in the wind,' answered Donal, levelling his gaze upon the mounted warrior. 'Any fella who wished to address a nobleman would do so face-to-face and not babble nonsense from the back of a flea-bitten nag.'

Iollan glanced at his companions and gave a warning shake of his head. To Conor, he said, 'My king and his brother lords have taken an interest in what you are doing here,' he continued, 'and they would have a ready accounting.'

'A ready accounting . . . ,' Donal repeated. 'To my ear that sounds more like a summons to answer for an offence.'

Iollan's eyes narrowed. 'I cannot answer for the sound in your ear, but you would not be far wrong to think that.'

'We have been here since the night of the massacre these many months past,' Fergal pointed out. 'All this time and you only just now come to us with this?'

'Your presence here has naturally raised many questions,' intoned the messenger, '—questions that require answers. In fact, accusations have been made that cannot be ignored. The kings considered that an airechtas is the proper way to give you a chance to explain yourself. I need not point out that failure to attend will be considered an admission of guilt.'

'Guilt implies a crime,' said Conor, his tone growing flat. 'And what crime is it they think me guilty of?'

'Stealing land sacred to Eirlandia—a crime that will be most forcefully punished.'

'Say that again and slowly,' Fergal said, his voice low and laced with menace. 'Better still, choose softer words for they will be the last you utter through those foul teeth of yours.'

The warriors on horseback drew their swords and started forth, but Iollan raised a restraining hand. 'Enough!' he said. 'We have done what we came to do.' To Conor, he said, 'We are leaving now, but know this—Lord Corgan will host the airechtas at his ráth at Bennáel three days following the next full moon.' He turned, walked to his horse, swung up onto its back, and, with a nod to his men, rode away.

As soon as they had gone, Conor turned to Fergal and Donal. 'Let's talk.'

Fergal called to Médon and said, 'Continue with the training. We will join you in a moment.' He followed Conor and Donal a few paces away where they would not be overheard.

'What do we make of that?' wondered Conor, watching the fianna resume their weapons practice.

'High-handed rogues,' replied Fergal. 'If anyone should ask me.'

'You were right to remind them, brother,' suggested Donal, 'we've been here for a goodly length of time, and only now do these lords find cause to object?'

'Aye, and after all you did for them during the battle?' He spat onto the ground. 'Disgusting.'

'They are worried,' Donal pointed out.

'About what?' said Fergal. 'What is there to worry about? We're not doing anything now that we haven't done from the beginning.'

'We were just a few wandering warriors camped out on the hill when we began,' Donal pointed out. 'Now we are a fair-sized warband building a substantial settlement.'

'Aye, so?' wondered Fergal.

'Our numbers continue to grow—and so, too, the threat in their eyes. We can no longer be conveniently ignored.' Lifting a hand to the fianna spread across the practice field, Donal said, 'We are a veritable tribe possessing what is soon to become—if not already—the largest warband in Eirlandia. I can well imagine that alone would be enough to make some of our brother lords anxious. Word of the fianna has reached all corners of the island. I doubt there is a Dé Danann clan that has not heard about what Conor and the fianna achieved on the night of the massacre. People talk, rumours grow. You know how it goes.'

'Ach, well, if *that* is what worries these tepid lords, then they are right to worry,' crowed Fergal. 'Our warband is the equal of any and better than most.' He looked to Conor and said, 'Do you mean to attend this council of theirs?'

Conor rubbed his chin thoughtfully for a moment and took his time answering. 'Aye, I do. It would be good to go and clear the air. This is not like the Corgan I know. I'm thinking there must be more to it than what we've been told so far.'

'A sad waste of time better spent here, if you ask me. They question your authority to take Tara, aye? Well, by what authority do they think to lay judgements on anyone? Answer me that.'

'Fergal's right,' Donal agreed. 'They have no authority over us, and you need not submit to their whims. Even so, might this be a chance to explain yourself—tell them what you plan to do here, show them you mean only good for the people and for Eirlandia.'

'Aye,' agreed Fergal, 'show them you are not another Brecan Big Brócs come to trample on their tender toes.'

'Poor dead Brecan wanted to be high king, so he did,' continued Donal, 'but even he did not dare seize the torc for himself. He knew he needed the support of his brother kings. So will you if you hope ever to live in peace on Tara Hill.'

'Brecan allowed his reach to exceed his grasp, and it drove him to commit an act of pure insanity,' Fergal pointed out. He squinted at Conor. 'We would not like to see that happen to you, brother.'

Conor smiled. 'It may be that all kings are a little mad. An otherwise sane man would never take it on.'

'So, are we going to this attend Corgan's council?' said Fergal.

'Aye, we will—but not because these worried lords demand it.'

'Nay?'

'We go because it suits me,' replied Conor. 'And if our luck is with us we may be able to bend it to our purpose.'

'Ach, but if you go at their bidding,' Donal cautioned, 'they will be seen to have authority over you. What is more, they will believe it.'

'Then we must go and show them the folly of false belief,' answered Conor. Shouldering his spear, he strode off to join the fianna at their training.

Fergal watched him for a moment—so easy in his stride, so full of confidence, grace, and strength, untiring in the face of all the trials ranged against them and their grand scheme. He glanced at Donal and said, 'He *is* a bit mad, you know.'

'Aye, so he is,' agreed Donal with a sigh. 'But his heart is in the right place.'

3

'How soon must you leave?' asked Aoife. It had been a long and eventful day—as each and every day had been since her arrival and marriage at Tara. This was her first opportunity to speak to him all day and, consequently, the first time she was hearing about the northern lords and their message.

'We'll not be leaving for some days yet,' Conor told her. He pulled off his siarc and untied the laces of his brócs before shucking off his breecs and sliding under the woollen cloak they used as a coverlet for their low pallet of a bed.

'I don't see why you have to go at all.' Aoife smoothed a hand over the slight swell of her belly. 'How long will you be away?'

'No longer than is needful,' Conor replied. 'But I must go. We need the support of our neighbouring lords if we are to survive. And if they continue to harbour doubts and suspicions of any kind . . .'

Conor saw the question in her eyes and continued, 'Think of Liam—'

'I would rather not.'

'My brother did what he did out of fear.'

'And jealousy,' she added crisply. 'Mostly jealousy.'

'Aye, fear and jealousy. It is the same with many of the other lords— *most* of the other lords maybe, come to that. They fear the power that is flowing to me, and at the same time they are jealous of it.'

'What if they refuse to listen? What if their minds are already made up?'

'All the more reason I must go'—Conor took her fidgeting hand in his—'and show them the error of their ways.'

Aoife squeezed his hand. 'You are meeting too many demands. You are dealing with so much—I would not say that I am worried for you, dear heart, but . . . there is only so much a man can bear, even you.' She looked down at his hand and kneaded it gently. Conor raised his other hand and brushed her hair.

'Aoife . . . I . . .'

'You go and do what you must, but do not be too disappointed if these other kings do not fall over themselves in their haste to pledge their fealty. It may take time for them to get used to the idea and see the sense of what you propose.'

'Wise words, lady wife,' said Conor, kissing her. 'But there is little time to spare. Summer moves on and harvest is still months away. We need supplies—and the sooner the better. We must make as many friends as possible.'

Nine days later, beneath a high, bright windswept sky, Conor and his ardféne—consisting of Donal, Fergal, Médon, Galart, and Calbhan—set out for the airechtas at Bennáel. Leaving Diarmaid and the rest of the fianna to protect the settlement, they rode north. As the weather was fine and the day warm, they proceeded at a leisurely pace so that Conor could stop and speak to the clan chiefs and headmen of the little dúns and settlements they passed and offer a reminder to any who might forget what he and the fianna had done for them on the night of the massacre. He also wanted to stop and pay his regards to Cahir, and ask about the possibility of acquiring some horses for his ever-needy warband.

Thus, through the tribal territories of the Brigantes, the Volunti, the Ulaid, and the Coriondi they travelled, receiving a mixed welcome at the places they visited. Some, like lords Cahir and Garbha, were glad to see them, and glad to know that such a large and skilled warband was abroad in the land, watching the borders, protecting them; but others, having heard about the settlement on Tara, were more guarded and suspicious of Conor's intent.

Nevertheless, Conor treated them all the same; without rancour or resentment, he reassured the doubters and encouraged the support of those who appeared more receptive. He told one and all that he was going to secure the agreement of a royal council summoned especially to approve the settlement at Tara.

'The way you speak,' Fergal pointed out as they left the yard of an Ulaid farming settlement, 'it sounds as if these northern kings have already granted their approval of your plan.'

'*Our* plan' Conor reminded him. 'What we do at Tara we do for everyone, for all Eirlandia.'

Not to be put off, Fergal insisted, 'You know what I mean. Do not pretend otherwise. And do not waste a moment thinking that Corgan and these northern kings—whoever they may be—have summoned you to grant you the golden torc of kingship. They mean to pluck your wing feathers lest you fly too high.'

'And is it that you think I do not know this already that you tell me such a thing?' replied Conor. 'Hear me, brother. This airechtas will become our triumph.'

'And if not?'

'Ach, well we will be no worse off than we are now.'

Donal, riding at Conor's left hand, had been listening to this discussion and spoke up. 'Even if they agree to tolerate a settlement at Tara, that doesn't mean the contrary lords will aid us in any way.'

'Perhaps not at once—'

'Perhaps not at all,' said Donal. 'Not now. Not ever.'

Conor thought for a moment, gazing at the rising trail ahead as if seeing into the future with Donal's second sight. 'They will,' he said at last. 'When it comes down to the question of who raises a ráth on Tara Hill—a choice between me or Balor Evil Eye—I expect they will choose me.'

Nothing more was said about the airechtas then, or the next day as their meandering northward journey continued.

The weather sweetened as summer deepened across the land, allowing them to camp beneath the stars and the slowly waxing moon. In glades and beside loughs, or at woodland borders, Conor and his ardféne gathered around generous campfires for simple meals and travellers' tales. Conor, Donal, and Fergal, having brought their faéry weapons with them, told about their sojourn among the Tylwyth Teg in the Region of the Summer Stars, and described life in Lord Gwydion's court in a way that held the other three spellbound. The bonds of brotherhood were strengthened; old ties to their former tribes further loosened and fell away. No one felt the loss at all. They only saw that, in Conor, they had a lord right worthy of their service and devotion. Once away from the constant demands of the builders and provisioners, Conor began to relax somewhat; he breathed easier, slept more soundly.

In this way, Conor and his modest escort arrived at Bennaél, the principal stronghold of Lord Corgan in the rough, wooded craggy hills of north-central Eirlandia. The ancestral lands of the Eridani spread in a wide band west and a little south of Conor, Fergal, and Donal's childhood home at Dúnaird—a region of the island Scálda raids had not yet penetrated.

So far as Conor knew, his father and Corgan had once enjoyed a neighbourly respect for one another. That friendship had faded over time, ending with Ardan's death in the Tara massacre. But now that he was here, Conor hoped he might find a way to rekindle some of that neighbourly regard. The travellers arrived near midday and dismounted a little way off; Médon, Calbhan, and Galart waited with the horses while Conor, Donal, and Fergal approached the fortress on foot. They were met at the gate by a square-jawed, muscular fellow with a bull neck, heavy shoulders, and a shock of black hair swept back and bound in a tight braid at the side of his head. He was clean-shaven and dressed in a red siarc and matching breecs; a torc of burnished copper gleamed dully at his throat. Standing with him were two other warriors—young men of similar age, size, and appearance—and all three seemed genuinely pleased to see their visitors.

'Welcome to Bennaél,' called the warrior, striding forward to take Conor by the arms in the warrior's greeting. 'Truly, Lord Conor, I am glad to meet you at last. We did not know if you would come at all—especially since . . .' His voice trailed off awkwardly.

The fair-haired warrior standing next to him spoke up. 'We have heard what you did on the night of the Tara massacre. It is an honour to offer hospitality to you and your men these next few days.'

'It is my hope that our time here will be well spent,' Conor said, somewhat taken aback by the effusive welcome. He introduced Donal and Fergal to the three Eridani and said, 'I was expecting to meet Lord Corgan.'

'I am Fáelán, Lord Corgan's son,' announced the warrior. 'And these are my friends Docha and Irél.' The two touched the back of their hands to their foreheads in formal acknowledgement of Conor's rank, and then the one called Irél blurted, 'Aye, we heard what you did on the night of the massacre. No less than a hero feat. It was the saving of many.'

'We yearn for the day when we can stand together with you on the battleground and fight the Scálda.' Docha confided, 'Truth be told, we would join your warband today if our king would allow it.'

Prince Fáelán put a restraining hand on his friend's arm. 'Do not let my father hear you say that—lest he take away your ale portion.'

'Is it true your spears are enchanted?' asked Irél.

'No more questions, you two,' interrupted Fáelán. To Conor, he said, 'Please, forgive my friends. As you can see, their eagerness has outrun their manners.'

'They are men after my own heart,' replied Fergal. He held out his spear to the warriors. 'Here now, have a closer look.'

Irél took the shaft of the spear across his palms and examined it and the intricately engraved blade closely while his two companions looked on in silent wonder. 'So light,' he said. He gave it a few exploratory thrusts and jabs. 'So quick, and supple. It almost feels alive.'

'Ach, but you should try it in battle,' said Fergal. 'That is when it truly lives.'

'Are your swords enchanted, too?' wondered Docha.

'Aye, it is true that our weapons are charmed,' Conor replied. Drawing his sword, he passed the exquisite blade to Docha. 'They were gifts from the faéry. How is it that you know this?'

'Those of our swordbrothers who survived the massacre brought back the tale. We didn't know whether to believe it,' said Fáelán. 'But now that I see the craft of these weapons for myself, there can be no doubt.'

'Will you tell us how you came to have them?' asked Irél.

'Again, too many questions,' said Fáelán. 'My father will not be pleased to be kept waiting.' He took the charmed sword from Docha, hefted it once, and then passed it back to Conor; Irél likewise returned the spear to Fergal. 'I see your men waiting nearby. Docha and Irél will go and bring them and see to the horses. There is food for you and fodder for the horses. You are to worry for nothing while you are here. My father is waiting to welcome you. He will receive you in the hall.'

With a word, the Eridani prince set his friends to their errands and then led the visitors through the fortress gates and into the yard—a somewhat cramped expanse due to the imposing size of the hall and the number of buildings contained within the high timber walls. Compared to the other kingdoms of the north, the Eridani were preeminent: their warbands larger, their lands more extensive, their wealth greater, and their power in the region unquestioned. With the enormous upheaval caused by the relentless predations of the Scálda, they were well placed to become Eirlandia's dominant tribe now that the Brigantes were no longer as strong as they had been under Brecan. This made Lord Corgan the most potent king in the region—a fact that was not lost on the visitors.

'That is a handsome thing,' Fergal remarked upon seeing Corgan's hall for the first time. Its round walls were washed with lime, its wide double doors painted green, and its high-pitched roof topped by a spear to which was attached a streaming red banner. 'I don't know when I've seen better. I always knew the Eridani lived well, but this. . . .' He indicated the cobbled yard, the row of large storehouses and roundhouse dwellings with a wave of his hand. He glanced at Conor and saw the bemused look on his face. 'Our young prince seems pleasant enough, eh? I was not expecting that.'

'Nor I,' replied Conor. 'And am I alone in thinking this very odd? Corgan's messengers treated us like horse thieves, and Corgan's son wants to join the fianna.'

'There is something curious here, you are right,' Donal agreed. 'But whatever it is, at least now you know that you have friends at the table. And if Corgan means for his son to succeed him, he will not be blind to the young man's admiration. Think on that.'

Donal would have said more, but Fáelán stopped as they approached the entrance to the hall; he turned and said, 'I will go and tell the king you have arrived.'

At that moment, the wide green door opened and out stepped Lord Corgan and two chieftains of his tribe, both white-haired men of advanced years, both wearing silver torcs and armbands. 'I only just now received word of your arrival or I would have come sooner,' declared Corgan in a terse but not unfriendly tone. 'Welcome to Bennaél. You have met my son—be pleased to meet my chief advisor.' He turned, and out stepped the flat-nosed messenger they had met before. The man inclined his head in a slight nod of acknowledgement. 'This is Iollan.'

'Him we've met,' said Fergal under his breath.

Corgan said, 'Iollan, Brenal, and Henda here will be joining me for our deliberations. I don't expect you will mind as I see you have brought advisors of your own. But all that can wait. Come along, you will be thirsty after your journey. Let us share the welcome cup and get to know one another better.'

The king led them into the hall, where, despite the warmth of the day, a damp chill still lingered. A fire burned in the hearth, and tallow candles lined the long board. Corgan took his accustomed chair, and offered Conor the place at his right hand. Donal and Fergal took places beside Conor and across from Brenal and Henda, and Médon, Galart, and Calbhan found places on the bench with Fáelán, Docha, and Irél. As they all settled around the table, three serving boys appeared; while two lads set cups and bowls upon the board, the third poured mead spiced with last autumn's blackcurrants and cherries into a large shallow bowl made of oak and set with a rim of hammered silver.

Taking up the cúach, Corgan thanked Conor and his men for answering the summons and expressed the hope that the next few days would yield a better understanding among the lords. He then offered the bowl to Conor, who took a drink and passed it back; the welcome cup was then handed on to Fergal and Donal, and then to Brenal and Henda in turn. Then Corgan commanded the other vessels on the board to be filled. Taking up the silver cup, the king drained it and handed it, empty, to Conor, who examined it for a moment.

Holding that cup, Conor was suddenly transported. He was once again that bare-legged boy, running through his father's hall, willow-switch sword in hand, waging battle with Fergal and Donal and younger brother Liam. His father was the newly made king of the Darini, and his brother Rónán had been taken away to be raised by the druids. He saw again the boards and trestles being set out for the evening's meal; and on a board at the back of the hall the cups and bowls stood waiting. His eye was caught by the gleam of a silver-rimmed cup; he went to it and, since no one was watching, took it in his hands to examine it more closely. He raised it to his lips, pretending that he had just drunk the portion of a great warrior. Someone entered the hall then. Quickly replacing the cup, he took up his pretend sword, and ran off to find Liam and the others once more.

'My father had a cúach like this once,' he mused quietly, tracing the silver band with a finger. 'I cannot think what became of it.'

Corgan's smile was quick and broad. 'Ach, well, that is easily told. The cup in your hands is that selfsame cup. Lord Ardan gave it to me many years ago. I came to visit him at Dúnaird on some business or other and when I remarked on this fine vessel, he made a gift of it.'

Conor nodded. 'No doubt he found in you a valuable ally.' He smiled and held the bowl out for Corgan to refill.

'Not an ally only, but an honest and trustworthy friend. I hope you will find me the same,' replied Corgan. 'Keep the cup. Consider it a gift from a friend who wishes you well.'

'A curious way to begin a friendship,' remarked Fergal after a moment. 'Your man here,' he nodded to Iollan, 'left us with the impression that this council was more in the way of a trial than a celebration.'

Corgan glanced sideways at Iollan, who, impassive, stared straight ahead. 'It seems my message was delivered in a manner you found offensive. I'm sorry. But you should know that each of the lords invited to attend this gathering have expressed serious concerns over recent developments at Tara. My purpose here is to allow everyone a chance to clear the air before things go too far and, perhaps, get out of hand.'

'If that's your aim, you'll find me agreeable,' replied Conor, shaking off any lingering feelings of melancholy or nostalgia. 'I welcome the chance to explain my intentions and, as you say, clear the air.'

The stiffness of the reception eased somewhat then and the cups were re-filled. The party drank, and talk drifted into other areas; after a while, Fáelán rose and announced that his duties called him away. To Conor, he added, 'Places have been prepared for you in the guest lodge. I will go and make certain all is ready for when you finish here.' Touching the back of his hand to his forehead, he acknowledged his father and Conor, and then left the hall.

'Your son is an impressive fella,' Conor observed. 'I can only hope to have a son as courteous and well-spoken one day.'

'You have no children, then?' asked Corgan, sipping from his cup.

'Nay, not yet,' replied Conor. 'But soon. My wife is expecting to deliver our first before Samhain.'

'I hope all goes well. Give her my best regards,' replied Corgan. He raised his cup to Conor, took a sip, and put the cup aside. Folding his hands on the table, he said, 'I was sorry to hear about your father. I did not see him at that ill-fated gathering and thought he had escaped the massacre.'

'The Darini were there,' Conor told him, 'but they were trapped on the plain when the attack began. They were never able to reach the top of the hill, so fought on alone.'

'Ach, well . . .' Corgan sighed and shook his head slowly. 'A very great pity that. We did not see as much of one another in these last years as I would have liked. I tried, of course, but something always seemed to get in the way.' The king smiled faintly and shrugged, as if to suggest things could not have been any different.

'Is that so?' replied Conor, suddenly wary. The Eridani lord's clumsy attempt at whitewashing his past allegiance raised Conor's hackles. 'It seemed to me that the Eridani always had time for Brecan mac Lergath. Perhaps it was your eagerness to pitch your tent in the Brigantes camp that kept the two of you from seeing one another as often as you would have liked.'

Corgan bristled at the reproach. In the sudden renewal of tension, talk around the table hushed, and all eyes turned toward the king, whose smile had developed an icy cast. For an awkward moment, it appeared the king would retaliate. Instead, he pulled his mead cup to him once more and took a drink. 'We may have spent time in Brecan's camp, but we were never in his keep. Be that as it may, everything changed when Brecan was killed.' He shook his head ruefully. 'And now the fortunes of many have changed again with the massacre . . . so many good men lost that night . . . too many.'

'Far too many,' Conor agreed. 'My father among them. But we survived, and now we have the chance to form new friendships and alliances.'

'I could not have said it better,' replied the king stiffly. An edgy mood settled over the table as the talk turned to insipid observations about herds, and crops, and weather—until a messenger appeared at the entrance to announce that other lords were arriving. Corgan pushed back his chair quickly and rose to leave, inviting his guests to rest and take their ease. Then, he and his advisors—and even the serving boys—cleared the hall in almost unseemly haste. Conor's men, just then entering the hall, stepped quickly aside lest they be trampled in the rush. 'Is the hall on fire then?' asked Calbhan as he came to the table.

'Nothing to worry about,' replied Fergal, staring into his empty cup. 'Our lord has been practicing his uncanny tact is all.'

4

'Would you mind telling me, brother, why you thought it necessary to insult our lordly host?' demanded Fergal. 'And this, considering he had just given you a valuable gift and all. A fella might have imagined that offending a king in his own hall was maybe a thing to be avoided.'

'Our host might be a king in his own hall,' Conor countered, 'but he was lying to me.'

'Eh?' said Fergal. 'From my seat on the bench, it appeared that he was more pleasant to us than we had any cause to expect. All the more seeing as how his man Iollan came on to us like a rabid cat.'

'Pleasant, maybe, but do not let the smiles and soft words sway you. The Eridani supported Brecan Big Breecs in all things—and that for several years. The whole world knows this. It is no secret.'

Fergal shook his head and clucked his tongue. 'Shame, brother.'

'So now, Corgan comes over all forlorn because he did not enjoy my father's company as much as he would have liked! That was a lie.'

'How so?' challenged Fergal.

'Dúnaird is no great distance from here and our *lordly host* could have gone to see my father anytime the notion took him. There was nothing preventing him—except his blind obedience to Brecan and his own grasping ambition. He considered my father unworthy of his attention and friendship, and that is the truth of the matter.'

Fergal stared at him, then rubbed a hand over his face. 'Ach, well, you have me there,' he conceded. 'But did you have to throw it back at him like that? And with his advisors looking on?'

Conor made no further comment, but drained the dregs, took up his

cup, and rose from the board. Médon and the others went to finish groom-
ing the horses, and Conor, Fergal, and Donal moved on to the Eridani
guest lodge: a large wattle-and-daub building across the yard from the hall.
As soon as they were alone, Fergal had rounded on Conor for insulting
their host.

'Insult? Open your eyes, man,' said Conor. 'Our Lord Corgan is not
above making fools of us. He sends his men to demand we attend this
airechtas or stand accused of a crime. He treats me as an apple-stealing boy
to be banished from the orchard and then treats me like a long-lost kinsman and lies to my face about how he regretted not spending more time
with my father.'

Donal, having listened to this exchange for a while, now broke in.
'Brothers, set aside your argument for a moment if you will. I believe I see
the shape of Lord Corgan's scheme.'

'Ach, now this is what we need,' said Conor, turning to Donal. 'Speak.'

'I'm thinking our host seeks to disarm us with courtesy,' Donal said simply.

'That is it?' cried Fergal. '*That* is your grand insight?'

'Kindness can be a weapon,' Donal told him. 'When allied to keen ambition it can become a most powerful weapon.' Fergal made a sour face,
but Donal continued, 'Think you now, we already know *why* we have been
summoned. You said it yourself, Fergal.'

'Remind me.'

'They mean to pluck our wing feathers lest we fly too high. Your words,
brother—and you were right. See now, the northern kings have become
alarmed at the prospect of a powerful new tribe arising in Eirlandia and
claiming Tara.'

'They tolerated Brecan Brigantes well enough,' Conor pointed out. 'They
didn't seem to mind him flashing his gold baubles around.'

'Maybe Corgan wants the high kingship for himself and thinks Conor
stands in his way.'

'Maybe,' Donal replied. 'But even if Corgan or any of the others have
no desire for Tara, that does not mean they are willing for anyone else to
have it.'

'Least of all me,' said Conor. 'Outcast and upstart that I am.'

'Least of all someone who flaunts ten generations of Dé Danann tradition and seizes the prize for himself,' amended Donal. 'This is what everyone

thinks you are doing. Corgan and his friends have decided it is time to slap you down.'

'Where does all this kindly courtesy come into it?' asked Fergal.

'Ach, well, I'm thinking Lord Corgan hopes to humble us and give us a taste of how well we could be treated if Conor will only agree to give up raising a settlement at Tara—and this before we become too powerful to stop without bloodshed.'

Conor took a moment to consider all that Donal was telling him. On the face of it, this did seem a likely explanation for their host's strange behaviour. 'So now, supposing it is as you say, I cannot see how this should change what we came here to do.'

'Nor should it,' Donal replied. 'I only tell you so you can be on your guard in the discussions to come.'

Just then Médon appeared at the door and said, 'Lord Conor. I thought you might like to know, your brother has arrived.'

'Liam is here?' said Conor.

'Himself. He just came through the gate. If you hurry you may still meet him before he reaches the hall.'

They left the guesthouse and stepped into the yard, where, as Médon had said, four riders had just reined up. Leading them was Liam mac Ardan. Conor had neither seen nor spoken to Liam since the day Conor had ridden to Dúnaird to claim his beloved Aoife and take her away to Tara. It was true that, for a time, Liam had imagined that in his brother's extended absence Aoife would come to accept him and warm to his affections. Her stubborn refusal had done much to stoke Liam's long-simmering jealousy and distrust of his brother. But surely, Conor reasoned, after these many months to reflect, Liam could see how badly he had misjudged the entire affair and that, perhaps, the time was right for a reconciliation.

They waited until the Darini delegation had dismounted, then walked over to meet them. Of those accompanying Liam, Conor recognised only one: Eamon, foremost among his father's hearth companions.

'Greetings, brother,' said Conor, extending his arms in welcome. 'I hope I find you well.'

'Conor,' said Liam, his tone flat. He stood unmoving beside his horse, gazing at Conor, his mouth tight, his eyes hard. 'Still playing king in that pretend kingdom of yours?'

Ignoring the insult, Conor said, 'I wondered whether we might see you here. Corgan did not tell me who would be attending this gathering.'

'I knew,' replied Liam, 'but I expected you would stay as far away as possible.'

Eamon, seeing how poorly this meeting between the two was progressing, stepped forward and, seizing Conor by the shoulders, pulled him into a firm, brotherly embrace. 'Conor, it is good to see you.' He thumped Conor on the back, then turned to Fergal and Donal, flinging an arm toward each of them, saying, 'And you, Fergal . . . Donal . . . ach, it gladdens the heart, so it does. You all look in fine feather. Not settling for the soft life yet, I see.'

'Nothing but work from sun to sun,' Fergal told him, grinning. 'But it keeps us trim and ready—eh, Donal?'

'So it does,' agreed Donal. 'Though it appears the soft life has claimed another volunteer in *you*, brother.' He slapped the Darini battlechief on the back. 'I have never seen you looking so fat and happy.'

'Not so, not so,' protested Eamon. 'I am fair run out of my brócs keeping the warband fighting fit. Our horses are another matter. We lost four foal last winter and two stallions have come up lame. We're trying to find some—'

'Enough!' growled Liam, glaring at them. 'Gabbling like old women at the well.' To Conor, he said, 'Do not expect to gain anything from our kinship, brother mine. You will not receive any consideration from me.'

Conor smiled grimly and shook his head. 'Remind me, Liam, when have I ever received any kindly consideration from you?'

Liam grunted and, snatching up the reins, led his horse away; he proceeded to the hall, where he was met by Lord Corgan and his advisors. 'Pleasant as the day is long,' muttered Fergal. 'I hope our man Corgan keeps a second guest lodge. I don't think I can sleep beneath the same roof with Liam.'

'Nay, not so,' scoffed Donal, 'you could sleep beneath the same roof with a herd of wild pigs and never stir a muscle.'

'Ach, well, I would *rather* sleep with wild pigs than anywhere that fella lays his head.'

Conor watched the reception his brother received from the Eridani king; it was both cordial and warm—intimate, even, an amiable exchange between two close friends—and it set Conor's teeth on edge. Turning away from the display of mutual regard, he said, 'I've seen enough.' With that, he stumped back to the guest lodge.

The meal that night was an awkward affair; Liam did his best to annoy Conor, and Conor pretended not to notice the slights and slurs his brother tossed his way. The next day was no better. Throughout the morning and into midday, other kings and lords arrived and to a man gave Conor a tepid greeting or ignored him altogether. When the last lord arrived, Lord Corgan announced a feast to mark the beginning of the airechtas—as if this was an event to be celebrated.

And a celebration it was, but one designed to impress those in attendance, not to fête them. A number of long boards and benches had been set up near the entrance to the hall. Out in the yard, several fire rings had been made and over the largest of them an entire ox sizzled on an iron spit tended by two cooks; stripped to the waist, one of the men turned the slowly roasting carcass while the other laved hot drippings over the meat with an enormous long-handled ladle. Silver smoke rose into the balmy evening air, filling the yard with a mouthwatering aroma. Elsewhere, members of the tribe were placing platters of bread and lobes of soft cheese on the tables, while others were busy setting up tripods for the ale vats and mead.

Médon and Galart, walking slightly ahead of Conor and the others, halted midstep to gawk at the display. 'Tonight we eat like kings,' said Galart, and Calbhan voiced similar sentiments. Conor, overhearing this, said, 'How many kings do you know who eat like this of an evening? Make no mistake, what you see before you is intended to win your approval and, with it, your allegiance. Take advantage of Corgan's generous provision. Eat and drink to your heart's content, but do not for a moment forget why we have come. Guard your tongues. Say nothing to anyone you would not care to have repeated in the council tomorrow. If you cannot do that, then take yourself back to the guest lodge and stay there.'

'Never fear, lord, Fergal told us what we might expect,' Médon assured him, and the others murmured their agreement. 'Aye,' agreed Galart, 'we know well enough when hands are turned against us.'

'Then by all means enjoy the food,' Conor told them, 'and make friends for yourselves among the Eridani warband if you can. Prince Fáelán seems an amiable sort. You might start there.'

The ardféne trooped off together, heading directly for the ale tubs with Fergal close behind. Conor and Donal stood for a moment longer, surveying the activity from across the yard. Several of the lords who had arrived earlier in the day already had cups in their fists; Lord Corgan moved among the newcomers, chatting pleasantly, while serving boys circulated, filling cups with ale or mead from jars. Other guests—noblemen and their advisors—were drifting into the yard, drawn by the ale and roasting meat. Conor surveyed the group standing with the Eridani king and said, 'Speaking of friends, which of these before us do you think we might count on for a good word?'

'Aside from our gracious host's watchdog Iollan, I don't see anyone I recognise,' Donal replied. 'I'm thinking these are lords new-made following the massacre.'

Conor conceded that this was probably so, and said, 'You may be right—which means they may not have had time to become hardened in their views and may yet respond to a little friendly persuasion. Brother, let us see what can be accomplished with the aid of an overflowing ale jar.'

The two made their way to where King Corgan was standing with a group of men; Corgan glanced around at their approach and, beaming a broad smile, declared, 'Join us! Join us and raise a cup—' He snapped his fingers at a passing serving boy. 'Here now, cups for our friends.'

Iollan, coming up just then, plucked vessels from the nearby board, and took them to the vat to fill them. Meanwhile, Corgan introduced the three newcomers to the other two lords standing with him and asked if they had met one another before. They had not, so he undertook to make the introductions all around.

'I would have you meet Lord Aengus of the Cauci, our neighbours to the east.' Corgan indicated a stocky young man with narrow eyes and a dense thatch of black hair; a livid scar pulled down the right side of his mouth and creased his chin.

'Excuse me for saying it, but that scar looks new,' said Conor after greeting the lord. 'Did I see you fighting alongside me at Tara?' he asked.

Lord Aengus grumbled a terse response and Conor introduced him to Donal.

Next, Corgan turned to the lord on his right—another young nobleman who, judging from the sparse moustache sprouting from his upper lip, was not long accustomed to the razor. Putting a hand on the young man's shoulder, Corgan said, 'And this is Lord Torna of the Volunti. But I think you may know one another already?'

Before Conor could respond, Torna said, 'Ach, I know him well enough—by repute, mind. We have never met.' The young lord fixed Conor with a hard gaze. 'It seems Conor mac Ardan here has lured away some of the best of my warband to join this fianna of his.'

Corgan raised a quizzical brow and looked to Conor. 'Can this be true?'

'It is true that a few Volunti have joined the fianna,' affirmed Conor, 'though I cannot recall luring anyone. Like the others in my warband, they came to us of their own accord—as I think friend Torna must know.'

The young lord bristled at this. 'Do you call me liar to my face?'

Conor put on a conciliatory smile and said, 'We have drawn many warriors to our number. I do not always know the reasons why they come, or the circumstances of their leaving. If you find yourself aggrieved by this, I am sure we can come to an understanding.'

Donal, watching this exchange, spoke up. 'Might it be that your sword-brothers left the Volunti warband *before* you began your reign?'

'Aye,' affirmed the young man. 'What so?'

Conor saw what Donal was hinting at. 'Would I be much mistaken to suggest that it was your father who gave Diarmaid and the others leave to join my fianna?' he asked. 'I suspect his decision does not sit as well with you as it did with him.'

'You have cut to the quick there,' replied Torna. 'If those men had not abandoned their king, he would still be alive today.'

'King Macha lost his life in the Tara massacre,' said Corgan.

'As did many another valiant nobleman that night,' said Conor. 'Full sorry I am to hear it. You must have heard that I also lost my father?'

The Volunti lord's manner became guarded. 'I had not heard that,' he muttered.

Lord Aengus, who had been following this exchange closely, spoke up, saying, 'I heard Conor abandoned his father and the Darini warband and fled to the hilltop to escape being trapped on the plain.'

The ruby birthmark quickened on Conor's cheek. He swung his gaze to the Cauci lord. *Was this what people are saying about me?*

'That never happened, friend,' said Donal, his voice low and laced with menace. 'It would not bear repeating.'

Iollan returned with two overflowing cups for Conor and Donal; Corgan passed them out. 'Ach, well, we all know there was a great deal of confusion at the time. Errors were made. Such is the nature of battle. On that, I think we can all agree.' He gestured for a nearby serving boy to bring the jar for Aengus and Torna. 'Fill your cups and enjoy this night,' urged Corgan, trying to lighten the mood. 'We are all friends here.'

As the jars were being poured, Corgan looked across the yard to where Liam, Eamon, and another nobleman were just then entering the yard from the warriors' house. 'Here are Liam and Vainche to join us. Excuse me, I must go welcome them.'

Leaving his guests to a chilly silence, the Eridani king moved off to greet the late arrivals. Conor and Donal tried to engage the two northern nobles in conversation about the state of this year's crops and cattle, hoping to coax them into a more affable outlook. The Cauci king, Aengus, made a few halfhearted attempts at pleasantry; from the Volunti lord, Torna, they received only grunts. All the while, Conor kept his eye on Liam and Vainche, who, even from a distance, he could see were already snugly wrapped in one another's esteem. As always, Vainche—the haughty usurper of the Brigantes throne—was richly and immaculately turned out in a fine new siarc and breecs of gold-threaded cloth; a bone-handled long knife was tucked into a wide leather belt ornamented with silver disks. Liam had arrayed himself in like fashion—in clothes Conor suspected of having come as gifts from his new patron king.

In the end, the effort to chivvy along the cheerless lords became too taxing and Conor abandoned the attempt. He made a lame excuse and then extricated himself from their company. Donal refilled his cup and followed. They found a relatively quiet place at the end of one of the long boards and paused to sip their drinks and reflect. Donal said, 'Well, *that* was a rough scramble up a steep hill.' He glanced at Conor. 'What do you think?'

Conor, his cup raised to his lips, took a long draught and wiped his moustache with the back of his hand. 'What do I think?' He looked across the yard to where Liam, Vainche, and Corgan were now head-to-head in conversation. 'I think it's going to be a long night.'

'Aye,' sighed Donal, 'and an even longer day tomorrow.'

Rhiannon

The bards of Tír nan Óg tell of a place unlike any other—an island in the western sea, far beyond the horizon of the setting sun. When I was a child I listened to the tales of this wondrous place and my heart burned within me with longing. The faéry folk of old, they told me, knew it as Í Ban. Some know it still as Ynys Gwyn, or even Hí Béo, the Blessed Isle. Though the names drift and change through the ages, the one that comes nearest to revealing the true nature of the place, and the best of them to my ears, is Tír Tairngire, the Land of Promise. Now, it may be that the stories about this mystical island realm number almost as many as those who tell them, few there are who have ever seen the island. Fewer still, those who have travelled there—for the reason that no one who sets foot upon those storied shores ever returns.

This, as the bards say, is the way of it:

In the elder time, when the dew of creation was still fresh on the ground, there were two men, kinsmen and cousins, Nuada and Gofannon. As the day was good and the sea bright and calm, Nuada went down to the shore and readied his boat. His cousin happened along a short while later and said, 'What—and are you going fishing without me?'

'Never say it,' replied Nuada. 'Here I was, hoping for good company. My boat is fair, as you can see—with two red sails and a stout rudder of yew and a mast of ash. There is room enough in the boat for two and for all the fish that we shall catch this day. Will you come with me then?'

'Aye, and here was I thinking you would never ask,' said Gofannon, 'If you cast your nets for sweet herring, I am your man.'

Together they readied the rudder and rigging, loaded a basket containing their food and drink for the day, and pushed the boat out into the gently lapping surf. The breeze was light and the boat lighter still for all it rode high on the waves like a feather. Out they went, beyond the cove and headland to where the sea grows deep and the fish big and fat. They dropped the net and waited to see what their luck would bring. Many things might have happened—a trove of silver herrings, a clutch of juicy mackerel, or a speckled sea trout or two—but none of those things transpired.

Instead, the lines grew taut and strained against the ties and, thinking they had drifted into a shoal of sand eels, they began hauling on the ropes. They heaved and pulled, the two of them together, but the net was too heavy. More than that—the net continued to strain against their pulling. More than that, the ropes remained taut and the boat began to move. And more than that, the boat swung about and was soon breasting the waves with a swift and wonderful speed.

Here was a thing neither Nuada nor Gofannon had ever encountered, and something no fisherman ever desires: his small boat overtaken by a force he can neither see nor control.

'I think we have snagged a great turtle,' shouted Nuada.

'Nay, cousin,' replied Gofannon. 'No turtle is so big that it can pull a boat under sail. It must be something larger—a very whale at least!'

'Turtle, whale, or something else,' cried Nuada, 'we are going out to sea!'

'We must cut the lines!' called Gofannon and, drawing his knife, he leaned over the side of the boat and began sawing at the nearest rope. Alas! His luck was not with him, for his hand became wet and the hilt slipped from his hand and fell into the emerald-tinted deep. He saw the brazen glint spinning down away from him and knew their fortune was sealed.

He gulped and gasped and turned to Nuada, saying, 'Cousin, my knife is gone and the rope still uncut. Your knife must finish the chore.'

'That would be a grand thing, to be sure,' replied Nuada as he collapsed upon the tiller bench. 'Had I so much as a fruit knife in my belt that rope would be severed even now.'

'What manner of seafarer puts out from shore without a knife?' wondered Gofannon.

'Well you might ask,' sighed Nuada. 'It was thinking of all the fine fish we were to get that drove all else from my mind.'

'Then we must untie the ropes and cast them over,' said his kinsman. 'Lend a hand and we'll soon put this right.'

But that was not to be. For the lines were stretched so tightly that, try as they might, they could not pull hard enough to gain so much as a thumb-width of slack to untie even one of the braided cords and there were four of them, and all four taut as bowstrings. They worked until their hands were chafed and red and sore, but it was no use. They could not free the net from the creature they had caught, and which had now caught them.

Over the white-topped waves they flew, over the broad and furrowed face of the briny deep; up and up, over the hillcrests of sea swells and down, down again plumbing the depths of the surging troughs. The earth and stone and verdant woodlands of their homeland receded behind them, growing small and then smaller until fading away in the blue-misted distance. And still they flew!

As the sun hovered high overhead, the two hapless sailors grew tired and took it in turn to sleep a little now and then; while one slept, the other watched the horizon always in the hope of seeing another boat or ship they might hail to their help. But all they saw was the sun-bright sea and the flying flecks of white seabirds wheeling in the salt-scented air. Over the boundless whale tracks and porpoise fields, over the wave-worried vastness the little boat ran westward, ever westward, always westward.

At long last, there appeared a dark smudge on the far horizon. 'Smoke!' cried Gofannon, waking his sleeping cousin. 'Where there's smoke, there is surely fire.'

'And where there is a fire, there is surely land,' said Nuada. 'We are saved!'

Both men watched eagerly and what they imagined to be smoke gradually assumed the form of a cloud-shrouded mountain in the middle of the sea. Closer and ever closer, they soon saw that the mountain was the high promontory of a large island—an island like no other they had ever seen. As they drew nearer, they saw lush green hills flecked with white sheep and goats and cattle, and long stretches of golden sand fronting sparkling blue waters, and tall spreading trees, and clean rushing streams. All they saw was fair beyond anything they had ever known. Indeed, every good thing desirable for a happy life was on that island and the two weary sailors cheered themselves that if they did not know what land they had come to, at least it was a fine and gladsome place.

The boat sped ever nearer and entered a wide and sheltered bay where shoals of fish sported in the shallow water. Here the boat—or the creature pulling the boat—slowed and as they neared the wave-lapped shore, a group of people appeared. Tall and elegant they were, graceful in every feature, richly dressed in sumptuous clothes of many colours. They came down to the water's edge and lifted up their hands.

Gofannon and Nuada, delighted to see other human faces after their long, mysterious voyage, raised their hands, too, and called out a polite greeting and asked, 'What place is this?' To which the answer came by way of a dark-haired woman wearing a torc of gold and six wide bracelets of heavy gold.

'You have come to a place with many names,' replied the comely maid. 'Which one would you hear?'

'We would hear the name most pleasing to our ears,' answered Gofannon happily.

'Since that is your desire, know this,' said the maid. 'You have come to Tir Tairngire, the Land of Promise. Where is your home?'

'Great lady,' called Nuada, 'we come from Eirlandia far away in the east. Early this morning we put out our nets for fishing and caught a creature that brought us here.'

'We are hungry and thirsty and tired,' added Gofannon, 'and we would be glad of your company and, perhaps, a drink and a crust of bread.'

At this the lady smiled and her silent companions murmured and looked to one another. 'You are a bold asker,' she replied, 'and it is well within my power to grant your wishes. However, you should know that to obtain even the smallest crumb from beneath our table and the tiniest sip of water from our stream would determine your destiny for ever and always.'

'That seems to me a steep price to pay for a mere crumb and a drop of water,' replied Gofannon. 'Why is that, I wonder?'

'Well you should wonder,' replied the lady. 'The reason is this: Anyone who sets foot on this island and eats from our table can nevermore return to the world left behind. Think you now, you would never see home and kinsmen again, never hear the gentle rain patter on the green woodland paths, or smell the sweet-smelling fields of broom and heather in the land dearest to your heart; never again would you see the sun rise in your beloved's eyes.' She leveled her gaze upon the pair of far-venturing youths. 'You are young men yet, so I ask you to long and thoughtfully consider: Are you prepared to abandon everything you have known and loved?'

Gofannon gulped and Nuada swallowed hard. They put their heads together and held a brief discussion. Before long, Nuada answered, 'We thank you for your forthright advice, great lady. We find that we cannot so easily forsake our kinsmen and home for the cost of a drink and bite to eat. We will not come onto your island.'

'Nor yet can we see how we are to return the way we came,' added Gofannon quickly. 'Unless the creature that brought us here can be induced to take us back, we cannot say how we will fare for the way is not known to us and we cannot long live in this bay, pleasant as it might be.'

At this, a tall and majestic man stepped forth. Dressed all in sapphire blue with a gleaming white cloak with chains of gold around his regal neck, he raised his hands. 'I am Manadan, and the creatures of the sea hear my voice and they obey. It is the work of a moment to send you home again if that is your true desire.'

The two voyagers assured the Lord of the Sea that retuning home was indeed their sole desire. 'Then go,' said Manadan, 'and take with you the knowledge of this place and remember that it is here waiting for those who tire of life in the wider world and would live in peace and harmony and plenty forever.'

The Sea King was still speaking as the boat began to move once more. Looking over the side into the shallow water, Gofannon and Nuada saw in their net the dark, fluid shape of an enormous rainbow-sided salmon. The King of Fish pulled them from the pleasant bay and out to sea once more. The two stood at the stern and watched as the Fortunate Isle dwindled and faded as a dazzling silver sea mist descended and stole it from view.

It was night and the stars were alight when the two ill-prepared seamen returned to the friendly shore of Eirlandia and to the homely cove of their departure. That night they told all their clan and kin about their seagoing adventure and their discovery of the Land of Promise—that realm beyond the farthest edge of the western sea. Everyone who heard the tale was amazed and filled with wonder at the telling.

This happened in the time of Lord Céthur the Undefeated, who after the Battle of Mag Teamhair became the first High King of Eirlandia and Albion together, for they were still one land in those days. In time, Nuada became king after Céthur and received the silver hand from the physician Dian Cécht and Credne the silversmith when Nuada lost his hand in battle. Gofannon became lord and king in Albion about this time and ruled so well and wisely that he became known as one of the three Wise Kings of Albion. It is said that as he approached the end of his life, Gofannon took ship and sailed back to the Land of Promise. This may be true, for he was never seen again by anyone, nor is his grave known to this day.

This is the tale our bards call 'The Wonder Voyage of Gofannon and Nuada.' I relate it here because my uncle Morfran, who is now King of the Tylwyth Teg, is of the opinion that it is time for our people to make that journey to the Land of Promise, nevermore to look upon the world of mortal men and their abhorrent works. He is not alone in this view, and though there are many who do not agree, sentiment in support of the idea is growing.

But it is also said, by wise druids and sages, that there will come a day when the Land of Promise will extend its reign into this worlds-realm so that all mortal flesh shall know the manifold blessings of the Kingdom of All Tomorrows.

5

Corgan's feast ended much as it began: in an atmosphere of somewhat strained cordiality. The Eridani king made a studied effort to play the genial host, but as the night wore on the temper of the gathering drifted steadily toward rancour and spite. Many of the worthies in attendance exhibited a crabbed suspicion if not outright resentment of Conor. It did not help that Liam and Vainche were seen to be deep in one another's embrace—drinking and laughing together like kinsmen at a wedding—an outright snub that was not missed by anyone in attendance.

Conor did what he could to show himself unaffected by the slight, maintaining a good humour throughout the meal. By evening's end, however, he could no longer sustain the pretence; he rose from the board dispirited and dejected—a mood that only deepened the next morning as the lords filed into the hall.

All the benches and boards for the feast the night before had been cleared, and a large ring of stools and chairs had been set up around the central hearth, where a small fire flickered—one seat each for a lord and his chief advisor. Any other advisors or counsellors were free to stand behind their lords to lend their support, or to come and go from the hall as they pleased.

Also present were lords Sechtán and Garbha, who, late arriving, had missed the feast. 'The Robogdi and Ulaid are here,' whispered Donal as the two entered with their men. 'We can count them friends, I think.'

'At least, they are not already against us. That may be our best hope in this place,' replied Conor, eyeing Vainche and Corgan, sitting opposite them on the other side of the hearth. Liam, not willing to waste a chance to openly offend his brother, took a seat at Vainche's right hand so there would be no doubt where his sympathies lay. Conor smiled and nodded to the lords as they took their places around the ring, but no one returned his smile.

When all were seated and settled, King Corgan began with a formal welcome and thanked those gathered in the circle for their participation; he then proceeded to recite the long-established rule of the airechtas. 'Be it known to everyone here that certain grievances have been aired and accusations made that require resolution. As summoner of this council of judgement, I will present the complaints and allegations so that all may hear. I will then invite any who care to speak to stand and make themselves known.'

He passed his gaze around the ring to make sure that everyone understood, then gestured to Conor. 'The subject of the allegations will be called to answer the complaints in any way he deems appropriate.' Conor nodded to show he understood.

'Finally, after hearing both sides, we will weigh the merits and render judgement. If fault is found, we will determine the appropriate remedies. Therefore, I ask each of you within this circle to remember that this airechtas has been called with the aim of healing all injuries, paying all penalties, making restitution, or levying compensation as may be decreed by the judgement of the airechtas. All members gathered beneath this roof will agree to abide by the decision of this council.'

Corgan paused to let his speech settle in the minds of the noblemen, then asked, 'Are there any questions before we begin?'

Conor rose to his feet. 'I have a question.'

Halfway to his seat, Corgan turned back, his eyebrows raised. 'What is it?'

'What if there is no fault to be found?' Conor spread his empty hands in a gesture of open honesty.

The Eridani king hesitated.

Conor jumped on the momentary lapse. 'If fault is found, you said, the appropriate penalties and restitutions will be assessed. But, if no fault is found, what shall be the compensation to the accused? For to be wrongly accused is injurious to a lord's good name and standing among the tribes, as everyone knows. And any who make allegations later determined to be false should bear the penalty for that loss.' He smiled and looked at the grim faces around him. 'Those with older and wiser heads than mine will no doubt recall that this, too, is ordained by the airechtas—as is only right and just.'

The silence that met this declaration resounded like dull thunder through the hall. At last, a lone voice spoke up. 'That is so. I do recall this provision.' Lord Garbha, one of the late-arriving kings, stood up. 'Lord Conor is right to remind that a man wrongly accused suffers a loss to his reputation and that cost must be compensated.' He sat down again, adding, 'A timely word of warning for us all.'

'That was well said,' Fergal whispered, leaning over the back of Conor's chair. 'But I wouldn't be counting my horses just yet.'

Corgan resumed in a slightly strained tone. 'We are grateful to Lord Conor for his reminder. The airechtas will now hear the allegations that have brought us here.' He turned and, in an appeal to the gathering, asked, 'Who will be first to speak?'

Awkward in his eagerness, Torna, the angry young Volunti lord, leapt to his feet. 'It is no secret to anyone here that Conor mac Ardan has claimed Tara and its three surrounding plains for his own—lands that have been sacred to all Eirlandia from long ages passed. I demand to know by what authority he has done this.' Although Torna appeared inclined to say more, he sat down to allow others to speak.

When no one did, Corgan, from his place at the hearth, announced, 'This, then, is the heart of the matter.' He turned to Conor. 'You stand accused of seizing sacred lands belonging to the tribes and people of Eirlandia and taking them for your own—a serious charge. What have you to say to this?'

Conor thought for a moment, then rose to his feet. 'Is it true that I have taken Tara and her surrounding plains for my own?' Conor said, looking directly at Torna. 'It is not. I have done no such thing.'

'Liar!' shouted Torna, leaping from his chair as if it had suddenly become too hot to withstand. 'He lies. He is building a fortress on Tara Hill! We have seen it!' He thrust a finger at Conor and shouted, 'Liar!'

Lord Aengus, coming to the aid of his friend, jumped to his feet and appealed to his fellow lords. 'I tell this assembly that I have seen the settlement he is raising! With my own eyes, I have seen it!'

The enraged outburst unleashed a commotion—some voices adding their comments to the accusation, others calling for quiet—and Corgan seemed in no hurry to quell the commotion. When he finally contained the uproar, he turned once more to Conor.

'Do you deny building a fortress at Tara?' asked the king.

'That was not the question before the council,' Conor replied evenly. 'Our young friend accused me of taking Tara Hill and the plains for my own. And I tell you and everyone here that I have not done so.'

This denial only served to stoke the fire of outrage higher. And though Corgan was not inclined to silence the protests, Sechtán, the Robogdi lord whom Conor had saved the night of the massacre, stood up and said, 'My lords, we seem to be wading into a bog. I say we allow Lord Conor to explain what he means lest we founder completely.'

Conor nodded and thanked Sechtán for his intervention, then said, 'I deny the allegation that I have taken Tara for my own for the simple fact that I am establishing a place of refuge for *all* the tribes and clans and people of Eirlandia. I am raising a settlement to be a haven and refuge for *all* the displaced of this island—all those made homeless by the raiding ravages of the Scálda.' He looked around at the faces of the lords, some angry, some thoughtful, some confused. 'Many of you will know the people I am talking about because many of you will have seen these exiles as they pass through your lands. Some of you will have even turned away these people yourselves, claiming you have no room for them.' Conor's voice took on a defiant tone. 'But, I do not turn anyone away. Tara is for all Eirlandia, and so we have families and clans from many tribes—just as I have warriors from many tribes serving in my warband. And to those who say I am building a fortress, Tara does not even have walls. I ask you, what kind of fortress would it be that doesn't have walls?'

A sudden chatter coursed through the gathering as various lords discussed what they had heard. Ignoring the sour looks and whispers of the lords and their advisors, Conor turned to his ardféne. Calbhan passed him a water skin, saying, 'Am I the only one thinking that fella Torna must have a wasp up his nose?'

The others laughed at this, and the tension they all felt since entering the hall eased somewhat. 'He's like a little yappy pup that cannot wait to jump up and bite you.'

'I cannot think why,' said Conor. 'I've hardly offered the man two words together since I met him."

'Clearly, something's bothering him,' said Galart. 'It might be well to find out what it is before his barking rouses the bigger dogs.'

'The big dogs are awake and growling already,' observed Médon, taking the water skin. 'You could see them talking behind their hands and giving one another nods and winks. They are only waiting for a chance to take over the fight.'

'Aye,' agreed Fergal, 'they'll be letting Torna and that Aengus fella worry at it for a little and then they'll rush in for the kill.' Nodding toward a knot of noblemen huddled tight around Corgan, he added, 'Look at them over there—plotting their next attack now.'

'Torna and Aengus are spoiling for a fight, true enough,' said Conor, eyeing the ranks of lords. 'Sechtán and Garbha may listen to reason. I'm not sure about the others.'

'Do not doubt for a moment that Vainche and Liam are honing their blades,' said Fergal. 'They won't be happy until they've sliced you to bloody threads.'

'It may not come to that,' suggested Conor hopefully.

*　　*　　*

'Ach, well—then you'll have to dance lively to stay out of their reach.'

Corgan, having allowed the chatter to continue, cleared his throat and took control of the proceedings once more. 'I know I need not remind anyone here that Tara Hill and its three fair plains comprise the most sacred and revered lands of the Dé Danann. We have heard Conor claim that he is establishing a refuge at Tara for the good of everyone.' Pulling on his chin as if deep in thought, he paced a few steps before his chair, then turned back to address the noblemen. 'I am of the opinion that whether this claim is true must depend on the character of the man making the claim. In other words, my friends, is Conor mac Ardan to be trusted when he says he acts for the good of all Eirlandia?' He glanced around the ring of seated noblemen. 'Who would speak to his claim?'

Lord Vainche rose to his feet and, as if the terrible weight of his testimony bore down upon his shoulders, he moved with slow, measured steps to take his place at the hearth in the centre of the ring of chairs. His smooth cheeks newly shaven, his hair neatly braided, he had arrayed himself in a costly cloak and now wore a golden torc around his neck—as if to remind everyone of the wealth and power of the Brigantes tribe he now ruled as king. 'I would advise this council not to be seduced by a few slippery words. You see, I know Conor mac Ardan. It is a fact that he once served in my warband.' Vainche turned and regarded Conor, then shook his head with a weary, lamentable air, adding, 'Indeed, it pierces me to the very pith of my being to say that as a warrior he served so poorly that I had no choice but to dismiss him for his incompetence and utter lack of honesty. And this, after he had been shown great kindness by the queen, seemed to me nothing less than a betrayal of her trust.'

This revelation caused an undercurrent of comment to swell through the hall. Corgan held up his hand for quiet. 'You say he had been taken in and given a place,' he said. 'For those who don't know the circumstances, can you tell us how this came to be?'

Vainche nodded. 'If you think it necessary to rehearse such a painful memory . . .'

'It would help in our deliberations,' replied Corgan, passing his gaze around the assembled lords.

'It is well known that Conor was cast out of his tribe for stealing valuables from unattended tents during the last Oenach of Brecan mac Lergath. I believe Lord Liam of the Darini—his own brother—can swear to the truth of this sad event. As a wandering exile, Conor came to Aintrén and, against sound counsel, Brecan took pity on him and gave him a place in the Brigantes warband.

'After Brecan was murdered . . .' Here Vainche paused and cast a glance to Corgan, who nodded as if encouraging him to continue. 'As many of you will recall, King Brecan was cruelly killed by a Scálda raiding party while on a circuit of his lands. It is also known that Conor was part of the bodyguard that accompanied the king, and that his role in Brecan's murder has never been satisfactorily explained. Yet another question that, in my mind at least, demands an answer.'

If Vainche's first pronouncement caused a flutter of comment, this one stirred a commotion. Fergal slammed his fist into his thigh and loosed a curse between clenched teeth. One voice cried out for justice for Brecan's murder.

Conor felt the fire flow up through his gut to his ruby birthmark, and it began to burn like an ember plucked from the fire and applied to his face.

Shaken by the cruel dishonesty of this spurious account, he nevertheless held his tongue and gazed in stony silence at Vainche and at the suddenly angry faces ringed around him. As the commotion subsided, another lord rose to his feet—one that Conor did not recognise.

'I, too, can speak to the contemptible character of this man.' He flung a dismissive hand in Conor's direction. 'I know him to be deceitful and greedy, little caring for the pains of others, or the injury caused by his vaunting ambition. . . .'

This assertion ignited the anger already smouldering in the hall. Lords threw their fists into the air and shouted loud condemnation: of Conor and his corrupt behaviour, of the Scálda and their evil blight, of all that was wrong in Eirlandia. There were cries for justice, for reckoning, for retribution, for revenge.

'This last rogue,' whispered Conor, leaning toward Donal, his voice strained and unnatural. 'Who is he? I have never seen him before.'

'Nor I,' replied Donal, and Conor looked to Fergal, who shook his head.

'I think that is Toráin, Lord of the Concani,' said Médon, leaning close to Conor's ear. 'One of his warriors joined us at Tara.'

'Joined us how?' wondered Fergal, also bending close. 'There are no Concani warriors in the fianna.'

'Fíol is not a warrior in the fianna,' Médon explained. 'He serves with hearth master Dearg.'

A faint memory floated into Conor's recollection; he dimly remembered talking to Dearg about a kinsman—a wounded warrior—he might ask to help him with his many duties. So much had happened since then, he had forgotten the conversation completely. 'You mean the fair-haired fella? The one with the limp?'

'Aye, lord, that's the one. He was sorely wounded the night of the massacre. He was in the Concani warband.'

'So now, this Toráin has his pointy nose out of joint because we took in one of his wounded?' said Fergal. 'This whole thing is a steaming heap of horse dung from beginning to end.'

Lord Corgan's pleas for silence went unheeded. Snatching up a jar of water from beside the hearth, he raised it and poured the contents onto the fire. A column of steam rose, hissing into the rooftrees. 'Quiet!' he shouted. 'We will have quiet!' When the irate lords had calmed themselves sufficiently to allow the proceedings to continue, Corgan thanked the Concani lord and dismissed him. Conor, a reply ready, made to rise, but Aengus, King of the Cauci, was already on his feet and moving toward the hearth.

'More trouble,' muttered Fergal as Conor dropped back into his chair.

Looking grave and thoughtful, the young lord began, saying, 'Unlike our friend Toráin, I cannot speak to the dishonesty and greed of this man.' He paused to point at Conor. 'But I do know something of his corrupt and unscrupulous rule. . . .'

'How can he know anything?' Conor muttered to himself. 'I never met the man before yesterday.'

'. . . and I know how he stole our friend Liam's betrothed and bore her away at spearpoint, and forced unwanted marriage upon her. This is not an act worthy of a lord or nobleman. It is, however, enough to earn the condemnation of this gathering,' concluded the young lord.

Donal and Conor exchanged a knowing glance as the source of Aengus's lies became apparent. 'Liam,' Conor grumbled. 'So that's how it is to be.'

Corgan thanked Aengus and offered sympathy for the loss of his uncle, Lord Credne, in whose place he now ruled. Returning to the hearth, he said, 'We have heard the grievous charges against Conor mac Ardan. As Lord Aengus has just reminded us, these crimes warrant condemnation of the offender and should rightly depose him of his lordship, usurped as it may be. Indeed, I am left wondering how anyone can answer these charges. Do we need to waste our time listening to whatever explanation a guilty man might offer?' He cast his gaze around the assembly as if defying anyone to disagree. 'Unless anyone has any further accusations to submit, I think we have heard enough—and more than enough. I know of no reason we should not now move to decide the judgement of the airechtas.'

'I would speak!' demanded Conor, his voice loud in the hall. He rose and advanced to the hearth, struggling to master his rage.

'The accused cannot stand assurance for himself!' shouted Toráin, leaping to his feet. 'Let the judgement be brought now!'

Before anyone could respond, Conor rounded on the outraged young lord. 'You have had your say, now I will have mine. Who among you would not demand the same if you were in my place?'

The older lords muttered grudging agreement that they would be willing to hear what Conor had to say. However, Vainche and Toráin and one or two others raised such a commotion that the more amenable among them were instantly drowned out.

'Let me speak! I will be heard!' Conor shouted above the tumult, barely making his words intelligible. 'Lord Corgan! I demand the right to be heard.'

Corgan stood and held out his arms as if to still the storm, but the dissenters only increased their uproar. One voice pierced the tumult. It was Vainche: 'What Lord Toráin says is true—the accused man cannot stand as witness for himself.'

Toráin, almost hopping with anger, pointed at Conor and cried, 'He will say anything to save his own skin! We can't trust a single word he says.'

'Judgement!' shouted Vainche. Others took up the demand and it became a chant. 'Judgement now!'

Conor felt his legs weaken; he steadied himself to face the onslaught, marvelling at the rage stirred up against him. In that moment, he saw the shape of the aggrieved kings' game: lure him in with the prospect of settling their differences, and then stick the knife in. He looked to Lord Corgan, who, having set himself up as an impartial arbiter, then abandoned that duty when it was most needed.

'Why are we waiting?' shouted Vainche. 'What more do we need to hear?'

Corgan, nodding gravely, intoned, 'Unless anyone has a reason to delay, I see no reason judgement should not now take place.'

The words were still hanging in the air when there came a sudden commotion at the entrance to the hall, followed by a flurry of motion, and a loud voice boomed, 'You ask if anyone knows a reason why judgement should not now take place. I have a reason.'

'Who is it that disrupts this lawful assembly?' demanded Corgan as the ruckus at the entrance continued.

Another voice, low and angry, growled, 'Take your hand away at once, friend—or lose it!'

A tall figure dressed all in green and grey strode into their midst. His long, dark hair was shaved high on his head in the distinctive style of the bards, and he carried a long staff of rowan wood with a silver top in the shape of a ram's horn; a large leather sparán hung on a strap across his chest, and his wide cloth belt was richly ornamented with tiny pearls and intricate patterns traced in silver thread. Soft brócs, laced high, were on his feet, a silver torc thick as an infant's arm adorned his neck, and a fist-sized casán of carved carnelian fastened his cloak at his shoulder. Head erect, exuding confidence and authority, he moved through the gathering looking neither right nor left.

In all, he looked like a king of the druid kind and took his place at the hearth like a monarch claiming the place of honour at the board.

'Rónán!' gasped Fergal. 'How is it that he's here?'

6

Conor took in the regal bearing and aspect of his younger brother, and his heart swelled with pride to see a man so secure in his power and authority. Conor had not seen him since the day of his wedding, almost a year ago, and Rónán seemed to have grown in dignity and stature since then.

Rónán stood for a moment, taking in the unhappy company gathered around the empty hearth. When he spoke, his voice resounded through the hall. 'You ask who it is with the right to disturb this assembly?' said the man. 'Know you, I am Rónán mac Ardan, a brehon in Eirlandia, and I pose a question to you, Corgan Eridani. By what right do *you* convene an airechtas without first securing the consent and attendance of a druid?'

Corgan stared, speechless; Vainche, his mouth half open, halted, the challenge still on his tongue. Behind Rónán appeared King Cahir; the Coriondi lord advanced to take his place beside the druid. 'My excuses to you all,' said Cahir. 'But it seems the messenger sent to summon me got lost on the way and failed to deliver his message. Otherwise, I would have been here sooner. Fortunately, I found out about this tidy little gathering of yours in time'—he half turned and gave Conor a furtive wink—'in time to fetch a druid to oversee these proceedings—as is only right and proper.'

'We were just about to begin our deliberations,' mumbled Corgan. 'You have come too late.'

Lord Vainche charged in. 'As a well-known ally and supporter of Conor mac Ardan, you were not summoned, Cahir—lest your blind, unthinking bias prevent you from making a proper assessment and judgement.'

'Is that so?' Cahir passed his gaze slowly around the ring of familiar faces. 'Am I to assume that this is the reason you also failed to summon

Cruim and Celchar?' The Coriondi king, his tone taking on a darker note, continued, 'The Venceni and Laigini also lean toward Conor and they are not among us.' He looked around as if expecting to see them; when he did not, he concluded, 'But I see that this blind, unthinking bias you profess to fear has not prevented you from summoning Conor's well-known opponents. Why is that, I wonder?'

'You have no place here,' Vainche insisted. 'The airechtas is nearly finished. You come too late.'

Corgan put out a hand to the Brigantes king and tried to calm him, saying, 'Lord Cahir is here now. There is nothing we can do about that. But, he will have no part in the discussions, nor any voice in the judgement.'

'We shall see about that,' replied Cahir. 'Bring me a chair!'

While the serving boys raced away to find another chair, the Coriondi lord nodded to Rónán, who stepped into the centre of the ring and said, 'As to any further deliberations and judgements, everyone here will have his say. But I tell you now that I alone will judge.'

'Outrageous!' shouted Vainche. 'Do you think—'

Rónán slammed the end of his staff on the floor, and a sound like a peal of thunder boomed through the hall. He advanced further into the ring of chairs around the hearth, and appeared to grow taller and more formidable with every step. 'Beware!' he roared. 'You are speaking to a brehon—one who holds the power to overthrow you with a word! Anyone here who cannot behave with courtesy and restraint will be removed from this place.' He stared with cold, pitiless eyes on the seething Brigantes lord, who at last allowed himself to be pulled back to his seat by his advisors.

'As to the deliberations—as you call them,' continued Rónán, speaking slowly, as if to truculent children, 'we will rehearse the grievances and allegations again for the benefit of Lord Cahir. Then, I shall consider the accusations and evidence, and I will render fair judgement.' He passed his stern gaze slowly around the ring of chastened faces. 'And, know you, that judgement will endure in this age and in the age to come.'

Rónán tapped the end of his staff on the floor three times and then said, 'Since many of you seem to have forgotten, I will enumerate the laws and customs of this assembly.'

To the sound of muttering, shuffling of feet, and one or two moans, Rónán undertook a long and detailed discourse on the ancient legal statutes relating to the rights and responsibilities of kings and the proper conduct of a judicial gathering. These edicts and rulings had been handed down and refined through the ages and memorised by the high-ranking druid caste called brehons. All the while, Rónán stood before the lords, upright as the rowan rod in his hand, stern and unbending, until he had delivered the law and all those present understood their responsibilities and limitations. After that, the grievance and accusations that had been levelled at Conor were quickly stated and judgement rapidly followed.

The initial charge was simple: Conor had taken unwarranted authority to himself by making himself king, seizing Tara, and establishing the sacred precinct as the centre of his realm. It was, as Rónán quickly surmised, an allegation born primarily out of jealousy and envy. But did it have legal validity? That was his main concern. 'I have heard your complaint and listened to the reasons for your grievance,' he declared. 'Has anyone anything to say now that will add to what has already been said?'

He paused, waiting for someone to speak. No one did. Perhaps out of caution, or mere exhaustion, no one raised any further points of clarification or contention.

'Well and good,' concluded Rónán after a moment. 'I will now render judgement.'

So saying, he drew his cloak over his head and stood at the hearth, gripping his staff before him with both hands. He remained motionless and silent for a long time, to the utter fascination of those looking on. The hall remained silent; rapt, unwilling to interrupt his curious meditations. After a time he was heard to groan. His grip on his staff tightened, his knuckles turned white, and his body trembled and rocked from side to side. More time passed and he relieved himself of another groan, and then pulled back his cloak and looked up, his face red, sweating from the effort expended. 'Hear, O Eirlandia, the judgement of a true brehon.'

He put out a hand to his brother. 'Rise, Conor mac Ardan, and receive the justice you deserve. Accusations have been made within the hearing of those present that your lordship is unlawful and, further, that in pursuit of this illegal nobility you have transgressed the laws of the realm by seizing the sacred precinct of Tara, its hill and ancient tombs and dwellings, and taking them for your own.'

Turning once more to the assembly, he continued, 'Regarding the legitimacy of Conor's lordship, I find that he has not violated any laws. For, as in the time of Céthur mac Gréine, so it is now. This is the way of it. Let everyone hear and remember.

'Céthur was a bold and cunning warrior. He fought with valor and pride against the enemies of his people and of Eirlandia. Following the great Battle of Mag Teamhair, in which his warhost, combined with those of his brothers Éthur and Téthur, emerged victorious, he and his men retreated to Cnoc Teamhair—as it was called in those days—and there he rested to heal his wounds and allow his people to enjoy the peace he had won by the strength of his arm and the edge of his blade.

'As he rested there to restore himself, he found it pleasant and, because it belonged to no one, he decided to erect a dún for himself and a ráth for his people. He and his clan dwelt there for a year and two seasons. When in time Céthur gained the high kingship—which he shared with his brothers, each in his turn—he made of Tara Hill a haven and refuge. Any man, woman, or child needing such a home could find a welcome there. And this . . . *this* is what made of Tara a sacred place. Not its stones and tombs and dolmens—for sanctity does not reside in stones and such as that, but in the care and concern we have for one another.'

Rónán paused and looked around at Conor, and the shadow of a smile flitted across his face. 'As it was then, so it is now.' Turning back to address the assembly, he said, 'It is my judgement that Eirlandia has been too long divided by our tribes and territories, our realms and kingdoms, and that Conor has revived an ancient and honourable tradition, restoring a practice long forgotten and too long neglected in this worlds-realm—unstinting hospitality to those fleeing oppression. I find no transgression in this.'

There was some muttering among the lords, but Rónán smacked the floor with his staff and silenced them.

'My judgement is this: Against the accusation that Conor has seized the kingship and made himself lord, I find no charge to answer. The reason is well established, and self-evident. Any man or woman is sovereign only so far as his people are willing to serve and follow. Wearing a torc of silver or gold does not make a lady queen, or a lord a king. Rather, it is the will of the people who submit to the rule of a leader, who grant and bestow the rights and privileges of sovereignty.

'In this, I find that Conor mac Ardan has not claimed another man's throne, nor forced anyone to serve him as lord. People have chosen to follow him and it is they who have given him the power and authority to rule over them. Thus, Conor is lord, not by imposition of his will on others, but by acclamation of the people who serve him. In this, he is blameless.'

In the shocked silence that followed this pronouncement, a single voice cried out. 'Unfair!'

Rónán turned around slowly. 'Someone among you deems this unfair? Who said that?'

'A real brehon would know who said it,' quipped one of the lords.

Rónán drew himself up, growing formidable. 'Let me remind you all— since some among you seem to have forgotten—that questioning the legal judgement of a brehon is an offence worthy of a fine and punishment. If I show leniency for your ignorance, Aengus mac Alpan,' he said, turning to speak directly to the offending lord, 'it is only out of pity for your people who must endure your belligerent stupidity. Keep your tongue from flapping or, I tell you the truth, I will have it tied as a trophy to my belt.' Rónán made a small pinching motion in the air with his thumb and forefinger, and Aengus gave out a little squeal and put a hand over his mouth.

Then raising his hand—palm outward at shoulder height—Rónán thumped his staff on the floor three times. 'The judgement of the airechtas has been made. Let all Eirlandia hear and obey.'

He made to dismiss the lords, but Conor, who was still standing just inside the ring, spoke up: 'A word if you please, wise brehon.'

'I will allow it.'

'Before your arrival, it was agreed by everyone here that compensation should be paid if the accusations against me were judged false. Since that eventuality has come to pass, I request a fair judgement. What compensation shall I have?'

This did not sit well with the assembled lords; they grumbled and squirmed in their chairs; having failed to obtain the judgement they sought, they were not keen to have to pay for their failure. 'I protest!' shouted Vainche, leaping from his chair. 'We have done him no harm.'

Corgan and others loudly echoed this assertion, but Lord Garbha, who had previously endorsed the principal, came to Conor's defence. 'We have heard enough from you, Vainche,' he called, thrusting a finger at him, 'and you, Corgan. We would not be here now if you had not kicked this hornets' nest. Conor came here in good faith. He is right to remind us that we all agreed to provide payment if the accusations failed. And I will remind you now, that we all agreed in order to allow the airechtas to proceed. It ill serves us now to refuse out of umbrage or spite.' He put out a hand to Rónán and said, 'I say we must pay what we owe.'

Rónán agreed and thanked the Ulaid king for speaking so directly to the point. Turning to Conor, he said, 'What compensation will you have?'

'I seek nothing for myself,' he replied. 'My name is my own and will rise or fall according to my deeds. But the raiding season is upon us and already the Scálda are pressing our farms and settlements along the southern borders and eastern coast. In order to best protect our people, my warband needs horses.' He turned to Garbha and said, 'You ask what compensation I would have? It is this: seven horses from each lord here beneath the roof of this hall.'

'This is fair and reasonable,' agreed Rónán. 'Seven horses from each lord here. That shall be the recompense in settlement of this judgement.'

'Seven horses!' the lords cried. 'It is too much!' Others shouted, 'Too much by far! We need those horses for our own warriors.'

Lord Cahir entered the fray with a smile on his face, saying, 'If you find this compensation too rich for you, Corgan, perhaps you should have had a care before summoning so many—not all, mind, but many—to condemn a man you should by all rights befriend. As for myself, I will pay the compensation—and pay it gladly—considering it fair exchange for the protection Conor and the fianna provide for our southern borders.'

'I stand with Cahir Coriondi,' said Lord Sechtán. 'The Robogdi will do our part.' To Conor, he said, 'I will deliver the horses to you at Tara as soon as the mares have foaled.'

Corgan, red-faced, found his voice at last, and said, 'Some of us are not as wealthy as Cahir and Vainche. Seven horses is a price we cannot meet without destroying both the herd and the ability to protect our tribe.'

'It is not a question of what you can afford,' Rónán told him bluntly. 'If you feel the pinch it may prevent you from wickedly defaming another in the future.'

'And I tell you it is too much!' cried Torna, the young Volunti lord, shaking with anger.

'Nevertheless, that is my judgement. If you—' began Rónán.

Conor, who was enjoying the sight of the chastised lords trying to wiggle out of paying him his due, nevertheless decided he had made his point. 'How much *can* you afford, Torna?' he said, breaking in.

'How much?' The Volunti lord looked around as if he might see a number he could name.

'Three horses,' suggested Aengus, and this was quickly endorsed by Toráin of the Concani. 'We can pay three horses . . . untrained,' he added.

'Six,' countered Conor. 'Six horses, three of them trained, and you will bring them to me.'

'Four . . . ,' suggested Sechtán cautiously. He glanced around the ring, gathering approval for his counteroffer, receiving both nods and frowns.

Fergal, grinning now, leaned over the back of Conor's chair and whispered to Donal. 'This is rich fare. See now, they no longer contest the judgement. Our Conor's got them haggling over the price. We're going to get those horses.'

'Patience,' replied Donal. 'We don't have them yet.'

'They are as good as ours. Rónán will make sure of that.'

The horse-dealing went on a little longer, and in the end the reward for the damage to Conor's dignity and reputation was agreed at five untrained horses for each lord taking part in the airechtas—these animals to be chosen by Conor or one of his men from among those in the herd at the time of collection. Fergal, almost hugging himself over this sudden increase in wealth, strode from the hall, counting the horses to be added to the herd for the use of the fianna.

7

The last to leave the Eridani king's hall, Donal walked out with Rónán, and Conor with Cahir. The other lords, peeved and embarrassed by the thumping they had received, nevertheless held their tongues and marched in sullen lockstep into the shifty light of a sky grown overcast and gloomy.

Most began fleeing the scene of their drubbing as soon as their horses could be readied and their men mounted. They would, it seemed, prefer a night out on the trail to spending another moment amid the ruins of their overweening pride. One such was Liam. While Eamon saw to the men and horses, Conor sought out his brother to offer a modest reconciliation. 'I'm not your enemy, Liam. I want you to know that.'

'Should I care a piss for what you want?'

'We could at least agree to leave our differences here and go our separate ways in peace. I'm willing if you are.'

Liam swung around and put his face close to Conor's. 'Feeling all high and mighty, are you?' he sneered. 'Think you've won some kind of victory here? You haven't. You are still just an outcast on a small hill crawling with outcasts. Go back to your refugees and rag-wearing exiles and leave the real kings to do what is best for Eirlandia. Better still, go join Balor Evil Eye—and take your stinking rabble with you. That way we'll be done with you once and for all.'

Having delivered himself of this hateful screed, Liam turned on his heel and stalked away. Conor, birthmark blushing crimson with the heat of anger and frustration, watched him go. *Hag take you, Liam,* he thought. *What did I do to make you hate me so? We never were so close, but when did we become enemies?*

Conor turned away and caught sight of Rónán talking to Cahir across the yard and hurried to join them. 'Thank you, Rónán, for what you did for me in there. That was well done.'

'I merely interpreted the law as I am duty-bound to do—no more, no less.' He smiled. 'But if you would thank someone, thank your man here. If Lord Cahir had not sent word, I would never have known about Corgan's ill-begotten scheme in time.'

Cahir, smiling at his own cleverness, professed himself more than happy to be of service to a friend; he took his leave and moved off to allow the brothers to talk. The two walked a little apart and Conor said, 'If I thought you would agree, I would ask you to come and join us at Tara. I could use the wise counsel of a druid.'

'If I thought my ollamh would approve, I would accept your offer.' He spread his hands and shrugged; it was a gesture Conor had seen his father make when confronted with a situation beyond his control, and Conor felt a pang of longing for his dear departed da. It must have shown on his face, because Rónán quickly added, 'I see you are disappointed, but I expect it is for the best. From what I've seen here today, you will benefit from my services as brehon far more than you would a druid advisor.'

Conor clapped his younger brother on the back. 'I reckon you're right. Even so, you'll come to me from time to time? I would like that. It is good to see you and, truly, those of us trying to make a home of Tara could use your wise counsel.'

'I will come when I can,' Rónán agreed. 'Until then, I wish you well, brother.'

'Must you leave so soon?'

Rónán indicated a young druid standing a little apart holding the reins of two fine horses. 'Ovate Milbél, over there, is waiting for me. This visit was unplanned and there are urgent matters elsewhere that require my attention.' He smiled sadly. 'Such is the life of a brehon in Eirlandia.'

Conor embraced his brother. 'Farewell, for now—but do come to us at Tara. Aoife would like to see you—she is with child, you know.'

'Glad to hear it. Give her my best regards.' Rónán stepped away. 'I'll come when I can. You have my word.'

Conor watched him stow his staff beneath the horse cloth, mount his horse, and ride from the yard with his assistant. Donal and Cahir moved to join him and all three conferred for a moment. 'Will you stay the night?' wondered Cahir.

'I'm thinking we've had the best of what welcome we received,' replied Conor, 'and we will be needed at Tara. Are you staying?'

'Ach, nay, it would be a bleak and cheerless night of it—friend Corgan would see to that. We'll leave as soon as the horses are ready.'

'Thank you, Cahir. Once again, your friendship has been the saving of me. Certainly, your intervention here has spared us all a great deal of trouble and difficulty—'

'And bloodshed,' added Donal. 'It likely would have come to blows if not for you, Cahir. I, too, thank you.'

'Pure pleasure,' replied Cahir. 'I have been itching for a chance to slap down that Briéfne upstart. I expected more from friend Corgan, though. He at least is made of finer stuff. He should have known better than to ally himself with a preening magpie like Vainche.'

'Like all birds of his feather, Vainche is able to charm and beguile even the most perceptive. I've seen him do it before. If it had not been Corgan, no doubt someone else would have fallen under his sway. All the same, I had hoped to convince a few lords to see the settlement of Tara in a different light—maybe change a few minds. But now it looks as though I have driven some potential allies further away from me.'

'Don't be thinking the worst. You made a good accounting of yourself today. And those that were against you will stay against you, and likely always will. Some of the older, wiser lords, those who do not know what to make of you yet—I imagine they will have been impressed by you.'

'I hope that is true.'

'So you are determined to keep the hill?' asked Cahir.

'Was there ever any doubt?'

'Ach, well, I can think of worse neighbours.' Extending an arm to Conor, he said, 'You have my support, son. Trust that I will do whatever I can to aid you.'

'Again, my friend, I thank you.' Conor took the extended arm and gripped it firmly. 'I have no doubt I will be calling on that friendship before too long.'

'Nor do I,' laughed Cahir. 'And you'll be wanting horses when you come.'

'That's not what I meant,' Conor told him. 'Cahir, I gladly relieve you of the burden to provide—'

'Stop right there! Fair is fair. I am no different than all the rest who owe you compensation, except . . .' The aging lord's voice took on a sombre tone and his gaze became direct. 'Except, I do it proudly and in eager anticipation of your success in making Tara a haven and refuge for Eirlandia in these anxious times.' He released Conor then and moved away, calling, 'Make us proud, Conor mac Ardan. Make us proud.'

Conor watched him walk away. 'A true friend,' said Donal.

'Aye,' agreed Conor. 'We could use a few more like him.'

They moved on to find Fergal and the ardféne and make their own departure, but had only gone a few paces when a rancid voice called out from across the yard. 'You squirmed out of it this time, worm. Next time, you won't have your brehon brother to pluck you from the fire.'

'One kinsman to support me, aye,' replied Conor, turning back, 'just as you had one of my kinsmen to oppose me. I'd say that levels the board, wouldn't you, Torna?'

'You won't succeed,' shouted the Volunti lord. 'You'll fall off that hill of yours soon enough and I just hope I'm there to see it.'

'We'll meet again soon enough—when I come to collect my horses. Be sure to have them ready for me. I don't want to be kept waiting.'

'The Hag Queen take you!' spat the young lord, and stomped off.

'Ignore him,' Donal advised. 'He's a fool who doesn't know head from arse. Let him fret and fume. It means nothing.'

'Do not think the worse of us,' called Sechtán, hurrying forward. 'You know we were honour bound to obey the summons, but not all of us were against you. Remember that.'

'I'll not be forgetting what happened here,' Conor assured him. 'But perhaps we can sit down and share a cup together next we meet and put all this behind us.'

Fergal appeared with their mounts then, and Conor and his ardféne departed as soon as everyone was mounted. They rode from Bennaél and out into the rolling green expanse of Úaine Coll, a hilly range of smooth moors. The day was fair and so they rode with swift purpose through the Eridani territories. Conor gave Búrach his head and the stallion took the low hills at a flying gallop. The next day they edged Volunti lands and came in sight of the Brigantes' borders. Two days later, Tara Hill rose on the southern horizon. Just the prospect of the place and what awaited them there lifted the heart. Leaving Fergal and the ardféne behind, Conor raced across Mag Teamhair and up the long, steep slope to the hilltop, urging

Búrach faster with every galloping stride. Heart racing with anticipation, he came pounding into the wide oval yard, where he found the ordinarily busy yard in turmoil: heaving with people and animals, and strewn one end to the other with tents made of rags and branches. Wagons, carts, and barrows stacked with baskets of household objects, clothing, and tools, and bundles of provisions of all kinds—an entire settlement plucked up and dropped in the centre of an already-crowded yard.

8

Such was the upheaval on the hilltop, Conor's sudden arrival went unnoticed. He paused for a moment to appraise the disarray and then slid down from his mount and began picking his way through the teeming jumble. Upon reaching the hall, he called out to announce his presence and was met at the entrance by Dearg, his hearth master, who greeted him and welcomed him back. 'And the council?' he asked. 'It went well?'

'Where's Aoife?'

'Lady Aoife has been staying in the women's house these last few days,' he explained. 'It is quieter there and . . .'

Conor thanked him and hurried through the sprawl to the yet-unfinished house and pounded on the door post. After a moment a hand pulled aside the cloak used as a door covering; a fresh face peered out, then disappeared—replaced a moment later by that of his own dear wife.

'Conor! I was just thinking about you and here you are.'

'I'm back and with good news.' He gathered Aoife into his strong embrace and gave her a tight squeeze.

'Ouch! Be careful.' She kissed him and then held him at arm's length and made a face. 'Did they have no soap and water wherever you were?'

'So eager were we to get home,' replied Conor, 'we did not stop to bathe.'

'The ardféne,' she said, glancing around, 'what have you done with them?'

'They're right behind me.' He turned and, with a wave of his arm, indicated the ramshackle mess that filled the yard and the strangers—some of whom who now stood looking on amid a welter of stuff: high-sided wagons full to groaning with tools and utensils, cloth and fleeces, bags and baskets crammed with provisions of all kinds; here and there cattle were tied to stakes in the ground; pigs and goats wandered freely; there was even an anvil and bellows for a forge. 'What's all this?'

'Ach, well, the Auteini have been driven from their lands,' she explained. 'They have come seeking refuge here.'

'The Auteini,' Conor repeated dully. He passed his gaze around the crowded, teeming hilltop. 'How many have come?'

'All of them,' she replied crisply.

'*All* of them? What do you mean?'

'Their lord and battlechief is here, too, and he is that anxious to see you. I expect he will have better answers for your many questions.' She turned and motioned Dearg forward and said, 'No doubt you'll find the man himself in the hall where he has been the last two days when he's not out here demanding food and supplies for his people.'

Conor sighed. 'Just when I was hoping for a space to draw breath.'

'Go see him and hurry back, we will talk later.' She gave him a quick kiss and sent him on his way.

Conor turned away and, taking his hearth master by the arm, said, 'Now then, Dearg, let's go see his lordship and find out what is to be done about all this.'

At the entrance to the hall he was met by a gaunt, hollow-eyed warrior wearing a silver torc and a much-abused yellow siarc with a frayed red-and-white-checked cloak that still bore the traces of recent bloodstains. 'My lord, Conor,' he cried, bounding forward. Two haggard warriors followed in his wake; both were as dishevelled and way-worn as their lord, both wore torcs and armbands of tarnished copper, and both had visible bruises on their forearms where shield grips were likely to rub. 'Tobha, here, brought word you had returned.' He indicated a sandy-haired man beside him. 'As you see, we have taken you at your word.' He offered an embarrassed smile. 'Later than planned, but the Scálda scum gave us no choice.'

'*My* word?' said Conor, glancing at Dearg.

Seeing Conor's uncertainty, the stranger asked, 'Don't you know me, lord?'

'You have me at a disadvantage, friend, I—' Conor broke off as the memory came flashing back: the night of the massacre . . . warriors on a rain-soaked battlefield huddled around the body of their dead king . . . and himself speaking earnestly to them, trying to convince them to abandon the corpse and join the fight elsewhere . . . the battlechief pointing to the cloak-shrouded body of his lord and saying, '. . . *leave our king behind? That we will never do.*'

Then you will soon join him, he had told them. 'Dead, you can do nothing for your lord. Stay alive and you can avenge him,' Conor repeated aloud his words of that fateful storm-racked night. 'You are the Auteini battlechief who took command when your king was killed.'

The lord smiled. 'Aye, and you said we must think what is best for our people—that they would be needing us in the hard days ahead.'

'And it is right you were there, lord,' said the sandy-haired warrior. 'From that day to this it has been one hardship after another. Until this last—'

'So it is,' resumed the lord. 'I am Morann mac Mahon, King of the Auteini. And this is my battlechief, Ruadh, and with me, my chief advisor, Tobha.'

'We are at your service, lord,' said Tobha, touching the back of his hand to his forehead.

Turning to Dearg, Conor said, 'The ardféne will be arriving any moment. Go and bring Fergal and Donal as soon as they get here.' To Morann, he said, 'So much has happened since then, that terrible night seems more and more like a bad dream.'

'All that and more,' agreed the Auteini lord. 'We offered you command of the warband and would have joined you then and there. But wisdom prevailed, and you sent us home to seek the counsel of our people.'

'Do you remember?' said Ruadh. 'You said to come to you in the spring if all the tribe agreed.'

'We would have come to you sooner,' Morann told him, 'but it has taken a little more time to settle the question. Some of the elders and old ones opposed giving up our clan's homeland of these many generations. They were most reluctant to see us go.'

'What changed their minds?' asked Conor, almost dreading the answer.

'Ach, now, that is why we're here,' Morann said gravely. 'Not ten days ago, Black Ships, seven or eight of them, were sighted off the coast. Four came into the bay and the others continued north.'

'Did you follow them to see where they went?'

'Aye, to be sure. But we lost sight of them during the night,' said Ruadh.

Morann went on to explain how they engaged the first wave of Scálda on the strand, but were beaten back; by the time the Auteini were able to regroup and organize a better defence there were even more enemy on the beach and still the boats were coming ashore. 'We saw then that it was no raid. The dog-eaters meant to claim the land and everything in it. We sent word to all our settlements and holdings to gather whatever they could and flee.'

'We stayed to the last man and fought to cover the retreat,' said Ruadh. 'We lost half the warband to them and many cattle, but we were able to make good our escape.'

'They meant to drive us out,' offered Morann. 'Having done that, the dog-eaters did not care to pursue us further.'

'And so you came here,' concluded Conor.

'As you see,' replied Morann. He passed an embarrassed glance around the yard. 'We had nowhere else to go, and to stay any longer was death, I know it.'

Conor assured the Auteini lord of his welcome and the three fell to discussing what was to be done for his people in the days ahead. They were deep in conversation when Fergal and Donal came threading their way through the confusion. 'What is this we're hearing of a Scálda attack on the Auteini coast?' said Fergal. He took one look at Morann and his two advisors, and said, 'I see that it is true. How many? How long ago?'

'Seven ships,' replied Ruadh. 'We were just telling Lord Conor that four made landfall in our bay and began unloading things—not weapons or men only, but all manner of gear, too.'

'Yokes and harness and large wicker chests,' continued Morann, 'and wheels—very many wheels.'

'Wheels,' repeated Conor. 'Thin wheels? Too slender for wagons? Iron-rimmed and about half a man high?' He held his hand to his waist to show the height. He glanced at Fergal and Donal and all three said together, 'Chariots.'

'I cannot say what they were, but the dog-eaters put the pieces together to make little war carts,' Morann explained. 'Very fast and able to carry two or three warriors into battle.'

'Aye, chariots,' agreed Fergal. 'The Scálda have been making them by the hundreds.' He passed a hand over his moustache and mouth and said, 'And now it seems the dog-eaters are bringing them into battle.'

'How do you know all this?' wondered Tobha. 'You've seen them before?'

'We've seen them,' replied Donal. 'We've also seen the forges where the iron for the rims is smelted. We have seen the rims and the finished wheels. We have even seen how these carts are to be used in battle.'

'You saw them unloading all this,' said Conor. 'What else did you see?'

'Very little,' answered Morann. 'We attacked then, hoping to keep them in the cove with the sea to their backs. We thought we could contain them there and drive them out before they could get more men and weapons ashore. But that was not to be.'

'We made two forays against them,' Ruadh told them. 'We could not get in close enough to make good the assault.'

'Our third attempt fared no better,' Morann said, the pain in his voice still raw. 'By then, they had horses ashore and were mounted. We fought hard, but were driven back.' He gave a gloomy shake of the head. 'They carried the fight to our very gates.'

'The battle lasted all day,' said Ruadh. 'We held out until nightfall when it became clear we could no longer defend the stronghold—much less the farms and settlements along the coast. We sent riders to all the holdings and told the people to flee with whatever they could carry.'

'The dog-eaters were burning everything they could set their filthy hands to,' said Tobha. 'We had no choice. It was save what we could, or be slaughtered. We were lucky to get away—those of us that got away, that is. We lost many during the night.'

'The barbarians took no slaves. Old men and women, children too young to lift a blade—all of them cut down where they stood.' Morann looked hopefully to Conor. 'Whatever tribe we have left is yours, lord. Our people are your people—if you will be having us.'

Conor merely smiled and said, 'As I said the night you lost your king, anyone who will join us is welcome. We need every man, woman, and child working with us to defeat the Scálda and rid Eirlandia of their curse. Will I have you? Aye, I will.'

Conor told Morann to go and gather the elders of the tribe to come and meet him in the hall to discuss their future at Tara. Morann and his men moved off to speak to their people. When they had gone, Fergal and Donal stepped close to Conor. 'Are you certain you want to do this?' asked Fergal. 'It will stretch us tight as a bodrán skin.'

'I know it,' agreed Conor. 'But, I stood before the gathered lords and noblemen and swore that Tara is for everyone or it is for no one at all.' He put out a hand to the refugees scattered across the hilltop. 'These people are Dé Danann like you and me, and you heard what Morann said—they have nowhere else to go. That is good enough for me. It should be good enough for the rest of us who call this place home.'

Fergal and Donal glanced at one another and nodded in reluctant agreement. Donal said, 'Aye, you're right. So now what?'

'Send word to the northern lords and warn them that the Scálda have taken a stronghold on the western coast.'

9

Over the next few weeks, the Auteini were moved from the hilltop down to Mag Rí, north of Tara Hill, where there was a ready supply of timber from the nearby woodlands, and water from the streams. Their cattle were folded into the herds being reared by Conor's herdsmen, and Morann and his warriors joined the fianna and began training with them.

Throughout Tara and its surrounding lands, activity of all kinds—from barn raising to sheep shearing—kept every hand employed from first glimmer in the east to last glow in the west. For the fianna that meant weapons practice, scouting parties, hunting, and, most important of all, collecting the tribute horses Conor had won from the kings in the airechtas judgement— a chore that turned out to be more onerous than anyone imagined at the time.

The collection teams rode out to the ráths and dúns of the lords, returning, days later, with the tribute—albeit only rarely in the form of the promised five horses. This failure was not viewed as the misfortune it might have seemed, however; such were the needs of the new settlement and its burgeoning numbers that the equivalent values in the form of seed, or lumber, tools, cloth, or cattle, were happily bartered. Two good milk cows, for example, were considered equivalent to one untrained horse; or, a cow, ten cloaks, six bushels of seed barley, four pigs, and a plough might be negotiated in payment. Thus, the return of the tribute collectors quickly came to be greeted with keen and enthusiastic interest and Eirlandia's newest realm began building up its stores and bolstering its ability to provide for its increasing population.

As Tara gained greater substance, its resemblance to a transient camp faded, taking on the lines and definition of an established ráth. Conor increasingly found that he was entangled in lengthy discussions regarding some detail or other concerning the ordering, planning, or allocation of this or that structure, division, commodity, or provision. Each day had fresh demands: supervising the various building works; visiting the new farms and holdings to gauge the progress of the fields and herds; meeting with Dearg and Fíol on apportioning provisions, and with Fergal about the training and readiness of the fianna—all of these necessary and important in their own way, all of them distractions of varying degrees. And, now that spring was marching resolutely toward a long, hot summer, the demands on him came thick and fast as decisions multiplied, each one begging for individual attention. Any spare moment, he spent with Aoife, making sure she was not overtiring herself with all the tasks she was undertaking with the women of the tribe.

Improved weather also brought increased raiding and enemy incursions into tribal territories along the coasts. Oddly, although the raiding season dawned fair, all remained quiet and peaceable along the southern borders and elsewhere. Fergal said it was because the Scálda were busy strengthening their hold on the Auteini coastal lands. Having driven out the native population, the dog-eaters had secured a prime place from which to launch new forays into the very heart of Eirlandia. This, he said, was an outrage that could not be suffered to continue.

Fergal was not alone in this opinion. In the middle of one particularly fraught day, word reached Tara from the Laigini that the lords of the north and west were raising a warhost to go and confront the Scálda and drive them from the region. Conor agreed to support the effort. Fergal and Donal were with him, and as the messenger departed, Conor ordered his battlechief to ready the fianna to ride.

'How soon?' asked Fergal.

'As soon as enough supplies and pack animals can be prepared,' Conor told him. 'I'll see to it.'

As Fergal moved off to find Médon and Galart to tell them the news, Donal said, 'You look like a fella that's just been kicked by a horse and is looking for a place to fall.' Conor opened his mouth to protest, but Donal continued. 'Don't bother denying it, brother. I can see it in your poor haunted eyes and pouty mouth.'

'I do not have a pouty mouth,' insisted Conor. 'Do I?'

'You do, you know, but I think I know the cause.'

'Ach, aye? And what would that be?'

'Walk with me and I'll tell you,' said Donal. Taking Conor's arm, Donal turned him around and started toward the rim of the plateau and the path leading down to the surrounding plains. At the hill's edge he stopped to look out upon the land below. What had once been only great green swaths of grass and small clumps of elder were now ploughed fields and cattle pens and the beginnings of two separate holdings with dwellings and barns and storehouses. Out on Mag Teamhair were a breeding pen and a training ground, and on the edge of Mag Rí, near the river where the Auteini were erecting their settlement, the beginnings of a forge.

They stood gazing down upon all this for a moment and then Donal said, 'Before the airechtas, we walked these boundaries, you and I—do you remember?' He indicated the plains below with a broad sweep of his hand. 'That walk would take longer today. See what you have done—what we all have done?' He turned and smiled at Conor. 'All this, brother, in so short a time. Aye, and it grows.'

'It grows, so it does.'

'And it does not take my second sight to see that Tara will become even larger—and so, too, the duties and obligations of its lord.'

Conor looked out upon his burgeoning realm and felt the pride of this achievement and, at the same time, the fatigue of so many demands to be met, decisions to be made, difficulties to be resolved. His spirit plummeted once more.

'It is too much for one man alone,' Donal told him. 'And I would not be a true friend if I stood here and told you otherwise.'

'Other kings and lords do it.'

'Perhaps they do,' agreed Donal. 'But other kings are not having to raise both a ráth and tribe from a scrap of bare nothing. They are put to rule with a realm already established and a people long in the land. Only very rarely must they create a settlement where there was none—and even then they have the help of their kinsmen.'

Conor glanced around and saw Donal looking at him with a curiously determined expression. 'What is it? What are you seeing, brother?'

'I see a man sinking in a bog that will soon pull him under and drown him if he does not reach out and take hold of the stout branch offered to him by the hand of a friend.'

'I take help when I need it,' Conor declared. 'You should know. You are always by my side. We've discussed this already.'

'I can do more.'

'Nay,' said Conor, dismissively. 'I thank you for the thought, but it is for me to—'

'I can do more,' Donal insisted, 'but *you* must allow it. In short, you must give me authority.'

Conor frowned and crossed his arms upon his chest. 'I need you with me, brother. When we take up arms and ride into battle—as soon we must—I look for your strong arm beside me.'

Donal shook his head gently. 'Once of a time that might have been true, but not anymore. And, truth be told, not for some little time now. You have the fianna to ride with you and fight beside you. With the addition of Morann and the Auteini, you now have the largest warband in Eirlandia. Think of it! Fifty-six men, Conor—men who will brave the vile enemy and death itself at your merest word, aye—men who will stand beside you in every battle and defend the realm with their last breath.' Donal offered a wry smile. 'All that, brother, but you do not have a solitary soul who will stand beside you and defend you from the carpenters.'

'True enough,' Conor conceded with a smile.

'I can be that man,' Donal said. He could see Conor thinking, and pressed home his argument. 'Who else knows you as well as Fergal and myself?'

'No one,' said Conor. 'Aoife maybe.'

'Aye, not anyone at all—save only Aoife, to be sure. And Fergal you have on the field in battle.'

'And Aoife, my lady, helping here when I am away.'

'But your lady is soon to have your child who will be all her care, and the demands of a new ráth and settlement should be the least and last of her daily concerns. See now,' said Donal, adopting a grave and solemn tone, 'I learned long ago that as much as you like to pretend otherwise, Conor mac Ardan, you cannot be in two places at once.'

'And is this not what Aoife is saying, too?' Conor laughed. 'Tell me, now—what is it that you're asking of me, old friend?'

'Only this,' he said, 'that you make me ail-duinn of this new realm of ours—with the power of your name and authority to carry out your will and have my commands obeyed as if they were yours.'

'Ail-duinn . . . second-chief . . . ,' mused Conor. To share his many burdens a little, to be able to rest of a time, to have a quiet meal with Aoife now and again . . . modest pleasures, to be sure, but ones that he had denied himself far too long. And, no doubt, new demands would rise soon enough. With two of them managing the new settlement, twice as much progress could be made in its development.

'I like this,' Conor said, feeling the heavy low clouds lift a little. 'I like it right well.' Beaming, he slapped Donal on the back. 'Ail-duinn it is! When do you propose to start?'

'Here and now,' Donal told him. 'I will see to the packhorses and provisions for the fianna. Leave it to me.'

10

Five days of hard riding brought Conor and forty-seven of the fianna to Laigini territory where they soon learned that King Laegaire and his warband were fighting up near Lough Emain. Morann and Ruadh guided them swiftly and unerringly to their former homeland: a region of lumpy hills covered in gorse, scraggy rocks, low boggy marshes around shallow loughs, and many-fingered bays spattered with tiny islands.

As they came in sight of the spreading grey waters of the reed-fringed lough, they met four Laigini clansmen with a low wagon bearing wounded warriors away from the battlefield; the clansmen told them the fight was now concentrated on a muddy plain to the south and west nearer the coast.

'Aye, that will be the place,' Morann told Conor and the ardféne when he heard the news. They had stopped to rest the horses and talk. 'There is a plain beyond the lough—Mag Cró it is. No doubt that is where they'll be fighting.'

The sight of the wounded languishing in the wagon sobered some of the younger warriors, but made the more experienced among the fianna angry. They shouted encouragement to the suffering warriors as they passed along the wagon and continued on to the battlefield.

Mag Cró lay between two scraggy hills; an expanse of damp ground dotted with tussocks of saw grass, it sloped gently westward toward the sea, the gleaming silver arc of which could be glimpsed in the distance.

The plain itself was abandoned; the current skirmish was over and both sides had withdrawn to regroup. The struggling Dé Danann warhost—made up of Laigini, Cauci, and Concani warbands—had withdrawn to the edge of the plain below the hills and, away to the southwest at the farthest end of Mag Cró, the Scálda camp could be seen as a wide dark splotch with the glimmering sea beyond. The fianna reached the crest of the last low hill and paused to take in the situation before riding down to meet the defenders who were clustered into three groups below. Two more wagons carrying wounded from the fray lumbered up the hill as they passed. Fergal halted the fianna and ordered Médon to take charge and see to the horses while he and Conor and Morann made straight for the central body of warriors where they reckoned they would find the warleaders. Word of the fianna's arrival flew before them, so that by the time they reached the place where the commanders had gathered, Aengus mac Millan, King of the Cauci, hailed them and beckoned them to join the war council.

All Conor knew of the broad-shouldered lord was what he had observed at the council, where the young nobleman had sided with the lords determined to force Conor to relinquish his claim on Tara Hill. Standing beside Aengus was his truculent, thin-faced friend, Lord Toráin of the Concani, and next to him a lord Conor did not know; slightly older, he had long hair pale as wheat and a gleaming torc of twisted gold strands. Neither of the two noblemen Conor *did* know had forgotten the heated exchanges and accusations aired during the airechtas, and it made for an awkward and uncomfortable few moments.

'Come to save us, have you?' was the first thing out of the Concani king's mouth.

'Three wagonloads of dead and dying,' replied Fergal bluntly. 'It looks to me like you could use a little saving maybe.'

'We have things well in hand,' huffed Toráin, dragging a sleeve across his nose and mouth. The Concani lord had a cut on the side of his face and one on his upper arm. Blood stained his siarc at the neck and arm, but he appeared in no hurry to have his injuries tended. He thrust a finger at Morann as the Auteini lord came up. 'We wouldn't be here at all if the Auteini hadn't abandoned their fortress and fled for the hills.'

Morann's bristled at the taunt; his nostrils flared. 'We fought them for two days and we fought alone, you insolent young—'

He started forth on the balls of his feet, but Conor pulled him back, saying, 'We're delighted to hear you're doing so well. Even so, we bring forty-seven keen new blades to the fight. Would I be wrong in thinking they might yet find some worthwhile service?' He looked from one lord to the next for an answer. When none came, he shrugged. 'Well, you say you have things well in hand. We are happy to go back the way we came and leave you to reap the rewards of victory that you so richly deserve.' To Morann, he said, 'Go tell the fianna we will not be staying.'

Morann, shaking his head at the ill-tempered Concani king, turned and started away.

'Wait! A moment . . . a moment, if you will,' blurted Aengus. 'I'm more of the opinion that it would do no harm to include a few more warriors fresh to the fight. And I'm sure my brother kings would agree with that at least—seeing as how they agree on little enough of anything else.' This last was said with a stern look at the quarrelsome Toráin.

'What say you?' asked Conor, looking at the unknown nobleman. 'Do you think we might find some practice for the weapons we've brought all this long way?'

'For a fact, I do,' replied the fair-haired lord. He glanced at Toráin and then offered his arm to Conor, saying, 'I am Lord Laegaire, King of the Laigini. You don't know me, but I know you. My father and his advisors were at the doomed Oenach. He was killed during the massacre, but you were the saving of our battlechief and the others.'

Conor took the offered arm and said, 'What a cursed night that was. I lost my father, too. I hope we fare better today.'

Morann, looking along the hill line, said, 'From the hilltop, we saw three battle groups. Who else is here?'

'Vainche and the Brigantes,' answered Aengus; he gestured to the north where, some way off, another warband had gathered. 'Liam and the Darini warriors are with him. They arrived a short while before you did and Vainche has been leading the warhost.'

'Has he now?' mused Conor. 'If that is so, why isn't he here now?'

'After this last retreat he said he needed time alone to think,' explained Laegaire. 'We were to wait here while he argued with that battlechief of his over what to do next.'

Conor looked to where the Brigantes and Darini were drawn up some little distance away, shaking his head in disbelief. Then, dismissing the insufferable lord, he turned away and asked about the strength of the enemy—how many footmen and how many riders?

'Too many to count,' replied Aengus. 'A few hundred at least, I'd say.'

'You don't know for sure?' wondered Fergal.

'We could not get a good count,' explained Laegaire. 'They are using a thing we have not seen before—little horse carts with warriors—'

'Chariots,' said Conor. 'Yes, we know. Morann told us.'

'War carts, they are. Very fast,' added Fergal. 'The dog-eaters have been making them for some little time.'

'Whatever they are,' said Aengus, 'they are impossible to stop. We can't get near the things.'

'We'll find a way,' said Fergal. Looking at the lords and warriors gathered around, he asked, 'Who is leading the warhost?'

'Now you're here you probably think that it should be *you*,' muttered Toráin, his derision thick as it was unpalatable.

Conor turned on him. 'Hear me, you impudent pup. We don't have to be here at all. We could more easily have stayed at Tara and let you earn your great victory all by yourselves. Nevertheless, we have ridden hard for five days, eaten little, and slept ill in order to risk life and limb for the protection of our people—'

'And what do we find?' snarled Fergal, breaking in. 'A sorry bunch of beaten dogs with their tails between their legs growling at each other and the enemy in full possession of their strength and the lands hereabouts! It is enough to wring tears from a stone.' Glaring at the lords, he said, 'How long have you been here, anyway?'

'Only since this morning,' Aengus told him.

'By the Hag, we received word five days ago!' hollered Fergal. 'You, Aengus—you are closer to the Auteini than we are at Tara. And you, Toráin . . . and you, Laegaire. . . . You *all* should have been able to get here well before the dog-eaters could claim the land hereabouts—*if* that was your aim. Where are the Nagnati? They are only a spear's throw away! They should be here. And where are the Ulaid and the Robogdi, eh? Where is Corgan and Cahir? Why aren't the Eridani and Coriondi here?'

'Were they even summoned at all?' asked Conor. When no one answered, he demanded, 'What happened? Why the long delay?'

He stared with hard eyes at the suddenly reticent lords. 'Well? I want an answer and I will have one.'

'We were waiting,' Aengus conceded at last. He cast a hasty, sidelong glance at his fellow lords and warleaders.

'Waiting!' Fergal shouted, fairly exploding in righteous indignation.

'Man, what was more important to you than preventing the enemy from camping at your gates?'

Fergal's righteous outrage cowed them, and all shifted uneasily under his withering glare.

'It was Lord Vainche,' blustered Aengus, giving way at last. 'We were ready to ride out—' He glanced at Toráin and said, 'We *were*, you know. But Vainche sent word that he would bring the Brigantes warband to aid us and said we were to wait until he got here.'

'So you waited? For Vainche?' said Conor, shaking his head in disbelief. 'Why?'

The lords looked down, refusing to meet his gaze or answer his question.

'If you had ridden out the moment you received the call, it is likely you would not have needed Vainche's help at all!' snarled Fergal. 'If you had—' he began, then broke off, saying, 'What's the use?'

'Fergal's right,' said Conor. 'If you had acted sooner, you would never have needed the likes of Vainche.'

'Ach, well, we're paying for it now!' snapped Toráin.

'You're not paying at all,' Conor told him coldly. 'Your men are paying! The Auteini are paying. Lands lost, good warriors wounded and dying . . . and for what?' No one spoke. 'For Vainche's insufferable self-importance!'

A sulky silence settled over the group then. Conor was right and they knew it. There was not one among them who did not feel in his bones that the error of judgement was a failing of grave and terrible consequence, and the guilt was drawn on every face.

Finally, Conor, having made his point, did what he could to revive their courage and conviction. 'Hear me. What's done is done. We'll deal with it later,' he told them. 'Now we must all pull together or we will lose even more territory to the Scálda. And if our luck is with us, maybe we can reclaim what's been lost.'

They fell to discussing how best to do that and were putting the finishing touches on a basic battle plan when they were interrupted by the sudden arrival of Lord Vainche and his odious, beetle-browed battlechief Gioll. Following in his wake rode Liam and Eamon. The four came trotting up on their horses and stopped a few paces away. Vainche, already scowling with displeasure, looked at Conor and demanded, 'What are *you* doing here?'

'We came to help,' replied Conor evenly. 'A fella might have thought that was obvious.'

'We don't need help from the likes of you,' sneered Vainche. 'We are perfectly able to defend ourselves. So you, Conor mac Ardan, you can take your mongrel fianna and go back to Tara—back to the land you stole from the Brigantes. But you, Morann,' he said, turning to the Auteini king, 'you can stay and watch real warriors clean up your stinking mess.'

Conor, a sharp reply on his tongue, swallowed it and instead looked to his brother. 'Greetings, Liam. Still suffering the insufferable, I see.'

Liam glared at him, but said nothing. Eamon, looking decidedly ill at ease, muttered a lame greeting, and Gioll gazed out from beneath his heavy brow, a look of gloating malice gleaming in his little piglike eyes.

'I came to tell you we are ready to mount another attack,' Vainche informed them. 'Gather your men and ride on my command.'

Conor felt the side of his face begin to burn as his birthmark kindled with the heat of an anger he could barely contain. The smug arrogance of the Brigantes king stole the words from his mouth. He could but stare hot blades at the haughty lord. Liam saw his brother's face darken and knew the look only too well: he put out a hand to Vainche to forestall any further comment and said, 'Now that they're here, I'm thinking the extra blades would be of some value.'

'So they would,' volunteered Laegaire readily, and the others nodded their agreement. 'In fact, we have just been discussing how to make best use of our combined warbands.'

Vainche sniffed heavily. 'Do what you will,' he said, affecting a tone of weary indifference, 'just keep *him* and his men far away from us. We might mistake them for the enemy and I, for one, won't be responsible for what happens.' With that, he lifted the reins, wheeled his horse, and rode away. Liam hesitated a moment as if he might join the other kings, then abruptly changed his mind and, without a word, turned and rode away, leaving a shamefaced Eamon to offer a limp apology. 'I'm sorry, Conor. I would happily join you if—'

Conor stopped him. 'Never mind, Eamon. Stay with Liam and do what you can to keep him from falling any lower.'

Eamon raised his spear in farewell, and rode back to the waiting Darini and Brigantes warbands.

'I don't think we can expect any real help from them,' observed Conor, watching them go. Then, turning back to the lords around him: 'If any of you think Vainche has a better plan to defeat the Scálda, then you are free to go to him now. Otherwise, let us proceed with the plans we've made and hope for the best.'

When no one spoke up for the arrogant Brigantes lord, Fergal said, 'Right so. What can you tell us about these chariots? How are they used?'

'I thought you said you knew all about them,' said Toráin.

'We've seen them being made, and somewhat of how they are driven,' replied Conor. 'We have never seen them in battle.'

'Then you will soon learn to fear them.' The Concani lord pointed out across the plain to a broad dark line flowing out across the centre of Mag Cró like a contaminating stain, or a storm tide engulfing the strand in a flood of filthy water. 'Here they come!'

11

The first thing Conor noticed was how very fast the chariots could move. While striking, it should not have been surprising; after all, the carts were light in weight—little more than a sturdy wickerwork basket on slender wheels—and pulled by two fast horses. Conor, Fergal, and Donal had briefly glimpsed a chariot under harness the day they snuck into a Scálda ráth. All the same, a broad line of swift war carts streaking into battle across an open expanse was a sight to behold. The ground trembled beneath the pounding hooves, the thin, iron-rimmed wheels carved grooves in the soft turf, and distance disappeared at an alarming rate. A hurtling chariot seemed to close on its target with all the speed of a spear in flight.

From what Conor could see, each war cart held two men: one to drive the horses and one to fight. Principally, the Scálda used long-shafted spears as their weapon of choice; each chariot carried several of these in wicker holders strapped to the frame of the cart. With one hand, the warrior hurled the missile, and with the other he employed an oversized round shield to protect both himself and the driver. It was an impressive, if not terrifying, practice that worked only too well and, as Conor was soon to discover, required enormous courage on the part of any defender placing himself in the chariot's path.

Facing a chariot in full flight in battle took an enormous amount of skill, luck, and an almost reckless disregard for life. It was the rare warrior who did not look upon the sight of a two-horse battle cart bearing down upon him and suddenly wish he was somewhere else far away. Nor did it take much imagination to see that the damage a chariot attack could inflict would be devastating: equally so the fact that a spear thrown from a fast-moving war cart seemed to gather all the speed and strength of the horse and cart itself—something Conor and the fianna learned in the very first moments of conflict.

Seeing the Scálda advance, Conor ordered the fianna to mount their horses and form their battle groups: two separate ranks, one behind the other. Each warrior was armed with a throwing spear; a long wickerwork shield covered in toughened leather with a large iron boss; a short sword with a tapering blade. Fergal led the first rank and Conor the second. The warbands of Aengus, Toráin, and Leagaire fell into place in either of the two ranks, and they all advanced together—slowly to begin, but gathering pace as they went. Meanwhile, the Scálda chariots sped over the plain, and the distance between the two sides closed with breathtaking speed.

The resulting clash would have been catastrophic for the Dé Danann horsemen, but the chariots remained in tight formation. On they rushed, wheel-to-wheel, the hooves of the two-horse teams chewing up the earth and flinging clouts of grass and dirt into the air. Seeing no space wide enough for a horse and rider to pass between the oncoming vehicles, Fergal broke off the charge, swerving aside to avoid a disastrous collision.

Even so, the hastily aborted attack cost the Dé Danann warhost, for as the line of defenders turned, they presented a vulnerable side to the Scálda spearmen, who loosed a barrage of spears, catching more than a few Dé Danann as they scattered to get out of the way. The canny warriors sought to deflect the thrown weapon with their shields—only to have the iron spearhead penetrate the shield to inflict a wound anyway. Most of the Dé Danann escaped serious injury—some by only a hair's breadth—but others were not so lucky: several received puncture wounds from hurled spears, and one a broken arm when the enemy blade punched through the shield near the boss; two riders were thrown from their mounts by the force of the blow and both fell beneath the wheels of the onrushing vehicles.

The rout of the Dé Danann defenders was complete. The attack collapsed and, within moments, all were in full retreat. The Scálda, having easily won the clash, offered only halfhearted pursuit. The defenders returned to their marshalling place at the foot of the hills, where they dismounted to rest the horses and regroup. 'That was no good at all,' spat Fergal, wiping sweat from his face. 'How many did we lose?'

'Three from our rank,' answered Médon, joining them just then. 'Two wounded and one dead.'

'And the wounded?' asked Fergal.

'Concani, I think. They'll live, but won't fight any more today.'

'The front line lost seven,' said Conor, sliding down from Búrach's sweaty back. 'One dead. Six wounded—I can't say if any of these will be fit to ride again.'

Lord Aengus came running up. 'You see the difficulty. They are fast, those war carts. And if they hold the line like that, there's no way we can get in close. We can do nothing.'

'Not if we persist in attacking like that,' said Fergal. 'Is that what you did last time, too?'

'It doesn't matter,' declared Conor, thrusting the point of his spear into the ground. 'We won't be attacking like that again. On my life, what a balls-up!'

'I didn't know they could move so fast.' Médon, shaking his head. 'And so many!'

'Go and see to the fianna,' Fergal told him. 'Tell them to prepare for another assault.' To Aengus, he said, 'Go tell the other lords to come and hold council. We have to talk.'

Thus, while the warbands saw to the wounded and tended their mounts, Conor, Fergal, and the other warleaders met to plan the next assault—all, that is, except Vainche and Liam, who refused to stand close enough to even overhear Conor.

'Clearly, we cannot break the enemy line with a blunt charge,' Fergal told them. 'But if we could get around the flanks we could attack from behind—strike before the dog-eaters can turn the carts around.'

'Aye,' agreed Laegaire, 'it might work.'

'How do you propose to get in behind them?' asked Aengus. 'We tried before but couldn't do it. Those war carts are too fast and they turn in a blink.'

'We have more men now. We can stagger the charge. Attack on three fronts,' suggested Conor. 'Begin the charge like before, but hold two wings back. When the Scálda commit to the centre, we bring in the wings to attack from the side. That way we can get in behind them.'

'Aye,' agreed Médon, 'the field is broad enough and if they stay bunched in the centre, we could get a warband around each side if we were in position.'

'That's what I'm thinking,' Conor confirmed.

'Ach, but they're not blind,' scoffed Toráin. 'They'd see that coming a long way off.' He turned to Fergal, who stood pulling on his moustache, his brow wrinkled in thought. 'Well? You are very quiet all of a sudden. All froth and no ale?'

'It could work,' replied Fergal at last. 'But you're right—the dog-eaters would see the feint unless we could hide our intentions from them somehow.'

'Aye, fair enough,' agreed Laegaire. 'But how to hide such a thing?'

'We might be able to use the speed of their chariots to our advantage,' Conor said. 'What if we ride out in force and break ranks once the Scálda have committed to the attack?'

'One battle group holds the centre,' said Fergal, 'and two wings to come in from either side.'

Laegaire was already nodding. 'If the centre collapsed, drawing the dog-eaters into pursuit, it would make it easier to get in behind them.'

'Then we can do our work,' said Médon. 'I like it.'

They went over it again, refining it a little, and when everyone understood the plan, Conor turned to the other lords and said, 'Now, then, one of you must go and explain it to Vainche and Liam. We need their warbands to do their part or the attack will fail.'

'I'll go,' volunteered Aengus.

'Nay, brother, let me,' said Toráin. 'Vainche will listen to me—Liam, too. I'll make them understand.' He hurried to his horse and rode to where the Brigantes and Darini had drawn up. The others watched as the three held a brief conference that concluded with nods all around. Toráin returned to say, 'They will do what is necessary.'

'Good,' replied Conor with a nod. To the others, he said, 'Prepare to ride. We'll attack on Fergal's command.' The lords hurried off to ready their men, leaving Conor and Fergal alone for a moment. 'Are you content with your part, brother?' he asked.

'As content as any fella can be standing on a battleground,' replied Fergal. Looking Conor in the eye, he asked, 'And are you content with the portion you have taken on for yourself? Or has all that high living made you soft?'

'Never say it! In truth, brother, I feel more myself on the battlefield than I do in a cornfield.' Conor held out his arm to Fergal. The tall warrior gripped it and the two exchanged a last word, then went to take up their

weapons and mount their horses for another assault. When all the Dé Danann were mounted, Conor nodded to Fergal, who gave the signal to ride
out.

This time, the combined warhost moved onto the plain in a long line
that stretched from one side of the field to the other. As expected, the
Scálda saw the Dé Danann advance and responded in kind, quickly rolling out to offer battle. The warbands of Aengus, Toráin, and Laegaire, and
Morann, held the centre, with Conor and the fianna on the far right flank;
Vainche and Liam with the Brigantes and Darini warbands anchored the
extreme left. As before, the Scálda kept their chariots in a tight formation
so as not to allow anyone to slip through the line. Both sides raced to join
battle and the dull thunder of horses' hooves and the rumble of chariot
wheels resounded across the plain.

As soon as Aengus saw that the enemy were committed to the impending clash, he raised his spear and waved it above his head—giving the
prearranged signal to retreat. But, in the rush of motion, the signal went
unheeded. The two sides closed on one another in a shuddering clash.

Aengus and Cauci, leading the charge from the centre, suffered the impact of the collision with riders overthrown and trampled; a number of
chariots were upset and this added to the carnage. All along the line, defenders fell to enemy spears or were thrown from their mounts and crushed
by enemy chariots. It seemed as if the battle would be over almost before it
had begun. Desperate, Aengus signalled the retreat once more. This time
the sign was received. All along the line, riders wheeled their horses and
the Dé Danann withdrew from the field, leaving the outer wings separated
by a great gaping hole.

Alert to the collapse of the centre, waiting for it, Fergal and the fianna
making up the right wing swerved hard to the right, galloping for the distant boundary of the battleground as if they would retreat that way. The
Brigantes and Darini performed the same manoeuvre, swerving sharply to
the left, riding hard for the opposite side of the plain. The chariots, in tight
formation, swept past in a flurry of pounding hooves and spinning wheels.
At that moment, Fergal gave out a cry and the fianna turned back—driving
once more toward the centre of the plain; only, this time, they were behind
the chariot line and were soon in swift pursuit. Faster and faster they flew,
lashing their mounts mercilessly, gaining ground on the Scálda from the
rear.

Fergal gave out a battle cry and let fly with his spear.

Instantly, twenty more spears took flight. Only a few reached their marks, but one of these struck a Scálda driver, causing him to lose control of his team. The cart slewed sideways, slamming into the next chariot. The fast-spinning wheels of the two vehicles tangled, the slender spokes splintered and gave way, and the wheels broke. Drivers and warriors spilled onto the ground in a mad jumble of wicker and flailing limbs. The horses charged on, dragging the wreckage. Fianna swords made short work of the warriors, and the chase moved on. Two more drivers fell to the fianna's counterattack in quick succession. The sudden loss of four chariots from the line alerted the enemy that a Dé Danann battle group was now behind them.

One of the Scálda battlechiefs shouted a command and an entire rank of chariots on the outer wing of the formation slowed, turned, and swung onto a new attack course. At the same time, a second wave of Scálda appeared behind them and began hurling spears at the defenders' unprotected backs.

Fergal saw what was happening and instantly broke off the chase, changed course, and streaked toward the centre of the plain to join up with the Brígantes warband driving in from the left.

Even from a distance, however, Fergal could see something was wrong: the Brigantes battle group was nowhere in sight. Fergal pulled up hard. 'To me!' he shouted. 'To me!'

Conor came pounding up beside him and reined in. 'Where is Vainche?'

'The Scálda left flank is intact,' cried Médon from somewhere behind them. 'The Brigantes didn't make the turn.'

Conor quickly cast his gaze across the battle field. The entire left-hand side of the Scálda chariot formation was not only intact, it was now in the process of turning inward to challenge the fianna from that side. The centre of the plain was now occupied by two enemy chariot lines—the first wave in full pursuit of Aengus's retreat, and a second wave coming up fast behind them. The fianna were trapped in a pocket between the three converging lines with no way out.

'Form up! Form up!' cried Fergal. The fianna quickly reined in around him. To Conor, he said, 'Fight or run, brother—which is it to be?'

Conor, his eyes on the chariots rumbling closer, hesitated. Búrach, sensing the tension in his master, tossed his head and stamped a hoof. 'My good horse wants to fight,' he said. He looked to the centre of the plain where the enemy was still in fast pursuit of the main Dé Danann battle group. 'That way,' said Conor, pointing with his spear.

'We'll be trapped!' exclaimed Diarmaid. 'Between the—'

Fergal cut him off. 'We go!' Raising his spear, he signalled the fianna to move out. Within two heartbeats, they were once again in flying pursuit of the Scálda chariots dead ahead. The Scálda behind them were not slow to react; they altered course to head off the fianna. The charge swiftly transformed into a frantic race to get between the fianna and two opposing chariot divisions—one to the left and one to the right, and both intent on cutting off the fianna before they came within striking distance of the main Scálda force as it chased the Dé Danann retreat.

Conor on Búrach held a straight and steady course, with Fergal hard on his right hand and Médon on his left; in a tight cluster on either side came the fianna—all of them low on their mounts and riding for their lives as the twin enemy battle groups rumbled toward them from either side. The chariots on the right flank were in the lead of those closing in from the left, so Conor veered slightly toward the left and, lashing the grey stallion hard, raced for the gap between the two wings—leading the fianna through the opening as if between two swiftly closing gates.

They nearly made it.

The lead chariot closed on them with astonishing speed. The first Scálda spear sliced the air a mere hand's breadth before Conor's face. 'Hie! Búrach! Hie!' he shouted, trying to coax a little more speed from his mount. The second spear struck the stallion high on the shoulder, penetrating the thick horse cloth and biting deep into the withers. Only a little higher and the blade would have found Conor's thigh. Búrach, enraged by the sudden flash of pain, put back his ears and surged forward in an effort to carry his rider out of danger.

Conor seized the iron-studded shaft of the spear and plucked it from the stallion's wound; he turned it and, casting a fleeting glance around behind, saw the enemy charioteer reaching back, steadying himself for a third throw. Without so much as a moment's hesitation to aim, Conor simply swung the spear shaft sideways and flung it behind him.

The spear spun in a crazy circle across the intervening space to smack the oncoming team, catching both animals a blow across the foreheads. Distracted, unnerved, the creatures jerked hard to the right to avoid getting hit again. The chariot driver reared back on the reins in an effort to get his team back under control. The horses resisted and the chariot lurched farther to the right, unbalancing the Scálda spearman, slamming him against the side of the cart. He grabbed the rail to keep himself from falling from the wildly lurching vehicle and the spear in his hand tilted down; the spearhead came in contact with the spinning wheel and caught a spoke. The force yanked the weapon from the warrior's hand and sent it spinning away to be trampled by the chariots coming on behind.

The disruption caused by the out-of-control chariot rippled through the chariot ranks as the others swerved out of the way—not by much, but enough for Conor to gain a little distance on the pursuit. Búrach sped through the gap and out onto the open field. Those behind Conor were not so fortunate.

Médon and Fergal were able to avoid the careering chariot, but those in full gallop behind them could not. The speeding war cart veered into their path, forcing them to rein aside. This deviation, however slight, proved enough of a lapse. Spears flashed out, tracing bright arcs in the air, striking home with deadly accuracy, and three horses sped on without their riders. Two more ran on with their riders slumped low, clinging to their galloping mounts.

Again the spears flew, and again riders fell.

Conor heard the wild whooping cries of the Scálda and the screams of spear-pierced horses, the shouts of the Dé Danann and the metallic clash of weapons. Cut off now from Fergal and the fianna, he raced on, hurtling toward the line of enemy chariots directly ahead. Those behind him swooped in to close the gap. Two of the nearest vehicles did not succeed in completing the turn. Unable to slow enough when those around them suddenly turned, the two carts slewed sideways as the wheels skidded on the grass; the iron rims bit into the soft earth and caught.

Over went the chariots, hurling their occupants to the ground. The horses galloped on, dragging the upturned vehicles behind them. But the necessary turn slowed their vehicles and the Dé Danann defenders seized on the momentary lapse. Fergal broke off the attack, turned, and fled. The Scálda gave chase, but the mounted warriors were faster and the distance between them and the fianna slowly increased. The fleeing fianna could not be caught. The best the chariot drivers could do was continue the pursuit and hope to get close enough to cast a spear or run down a wounded or unwary adversary.

Conor glanced behind him, saw the war carts giving ground, and urged the stallion on with strong words and praise. The grey's hooves drummed a quickened beat upon the earth, and the wind of their passing lashed the stallion's mane and tail like a streaming battle flag.

As soon as the rearmost chariot came within striking distance, Conor, leaning low on the neck of his galloping mount, gave Pelydr a mighty thrust. The charmed faéry spear struck deep. The sleek razor point buried itself between the shoulder blades of the chariot driver. Conor darted away again. The driver gave out a cry and sank to his knees on the floor of the fast-moving vehicle; his warrior companion tried with his free hand to take the reins from his dying partner, but could not reach them. The reins jerked free and the chariot started drifting off to one side, veering out of the tight wedge-shaped formation.

The struggling spearman, unable to regain control of the horses, made an awkward swipe with a blade, but Conor was already out of reach. The chariot continued its uncontrolled arc and Conor remained right with it. Driving in close, he delivered another blow: a rising slash that caught the enemy warrior between the elbow and shoulder. The warrior cried out and scrabbled for another spear. Drawing it from its holder, he half turned and made to let fly. At that moment, the speeding war cart hit a clump of saw grass and bounced, throwing the warrior off balance. He made a flailing grab for the cart rail. His hand, bloody from the cut, slipped and he fell out of the vehicle. Conor saw the wounded warrior hit the ground and then Búrach trampled the body.

The war cart with its dead driver swung farther out of formation, opening another gap in the flying wedge and forcing the nearest chariots to swerve to keep from colliding with the loose vehicle. Conor saw the breach open before him and, in the near distance beyond it, the main body of the Dé Danann warhost. Laegaire and the retreating defenders had reached the base of the hills at the far end of Mag Cró. Through the open space before him, Conor willed them to turn around and see the yawning rupture he had forced in the Scálda chariot line. But they rode on, so Conor went to work trying to widen the gap.

He made for the nearest chariot and soon caught up with it. Leaning out, he came abreast of the driver and made a great swooping slash with Pelydr. The swipe did not connect, but proved a distraction nonetheless. The Scálda warrior lunged with a spear, but missed—and then hurled the spear instead. Conor saw the movement of the warrior's arm and threw himself down flat against Búrach's neck as the blade sliced the air a spare hand's breadth above his head. Conor pulled hard on the reins; the stallion swung to the right. The Scálda spearman plucked another spear from the carrier, drew back his arm, and tensed to throw. Conor saw the movement and raised Pared; the faéry shield took the blow an instant later without so much as a quiver. Conor jerked the reins to the left, bringing Búrach back in line with the chariot team. Conor jabbed at the straining neck of the lead horse. The animal shied away from the thrust and the vehicle lurched, slamming the driver into his warrior companion. The warrior staggered back, lost his footing, and toppled full length from the chariot. The driver fought to regain control of the fast-moving vehicle, but the horses continued pulling against one another, slowing the war cart further and opening the gap wider. It was now big enough for one horse to pass through . . . then two . . . and three . . . and more.

'Hie, Búrach! Hie!' Conor cried, lashing the stallion faster. The grey lunged forward and Conor made for the opening, galloped through it and away. The Scálda shouted and threw spears, but none struck home and Conor drew swiftly away and out of reach.

Once begun, the collapse of the enemy wedge formation proved irreparable. The Scálda warleader chose to fall back to regroup. This gave the harried Dé Danann defenders time to escape and return to their mustering place to the east. Conor made directly for the Dé Danann muster point at the foot of the low hills on the edge of Mag Cró; he threw himself down from his winded mount and ran to confer with Laegaire and the others.

'What happened out there?' Conor demanded, his scarlet blemish flaring with the heat of his anger. 'You were supposed to make the Scálda chase you, not engage them!'

'I gave the signal! No one saw it!' shouted Aengus. The broad-shouldered young lord, breathing hard, wiped sweat and blood from his face with his sleeve. 'I had no choice!'

Conor clenched his teeth in frustration, but held his tongue. He drew a hand across his sweat-beaded brow and looked around. 'Where is Vainche?'

Laegaire, breathing hard, shook his head. 'Was he not out there on the battlefield?'

Conor turned and scanned the plain. He saw the wreckage of several chariots—one with a wheel still spinning and others a tangled mess of wickerwork and iron—and, here and there, a few Scálda dead: both horses and men lying still on the lumpy ground. There also, in grass stained with their own blood, lay the Danann dead. Conor did not have the heart to count them, but knew the tally would be more than he could stomach just then. Instead, he watched as the Scálda came streaming back onto the battle ground to retrieve weapons and strip the dead—both their own and Dé Danann. Farther out on Mag Cró, he saw Fergal and the fianna working their way back along the edge of the plain to rejoin the warhost. Raising his eyes, he quickly searched the slopes and heights of the hills west of the battlefield. There was no one to be seen. 'They're gone,' he concluded.

'Who?' wondered Morann, hobbling up just then. He was bleeding from a nasty cut to his leg where a blade had slid off his shield. 'Who are you looking for?'

'Vainche, of course,' growled Conor. 'Who else?'

'Both the Brigantes and the Darini gone,' reported Toráin. Red-faced from his ride, he bent at the waist and gulped air. 'I didn't see them on the field, either.'

Lord Morann came running up just then. 'What happened? Why did you break off the attack? We could have turned them. We could have driven them back.'

'What happened?' snarled Conor. 'I'll tell you what happened. Vainche withdrew his men from the fight and abandoned the field. He deserted us in the midst of battle—'

'Aye,' said Toráin, 'and he took the Darini with him.' He spat on the ground. 'Traitor. If I see him again, I'll kill him.'

'Betrayed us?' said Morann. 'Is that what you're saying? Could he do that?'

'Could and did,' said Toráin, his voice thick with rage. 'Vainche has betrayed us and all of Eirlandia into the bargain.'

'They would never do that,' said Aengus. 'No Dé Danann warrior could do such a thing to a swordbrother.'

'Truly?' demanded Conor, his voice shaking with rage. 'How little you know that double-faced rogue Vainche.' He jerked a thumb in the direction of the plain behind him. 'Unless you find his corpse on the field out there, that is exactly what he did.'

They were still cursing Vainche's betrayal when Fergal and the fianna reached them. 'Look at them out there!' shouted Fergal, throwing himself down from his mount. 'Look what they're doing! The animals!'

The lords turned back to the battle ground, where the Scálda, having stripped the Dé Danann dead, were cutting off the heads of the warriors and were putting them on spears driven into the ground. All across the plain, spears were being raised, and the blood of good warriors was being smeared on the horses and shields, faces and torsos of their victorious foe.

Humiliated, shamed, the defenders stood shaking in rage and dismay as the bodies of former friends and kinsmen were cruelly, wickedly defiled: the hands, feet, arms, and legs of their dead swordbrothers were lopped off and heaped in piles while laughing Scálda urinated into the ragged wounds. Then the victors began dragging the bloody remains behind their chariots. Back and forth across Mag Cró they rolled, whooping and ululating in triumph as they hauled the headless, limbless corpses through the battle-churned dirt.

'Taunting us!' cried Aengus. 'The shit scum are taunting us!' He lofted his spear and shouted, 'To your weapons, brothers. Let's ride!'

'Stop!' Conor grabbed hold of the young lord's arm and spun him around. 'Look out there. They've claimed the battleground. It's over.'

'We can attack while they're—'

'Shut up!' snapped Toráin. 'Conor is right. They dog-eaters have won. It's over.'

Conor, still restraining Aengus, said, 'Listen to me, brother. We were outnumbered today. With the Brigantes and Darini we had a chance. Without them, whatever chance we had is gone. The Scálda know it. That's why they taunt us now—hoping to draw us into a fight we can't win. It's over.'

Morann, leaning on his spear, spoke not a word, but the expression of grief and rage over having lost his tribal lands again spoke for them all. They had been beaten by a superior host with a superior weapon. All the Dé Danann could do was to slink away while they still had life and strength enough to cover their retreat.

By the time the defeated defenders left the battlefield, the smoke from the burning bodies was already curling black and pungent into the clear blue sky.

Sceana

The first time he hit me came as a shock. To think that anyone would dare raise a rude hand to a reigning queen in Eirlandia was outrageous. As queen of the Brigantes, no one had ever put a hand to me in anger—not my father, nor my lord Brecan even in his most savage bouts of rage. The thing was unthinkable.

When it came, the storm roared in out of nowhere. I had dallied with some of my maidens and kept him waiting overlong. My lord had expected us to dine together and had returned from his hunting earlier than I knew. By the time I learned he was waiting and joined him, Vainche was already well and truly enraged.

At the first words out of my mouth, he seized me by the arm, his hand flicked out, and he struck me hard on the cheek. 'Who are you to keep me waiting? You are my bitch and I expect you to heel when I call!'

I could not answer. So appalling were his words . . . so hateful and cruel. It fair stole the breath from me. If the earth had opened and swallowed me whole, I would not have been more stunned. I fell back, cowering like the dog he said I was.

At this, he leapt to my side, instantly tender and attentive. He took me in his arms, comforted me with kisses, and told me that I must take heed not to rouse his anger. He said he loved me, adored me more than life itself and would never want harm of any kind to visit me.

I believed him. How could I not? He had never behaved in such a way before and I thought he would never do it again. We resumed our life together in all the pleasantry and harmony we had enjoyed before.

But, little by little, he began to behave in ways I had not seen before.

He would make demands—deciding who among my ladies and maidens I could confide in, talk to, which could serve me. He convinced me to dismiss all but two of them—the two he approved and trusted.

He told me what to wear—only the merest suggestion at first, but if I disagreed and chose a mantle or girdle he did not like, or a brooch he thought unsuitable, he was quick to make his displeasure known—sometimes with the back of his hand. In this way, he enforced his will in most other things as well. If I wanted to ride, he told me which horse I could take, where I could go, and, eventually, whether I was allowed go out at all. Over time, he gave me to know that he did not like me venturing beyond the gates of Aintrén without someone with me. That someone was, as often as not, his battlechief Gioll—a man whose company I found so repugnant that I chose not to ride at all rather than have that leering pig following me, watching my every move. All this time, as I later learned, he was working to turn my own people against me. He told them things—insane things I will not repeat—that gave them to know I was not in my right mind, and so never to be believed or trusted by anyone.

Through all this, my lord Vainche gave me to know that it was displeasing him that roused his anger, and that we might both avoid the unpleasantness of a slap if I merely obeyed him in all things as, after all, he was only acting in my best interest. He convinced me that it was no one's fault but my own that he struck me. If I had not angered him so, he would not have lashed out at me. Thus, it was up to me never to cross him again.

If I doubted this, it was a lesson I was soon to learn in earnest. Once again—as ever was his wont—he had been out hunting with Gioll and some of the warband. I had gone to the hall on some errand or other and on emerging saw Elidhe, one of my former maidens. The side of her face was swollen and discoloured by a nasty bruise. Naturally, I asked about how it happened, and she made light of the matter, saying it was her own fault and that she had been clumsy the night before. She had been serving ale to his lordship and his warriors, and had tripped over her own feet. She had fallen against a bench, she said. It was nothing, she said.

As it happened, Vainche and the hunters returned just then. They came pounding into the yard and my lord saw me with Elidhe. He flew into a rage and ordered us both to our places. I refused. He dismounted, seized me by the hair, and began dragging me across the yard to the women's house. I screamed and struck out at him—hardly knowing what I did. He halted, jerked me upright, and swung his fist into my jaw, knocking me to the ground.

Ach, well, the next day I had the selfsame bruise on my face that Elidhe wore on hers. And I knew full well how she got it.

Shamed, humiliated, mortified beyond words that he should treat me so before my people, I did not show myself outside the door of the women's house for two days. I remained inside, unwilling to let anyone see what he had done, stewing over it, refusing food, fretting myself sleepless. It came to me as I lay on my bed that Vainche had not changed at all, that he had always been this same scheming, deceptive creature revealed in the yard, and that he was only beginning to show his true nature.

I also determined that I would never allow him to raise his hand to me again.

I have obeyed his whims. I have agreed to his ill-conceived plans. I have been meek and mild to him beyond all his desirings. In this, I have been scrupulous. I have also been vigilant—awaiting my opportunity to free myself from this self-obsessed tyrant. When that opportunity presents itself, I will be ready and I will act. Though it cost my life, I will see him suffer the dishonour he has earned for himself and face the justice he deserves.

12

These are the names of the Dé Danann who fell at Mag Cró: Lúgaid mac Lóann, Carillán mac Fiachna, Uisni mac Floda, Rofessa mac Dátho, Briccir mac Bricrú; Ferbaeth mac Rónán and Blai Orlám of Sliabh Cuilinn; Sualdaím mac Buan, Conal mac Cernach, Cimling from Clan Banbha, Senlobar of Clan Celtchar, and Bruchar, Alamac, and Amargin of Clan Muire; Dredas mac Drenhan, Tibraíd mac Rus, Fergus mac Sencha from Clan Cerno Tum, and Tuam mac Dáithi, Malen and Griann from Clan Ess Ruadh; Tibraidh mac Gall, Dorda and Seirid and Serthe from Druim Oblan; Láráin mac Mathar, Ferdia mac Damach, Lúgaid Lechmor, Cúroi mac Conad, and Conall mac Roth.

These were the dead left on the blood-soaked ground and over which their clans and kinsmen mourned. The warbands of the Concani, Cauci, Ulaid, and Laigini were each diminished and each grieved for their slain swordbrothers. Three of the fianna fell to Scálda blades, too: Torban mac Cael, Uail mac Duri, and Reith mac Rotha.

In all, thirty-two died in that ill-fated battle that day. Others would later succumb to wounds received in battle, and they were no less mourned. Conor and Fergal reckoned each death and every injury a defeat and a failure. The only kings who did not suffer any loss were Vainche and Liam; their betrayal added to the heavy hearts and sour mood of the survivors and made their defeat that much more intolerable. Thus, when the low clouds turned the sky grey and heavy with rain, it matched the desolation they all felt.

Tired, disheartened, aching in mind and heart and body, the Dé Danann warhost came to Glasbrú, a small Cauci farming settlement near the

IN THE KINGDOM OF ALL TOMORROWS ✣ 113

green, reed-fringed banks of Lough Glas on the border of the Lord Toráin's territory. The clan chief and two of the elders came out onto the trail to greet them, displaying an awkward regard for their lord, and he for them—which served to remind Conor just how inexperienced was the young nobleman as a ruler.

Toráin quickly explained to his clansmen about the battle that had taken place at Mag Cró and the need for a place to rest and heal their wounds. Daragh, the chieftain—a brusque fellow with a brown, weather-worn face and large, splay-fingered hands—pointed out that it would be tight quarters but they would do their best by their lord. Some of the settlement's boys had gathered to gawk at all the warriors and their horses, and the chieftain sent them running back to the ráth to alert the women that food and drink would be needed—and that soon!—for upward of sixty or seventy hungry and thirsty men.

'I would that you slaughter a bullock for us tonight,' the lord said, 'and bring out your best ale—and mead, if you have it.' The head man nodded agreeably, but rubbed his chin with a thoughtful expression. Toráin, mindful of the man's hesitance, said, 'I will replace the beast from my own herd as well as anything else you provide.' Still the chieftain hesitated. 'Man, we have come fresh from battle and care nothing for the cost,' Toráin told him in tight, exasperated tones. 'We have wounded with us and many already faint from hunger. Do as I say, and be quick about it!'

This propelled the whole settlement into motion as the clan set about preparing food and lodging for the warriors. Glasbrú, the sleepy farm holding, was transformed into a crowded and busy armed camp. The boys and young men ran to help take care of the horses, and the older men put up boards and set cooking fires in the yard and hauled provisions from the storehouses. While the food was being prepared, several of the older women who had experience of treating and dressing injuries of various kinds directed the wounded to be brought into the steading's hall, where their wounds could be washed and bound. Some of the younger women filled tubs and vats with water and brought out fist-sized lumps of soap for the warriors.

Conor and the fianna took full advantage of the soap and water to wash away the sweat and grime and gore of the day's fighting. They spoke little and haltingly, and went about cleaning themselves with a sort of grim determination—as if to remove the awful stain of defeat. Then, bone-weary, but grateful for the small comfort provided, the warriors went to join their swordbrothers at the ale vats and Conor and Fergal found a quiet spot on a bench under the sheltering eaves of the chieftain's modest hall to talk and share the first of many cups that night. Toráin and Morann joined them for their discussion.

'I hate losing a battle,' said Fergal, as Daragh's youngest son offered two jars to them and then ran off to fetch more cups. 'All the more because this is one we should have won.'

'Aye,' agreed Morann unhappily. 'If not for Vainche we would be celebrating a victory tonight.'

'How many men did we lose today?' asked Toráin.

'Counting the six from the fianna, I make it thirty-two,' answered Conor, staring into his jar.

'And at least half that many wounded,' added Fergal. 'How many wounded among your men?'

'Nine—including five before you came,' said Toráin. 'But we were luckier than Aengus and Laegaire, I think. I saw them only briefly after the battle. They could not wait to leave Mag Cró.'

'Do you blame them?' said Morann. 'I would we were home, too. But that is not to be—at least not anytime soon.' His sigh of frustration and fatigue spoke for them all. 'If not for Vainche—the Black Hag take him! I curse his name.'

'Touching on that,' said Fergal, 'I know Vainche holds us low in his sight, but I would never have expected him to abandon the battle—and all for the sake of dealing us a blow.'

'Me, you mean,' suggested Conor. 'He wanted to deal *me* a blow.'

'What can Vainche have been thinking?' wondered Morann.

Fergal gave a snort of sharp disdain. 'It is rank treachery—that's what it is. And treachery in the midst of battle, as any druid would tell us, is one of the three loathly treasons.'

'Aye,' confirmed Morann. 'Treason it is, and death is the proper punishment.'

'You're right,' said Conor, swirling the ale in his cup. 'Any warrior in my fianna who behaved so would not be drawing breath in the Land of the Living even now.' He raised his eyes to Morann and added, 'But you have stirred my curiosity. I want Vainche punished, but I want to know *why* he did such a contemptible thing, aye, and what he hoped to gain by it.'

Daragh's boy appeared with more foaming jars and passed them to the lords and all drank in silence.

'Where were the Coriondi?' wondered Morann after a moment. 'They should have been here. With them at least, we might have carried the day without the Brigantes at all.'

'And the Eridani,' said Fergal. 'Corgan should have been here, too.'

'And what of your kinsman, Liam?' asked Toráin, a hint of his old, sly insinuation edging into his tone. 'Do you plan to invoke the justice of a brehon for Liam's part, too?'

'Whatever judgement is meted to Vainche will be shared by my wayward and unwise brother,' Conor replied darkly. 'Liam chose his portion when he sided with Lord Vainche and so must suffer the consequences accordingly.'

Lord Toráin regarded Conor for a long moment and his demeanour altered. He took a drink and gazed into his cup, saying, 'I was wrong about you, Conor mac Ardan. After what happened at the council, I would not blame you if you had planted a spear between my shoulders.'

'Nay, brother, I never would,' Conor told him lightly. 'My spear knows only one enemy and that is the Scálda. You have nothing to fear from me.'

'Too many Dé Danann have died today already, we would not be about adding to that number,' Fergal said.

'Now we have the enemy here on the coast, we must look to strengthen the defence of our borders,' observed Morann, bitterness edging into his tone. 'At least those of you who still have settlements and strongholds to defend.'

'Aye, and for that my people owe you our thanks, Conor mac Ardan. I am sorry for doubting you. Believe me when I tell you that I was influenced by some very bad advice. I'm finished with Vainche and I will never seek his aid or counsel again. Twice I've trusted him and twice been led astray against my own best interests. I have learned a hard lesson this time, and no mistake. I hope you'll accept my apologies for my part in Corgan's airechtas. I was a fool.'

'All that is behind us,' Conor told him. 'We need speak of it no more.'

'If anyone deserved to be judged it is surely Vainche,' said Morann. 'After his behaviour on the battlefield . . .' He spat. 'Disgraceful.'

'Criminal,' agreed Toráin. 'It's him we should be raising a charge against and this time get a druid or two to stand as judge. That's what he deserves.'

'He deserves to be stripped naked and horse-whipped to within a hair of his life. *That's* what he deserves,' said Morann.

The talk went on like this and the day closed gently around them. The exhausted warriors sat and watched the Cauci clan prepare the meal and allowed the sweet ale to ease the pain in their battered bodies.

The pain of defeat would take much longer to heal.

The defenders had lost good men and Conor did not know which hurt the more: being unable to recover the bodies for a warrior's burial, or that those warriors were betrayed by one of their own. Conor carried the hurt like a wound and he knew that, like a wound, it would leave a scar. Every wound left a scar, and every scar a lasting memory.

Later, after a morose and melancholy meal, Conor went off to sleep in the overcrowded barn. Anxious to be on his way back to Tara, he rose at dawn and ordered the fianna to get ready to leave. 'You'll be stopping by Dúnaird on the way home?' Toráin asked as Conor and Fergal waited for their horses to be brought out.

'Nothing good would happen there,' Conor replied. 'My brother knows what he did, and there will be a reckoning one day soon. This is far from finished.'

'Then I wish you all speed,' the Cauci lord told him. 'I'm certain we will be meeting again very soon.'

'Count on it,' said Conor. 'Perhaps sooner than we know. The Scálda are on the move again, and I doubt they'll be satisfied with the gains they've made. They'll try for more. We can only hope that next time, we're better prepared.'

With that grim pronouncement hanging over them, Fergal led the fianna from the yard. Six days later, they glimpsed Tara Hill in the distance and Conor's spirits rose at the sight. It lifted a little more when he saw Donal and Calbhan riding out to greet the returning warriors. Seeing them from a distance, Conor urged Búrach to quicken his pace and galloped to meet them. As he drew nearer, a thought occurred to him: what if all was not well? They had been away almost a fortnight; what if some disaster had occurred in his absence?

'Welcome, lord,' called Calbhan as Conor came within hailing distance. 'The battle went well?'

Conor meant to return the greeting and relay the sorry news, but the first words out of his mouth were 'How is Aoife?'

Donal laughed. 'Good to see you, too, brother. Allow me to relieve your misery. Your *son* is not yet born. . . .'

'Is he not? Then there is still—' It was then he caught the odd emphasis in Donal's reply. 'Why? What has happened?'

'You have a daughter.'

'A daughter!'

'Aye, a daughter,' replied Donal, beaming such uncontained joy anyone would have thought the child his own, 'dark-haired like her mother and sweet as honeyed milk.'

'A daughter . . .' Conor lifted his eyes to the flattened top of Tara Hill. Then, with a sudden slash of the reins, the stallion leapt away.

'Aoife is well, too, since you ask,' Donal called after him, but Conor was already gone.

A wild dash to the top of the hill brought Conor pounding into the yard. He hit the ground as soon as Búrach juddered to a halt and, without thinking, ran to the hall—only to be met there by Fíol, Dearg's second, who was busy strewing clean rushes onto the floor. 'Your lady wife is not here, lord,' explained Fíol.

'Not here!' cried Conor. 'But I thought . . . Where is she? Where is she?'

'All is well, lord. She is in the women's house. She is . . .' Conor was out the door again before he finished.

Racing across the yard to the still-unfinished house, Conor shoved through the oxhide covering, shouting, 'Where is she? Where's Aoife?'

He was met by Noirín, a young Auteini woman Aoife had adopted as one of her handmaids. 'My lady is within, lord,' she replied, raising the back of her hand to her forehead. She half turned and pointed to a corner of the room that had been hastily partitioned off by a grouping of cloaks hung upon a wooden frame to form a temporary chamber.

Conor hurried to this crude bower and, throwing aside one of the cloaks, stepped in to find his wife cradling his infant child to her breast and crooning softly. Aoife was sitting on a pallet piled with fleeces; her long dark hair was combed and neatly braided, and she was wearing her best blue mantle and her silver torc, looking regal in every line. 'Conor!' she gasped upon seeing him.

'Aoife! I'm here,' he said. 'Are you well? Are you—'

The infant stirred and gave a little squeak. 'Shh! She's trying to sleep,' Aoife told him. 'Keep your loud voice down.'

'But I want to see her,' protested Conor. 'Here—' Kneeling down beside the pallet, he held out his hands for the cloth-wrapped bundle.

'Ach, well, then I suppose you must. Here, my husband, meet your new daughter.' Smiling proudly, she withdrew the baby from her breast and gently placed the newborn in her father's hands.

The little bundle, wrapped in a scrap of well-used cloak, weighed nothing and seemed barely big as a new-baked loaf. 'Careful,' Aoife told him, smoothing the fluff of hair, 'you'll be squashing her in those big rough hands of yours.'

'Never that,' Conor whispered, gazing into the tiny scrunched-up face as a mixture of strange emotions swirled through him: wonder and delight, and an awe tinged with terror. How was he to protect and provide for one so small and defenceless? How could he not?

'She is . . . she is . . .' Words failed him and he reached for the first thing that came into his head. '. . . so *red*!'

Aoife laughed and cupped a hand to the tiny head. 'She is not!' she chided. 'A little warm maybe, but beautiful all the same. And will you just look at all that dark hair!'

'Aye, beautiful—just like her mother.' Conor reached out a finger and stroked it across the infant's brow.

At his touch the child squirmed and opened her eyes, looked up with a somewhat milky gaze, then promptly closed them again.

'What are we to call her?' wondered Conor, gazing in wonder at the tiny face.

'I thought we might call her Ciara.'

'Ciara,' Conor repeated, smiling. Then, with a shock, he glanced up into his wife's smiling face in surprise as a memory surfaced from long ago. 'Ciara! But that was my mother's name.'

Aoife laughed at his reaction and nodded. 'And I know it, do I not?'

'How?' wondered Conor, gazing on the child with renewed respect and wonder. 'I'm certain I never told you.'

'And it's certain I am that name never crossed your lips, husband. But I was that many years a master of song in your father's hall, if you spare a thought to recall. Of a time, Ardan would speak of her—when a song touched him, or stirred up a memory. And then,' she added, 'Rónán reminded me.'

'Rónán . . . my brother Rónán?'

'Is there another hereabouts? Aye, your brother Rónán. He's here at Tara. He came to see you and arrived in time for Ciara's birth, and I am that glad of his help.'

'Rónán is here,' said Conor.

'Is that not what I am saying?' Aoife laughed. Little Ciara squirmed and squeaked again; Aoife motioned for him to return the baby and Conor carefully placed the bundle in her hands. 'He says he has news.'

'Aye? What is that then?' asked Conor absently, unable to take his eyes from the newborn infant, now snuggled in her mother's arms.

'No one knows save Rónán alone, and he is being most mysterious about it—saying no one can hear this news until he has told you. So, you best go find him and see what it is. Then come back and tell me what he said.'

Conor agreed, but made no move to rise or leave; he remained kneeling beside his wife and new daughter.

'Today at all?' asked Aoife after a moment, immensely enjoying the sight of her lordly husband so awed and stricken by the newborn child.

'She is so beautiful,' he said, reaching out to stroke the tiny head once more.

Aoife laid a hand on his and gazed at the newborn in her arms. 'Aye, my heart, she is that.'

13

'Donal told me what happened,' said Rónán. 'I'm sorry.'

Conor regarded his younger brother curiously. He felt he had been living as one in a dream lately. That any nobleman could act out of such pettiness and spite as Vainche did—betraying his swordbrothers and delivering them to the slaughtering spearheads of a merciless enemy . . . Conor would not have believed such a thing possible if he had not been there to see it. Nevertheless, this was the world in which he lived; a world as real and strange as any faéry realm, but twisted and poisoned at the root. 'Aye,' he murmured, 'and so am I—sorry to the blood and bone of me. We lost the battle. Thirty-two men dead and seventeen wounded!'

'You did your best, Conor,' Rónán replied. 'How were you to know the depth of Vainche's duplicity?'

'I *should* have known,' snapped Conor. 'He has ever been a liar and deceiver. By my sword, I never imagined he would perform some trickery to mock me and show me for a failure.'

'You should have known?' said Rónán, thrusting himself back in his chair. 'Aye, and the Scálda should never have come to Eirlandia.'

They were sitting alone in the temporary dwelling Conor and Aoife used for their lodging before the baby was born. 'Or, are you responsible for the arrival of the Scálda, too?'

'I hardly know what to think anymore. Do you know what I have been asking myself? I have been asking myself if I have been deluded all my life. Maybe I was only seeing the world as I wished to see it, and not as it is. Because it was not just Vainche that stabbed us in the back on the battlefield, it was our brother, Liam.' Conor gazed at Rónán, a note of pleading in his voice. '*Liam!* And not those two only, but every one of our swordbrothers who deserted the field with them. Men that I know, that I have lived with, our kinfolk, and Aoife's, too. I have sat beside these men at the feast bench, passed the cup of welcome with them, trained with them. These selfsame men fought together on this very hill not so long ago. Bold souls of Eirlandia! And yet a word from their master—a word they must have known was death to honour and dignity—and they left us. Left us to fall beneath the blades of our common enemy.

'It hurts, Rónán. It hurts and the ache is deep. . . .' Conor paused, choked up and blinded by the tears that suddenly filled his eyes and began coursing down his cheeks. And had he been able to see through them he would have seen tears standing in his brother's eyes as well.

'And I wonder,' he continued after a moment, 'I ask the same question over and over, with no answer . . . Did they turn back?'

'What do you mean?' asked Rónán.

'I mean, did even one of them feel a pang of conscience, or regret, and turn back to see how we fared? I could believe it of Vainche that he rode away with a high, stiff neck—I can well believe that. But did any of the others so much as glance over their shoulder to see us run down by enemy war carts? Did any of them turn to watch the slaughter they arranged for us?'

'Would knowing make a difference?' Rónán said after a time. 'Let it go, brother. If it is as you and Fergal have said, Lord Vainche will be brought to justice.'

'*If*? What do you mean by this *if*? Is it me or Fergal you doubt?'

'I only meant—'

'Where is Fergal?' Conor jumped to his feet. 'Let's go get him and let him tell you to your face.'

'Conor, wait—'

Out in the yard, Conor saw a few of the fianna moving toward the gate. He called to them and was told Fergal had gone down to the washing stream with some of the others. 'Let's go,' he said to Rónán. 'We can talk on the way.' Rónán rose and fell into step beside him.

Crossing the yard, the two started down the long sloping path to the plain below. Rónán steered their talk toward Conor's plans for the Tara settlement and the surrounding lands: the farms and holdings, the horse breeding stables and pens, and building up the fianna, and all the rest until, approaching the river, they began meeting warriors on their way back to the hill. 'Where's Fergal—have you seen him?'

The warriors pointed to a section of the river screened off by a stand of young birches, and there they found a few warriors stretched out on the mossy bank to dry in the sun, talking in low tones as they enjoyed the warmth of the day. Conor hailed Fergal, who was standing out in the middle of the stream, and called him to the bank. But Rónán, seeing the warriors so enjoying themselves, said, 'Our talk can wait a little. Go join your men.'

Conor, still agitated, made to refuse, but Fergal called out that he was almost finished. At Rónán's urging, Conor shucked off his siarc, breecs, and brócs, and splashed into the shallow water. Rónán found a lump of soap one of the warriors had left behind and tossed it to his brother, then settled on the bank to wait.

Something about the mundane task of bathing in a cool, slow-running river put Conor in mind of all the times he and Rónán, and Fergal and Donal and the other boys of the clan, had enjoyed swimming and sporting in the rivers near Dúnaird. From the earliest times he could remember, Rónán had always been there—more so than Liam, who never seemed to have much time to spare for him, nor for the youngest of Ardan's three sons.

As he sluiced the water over himself the years seemed to fall away and, if only for a moment, he was that boy again. Conor smiled to remember those far-off happier days from a time before the Black Ships came and the Scálda spread death and destruction across the land.

'There is a big fat rat in the ale tub,' Fergal announced, striding up out of the water. 'What are we going to do about it, eh?' Snatching up his cloak from the bank, he flopped down on the ground. 'Vainche is that rat and what he did cannot go unpunished.' He looked to Rónán. 'So now, I'm asking you, my druid friend, what are we going to do about it?'

'And have not Conor and I been discussing this very thing?' said Rónán.

'Tell him what happened up at Mag Cró.' Conor shook water from his hair, picked up his siarc, spread it next to Fergal, and sat down. 'I told him already, but he wants to hear it from you.'

'That is not what I said, and not what I meant,' Rónán replied evenly. 'There is a remedy for treachery of the kind you describe,' Rónán explained.

'But in such cases it requires the witness of two lords. Conor can be one of them. Who else?'

'Ach, well, everyone saw it—Lord Morann, who was with us, and Toráin, Aengus, and Laegaire. They were all in the battle. They all know what happened and all lost men because of it.'

'We will leave that aside for now,' Rónán told him, 'and determine who would be best to speak to what happened on that day.'

'Leave it aside? Why!' demanded Fergal. 'Good men died because of Vainche's treachery. That is the very heart of the matter.'

'I'm not saying they didn't,' Rónán replied patiently. 'But it was a battle and men are killed in battle—are they not? There is no way to say how many would or would not have been lost if Vainche had or had not done what he did.'

Conor gave a mirthless bark of laughter. 'Only a druid would see it like that.'

'Be that as it may,' continued Rónán unperturbed, 'I will speak to these other lords and hear from them what happened.'

'You can start with Morann—he and his people are at Tara now,' said Conor. 'The battle took place on Auteini land and he fought alongside us.'

'Then that is where I will begin. I'll speak to him today.'

'And then?'

'Once I have spoken to the lords who were present, then I will personally make the case against Vainche before the brehons.'

'What about Liam?' said Fergal. 'He sided with Vainche.'

Rónán's eyes narrowed. 'If he aided in the betrayal, he must suffer the consequences. But, tell me now, from the beginning, everything you can recall of the battle and what happened on the field.'

Conor rose and began pulling on his clothes. While he dressed, he explained about the Scálda landing on the Auteini coast and driving Morann's tribe from their fortress, and how the neighbouring lords had gathered to turn back the incursion. He described the battles and how, in the second foray, Vainche had agreed to aid the attack, but had removed his battle group during the most perilous phase of the battle, leaving Conor and the fianna exposed and on their own behind the enemy chariot line. He concluded, saying, 'We were able to breach the chariot line and make good our retreat,' Conor concluded. 'We left thirty warriors behind and could not even retrieve their bodies to offer them a warrior's burial.'

Conor finished and Rónán drew a deep breath and looked to the sky and the bright clouds drifting over. 'This is how it will be,' he said after a moment. 'I will speak to the lords, as I said, and then I will bring the charge before the brehons. They will hold council and determine how best to proceed.'

'A council?' wondered Fergal. 'What good will that do? Treachery demands punishment—swift and severe.'

Conor rose and took up his cloak. 'We will leave it in your hands, brother. Just know that Tara's gates stand open to you if you wish to hold your council here. In fact, I would welcome it.'

'Let it be as you say.' Rónán bowed his head slightly. It was not a brother's assent that he saw; Conor understood that he was looking at Rónán the druid now.

Later that day, Rónán gathered everyone together at the burial mound and, as the dying sun set the cloud-fretted sky alight with flames of red and yellow gold, he observed the funeral rite for a warrior fallen in battle. There was no corpse to place in the dolmen; there would be no bones to gather and wrap in rich cloths and carry to the tomb: this was a rite for warriors whose bodies could not be recovered, whose corpses had been defiled and destroyed by the Scálda. So, the brehon improvised the rite and substituted new words for those traditionally spoken at the death of a ruler, and he substituted a damaged shield and a broken spear for those whose sacrifice he honoured.

As the starry legions claimed the night sky, the people of Tara left the tomb more unified than when they first arrived at the burial mound. In this way, the healing of the loss and the recovery of the dignity and pride of the survivors was begun.

The next morning, Rónán departed on his errand to visit the northern kings to obtain evidence of Lord Vainche's treacherous act.

14

Work at Tara proceeded much as before, only now there was a distinct feeling of kinship among the groups from various tribes. Slowly, the season of Lughnasadh approached and people began to wonder if this year, as in the one just past, their lord would observe the festival that marked the beginning of harvest. Conor heard the whispers and, although the idea appealed to him, there was the cost to be reckoned. He and his ail-duinn had just begun to discuss this very thing when Rónán returned from his circuit of the northern kings.

He appeared without warning one day as the fianna had just finished their morning's training. Conor had been with them and was on his way to the bower he and Aoife still shared until the inner chambers of the hall were finished. He halted when he heard a voice calling to him from across the yard. 'Rónán!' he cried, and hurried to greet his brother. 'I was just on my way to see Aoife and the baby. Come along, Aoife will be glad to see you—and you won't believe how much little Ciara has grown.'

Rónán embraced his brother and fell into step beside him. 'Well?' said Conor expectantly. 'How was your journey? You were gone a long time.'

'I not only gathered the information I required, I have also been to Clethar Ciall to speak to our chief brehon.' He beamed with pleasure at his news.

'And?' Conor stopped walking. 'What did he say?'

Rónán gave a quick nod. 'He has decided that the brehons will hear the case against Vainche.'

Conor smiled. 'Was there ever any doubt?'

'Not much—and not after I told him I had been to see all the lords involved and even talked to many of the warriors who were in the battle that day.' They started walking again. 'The charges will be heard at Lughnasadh.'

Conor attempted a quick calculation, adding up the days. 'That is still a month or more away.'

'It is that. But in matters of such grave and terrible consequence, there must be nine brehons to sit in judgement.'

'Nine!' said Conor.

'Aye, nine. Three threes it is—for an Ard Airechtas. Lughnasadh is a propitious time.'

Conor frowned. 'If you really think it will take that long. . . .'

'The deliberations will be undertaken according to brehon law. That being the case, I can tell you they will wish to call on some of those who witnessed this offence and seek to obtain any evidence for or against this complaint. Naturally, all this takes time to arrange. Trust me, you wouldn't want it any other way.'

Conor nodded thoughtfully and stroked his moustache; Rónán saw the glint of a sudden idea spark his brother's gaze. 'What are you thinking, Conor? What is it that has set your eyes agleam?'

'A stray thought,' replied Conor. 'Perhaps you might care to delay your journey to the druid house and come with me instead.'

'Where?' wondered Rónán, suspicion edging his voice. 'What are you thinking, brother?'

They had arrived at the bower and Conor said, 'I'll tell you later. For now, come in and greet Aoife and the baby.'

Once they were inside the cramped little structure, Conor gave Rónán the chair and settled on the sleeping pallet. Aoife, cradling tiny Ciara to her breast, welcomed Rónán and asked how he had fared on his travels north. He told her that his northern visits had produced better than expected results and, reaching out to stroke the baby's head, added, 'I have told Conor that the brehons have agreed to judge Vainche's betrayal.' He went on to explain that this special council, the Ard Airechtas, would be conducted at the druid school at Clethar Ciall during Lughnasadh. 'The lords present at Mag Cró will be summoned to attend, and I will need Conor and Fergal also—and perhaps a few of the fianna if they can be spared their duties for a few days.'

'As to that,' said Conor. 'The Brigantes owe five horses and they have not paid yet. Lughnasadh is soon upon us and I'm thinking we should go collect what we're owed before Vainche is put to the brehons.'

'Lest in facing one judgement the falsehearted rogue eludes another?' said Aoife.

'We should collect what we're owed before any other claims are made against him.'

'Very shrewd, husband.'

'Shrewd perhaps,' allowed Rónán cautiously, 'but I strongly advise you against making any such demands or advances lest you be giving Vainche an excuse to attack you.'

'But he *owes* us those horses,' Conor replied sharply. His elevated tone disturbed the infant and she began fussing.

'My love, Rónán makes a good point. We both know Vainche is not to be trusted,' said Aoife, rocking the baby gently. 'Why risk an unnecessary confrontation? We have enough trouble one day to the next, why stir up more?'

Conor regarded the two of them dubiously. 'We could use those horses,' he insisted. 'And it is but the work of a moment.'

'If so, then send Médon and any of the other Brigantes in the fianna,' suggested Rónán. 'But do not go yourself. That is my strong counsel. Send Fergal or Donal to Vainche if you must—but do not go yourself.'

Conor saw that it was no use pushing the matter further. 'Who am I to argue with a druid? I'll send Médon and some of the other Brigantes.'

'Good. That's settled.' Rónán stood abruptly. 'And I must be on my way.'

'Now?' said Conor. 'You've only just arrived, man.'

Rónán expressed his regret, and said, 'I'm needed up near Lough Leagh where a dispute has broken out over an injury caused by a prize bull to a cow owned by a farmer from a neighbouring settlement. A battle is threatened.'

'A weighty case then,' remarked Conor, rising.

Rónán bade Aoife and the child farewell, and Conor followed him out of the hut to see him on his way. 'At least have something to eat before you go.'

'I suppose I might take a little something with me,' Rónán replied. 'And you take this with you, brother mine. Do not go to Aintrén and confront Vainche. Those horses are not worth getting killed over. Do you hear me?'

'I hear you, brother,' Conor answered, somewhat resigned to the argument. 'And I'm sure it's good advice.'

15

The high walls of Aintrén glowed in the bright midday sun beneath a high blue, cloudless sky. Conor sat on his stallion Búrach regarding the Brigantes fortress. It was much as he remembered, but there was something about it that had changed and he could not readily tell what it was. The walls were still just as high, the ramp leading to the gates just as long, and the fields round about just as verdant as any he recalled. Even so, something was amiss. Perhaps, he thought, it was just the stillness. Here it was the heart of day and he could not hear a sound nor see any activity anywhere— neither in or around the stronghold, nor in the surrounding fields.

'Seems quiet up there,' mused Fergal from his place beside Conor. 'There's still time to turn back.'

'Why would we be wanting to turn back?' said Conor. 'I didn't come this far to be turning back.'

'Rónán said to stay away from here to avoid picking a fight with Vainche.'

'That's why I left the fianna behind,' Conor countered. 'Anyway, it's horses I want, not a fight.'

'Ach, well, it's a fight you'll be getting if I know Vainche at all.'

Conor glanced around at Médon, silent beside him. 'What do you think? Should we be going home to avoid a fight?'

The warrior glanced sideways at Fergal, who was shaking his head. 'We're here now. We might as well see it through.'

They had left Tara in the middle of the night, just the three of them, and had ridden hard to reach Aintrén before the day was out. Conor had kissed Aoife and told her to go back to sleep as he crept from their bed. He then met the other two outside the stable and they set off.

From his extensive knowledge of the place, Conor assumed their approach had been seen and that Vainche had been duly informed; but there was no sign from the ráth, no warriors had put their heads above the walls, and the gates stood open.

'Soon done is soon home,' said Conor. 'Let's make a start before the day is too much older.' Lifting the reins, Conor gave Búrach a gentle kick with his heels and started up the long ramp to the Aintrén entrance. The three rode through the open gate and into the yard, paused to take in the state of the place. There were a few folk going about their affairs, and though several of them stopped to see who had arrived, no one challenged them. As they stood waiting, two warriors came out of the hall, saw the strangers, and ran to meet them. 'You there!' shouted the first one. 'Stand where you are.'

Médon stepped forward. 'Feobhil!' he called. 'Is that you, lad? You remember me, aye? And you—Mongan . . . you know me—swordbrother and battle leader to you of a time.'

'Médon,' said the one called Feobhil. 'What are you doing here? And who's that with you . . . Conor? Fergal?'

'So you do remember us,' said Conor, stepping up beside Médon. 'We want to speak to your lord. Maybe you could go tell him we've come to see him.'

'If that's why you've come, then your luck is not with you,' said Feobhil. 'Lord Vainche is not here.'

'He went out hunting with some of the men,' Mongan told them. 'They left early this morning and won't return until nightfall—if they hold to the usual run of things.'

'Ach, well, too bad. He will miss the chance to share a welcome cup with us weary travellers,' said Fergal. He looked to Conor, who said, 'If the queen is here, maybe you could go and tell her we'd like to talk to her instead.'

'You want to talk to the queen?'

'Aye, that would be grand,' said Conor.

The two exchanged a brief word, then Mongan gave a shrug and strolled off in the direction of the king's house. As soon as he was gone, Feobhil joined his former friends. 'Why do you want to see the king, anyway?'

'It's about the horses,' Médon told him. 'We've come for the horses.'

The warrior appeared confused. 'What horses are those then?'

'The five horses we were granted at the airechtas,' said Fergal.

Feobhil again looked confused.

'You don't know about the judgement of the airechtas?' asked Médon.

'I don't even know what an airechtas *is*.'

'Ach, well, it wouldn't do to start worrying about it now,' replied Fergal. 'You'll find out soon enough.' He nodded toward the royal residence, where Queen Sceana had just appeared in the yard. 'Here comes your lady.' Turning to Conor, he said under his breath, 'They know nothing of Corgan's airechtas. Vainche didn't tell them about the horses.'

'Or much of anything else, I'm thinking.'

Conor watched as the queen, her brow creased with concern and curiosity, crossed the yard to meet them. Slender and regal as ever, her long russet locks curling down along her neck, her thin gold torc gleaming, she was dressed in a fine linen gown of new grass with a richly embroidered girdle of red and blue and gold about her waist and a light yellow mantle over all. Yet despite the splendour of her clothes, Conor noticed a darkness behind her eyes and she possessed an air of sorrow, or weariness—or perhaps, Conor thought, even desperation.

Behind her appeared an older, grim-faced woman who hurried across the yard to join her, and quickly fell into step beside her. Before the queen could speak, the woman demanded, 'Who is it that would disturb the peace of this place?'

Conor dismissed her with a glance and Conor stepped forward, saying, 'Lady Sceana, forgive our unexpected intrusion.' Handing his spear to Médon, he raised the back of his hand to his forehead in acknowledgement of her sovereignty and thanked her for agreeing to meet them.

'If you had sent word, I am sure his lordship would have wanted to receive you in the manner you deserve,' replied the queen primly.

Conor smiled at the double meaning of her words. 'I have no doubt of that whatsoever.' Still smiling, he said, 'I see you are thriving here. It is good to see you looking so well.'

She stiffened slightly and that, to anyone looking on, told the tale.

'You would do well to leave now and come back when the king is here to receive you,' said the queen's stern companion.

'This is Lord Vainche's sister,' explained Sceana. 'She is become companion to me and mistress of the hearth.'

'Why are you here?' demanded the woman. 'It is not, I think, to see how we fare at Aintrén.'

'Indeed not,' Conor told her. Turning once more to the queen, he said, 'We have come to collect the horses granted me in the airechtas judgement.'

Sceana pursed her lips and regarded the three before her with a wariness approaching apprehension. To Conor, it seemed as if she sensed a nasty jolt coming. 'And what airechtas judgement would that be?'

'Five horses in compensation for the false accusations made against me by Lord Corgan and several others—Lord Vainche among them.'

Again, a look of concerned uncertainty passed over the queen's features. She gave a sidelong glance at the frowning woman beside her. 'I know nothing about any such accusation or compensation.'

'Then I must beg your pardon, lady. I had assumed your lord would have told you,' said Conor. 'If I had known—'

'My lord keeps his own counsel,' interrupted the woman shoving up beside the queen. 'We should all be so wise.' She put a hand to the queen's arm as if to pull her away. 'I think we've said enough here.'

'And yet, my question remains unanswered,' insisted Conor.

'What question is that?' said the queen's sour-faced companion.

'Where are the horses I was promised?'

'This airechtas judgement you mentioned,' Sceana said. 'What was it?'

Conor drew breath to reply, but Médon interrupted. 'Allow me to answer, my lord. I was there and I can tell what happened.' Conor assented and the former Brigantes battlechief quickly told how Conor had been summoned by a gathering of northern lords who accused him of stealing Tara Hill and surrounding lands for his own, and how these kings—Vainche included—told lies about Conor. He described the late arrival of the brehon to take control of the proceedings and ensure that true justice was delivered. The former Brigantes warrior concluded, saying, 'The accusations against Lord Conor were shown to be baseless and without merit. My lord was vindicated and was awarded reparation in the form of five horses from each of the kings who took part in the gathering. It is these horses we have come to collect.'

While he had been speaking, a small crowd assembled in the yard—mostly warriors, but others as well. Médon finished and the queen regarded the three visitors for a long moment, then said, 'If horses were promised, then horses shall be given.' She turned to the warriors who stood looking on. 'You there, Irchel, go and tell the stable master to bring five horses.'

'My lady, I think it best to wait until—' began the elder woman.

The queen waved her to silence. 'I have spoken.' To the warrior, she said, 'Go now and fetch the horses.'

The warrior departed on the run and Sceana turned back to Conor. 'I trust this act of good faith will suffice to mend whatever hurt you have suffered.'

Something about the way she said it—as if belittling the harm caused by Vainche—rankled, and Conor felt his scarlet blemish begin to prick and burn. 'The small obligation to me will be satisfied. But the hurt to the men he betrayed at Mag Cró will take more than five horses to heal.'

'Why?' The queen's back stiffened and her green eyes narrowed as she feared the answer. 'What happened at Mag Cró?'

'You don't know?' said Conor. 'I thought Lord Vainche would have told you all about our great battle in the north.' He glanced at Vainche's sister, and added, 'No doubt he withheld any mention of his cowardly action on the battlefield.'

'Very wise,' snorted Fergal. 'The man is a very champion of wisdom it seems.'

Ignoring him, Conor said, 'Some few weeks ago, Scálda ships made a landing on the western coast and took Auteini territory. Neighbouring kings rode to help reclaim the stolen lands—the Brigantes warband and the fianna of Tara foremost among them. You will recall that Lord Vainche and his warband returned unharmed—'

'Owing to the skill of the brave Brigantes warriors,' said Sceana's companion. 'Yes, we know of the battle.'

Conor was shaking his head before she finished. 'Nay, lady. The safe return of your warriors was owing to the fact that Lord Vainche perpetrated a foul act of treachery and deceit. He abandoned his brother kings in the midst of battle and removed the Brigantes warband from the field.'

The crowd began muttering among themselves, and the colour fled from the queen's face. 'That could not happen,' she said, her voice growing small.

'It is the truth, my lady,' said Médon. 'I was there in the leading rank. With these eyes in my head, I saw this treachery committed.'

'You need not rely on our word alone,' Conor continued. Lifting a hand to the warriors standing nearby, he said, 'Ask *them*—your own men will tell you.' Raising his voice, he addressed the warriors. 'Who among you rode north to Mag Cró? Who among you was there on the battlefield the day we met the Scálda chariots?'

Most of those looking on either shrugged or looked away.

'No one?' said Conor. 'None of you were there?' He glanced at Médon, and said, 'Why am I finding that difficult to believe?'

'Difficult, perhaps, because it is not so.' Turning to the warriors ranged behind the queen, Médon said, 'For a fact, I know that you, Comgall, were there—and you, Mongan. I saw both of you among your swordbrothers before the battle began. Not so?'

Comgall glared at Médon, then jerked his chin down. 'I was there, aye.'

'And you, Mongan?' The warrior muttered something in reply and Médon said, 'Speak up, man, we did not hear you.'

'I was there. Everything Conor said is true, but we were sworn to tell no one what happened that day.'

'Who forced you to make that vow?' asked Conor.

'Who do you think?' muttered Mongan darkly.

'Never fear,' Conor told them, 'I will not ask you to break your vow.' To the queen, he said, 'The battle plan required the close cooperation of every battlechief and warband. We all had our work to do. Yet, when the charge began and the Dé Danann joined battle with the enemy, Lord Vainche removed his warband and that of the Darini from the battle. They fled the field, leaving those of us in the thick of the fight at the mercy of an enemy that has never been known to show the least mercy to anyone.' To the two Brigantes warriors, he demanded, 'Isn't that so?'

Again, the two stared at one another glumly.

'Say nothing more to these men,' said Vainche's sister, her voice taking on an ominous tone. 'Or you will answer to your lord for your insolence.'

'You will answer to your queen first,' Sceana told them. 'Tell me—does Conor speak the truth?'

Mongan drew a long, shaky breath and confessed, 'Aye, my lady. To my shame, I confess it is the truth. Lord Vainche withdrew from the fight and ordered us from the battlefield. We rode for home without looking back.' Having spoken he lowered his head, waiting for the wrath to break upon him.

Queen Sceana—shaken, and shamed to silence—stared in forlorn disbelief at the two warriors. After a long painful moment, Conor, his voice gentling, said, 'Good men lost their lives that day and Vainche's treachery will be exposed. He is to be summoned before the brehons of Eirlandia.'

The stable master and two of his grooms entered the yard just then, leading five horses on halters. The queen's companion, humiliated, her voice quivering, took charge and commanded the stabler to deliver the animals into Conor's keeping, and then said, 'Accept these horses in payment of the debt you are owed. Take them and go.'

Conor motioned Fergal and Médon to take the animals and thanked the queen. 'But I would not like to leave here without—' he began.

Sceana raised a hand to prevent him saying any more. 'You have what you came for,' she said, her voice almost breaking. 'Just go now and never come back.'

Conor nodded and, taking hold of one of the halters, followed Fergal and Médon to the fortress gate, where the three paused to collect their own mounts. The Brigantes watched them depart. The three had almost reached the road at the bottom of the hill when they heard a shout behind them. Conor glanced over his shoulder to see the two warriors, Mongan and Comgall, dart out from the crowd and run after them. 'Wait!' shouted Mongan. 'We want to come with you.'

'We want to join your fianna,' said Comgall.

'You would choose the fianna over your kinsmen and king?' said Fergal.

'Nay, rather say we choose not to live in dishonour anymore,' Mongan replied. He raised hopeful eyes to Conor and said, 'Will you be having us at all?'

'I will,' replied Conor. Putting a hand to the warrior's shoulder, he handed him the halter and said, 'You can start by taking care of our new horses.'

Conor cast a last look at the Brigantes fortress, then took up the reins, swung himself onto Búrach's back, and rode away.

16

As soon as the Aintrén fortress was out of sight, Conor halted and called to Médon. 'You and Mongan and Comgall take the horses and ride for Tara and don't stop until you're out of Brigantes territory. Fergal and I will hold back a little while to see we're not followed.'

'In case Vainche comes back and wonders where his horses have gone?' Médon said with a smirk.

'Just go,' Conor ordered. 'We'll linger behind awhile just to make sure, and join you later.'

Médon and the two newest fianna recruits rode on, leaving Conor and Fergal to resume at a slower pace, pausing every now and then to watch the road behind for any sign of pursuit. Easy in one another's company, they fell to discussing the various ways to order Tara's ever-growing warband, and the day slowly faded around them.

By the time the sun began to lower in the west, Conor pulled up at the edge of a stream in a wood near the western border of the Brigantes lands. 'We should be thinking of a place to camp for the night,' said Conor, looking around. 'I say this place is as good as any.'

'We've a fair bit of daylight left,' observed Fergal. 'We might still be able to catch Médon and the two new fellas. Maybe make camp with them. They've got most of the food anyway.'

Conor nodded. 'After we rest and water the horses. We'll let them graze awhile and then move on.'

Dismounting at the streamside, they let the animals drink their fill and then tethered them so they could nuzzle the greenery; after replenishing their own water skins, they settled back under the wide-flung boughs of a large old elm to rest. As they waited, they ate a little dried beef bósaill and hazelnuts from their sparáns, and the sun dipped below the treeline on the horizon and an early twilight fell across the wood.

'So then, you must be feeling very pleased with yourself just now,' said Fergal. 'But what will Rónán say when he finds out you went to Aintrén? I cannot think this little frolic was really about collecting a debt.'

'It was that and nothing more.'

'I know you, Conor mac Ardan. You could not resist a chance to poke Vainche in the eye.'

'It was only ever about collecting that debt,' maintained Conor.

'Ach, aye, because not even you could be so feckless as to go against a druid's strong advice. My mistake, I see that you are not the brash hothead that you once were.'

'And I know it,' replied Conor. His voice took on a wistful note as he watched the shadows deepen through the wood. 'I suppose I must seem a different man. Becoming a lord . . . becoming a father . . .'

'Aye, that might have something to do with it,' agreed Fergal. 'What with all the feasting and drinking and cavorting of a night.'

'Too true—for life is all one endless celebration for the Lord of Tara— as you well know.'

'Not to mention having to set the sun alight and hang it aloft every morning and receiving the endless praise and adoration of your people.' He made a wry face. 'I would not be wishing it on anyone!'

Conor laughed. 'But tell me now,' he said. 'Am I really that much changed?'

'We are *all* of us changed, brother,' said Fergal. 'How not? Even take away our banishment, the constant reavings and wearings of the Scálda, being spirited away to the faéry realms—what man is not changed by the years? Aye, you are changed—but not so much that I would not know you by heart and deeds.'

Conor considered this. 'Thank you, good friend. In truth, I sometimes think this lordship will be my undoing.'

'Heavy burden, is it?' scoffed Fergal. 'The way I see it is if ever I'm in need of a light in a dark place all I have to do is ask you to bend over and crack open your cheeks a little.'

They laughed raucously at this, and when they rose to resume their journey, they noticed that a thin mist had risen and was coursing along the stream, drifting through the trees, and sifting along the wooded pathways like ghostly fingers, building and deepening until it formed a wall obscuring everything but the sky above, which still held the violet glow of the setting sun. And then that, too, disappeared.

'I'm thinking it's fixing to be a damp night,' observed Fergal. 'We'll have to make a bit of speed if we're to find the others before dark.' He glanced around at the silvery white mist deepening around them. 'Didn't this fog come up fast, though?'

'Conor mac Ardan!' The call, muffled by the mist wrack, seemed to come from everywhere and nowhere.

'Who was that?' Fergal. 'Vainche?'

When Conor did not answer, Fergal turned to look at him and saw Conor's face and hands lit by a strange, green-white glow and his eyes agleam with a spectral light—as if he might be staring at the beam of a distant star.

The voice came again. 'Conor mac Ardan . . .'

'I am here!' he replied, his voice hushed by the deadening fog.

'There!' whispered Fergal. 'In the trees.' Spear in hand, he pointed into the mist.

Conor followed Fergal's gaze and saw shapes emerging: three tall, thin figures that seemed to be forming out of the glowing mist itself. They were wrapped almost head to foot in long cloaks, so he could not make out their features or faces, yet there was something curiously familiar about them. They drew closer and Conor saw that the tallest of the three carried a long rod with a curled knob on the end of it and it was from this shell-shaped knob that the eerie green-white light emanated. In the gleam of that light the face of the stranger took on an aspect Conor remembered only too well.

'Lenos!' said Conor.

Fergal exhaled, releasing the tension in his body. 'Faéries!' he muttered. 'And not the pleasant kind.'

'Shh! They'll hear you,' Conor whispered. 'Try to be agreeable—at least until we find out what they want.'

Fergal gave a grunt of acceptance to the idea, but said no more. Conor moved to the edge of the stream and Fergal moved quickly to Conor's side, spear in one hand and the other on the hilt of his sword. They waited until the three faéry came to stand before them on the trail. The tallest wore a long, belted siarc and breecs and cloak the colours of shadows and night, his long flame-tinged hair knotted and braided at the side of his head. He stretched out his long-fingered hand, then slowly raised it and touched the back of his hand to his forehead. 'Greetings, Lord Conor. I hope we find you well and recovered from your wounds.'

'Lord Lenos, greetings. You must forgive us if we stare. Bearing in mind how we last parted, we did not expect our paths to cross again.' Conor gave a nod to his companion. 'You will remember Fergal, I think. He it was who came with Lord Gwydion to our aid that day we faced the Scálda on the strand.'

'Greetings to you, Fergal mac Caen,' replied Lenos graciously. 'You may remember my chief advisors—' He turned to the two beside him, one with fine, straight, silvery hair in a long braid upon his shoulder, and the other with short black curls like those of a fleecy ram. 'This is Armadal.' He indicated the silver-haired one, then turned to the dark-haired one and said, 'And this is Sealbach. They are my principal advisors and confidants, and worthy to be trusted through all things. You may speak freely before them.' The two gaunt beings gave low bows, but said nothing.

Conor cast his mind back to his singular encounter with Lenos and his people: prisoners bound in iron chains in a crude hut on the border of the deadlands. Like Rhiannon and her maiden before them, the Kerionid faéry had been captured by the Scálda to be killed one by one until they agreed to divulge the secret of faéry magic. Lord Lenos was the king of the Kerionid branch of the faéry race, but though the two with him seemed vaguely familiar Conor could not recall if they had been among those he had rescued. Then again, that night had been fraught with other, more pressing concerns—such as the murder of Brecan, to name just one.

'And you are right to remind me that we parted on less than cordial terms,' the king continued. 'The fault is mine and I own it. I want you to know that this lapse of gratitude has caused me pain whenever I reflect upon my behaviour toward you both—mortals who put your own lives at risk for ours. It was unworthy of me and a poor example to my people. For that I am truly sorry and beg your pardon.'

'There is no need,' Conor told him. 'I'm thinking we were all less than our better selves on that difficult day.'

Lenos spread his long hands in acceptance of Conor's generous assessment. 'Be that as it may,' continued the faéry king, 'I owe a debt of honour, and that weighs most heavily. It is my wish to repay it now.'

'Now?' wondered Conor. He glanced at Fergal. 'This seems to be a day of balancing accounts.' To Lenos he said, 'There is nothing to repay.'

But Fergal put out his hand to stay Conor's refusal, and said, 'Forgive my curiosity, Lord Lenos—but how do you propose to pay this honour debt?'

'What if I told you I possessed something of great value that would aid you in your fight against the Scálda?'

Conor and Fergal exchanged a glance. 'And are you offering to give me this thing?' asked Conor.

At this the stern-faced faéry king brightened and his pale lips formed a smile that, for all its rarity, did much to alter the solemn being's aspect for the better. 'What I propose to give you is the answer to a riddle.'

Conor and Fergal shared a baffled glance. Conor said, 'Did I understand you to say you are offering an answer to a riddle?'

Again, Lenos flashed his rare smile. 'You heard correctly, my friend. But far better, perhaps, to ask what is the riddle.'

'What, then, is the riddle?' asked Fergal, suspicion edging his tone.

'It is this,' replied the faéry lord. 'What is swifter than a spear in its flight, and sharper than a sword in the fight?'

'And the answer?' asked Conor.

'For that,' announced Lenos, enjoying his game, 'I must ask you to come with me.' He half turned as if to lead them away then and there.

'Go with you?' said Conor. 'Where?'

'To Eilean Ceó.' Looking back over his shoulder, the tall faéry king added, 'The answer lies in Albion.'

17

'We need a better reason than a tricksy faéry riddle to go sailing away to Albion with them. It is a mad scheme and I don't trust it,' protested Fergal. He cast a dark glance at Lenos and his companions, who stood looking on from across the stream, their elongated forms aglow in the shining mist. 'And I don't trust Lenos, either. Him and his sly faéry ways. This thing smells of lies and deception. I don't like it.'

'Then you don't have to go.'

'And you think this a good idea, do you? What about your lordly duties? You cannot go swanning off to some faéry island. Think of your people . . . think of your family! What about Aoife and your dear sweet infant child? And what will I be telling them when I turn up and you're not with me?' Fergal shook his head. 'We can't be going off with the faéry folk, brother. And there's the end of it.'

Conor contemplated this for a moment. 'You make a good argument. You are right to remind me of my duties.'

'Does that mean we'll not be going?'

'It means that we must obtain an assurance or two from friend Lenos before we agree to anything.'

The faéry lord, still waiting patiently on the other side of the stream, spoke up. 'Well, then? Shall we go?'

'A word first,' said Conor. He quickly explained his reservations and the faéry king listened patiently.

'I understand your hesitation, my friends,' Lenos said when Conor finished. 'You would be better inclined if this journey I propose could be accomplished in such a way to ensure your absence would be little noticed by anyone here. Is that right? As it happens, we have anticipated this very concern.' The king of the Kerionid nodded to the one called Armadal, who pressed his hands together in a curiously self-satisfied gesture and said, 'I can give you every assurance that no one in Eirlandia will think you absent from these shores more than a single night—if that. The space between sleeping and rising, shall we say?'

'And do you also promise that what you have to show us will be to our benefit in the war against the Scálda?'

'On that you have my solemn word,' said Lenos. 'What I shall propose will be of tremendous benefit to both of us. Otherwise we would not have come to you at all. Will you come?'

Clearly still resistant to the idea, Fergal stood gripping his spear as if throttling a foe. Conor put a reassuring hand on his arm. 'If there is a chance that we can gain an advantage against Balor Evil Eye, then we have to try. Come with me, brother. I won't be going without you.'

'You will, you know.'

'I won't,' insisted Conor. 'True, it might be chasing after wild geese as you say. But what if it comes good?' He shrugged. 'Anyway, no one will even know we're gone. What have we got to lose?'

'With the faéry, who can say?' Fergal gave one last glare at the king and his cheerless companions, then sighed and surrendered. 'Aoife would have the head clean off me if I let you go off with them alone. Aye, I'll be going with you—if only to keep *them* honest.'

'We'll come with you, Lenos,' Conor called across the stream.

'Bring the horses,' commanded Lenos, and Sealbach departed on the run.

From that moment, the night took on that eerie, dreamlike quality for Conor and Fergal—similar to the one they had experienced before with Rhiannon and the Tylwyth Teg when they had outraced the enemy riders to make their escape from deep in Scálda territory. Afterward, they would remember little but the blurred woods and fields, high rain-lashed hills, darksome dells and valleys, and an endless succession of shadows melding into one another. They would recall pausing by a lough to water the horses and then, later, riding along the high bluffs with the moon glinting off the sea far below and the waves booming as they smashed against the stony feet of the towering seagirt rock stacks. They would imagine they were led along the frenzied paths by the moon, or by starlight, or again, in rain and shadow-crowded darkness.

At last the travelling party arrived at a secluded bay somewhere on the northeast coast and improbably far from where they had begun. The night was far spent and the tide already running. Lenos's ship was waiting for them by the strand. A curious craft, the faéry vessel had a wide, low-sided hull topped by a carved rail, and a tall mast rising from a tentlike enclosure that took up most of the space in the centre of the flat deck. The pilot stood at the stern in command of a long, curved tiller oar. Lenos hailed the craft, and two crewmen appeared; they put out a wooden ramp and scrambled ashore to take the horses while the riders climbed aboard the ship. Conor and Fergal, bone-weary, sank down on benches that ran along the rails; bleary-eyed, they watched as the horses were blindfolded, led up the narrow walkway, and secured for the voyage. This was all accomplished with extraordinary speed and soon the faéry craft began to move out into the bay.

Riding on the waves lightly as a leaf driven by the wind, the ship reached deep water. The green sail billowed and the sharp, blade-shaped hull knifed through the waves, carving a wake of white foam on the blue-black sea. Conor and Fergal, exhausted by the night's ride, slumped on the bench and delivered themselves to the dip and roll of the vessel.

Conor woke sometime later to the keening cry of gulls sailing above the faéry ship's mast. The sun was a pale blot in a white sky, with low clouds scudding in from the north, and Fergal stood at the rail staring out at a flat grey sea. Conor rolled upright on the bench and yawned. 'Can't sleep, brother?'

Fergal, still staring out at the empty wave-rippled expanse, replied, 'Say what you will, *I* say there is more here than meets your little beady eye.'

Conor swung his legs off the bench, rubbed his face with both hands, and leaned his elbows on his knees. 'I know,' he yawned. 'So you've been telling me since we boarded this ship.'

Fergal cast a glance over his shoulder and then turned around to address Conor, crossing his arms over his chest. 'Do you not think it odd that sour old Lenos should appear out of nowhere all of a sudden with sweet promises of aid and friendship? And him a fella well known to never have two happy words for you or me when last we saw one another?'

Conor looked around to see if they were being overheard. The pilot at the tiller was the only faéry to be seen. 'Keep your voice down. They'll hear you.'

'I tell you the truth,' Fergal continued, dropping his voice, 'these Albion faéry are serving up bad fish. The stew smells rank to me.'

'You may be right,' Conor conceded. 'Then again, it may be just as Lenos says—that he regretted the unfriendly way we parted and saw a chance to make amends.'

'What so?' said Fergal; leaning close, he put his face in front of Conor's. 'These faéry folk have found a way we can all help each other? What does *that* look like on two legs? Tell me if you know.'

'I reckon we'll find out soon enough.'

'And I say we're making a very large mistake trusting them. We should tell Lenos to turn this boat around and take us back.'

'Too late for that,' said Conor, glancing toward the stern, where Armadal had just appeared and was coming toward them. 'We'll have to see it through.'

'You are awake,' said the silver-haired faéry, folding his long pale hands in front of him. 'Follow me. You will want to see this. . . .' He moved on, leading them around the central enclosure to the other side of the ship, where Lenos and Sealbach stood at the rail gazing at the high, rock-bound coastline of a verdant green island. The pale sky gave the water a silvery aspect over which a multitude of white birds sewed the air; looping and diving, they flocked to their roosts on the sheer cliffs and crevices, their mewing cries filling the sky with a melancholy sound; dolphins, pacing the prow, breached the shimmering surface chasing small fish. The rich green of the tree-lined hills and silver sea gave the island the appearance of a rare jewel in a costly setting.

'Behold!' declared Lenos, lifting a hand to the ruddy brown headlands and towering black crags rising before them. 'Eilean Ceó, our home.' The king pointed to a mountainous landmass rising out of the blue mist on the near-distant horizon. 'And there lies the Albion mainland. The Aes-sídhe have lands in both places. The Kerionid reside here. The island has everything we need for an agreeable life.'

The five remained at the rail as the ship bounded over the wave swell, closer and closer until gliding into the shelter of the high headlands, whereupon the pilot swung onto a northern course, passing along the rock-bound coast. Some little time later, the ship arrived in a wide, shallow cove and the water changed from stony grey-green to the blue of a sparrow's egg; the cove was ringed with a strand of sand as white and fine as snow leading to grass-covered dunes above. There was a scattering of small, stone-built beehive-shaped dwellings lining the crest of the dunes; blue nets were strung on poles between the huts, and a few deep-bellied boats were drawn up high on the beach.

The ship's pilot gave out a cry and his crewmen struck the sails. A moment later, the faéry craft kissed the strand with the soft whisper of the keel against sand. 'Welcome to Eilean Ceó in Albion, my friends,' said the Aes-sídhe king. 'You will want for nothing while you are my guests.' He put his hand to the rail and, with a lithe, graceful leap, vaulted over the side of the ship and landed in water to his knees.

Fergal and Conor followed their host's example, clambering over the side. The cold water rinsed away the dregs of sleep, and they waded onto the glistening beach to wait while the wooden walkways were put down and the horses led ashore. Lenos saw the two mortals eyeing the boats and fisher huts. 'You must be hungry after your long ride and voyage,' he declared. 'We will eat soon. And worry not—my people love fishing and you will be well supplied with food and drink suitable for your race.'

Conor turned a puzzled glance at his host. 'I thank you for your thoughtfulness, but we have eaten faéry food before and are more than happy to do so again.'

Lenos professed astonishment, and then understanding came to him. 'Of course! To be sure. I was forgetting you sojourned among the Tylwyth Teg for a time. And they allowed you to eat from their table?'

'For a fact they did,' replied Fergal. 'And we were all the better for it.'

Lenos's long face pulled a wry smile. 'I am certain that you are much the better for it. Any mortal would be. But did they not tell you the terrible price you pay for such indulgence?'

'I would not say it was an indulgence,' replied Conor. 'Donal lay for many months in death's shadow and that close to the door of the Hag Queen's hall he might have walked through at any moment. I myself was sorely wounded. We owe our lives to King Gwydion and his physicians.'

Fergal, his brow furrowed in thought, asked, 'You mentioned a price to be paid just now—what did you mean by that?'

'Do you not know?' wondered Armadal, coming up just then. 'Has no one told you what happens to any who touch food or drink of the faéry?'

'Ach, to be sure,' replied Fergal in a lightly scoffing tone. 'We've heard it said—by bards and such—that drinking from a faéry's cup means you can never leave the land where that cup was served.' He looked to Sealbach for confirmation. 'Aye, well we not only drank our fill at Lord Gwydion's table, but dined every day we were with them. And, as Conor says, we left them better than we came. If that is a cost, then it is a price I'll gladly pay any time.'

'Perhaps,' replied the faéry. 'But you should know the nature of the bargain you have made.'

Lenos, assuming his usual dour mien, added, 'The price is nothing less than your mortality.'

Donal

Last night I awoke to the screams of dying warriors. I started up out of my bed, the shrill and terrible cries hanging in the air. I looked around. The hall was dark and silent, the fire in the hearth burned down to embers. Those who slept in the hall, slept still. Was I the only one who heard the death agonies of Tara's brave defenders?

It took me a few moments to realise that the terrible cries belonged to a dream—a dream of my second sight. Since my sojourn among the Tylwyth Teg on the Isle of the Everliving, I have experienced such dreams and visions. They seem to have become more frequent and more vivid. This latest was a vision of such rare and vivid intensity that it awakened me and left me upright and shaking, my heart beating hard and fast. I waited—holding my breath and listening. . . .

The hall remained calm and silent, save for the gentle sough of men breathing like the ebb and swell of a distant sea.

Reassured, but still unsettled, I passed a hand over my face. My palm came away slick with sweat. I closed my eyes and lay down again, but could not rest. The echoes of the screams banished all thoughts of slumber. Instead, I rose, draped my cloak over my shoulders, and left the hall. Barefoot, I paced the yard, moving among the huts and shelters of our refugee citizens, hearing only the occasional night murmur, or snores of a sleeper. Above, the night sky was clear with a sea-foam spray of stars stretching from horizon to horizon, and the air held a hint of stale smoke from the evening before.

One of Tara's dogs saw me and came to nuzzle my hand. I patted the warm head and stroked the soft ears and, looking down, saw his glossy white coat aglow in the starlight, his blood-red ears erect as he stared out toward the rim of the hill; and I understood that the dog wanted me to go there. So, we walked together to the rim of Tara Hill and looked out over the darkened plains of Mag Rí, Mag Coinnem, and Mag Teamhair.

As I gazed over the starlit land, I heard a rustling movement behind me and the sound of many feet. Suddenly, I was standing in the midst of a warhost and the warriors streamed around me, running, racing down the hillside to the plain—Mag Teamhair, but the other two also, for when I looked again the lowlands all around the hill were covered in smoke and mist, which began flowing up the hillside from the plain—smoke from a thousand fires of the enemy camped out on the plain.

I could not see the Scálda for the obscuring wrack, but I could hear them. I could hear their shouts and jeers and wild ululations. I could hear them beating the iron rims of their shields with sword hilt and spear shaft. I could hear the rhythmic rumbling of their drums. It seemed to me that I had been hearing them all through the long, wakeful night— booming like the thunder of a storm about to break. And I knew we were powerless to avoid the impending conflict, much less stop it.

Even though I could not see them, I sensed somehow that we were fearfully outnumbered. Where were the other tribes? Where the other kings? What had happened to the fianna? Where were Médon and Galart? Where was Fergal? And Conor . . . where was he?

As I looked around for my swordbrothers, I heard the dog whine. I turned around to see that the dog was gone and in its place stood a woman clutching a tiny child tight in her arms and she was trying to quiet it, to comfort it. She stumbled out of the mist wrack and took her place beside me. I gazed at her and recognised her at last. 'Aoife, what are you doing here? Go back.'

'I am a queen in Eirlandia. Where else should I be but with my brave warriors?' she said, and when I looked again I saw she held not a child, but a sword. She gazed at me and I saw that half her face was daubed in blue: the ancient colours of a warrior.

'Go back to the women's house where you will be safe,' I told her.

'Think you any place on Tara Hill is safe?' she spat. 'I tell you, brother, no place is safe while the Scálda spoil and scream for the heads of Dé Danann warriors to adorn their spears.'

'Where is the king?'

Aoife was gazing down upon the plain—only this time it was Mag Tuired—and I knew that there had been another battle there, long ago. This battle, still remembered in the songs of bards, had determined the destiny of the island for ages to come.

Thinking she had not heard me, I asked her again, 'Where is Conor? Where is the king?'

The queen turned to me with tears in her eyes and shook her head. But I heard a voice from somewhere—behind me, above me—I know not where, saying, 'Conor has gone to the Land of the Everliving. His like will not be seen in Eirlandia again.'

The voice I recognised.

'Gwydion?' I spun around to see where he might be, but there was no one to be seen. The words chilled the warm blood in my heart. 'Did you hear that, Aoife?' I asked, turning back to the view of the valley.

Alas! Lady Aoife had vanished, too—as if, like Conor, she would be seen no more in this worlds-realm. Meanwhile, down on the open ground of Mag Tuired, the battle had begun.

The Scálda appeared, rolling out of the smoke and mist in their fast chariots led by Balor Berugderc, he of the Evil Eye. He rode in his wheeled war cart waving his iron spear and shouting to the bestial gods of his people while his driver whipped the double team of horses to a lather to serve their foul lord's bloodlust. Behind him, behind that lead chariot, came a vast sea of high-wheeled war carts sweeping over the wide, grassy plain, the hooves of the horse teams churning, the chariot wheels spinning. Like the storm-driven tide-rush inundating the strand, drowning the beach and rushing inland, they came. Rank upon rank, they came. And the sound of their rumbling filled the earth and drove the birds from the very sky.

But I bound courage to my heart, vowing within myself that I would not be ground beneath the wheels of a Scálda war cart like the carcass of a dumb animal. I was a warrior of the Dé Danann and I would go to my grave with my spear in my hand and send as many Scálda to the Hag Queen's hall as I could.

Suddenly, I was down on the plain with a shield on my arm and my faéry spear in my hand and there was a great warhost around me—many on horseback, more on foot—and we were flying to meet the enemy.

The clash when it came shattered the air with a horrendous concussion—the sound of ten thousand collisions as blade met shield and bone. The ground trembled. The sun dimmed. Faint stars glimmered in the sky. And then the screaming began. My ears were filled with the screams of triumph and of pain.

And then, strange to say, I was back in the yard at Tara. I was chilled from standing barefoot in the yard. The moon had set and in the east the sun was just tinting the horizon pale pink. I looked out at our settlement—still and quiet and at peace in the dawn of a new day. I was alone and wondering not only what had happened down on the plain, but what had become of the warriors and people of Tara?

18

A short journey inland from the shore brought the travellers to a steep rocky path leading up to a high, windy, gorse-covered moorland. Away to the east and north, the land rose higher still to form the crags and peaks of a serried mountain range. Atop one of the moorland's rounded hills stood a stone circle much like those Conor knew in Eirlandia: a series of enormous upright slabs linked together by horizontal lintel stones and arranged in a great ring surrounded by two deep ditches. But this stone circle was not only much, much larger, it was also topped with a steep, conical roof thatched with reed and perched atop the lintel stones like a hat. Each space between the many standing stones became a huge door; and each door was overhung by a curtain of heavy material woven into patterns of swirls and spirals in green and silver.

There were other structures, too. Scattered around the stone circle were several large round turf-covered barrows, a handful of dolmens, and several of the beehive-shaped structures like those seen on the shore—and all had doorways covered by the cloth hangings bearing the same spiral design.

Conor took in the strange settlement and it seemed to him a wilder, more austere and primitive place than any faéry habitation he might have imagined—and certainly far different from those inhabited by the Tylwyth Teg, which he knew well. Perhaps the Aes-sídhe settlement reflected both the severe nature of the storm-worried island and the otherworldly beings who lived there. To Conor's eye the contrast could not have been greater or more complete. Where the faéry of Tír nan Óg lived in a woodland paradise of tall trees and flowing water, the faéry of Eilean Ceó lived on a wind-blasted scarp of granite amid purple heather, bracken, and the perpetual heave and sigh of the restless ocean round about.

Unaccountably, the entire day had passed as they toiled up the long winding path, and the travellers arrived just as the sun broke through the haze in the west to paint the stone circle in a soft yellow light. A few early stars kindled in the wind-scoured sky to the east and from somewhere came the dull, clanking sound of a cattle bell.

Coming into the settlement, they were greeted with fine hospitality by the inhabitants, who showed a genuine, if reserved, esteem for their king, and a reticent recognition of their mortal visitors. The horses were taken away to be groomed and fed, and a young maid with hair white as eiderdown appeared with a silver bowl filled with mead, which she passed to the king, then backed away with a bow; another maiden followed bearing a silver platter with tiny flat loaves of sweet brown faéry bread. As the mead and bread were brought to the king, Conor noted the aspect of the people, most of whom gave every appearance of being just as dour and forbidding as their moorland surroundings.

'Welcome to Socair Sídhean,' said Lenos, passing the mead cup to Conor and Fergal in turn. 'May you find rest and good fortune in your sojourn here.'

When they had drunk and eaten a little of the bread, Lenos then led them over a short timber walkway across the double ditches and onto a paved pathway leading to one of the great circular structure's many doors.

'I can see why your Lenos is such a grim old charmer,' Fergal whispered, leaning close to Conor. 'He gets it from this mean ráth of his. I tell you the truth, brother, I am not liking this Socair Sídhean. Not at all.'

'A cheerless place, so it is,' agreed Conor, gazing around the massive stone circle and the barrow mounds and dolmens. 'The cave palaces of the Tylwyth Teg are happier by far than this. Why that should be, I wonder?'

'Ach, it is the nature of the beast,' remarked Fergal. 'These folk are as much like their king as I remembered. Every scrap and scrape as friendly anyway.'

One of their guides pulled away the heavy hanging over the doorway and they passed between the enormous standing stones and into a great hall with its heavy stone walls and huge carved pillars to support the timber roof. Each of the pillars was made from the entire trunk of a huge pine, and the roof was so high overhead it disappeared into the shadows.

The doors at the entrance opened onto a broad circle of stone steps leading down to a stone-paved floor. The outer walls were lined with nooks, some partitioned with hangings, others enclosed with wooden panels and doors. In the centre of the great round hall, a great bronze bowl on a tripod burned with a golden flame before a low dais on which sat a throne draped in green cloth embroidered with silver thread into the shapes of deer and boar, oxen and eagles. Other fires burned throughout the enormous room in smaller braziers and from large candles on bronze sconces affixed to the rooftrees. Unlike every other hall the Dé Danann visitors had ever entered, the fires produced no smoke, nor were the candles consumed by their burning. The lightly tinkling sound of a harp played among the stately pillars with the sound of a brook trickling through a wooded glade, yet no musician was to be seen.

Near the bronze cauldron, a semicircle of boards and benches had been set up with three carved wooden chairs placed in the centre. Lord Lenos took the middle chair and placed Conor and Fergal on either side. One by one, the Kerionid came to take their places and were introduced to the visitors. Conor soon gave up trying to remember who everyone was and how they were related, but did his best to greet each one with cordial, if subdued, courtesy.

When everyone was seated, the meal commenced, and while they waited for the food to be brought out, Lenos told his guests something of the long history of the Aes-sídhe and how the Kerionid had come to the island. He explained that Eilean Ceó was not always their home, but that long ago war erupted among the island faéry tribes and those of the Tír Galli across the sea. In what came to be known as the War of the Sun Bull, the fortunes of the various faéry tribes rose and fell many times as power shifted and alliances were formed and broken. Following one particularly brutal battle, a truce was negotiated and the combatants withdrew; on the way home, the truce was violated; the Aes-sídhe were ambushed and suffered a ruinous loss. Shattered, dispirited, bereft, they retreated to the high moors and mountains and the remote islands of Albion, leaving the wider world and its affairs to others. 'We have lived here ever since,' concluded Lenos somewhat morosely.

This glum recitation set the tone of the evening, and despite the ale and sweet mead and succulent roast pork served by the king's hearth master, the mood failed to rise much beyond the level of dull duty. The two visitors were relieved when at last they were ushered to the guest lodge in one of the nearby barrow mounds. Though largely underground, the barrow was warm and dry; the beds were high and soft, and the massive stone walls were whitewashed and lit with candle trees, making the interior of the single large chamber seem almost comfortable. As soon as they were alone, Fergal wasted no time giving vent to his suspicion that Lenos was up to no good.

'They are only trying to show us how much they value our friendship,' Conor told him, challenging Fergal's mistrust.

'Aye, so they are—trying too hard by half, it seems to me.' He grumped and stalked around the chamber for a moment, then said, 'And what is this Lenos is saying about *mortality*? Why is he throwing *that* in our laps like a scalded cat?'

'The faéry kind do not age as we do,' Conor mused. 'We know that right well. If eating the food of the faéry grants long life to a mortal—'

'What so? Most men would agree that is a good thing and much to be desired—to live long and not age with it.'

'Aye, so they would. But consider, brother. It is a boon with a curse wrapped inside it.'

Fergal stroked his moustache thoughtfully. 'To live long and never feel the tooth of age gnawing at your bones? I fail to find this curse you say is lurking there.'

'Do you not?' Conor stood and began pacing back and forth. 'Then consider how the years go by and, aye, you remain hale and healthy, never changing, but all those around you begin to succumb to old age, sickness, and death. Everyone you know and care about—your friends, your tribe, your wife and children and kinfolk—*everyone* you've ever known, brother. Old age takes them all down to their graves. Think now! How will you feel when you have outlived everyone you ever knew or cared about? How will it feel to place the bones of your last living friend in the tomb?' Conor's voice fell and he concluded in a hushed and broken voice. 'How will you feel about this great gift then?'

Fergal, head and heart aswirl with a swarm of conflicting thoughts and feelings, could make no reply.

'At least Lenos told us the truth,' continued Conor after a moment. 'There *is* a terrible cost to be paid—more, I'm thinking, than many a mortal can bear.'

Fergal nodded. 'Is that what Gwydion meant when he said we would always have a home in Tír nan Óg?'

'Maybe it was,' Conor allowed. 'Aye so, maybe it was.'

'And a sad day that will be.'

A dejected silence claimed the room and they sat for a time watching the flames glimmer in the torches and candle trees, listening to the rising wind fingering the chinks and hollows of their stone house. Finally, Fergal burst out, 'It was a bad idea we had coming here. Lenos and his tribe are a scheming lot, and I don't doubt they're scheming right now this very moment.'

'I don't say it is so,' replied Conor. 'But here is where we find ourselves and if we ever want to see home again, we must make the best of it and see whatever it is that Lenos thought important enough to fetch us here to show us.'

There the matter rested for the night. Nor was it revisited the next morning when, after breaking fast early, Lenos and his two advisors, Conor, and Fergal left Socair Sídhean and travelled up into the high hills and into the dark, fragrant green shadows of an enormous forest spread out upon the hills like a rumpled cloak flung down upon the land. They rode to the jingling accompaniment of tiny silver bells that had been braided into the manes and tails of their freshly groomed horses, speaking little, and maintaining a wary watch on their faéry companions. A narrow road had been cut through the trees, and it was to this they made their way.

Heavy boughs spread a roof high above their heads, crowding out the sky, allowing only a frail light to filter down through the latticework of branches. The air was redolent with the sharp, woody scent of pine bark, resin, and damp earth; and the road—soft underfoot, the colour of rust— was drifted deep with spent pine needles, hushing every step. No sound of running water, no chirp or cry of bird or chitter of squirrel reached them. Gradually, all talk ceased in the gloomy tomblike silence broken only by the jangly song of the horses' bells.

They had not gone far into the forest when they arrived at a wide clearing and the timber palisade of a small settlement, merely a few round huts and some storehouses—no cattle enclosure, or hall, and not much of a yard. What little space the place possessed was taken up by a fair-sized forge surrounded by stacks of firewood and baskets of charcoal. Smoke rose in a steady column from the forge, drifting into the cloudy sky.

'Welcome to Cuweem,' called Lenos as he dismounted in the cramped yard. From one of the houses two faéry emerged and hurried to greet their king and his guests. Two other faéry appeared and took control of the horses.

Like the other Aes-sídhe they had seen, the forest dwellers were tall and handsome, their clothes elegant, but muted in colour and more subdued in adornment, more sparing in style. The contrast between Rhiannon's people and those of Lenos was stark. Whereas the faéry folk of Tír nan Óg chose the deep, rich colours of rarest gemstone and jewels, those of Eilean Ceó selected the colours of the world around them: the forest with its many shades of green and its many-shadowed byways; the elusive silvers of rain and trickling water; the greys of clouds and stone.

The king made perfunctory introductions and, while the horses were led away, he spoke to the two faéry who had met them on arrival. Then, motioning Fergal and Conor to follow, they walked to the forge, where now the sound of heavy hammers on hard metal could be heard ringing like the tolling of a bell. At their approach, Sealbach hurried on ahead and, entering the forge, spoke to someone inside, emerging a moment later with a lump of pale white metal the size of a barley loaf.

'Silver?' wondered Fergal.

Sealbach handed the rounded chunk to Lenos, who turned and said, 'Not silver, my friends.' He passed the metal to Fergal, who hefted it in his hands, feeling the substantial weight before passing it to Conor. 'It is something, I think, you will find far more valuable.'

19

Inside the forge they saw four men hard at work. Short, stocky men, they were stripped of all clothing save simple leather loincloths and thick leather leggings, and heavy, boat-shaped wooden brócs on their feet. Odd as that appeared to Conor and Fergal, their attire was not the most curious thing about them, nor the first thing the Dé Danann noticed. The smiths were stocky men with long sleek black hair, broad faces set with round black eyes, and tawny buff-coloured skin. They all wore their hair bound tight at the back of their head and long, double-forked beards in tiny braids; tight around their foreheads they wore folded cloths to keep the sweat from their eyes. And if they noticed their visitors at all, they gave no sign and chattered incessantly to one another as they went about their labours.

A jumbled stack of cut logs ready to hand supplied fuel for the fires of three separate ovens. Behind the stone-built forge, four small huts made of deerskin stretched over willow hoops tied together with rawhide stood nearby. Outside two of the huts sat three women of the same, strange race; all three were kneading dough in shallow elmwood bowls; one of the women cradled an infant in her lap as she worked.

'These are my smiths,' declared Lenos, his voice tinged with a peculiar pride.

'They are not Dé Danann,' observed Fergal lamely, not knowing what else to say. 'And not of the faéry, either.' He looked to the king for an answer.

'They are not,' confirmed Armadal, speaking up. 'They have come from a land called Hatti far, far to the east—beyond where the sun rises.'

'And they work for you as slaves?'

The silver-haired faéry replied, 'Far from it! They are paid in fine gold which we value little enough, but they value highly.'

'The Dé Danann have a certain fondness for gold, too, I can tell you.'

'We persuaded them to come and work here in exchange for their weight in gold,' confirmed Lenos, 'so that we might learn the secrets of their forge craft.'

The faéry king turned and strode to one of the smiths—a squat, broad-shouldered man with thick powerful arms, a wide muscular waist, and short bowed legs. He hailed the man in his own tongue, the two spoke, and he called the others to join them. Lenos made a curious sign in the air, spoke a word in the faéry tongue, and touched the smith lightly on the forehead, then said, 'This is Hasammeli, Master Smith of Hattusa. He is chief among those working here.' At this the sweating fellow bowed and stretched forth his hands at the knee, then rose and looked expectantly to Conor and Fergal; Lenos introduced them by name and said, 'These are my friends, and lords in their own right. Like yourself, they come from a land across the sea. They have come to examine the fruit of your labour.'

Both Dé Danann greeted the smith and wondered at the hint dropped into the faéry king's words. Whatever this *fruit* might be, it was the reason they had been summoned to Eilean Ceó.

Hasammeli looked around to his men, who remained occupied with their labours. Indicating the activity with a wave of a muscled arm, he called out in the tongue of his people and one of the smiths pulled a burning rod white-hot from the flaming mouth of one of the ovens, carried it quickly to an anvil, and began pounding on it with a long hammer. Sparks scattered in every direction and the stink of burning metal filled the air.

'He says that the work goes well and they are soon finished,' Armadal told them. He then spoke to the smith, whose face split in a huge grin, revealing a missing tooth in his lower jaw. He turned and clapped his hands, calling to one of his workers; one of the younger-looking smiths dipped his head, put down his tools, left the forge, and hurried to a nearby hut, emerging a moment later carrying a long bundle wrapped in grass cloth. He brought it to his chief and presented it across his palms.

Hasammeli took the bundle and likewise presented it to the faéry king, who, in turn, delivered it into Conor's hands.

'Open it,' Lenos told him. 'I give you the answer to the riddle I posed to you in Eirlandia.'

Conor pulled away the wrapping to reveal a sword much like many another he had seen throughout his life, but somewhat longer, thinner, and made of the same pale whitish metal as the lump he had handled earlier.

'A sword?' wondered Fergal, unable to keep the disbelief out of his voice. 'You are paying them in gold to make swords for you?'

'A sword, yes, but unlike any weapon you have ever seen,' Lenos declared. 'The secret is in the metal which is itself unlike any other—harder than iron, and lighter than bronze. It is quick and supple, and will hold its edge in the fiercest fight.'

Conor touched the smooth polished surface and tested the edge with his thumb appreciatively. Then he took the blade by the hilt—unfinished, it was a simple tang of metal to which a suitable grip would be bound—and, raising the weapon, sliced the air with it. He handed the sword to Fergal, who waved it about and thrust at an imaginary opponent. 'It is sharp and light, I'll give you that' was his judgement. 'But we have good swords, too.'

'Those the Tylwyth Teg gave you,' replied Lenos. 'I have seen them. But this weapon is not charmed in any way. Its chief quality, its value, resides in the metal itself.'

'What is it called, this metal?'

'The Hatti call it *haranbar*, or *nakki*,' Armadal explained. 'In their tongue, it means "strong iron." We call it *sgriosadair* or, as you would say, *scristóir*. . . .'

'Destroyer,' echoed Conor. He looked to the faéry. 'Why this name?'

It was Lenos who answered him. 'We chose that word because that is what it does. In the hands of a skilled warrior, this blade will destroy any lesser weapon.'

Seeing Conor and Fergal exchange a dubious glance, the king turned to Sealbach standing nearby and said, 'Show them.'

The faéry counsellor spoke a word to the young smith, who ran to one of the small storehouses behind the huts, returning a moment later bearing an iron sword of a make and design that the Dé Danann did not recognise. 'This is a weapon made in Aégipt and very like those of the Scálda, from what I've seen,' Sealbach said. 'The smiths brought some of these with them.' He nodded to the smith, who took the sword by the hilt and held it upright out in front of him.

The master smith removed his head cloth and then, taking up the silvery haranbar blade, wrapped the cloth around the hilt to form a handle on the naked tang. He reared back and, with a roll of his heavy shoulders, swung the silvery blade at the upraised sword. The gleaming metal seemed to trace an arc of light through the air, and unlike the usual dull clatter of iron weapons, there came the clear, clean ring of a bell. The iron blade quivered; a deep notch appeared along one edge. Another hefty swing and the iron weapon snapped; the blade toppled to the ground and the smith was left holding the broken stub of a sword by the useless hilt.

Conor and Fergal glanced at one another in amazement. 'By the Hag's foul breath,' gasped Fergal. 'That is fierce.'

'Again!' said Sealbach.

The master smith spoke a word to his assistant, who ran to the wood stack and selected two sturdy logs and set them upright a little distance apart one from the other; he then scooped up the broken iron blade and placed it lengthwise across the top of the upright logs. Hasammeli offered the silver sword to the visitors and invited them to try it. Fergal stepped forward and took the offered sword. He strode to the suspended length of iron and, with a swift, practiced downward stroke, delivered a forceful blow. Again came the ringing sound and this time the iron blade bent in the middle. Fergal raised the sword and struck again. The inferior iron blade sheared in half and the pieces fell to the ground. On examination, the haranbar blade remained undamaged: no cracks, no notches or pieces missing, and even the edge was still keen and sharp. In all, the weapon appeared unharmed by the violent encounter.

Fergal and Conor both ran their fingers over the new blade and held it before their eyes, turning it this way and that, giving it a close and thorough inspection before passing it back to the smith. 'That blade is still as keen and sharp as new,' Conor declared, running his thumb along the unmarred edge. Taking the hilt, he swung the blade a few times and then turned to the king. 'Again.'

At a nod from Lenos, the smith selected one of the broken lengths of iron and set it on the uprights. Conor stepped up and, with the easy, fluid motion of a lifetime's experience in battle's arena, he drew back and loosed a formidable strike. Again, the pale metal traced a shining arc through the air, but instead of the clear metallic ring there came a timid crack, like that of a dry twigs breaking. To those looking on, the haranbar blade seemed to simply slice through the stubby length of iron without so much as a flicker.

There was a snap and the two severed pieces of the ruined weapon fell away as useless shards.

Conor examined the silver metal and found only a scrape of a mark to show the weapon had even been used. An iron sword would have been at the very least deeply scored, or bent, if not broken. He passed the extraordinary weapon to Fergal and picked up one of the severed lengths. There was a cut mark where the haranbar had bit deep into the iron before the Aégiptian blade had given way. 'Extraordinary,' he observed, shaking his head in wonder.

'It *is* extraordinary,' confirmed Lenos. He gave a satisfied nod to the smiths, thanked them, and sent them back to their work. 'Whoever holds a weapon like this,' he said, resting his hand on the silvery sword in Conor's fist, 'will be a warrior twice armed.'

'Twice!' hooted Fergal. 'More like ten times over, I'm thinking.' Taking the silver sword from Conor, he gave it a few swooping flourishes and proclaimed, 'No one could stand against the warrior with this in his fist.'

That, Conor reflected, might be claiming too much. Such were the fortunes of war that chance loomed large in the heated frenzy of battle. It was not always a man's weapons that tilted the balance toward victory or defeat. A slip on wet grass, a stumble, the unseen cast of a spear from a distance—even a well-aimed stone could fell the superior warrior, however well armed he might be. Skill, bravery, luck, even the weather also played a larger part than most warriors cared to admit. Nevertheless, Fergal had a point. Between two evenly matched warriors, the one with the haranbar weapon would likely emerge from the combat. His opponent would not.

'I am much impressed,' Conor told the faéry king. 'Master Hasammeli and his men are to be commended on their remarkable discovery and superlative craft.'

Lenos, beaming expansively, took up the sword and raised it skyward. 'What is swifter than a spear in its flight, and sharper than a sword in the fight?' he said.

'Scristóir,' answered Conor. 'Destroyer.'

20

'Iron is lethal to us. We cannot touch it, nor allow the vile metal to touch us. Naturally, a wound—even the merest scratch—from an iron blade quickly festers and poisons the blood. Just being near the metal weakens us unto death. All this, I think you know.'

'I do,' affirmed Conor. Indeed, he knew it only too well. Three times over he had found and freed captive faéry folk from Balor Evil Eye and three times thwarted the enemy's insidious attempts to obtain the secrets of faéry magic from his tortured captives. But each of those escapes exacted a deadly price. To Conor's lasting regret, individual faéry had succumbed to the deadly metal—Lord Gwydion himself was the latest and most appalling fatality—and Conor himself had paid in blood and pain.

'Knowing this, you will understand and fully appreciate the value we would place on discovering a superior material without any such dire effect on our kind,' Lenos continued. 'In the haranbar of the Hatti we found it.'

Following their return to Socair Sídhean, Conor and Fergal had gone to their barrow to rest and refresh themselves; once within the privacy of the thick stone walls, they engaged in a lively exchange over the demonstration they had witnessed at the Cuweem forge and the massive implications of this superior metal. Their discussion was far from concluded before they had been summoned to join their host at the board.

This time, there had been no festive reception for them, no feast in their honour. It was just the lord and his two advisors and Conor and Fergal huddled in one of the many smaller alcoves partitioned off from the main room. A supper of cold roast meat, bread, and cheese had already been laid;

there were no servants to attend them, but Armadal kept the platters moving and the jars refilled.

'Do not imagine I have forgotten your risk and the sacrifice you made to save us from captivity to the Scálda vermin,' the king continued. He extended a long, pale hand to Armadal to refill the bowls of his guests. 'For that reason, if for no other, you will appreciate the need that drove us to seek out the secret of this strong iron.'

'Am I right to be thinking that, apart from being far stronger than iron, this new metal causes no harm at all to faéry folk?' asked Fergal. 'You can handle the stuff without fuss or fear?'

'That is so,' replied the faéry king. 'Although this haranbar derives from iron, it also contains other materials that render its touch harmless to our race.'

'And am I right in thinking that you are willing to share the secret of this strong iron with us to use in our fight against the Scálda?'

Lenos inclined his head in regal assent. 'Out of gratitude for your rescue from the death awaiting us in Balor's cruel captivity, we would.'

Fergal's expression told Conor all he needed to know about what his swordbrother thought of the faéry king's simple explanation—nor was Conor wholly inclined to entirely believe it himself. It may have been true as far as it went, but Conor suspected there was something more he was not being told.

'Let me tell you what I propose,' said Lenos. Conor gave a nod and the king, leaning over the board, continued. 'Let us be clear. The new metal is derived from iron, as I have said, and which you also know to be deadly poison to us. We cannot touch it or even have it near us for any extended length of time. Yet, we need old iron to make strong iron. . . .'

'And you need mortals to supply and handle the raw iron for you to use to make this haranbar?' guessed Fergal.

'In a word, yes,' replied Lenos. 'And we need something else as well—'

'Craftsmen and smiths to work it,' surmised Conor.

The faéry king smiled and glanced at his two advisors. 'I told you they would not be slow to understand.' To Conor, he said, 'Yes. The Hatti are leaving soon to return to their homeland. They have completed their part of the bargain and have demonstrated they possess the secret of strong iron, and have been richly rewarded for their efforts. Before they sail for the east, they will teach us the methods and practices used in making strong iron and we will pass this secret on to you.'

'And in return we will supply the raw material required,' concluded Conor, 'and men to work it, and we will both share the proceeds.'

'That is the bargain,' Lenos told him.

Conor studied the faéry for a long moment, once more consumed by the very strong feeling that there was yet something he was not being told. On the face of it, the bargain made perfect sense: the Aes-sídhe had discovered a superior metal, but required help to develop it. Owing to their past history, Lenos had come to Conor and offered to give him the secret in exchange for that help. Simple. And yet . . .

Finally, Conor said, 'Impressed as I am with all you have shown us and the bargain you propose, there is one thing I still do not understand.'

'Tell me, my friend, and I will help you however I can.'

'Why do you need strong iron at all?'

Lenos sat back in his chair. '*Why*? Because it is a very useful material, very powerful—as you have seen with your own eyes.'

'But why do you need these weapons?' persisted Conor.

'To fight our enemies,' offered Sealbach. He had been silent through the meal and following discussion, but he spoke up now. 'We need strong iron for the same reason you Dé Danann need it.'

'So long as you remain here in Eilean Ceó, the Scálda are no threat to you,' countered Fergal.

Sealbach gave him a slighting look. 'The Scálda are a threat to every living thing so long as they live and walk and breathe the air of this worlds-realm.'

'You have bronze weapons already,' Conor pointed out. 'And charms to enchant them.'

'Strong iron is far superior,' Sealbach sneered. 'I thought that fact had already been demonstrated and placed beyond all doubt—even for one of such dim intellect as—'

'Please! Please, friends,' broke in Lenos, trying to recover something of the former civility. 'We seem to have drifted some way from the main current of our discussion.' He gave Sealbach a hard look and then turned to Conor and forced a smile. 'I think we are making this more difficult than it need be. We have something you want, and you have something we need.

It is as simple as that. I say we work together for the benefits we will both derive.' He put out a hand to Conor. 'What do you say?'

Conor stroked his moustache in thought. 'I say,' he replied, 'that it is a hefty decision and there are many details to consider—on our side of the bargain, at least—and this is new territory for us. Let us sleep on it and we will give you our decision in the morning.'

Lenos leaned back in his chair and gazed at his two reluctant guests, not bothering to hide the disappointment on his face. Finally, he sighed and said, 'Then let us leave it there for the night. We will talk again tomorrow morning.' He rose, signalling an end to the meal and discussion.

'I am sorry to say it must be an early start tomorrow,' Armadal informed them as they pushed back from the board. 'If we are to return you to Eirlandia in time, we must leave on the next evening tide and there is a long ride ahead of us to reach the shore.'

Conor thanked Lenos for the meal and promised to deliver his answer to the proposal without fail, first thing in the morning. Leaving the hall, they were accompanied to their quarters by Armadal. Though night was full and deep upon the land, the sky yet held a blush of ruddy light in the west through which a light sprinkling of stars glowed like individual candles. At the door to the barrow, they bade their faéry guide a good night and went inside. As soon as the door was closed, Conor began pacing. Fergal sat on the edge of his bed and watched him marching back and forth, his face scrunched into a fierce and thoughtful scowl. 'What is in your mind, brother?' he asked after a moment.

Conor was slow to answer, but when he did, he said, 'There is more to this than we know. I feel it here—' He struck himself on the chest. 'But for the life of me, I cannot say what it is.'

'Let's start with what we do know,' Fergal suggested. 'And it is clear that your fella Lenos and his folk have gone to enormous difficulty and expense in pursuit of this new metal—this Destroyer as he calls it,' Fergal observed.

'They have. For a fact, they have. Yet, here I am, asking myself to what end? Why? When the faéry kind can conjure up a charm for a sword or spear and shield superior to any iron blade. The weapons Gwydion gave us are proof enough of that.'

'They say they want weapons to protect themselves against the Scálda,' Fergal suggested. 'They could do that with charmed weapons of their own.'

Conor considered this for a moment and a thought occurred to him. 'Ach, but what if they can't? What if they can't conjure such a charm? Could it be they lack such a skill as the Tylwyth Teg possess?'

Fergal stood and began pacing, too. 'This lack might drive them to find a remedy—is that what you're thinking?'

Conor stopped and stared at Fergal, who also stopped. 'What? You look like a fella who just stepped in a badger hole.'

'You said it just now,' Conor replied. 'You said they wanted the strong iron for protection against the Scálda—'

'Aye, so I did.'

'But that's not what Sealbach said! Remember? He said "our enemies"— remember? He said they needed weapons of strong iron "To fight our enemies." . . .'

'Aye, his very words.'

'It was *you* who assumed that it was the Scálda he was talking about,' said Conor. 'But think you now—who are the enemies of the Aes-sídhe?'

The light of comprehension finally broke across Fergal's face. 'The Tylwyth Teg!'

'Aye, the Tylwyth Teg,' echoed Conor. 'Rhiannon and her folk. Exactly. Iron breaks bronze, and charmed weapons break iron. But haranbar is above them all.'

Silence claimed the barrow as both men considered the awful implications of the idea they had conjured. Finally, Fergal said, 'What will you tell his lordship? He expects an answer in the morning.'

Conor shook his head. 'I don't know. But I intend to do what I said I would do. I'm going to sleep on it.'

There was, in the end, very little sleeping for either of them as they continued to wrestle with the problem through the night. Dawn found them no better prepared to meet Lord Lenos and deliver a satisfactory decision. They were awake and pulling on their clothes when a knock came on the door and, a moment later, Armadal appeared. 'The king is asking if you would join him to break your fast before leaving?'

'Tell your king we will be pleased to join him,' said Conor.

They finished dressing and took up their weapons and went out. They found Lord Lenos waiting for them outside the hall. He had put off his splendid royal garments and was dressed in simple attire, the colour of trees and bark and leaves—the hues and tints of forest and glade. His mood seemed as subdued as his clothing, and Conor wondered if the faéry king already guessed the nature of Conor's reluctance to seal the bargain he had proposed.

'I hope we have not kept you waiting,' said Conor.

'It is of no consequence,' replied the king tartly. 'But we must go now if we are to return you to Eirlandia as agreed.' He lifted a hand and indicated Sealbach and two others leading their horses to them. 'We can conclude our discussions on the way.'

'I would like nothing more,' Conor replied, taking the reins of the grey stallion from the groom.

'What happened to breaking our fast?' whispered Fergal as he swung onto his mount.

'The same thing that happened to our glad welcome,' replied Conor under his breath. 'Here and gone.'

As soon as everyone was mounted, the travelling party departed. Sealbach and Armadal rode on ahead to lead the way, Lenos came next, and Conor and Fergal rode last. They crossed the empty moor under a grey sky and entered the forest, striking the descending trail leading to the shore. The tall trees soon closed around them and they rode through a resin-scented woodland on a trail strewn thick and soft with pine needles to the accompaniment of the occasional trill of a thrush or the tat-tat-tat of a woodpecker.

After riding in this way for some time, Lord Lenos half turned to Conor behind him and said, 'Come up here with me.'

Although the summons was more on the order of a command than an invitation, Conor put aside the insult and dutifully complied. 'What is your pleasure?' he asked as Búrach fell into step beside the faéry king's long-legged brown mare.

Fergal, not to be left out of the discussion, joined them, reining up a step or two behind Conor's left shoulder where he could hear and see everything that passed between the two. Lenos, of course, noticed the intrusion and appeared inclined to object, but Conor quickly intervened. 'Whatever you say will be repeated to my battlechief, so we might as well speak freely and openly.'

'As you will,' conceded Lenos. He paused, gathering his thoughts, and, with a last glance at Fergal, began. 'It appears that you do not trust me or my motives in bringing you here.' He held up a hand to forestall any disagreement. 'It is of no consequence. But I had hoped to achieve a better understanding between our peoples.'

'That is greatly to be wished,' Conor told him. 'You said you required these superior weapons to ward off your enemies—a need I understand only too well. Forgive me if I offend, but you refuse to join us to fight the Scálda—and the only other enemy of yours that I know are the Tylwyth Teg.'

'Do you deny that possessing such weapons for yourselves would be a great boon to you in your struggle against the Scálda?'

'I do not deny it at all—'

'Ach, then why do you question our need for the same boon that you would possess?'

Fergal, listening intently, spoke up. 'With all respect, lord king, that was not the question asked. Could it be that you intend using these weapons against the faéry folk of Tír nan Óg?'

Lenos reined to a halt in the path. His gaze grew cold as he turned to Fergal. Armadal and Sealbach, riding a little ahead, stopped and turned their horses. The king, this voice thick with disdain, replied, 'I do not see that is any of your concern.'

'The Tylwyth Teg are our friends and allies,' Conor declared evenly. 'We would do nothing to endanger them or our continued friendship. It seems to me that helping you to obtain strong iron would pose very potent threat to their safety and welfare. That I will not do.'

'Friends!' The faéry king pulled hard on the reins and jolted to a halt. 'Do not tell me about friendship. The Tylwyth Teg are not your friends! Morfran has no love for you. He despises the Dé Danann.'

'The same could have been said of the Aes-sídhe,' said Fergal. 'And yet, here we are. Could it be that you discovered a deep fondness and regard for us when you realised you needed our help?'

Lenos's face hardened. 'Who are you to teach me my business?' he shouted. 'Listen, little man, there are others who will leap with joy at the offer I make. I can easily find someone else to do my bidding. I *will* have strong iron. Whether you help or not, I will have it.'

Conor's birthmark flared with instant heat and it took all his strength to keep his voice steady. 'There will always be a sharper sword or a better spear, but if we abandon the virtues we esteem, then we are no better than those who would destroy those things. Indeed, we do their work for them.

Hear me, Lenos, we fight against the Scálda, to be sure—but not at the cost of becoming the very thing we hate.'

'Then you will never possess strong iron,' spat Lenos, no longer concealing his contempt. 'The secret of haranbar will remain with us.'

'So be it,' said Conor firmly.

Lenos regarded him with an icy glare. 'You would choose death and extinction over certain victory?'

'We may be defeated, aye. We may go down into the dust of annihilation. But the Dé Danann will be remembered for the high value we placed on the virtues of honour and nobility. If we must die, then let those who come after know us for the things we valued—the joys of song and beauty, the bonds of love and friendship—and not that we betrayed those things when we came to the test.'

'Only a fool places such a high value on transient things,' mocked Sealbach. He flicked his fingers at Conor. 'Friendships fail, songs end, beauty fades, love dies. That is the way of the world.'

'No more talk,' snapped Lenos. He turned a stony gaze on Conor. 'The only thing left to decide is will you set aside your petty qualms and seize the victory that is offered you.'

'It is not victory you offer,' replied Conor through gritted teeth, 'but death by another name. We will not be part of it.'

21

'This is not the end of it,' warned Fergal. 'They'll only be finding someone else to do their bidding—someone who won't care so much about the finer things such as honour and loyalty. Someone like Vainche maybe.'

'I cannot answer for what anyone else might do,' replied Conor. 'But I see my way clear enough.'

'Honourable as the day is long, to be sure. But, mark me, with us or without us the falsehearted faéry will be getting those weapons,' Fergal concluded. 'Did you ever consider that?'

'There was nothing to consider!' Conor swatted the air with his hand and gazed out across the white-capped waves as if at a massed warhost surging to battle against him. 'And I tell you the truth, if Lenos offers again, I will do the same in an instant.'

They were standing at the prow of the faéry ship on their way back to Eirlandia. Lord Lenos and his two advisors had declined to accompany their guests on their homeward voyage. After the bitter discussion on the way to the ship, the last thing either party wanted was to endure the trip in one another's company. So, after bidding Conor and Fergal a curt and frosty farewell, the king and his companions sent them away with a final admonition to think long and hard how much more swiftly the war with the Scálda could be ended with the acquisition of strong iron.

'I doubt you'll be getting another chance.'

'Do not waste another moment thinking about it,' Conor said. 'Lenos's offer was never made in good faith.'

Fergal pulled on his lip as he considered this, then said, 'Will we tell

Donal and the others what we've seen—about the strong iron, I mean—will we tell them?'

'Aye, we will. And why would we not?'

'There are those who may not understand your refusal. I expect there will be those who think you bartered away our victory when you should have joined an alliance with Lenos and the Aes-sídhe.'

Conor gave his friend and warleader a disgruntled look. 'Anyone who imagined such a thing would be wrong. Might we have gained a better weapon? Aye, maybe—*if* Lenos delivered his part of the bargain. But it would have been at the cost of our faéry friends who are as much a part of Eirlandia as the Dé Danann. Any man who betrays a friend is no better than a rogue and, in this case, worse than a bloody-handed murderer. Where is the honour in that?'

'Where is the honour of the grave?' replied Fergal softly, almost to himself.

'Ha!' scoffed Conor. He slapped Fergal on the back. 'Cheer up, brother, we are not dead yet.'

'So, then, what will you tell Donal and the others?'

'I'll tell them what I told you just now,' said Conor. 'And I will tell the Tylwyth Teg as well. Rhiannon and her people should know about this and what we suspect of Lord Lenos's intentions.' He turned his face to Fergal and added with some force, 'They have every right to know.'

'Do you hear me disagreeing with you?'

'Are you?'

'Nay, brother. I think they should know—all the more since you seem bent on telling everyone else.' He followed Conor's gaze to the stern, then looked back at the glittering waves. 'How do you mean to reach them with this warning?'

'Easily done, that. I have only to whisper her name and Rhiannon said she would come to me in times of need.'

'Well then?'

Still looking out at the far horizon, Conor, barely lifting his voice above a whisper, said, 'Come, Rhiannon. I must speak to you.'

The two watched for a long moment, but nothing changed: no green sail appeared, no dark speck of a sleek hull on the horizon. . . . Conor repeated the summons and they waited some more, but the sea remained a wide, empty expanse stretching away as far as the eye could see.

The remainder of the voyage, like previous sailings with the faéry, proceeded with the slightly unnerving quality of a dream and before either Conor or Fergal had time to mark the passing day the distant shore appeared; soon after, the ship came gliding into a secluded eastern bay. Judging by the sun, it was some little time before midday. With the help of the pilot and his two crewmen, the horses were led onto the pebbled shingle; the passengers collected their weapons and followed. Thanking their pilot and his men for their care, Fergal and Conor took their mounts and watched the sleek vessel immediately depart. As soon as the ship cleared the bay, they turned their horses and proceeded inland.

'Do you know where we are?' wondered Fergal. They had just gained the top of the bluff and had paused to view the low hills and woodlands rising before them.

'Somewhere on the Volunti coast, I think. Tara should be just to the east.' Lifting the reins, he started off. They reached the end of the moor and entered a pinewood and quickly found a game run to follow through the trees and undergrowth. A little while later, they came to a dell with a scattering of boulders large and small through which a fresh stream meandered. They gave the horses to drink, and stretched their legs.

'Do you think we'll reach Tara while it's still light?' wondered Fergal. 'If we—'

Conor held up his hand. 'Did you hear that?'

Fergal listened, then said, 'Wind in the trees and water—that's all. Why, what—'

'Shh! There it is again!' Conor glanced over his shoulder and looked back the way they had come. 'Someone's calling.'

Both men stared into the wood. In a moment, they sensed movement among the trees. And then . . . 'There!' Conor pointed into the wood just as three mounted strangers appeared as if taking shape out of the shadows.

The strangers moved closer and Fergal turned to his mount to retrieve his spear. Conor gave out a shout and started forward and Fergal turned back to see a lady dressed in a cloak and mantle the shimmering green of sunlit emeralds and, with her, two men in carnelian cloaks and breecs—all of them on fine black horses. 'Rhiannon!'

Smiling in welcome, the Princess of the House of Llŷr slipped down from her mount and extended her arms to Conor, taking his hands as he stepped close. 'It is good to see you, Conor,' she said, and then put out a hand to Fergal. 'And good to see you, too, Fergal, my friend.'

'You found us,' said Conor. 'After what Morfran said last time, I feared you might not come.'

'Please, forgive my tardiness,' she said. 'It is because of Morfran that I thought best to bring an advisor with me.' She turned to the gaunt faéry coming up to stand at her right shoulder. Like her, his hair was black as a raven's wing, and like her he wore a green-and-white-checked cloak that glistened with a gentle radiance in the dim forest light; but where Rhiannon's gown was green as pine needles, his siarc and breecs were blue as the ocean deeps, and studded with tiny silver stars.

Conor gaped openly at the tall, dark faéry, taken aback by his uncanny resemblance to the dead Lord Gwydion. If Conor had not seen the faéry king die and his bone-white ashes scattered to the wind like so much snow, he would have sworn it was his lordship healed and restored to life.

Taking the dark faéry's arm and pulling him forward, the princess said, 'Conor, I want you to meet Lord Gwyddno, he is my uncle. I asked him to come with me.'

Conor, still slightly unsettled by the apparition before him, nevertheless professed himself happy to meet another member of the House of Llŷr. Fergal echoed the sentiment and observed, 'I thought Morfran was your uncle.'

Rhiannon smiled at the mild confusion. 'My father had *two* brothers.'

'I am the youngest of the three,' said Gwyddno. 'And it is an honour to meet the renowned Conor mac Ardan, and is this Fergal?' He put out a hand and gripped Fergal by the arm. 'Rhiannon has told me so much about both of you, I feel like I know you already.'

'You might have met sooner,' Rhiannon explained quickly, 'but not all our kinsmen live in Ynys Afallon. Our realm extends to places on the mainland to the east as well and it took a little time for Gwyddno to join me.' She turned and gestured for the third faéry to join them. 'You will remember Eraint, I think. When he learned I would sail to Eirlandia, he wanted to be included.'

They welcomed the ship's pilot, who came with a bag of food and drink. At Rhiannon's insistence—and to Conor and Fergal's great relief—they sat down among the trees to refresh themselves and talk about all that had happened since the last time they were together following King Gwydion's death. Conor told about establishing a settlement at Tara Hill and the birth of his infant daughter; Fergal described their growing warband and the work of their training. Rhiannon told how her uncle, Lord Morfran, had moved the royal residence from the cave of the waterfall to a more remote, less accessible cavern farther away from the coast. 'Though it pleases me to see you both and hear of your latest achievements,' the princess concluded, 'I know you would not have called me unless it was a matter of some importance.'

She reached out and touched Conor on the arm; Fergal noted the gesture and recognised the natural intimacy behind it. 'We are here, my friends, and I sense there is trouble in your hearts and minds. How can we help?'

Conor thanked them again for coming and told them that it was not for his benefit alone that they had been summoned, but for their own as well. 'I fear that you and your people are in grave danger,' he told them, and went on to explain about their recent visit to the Aes-sídhe in Albion and what was revealed to them there. 'The Kerionid have smiths who are perfecting a new metal that is compounded of iron and other materials. They call it *haranbar*, or "strong iron," for it is all that and more.'

'Aye,' said Fergal, 'strong enough to break bronze and cut ordinary iron weapons. We saw them do it, and even tried it for ourselves. It is superior in every way.'

'But I don't understand,' said Rhiannon. 'The Kerionid have the same vulnerability to iron that we do.'

'That is true,' Fergal replied. 'And that is why they need mortals to supply the raw iron and to work it. Once the iron has been combined with other materials and refined in the forge, the stuff is no longer any danger to them. They can handle it with ease.'

'Lenos and his smiths are making weapons of the stuff to wield against their enemies,' Conor told them.

The faéry were not slow to recognise the implications of the new material. 'Weapons to wield against *us*, you mean,' said Gwyddno.

'That is my fear,' said Conor. 'We have seen what these weapons can do and, believe me, the threat is real. They have named it Destroyer.'

'The Aes-sídhe are preparing for war,' mused Gwyddno. He turned a stricken face to his companions. 'Grave news indeed.'

'Grave, aye,' agreed Conor, 'but not yet desperate. These craftsmen Lenos has found—men of the Hatti race from the east—they have made a few swords in order to test the strength of the metal and such—a sword or two only, and that is all. And now that the smiths have delivered the secret of making the haranbar, they will be going home. Lenos wanted us to supply the raw iron and men to work it and make the weapons. We refused. So, we still have time to act.'

'Aye,' said Fergal, 'a *little* time, perhaps . . .' He paused and added ominously, 'That is, until the Aes-sídhe find someone else to give them raw iron they need and supply workers to fashion it into the weapons they need.'

'We must act quickly,' said Rhiannon. She looked to her uncle, searching his face. 'But what can we do?'

Gwyddno only gazed back, trying to fathom the enormity of the threat. But Conor was ready with an answer. 'Join us. The Tylwyth Teg and the Dé Danann—together we can fight the Aes-sídhe, and the Scálda. Together we can free both Albion and Eirlandia from any who would threaten us forever.'

The faéry lord appeared doubtful. 'You know Morfran wants nothing more to do with mortals or their wars.'

'The war has now come to you,' Fergal told him. 'It cannot be avoided.'

'If the Scálda defeat us,' Conor said, 'the Tylwyth Teg will be next. They know of your existence and they will hunt until they find you. That is, if Lenos does not slaughter you first. Either way, the danger will only grow. As Fergal has said—war has come to you and there is no way to avoid it.'

Gwyddno shook his head slowly. 'Morfran will not be persuaded—and he has history on his side. Every time our race has become involved in the affairs of men, we suffer the hurt and it is everlasting.'

'That may be so,' agreed the princess. 'But I also know that the world has changed. We must act if we are to save our people. If we cling to our ancient ways, we will be destroyed. But if we adapt and unite, we can hope to survive.'

'If Morfran will not be moved,' Conor said, 'then it is for you to make the decision for him. We are willing to help in any way we can. If you like, Fergal and I will return with you to Tír nan Óg and speak to him. Perhaps when we tell him what we have seen and what the Aes-sídhe intend, he will be persuaded.'

'That, I fear, would only make it worse,' Rhiannon said. 'He holds you responsible for Gwydion's death.'

'Me!' Conor exclaimed.

'Morfran believes that if you had not appealed to Gwydion for aid, then Gwydion would never have embarked on the mission that killed him.'

'It was Scálda that captured him,' Fergal said. 'If Morfran would blame somebody, it should be Balor Evil Eye, never Conor.'

'I know it,' Gwyddno said. 'But that makes no difference to Morfran. He believes that death and destruction are the inevitable consequence of dealing with mortals.'

'I understand,' replied Conor. 'Yet, one way or another, you are already involved in mortal affairs. Better to join us who offer friendship and hope, than deal with Lenos or Balor, who only seek your destruction.'

'Conor is right,' Rhiannon said. 'The time has come to join the fight. Now—before it is too late.'

'I need no persuading. If it was my place to decide, I would make that pledge even now. But Morfran is king and he alone commands the warhost of the Tylwyth Teg. We can do nothing without the king's support, or at least his approval.' Gwyddno rose from his place and, turning to Rhiannon, said, 'We must go to Morfran at once. He must hear that Lenos is plotting our destruction.'

'Will that be enough to convince him?' wondered Fergal.

'I cannot say,' replied Gwyddno. 'But we will have to find a way.'

Conor rose slowly to his feet. 'You should know that the Scálda have a new weapon, too—war carts that allow them to strike with great speed and fury. And if they succeed in defeating the Dé Danann, there will be no one left to help you.' Conor fixed Gwyddno with a firm and steady gaze. 'You must make Morfran understand.'

Rhiannon stepped close and, taking Conor's hands in her own, said, 'Thank you for your timely warning. We will leave at once in the hope that when we meet again it will be in happier times.'

'Hear me, my friends, there may never be happier times for any of us unless we unite.'

22

Daylight was already fading by the time Tara Hill came into view over the treetops. A short while later, the travellers emerged from the wood at the edge of the plain and entered the rising expanse of Mag Teamhair. They were halfway across when they were met by a welcoming party made up of Donal and Médon. Donal greeted them and said, 'All went well? Médon said you would be coming along right behind.'

'We only got back at midday,' Médon told them. 'Vainche didn't give you any trouble?'

'Vainche?' wondered Fergal. So much had happened in the last days, it took him a moment to cast his mind back to Aintrén. 'Nay, nay, no trouble. We weren't followed if that's what you mean.'

Donal noticed Fergal's momentary confusion. 'But there is something else—besides faéry time, that is.' Donal glanced from one to the other. 'Not good news, I'm thinking.'

'I could wish for better,' replied Conor. 'Go to the hall and pour the welcome cup. I want to see Aoife first, then I'll join you at the board. There is much to tell.' Conor said this last while flicking the reins and sending Búrach into an easy trot.

'I expect *they* have much to discuss as well,' observed Fergal. 'As for me, I will happily make do with a welcome cup.'

'Then let us get that cup in your hand, brother,' Médon replied.

The three rode on, climbed the steps of the hill, and entered the yard, where they were met by some of the fianna, who put down the weapons they were repairing to welcome their battlechief home. Fergal dismounted, greeted them, and commended them to their work; Médon delivered their horses to the stable master, and Fergal followed Donal into the hall.

The two had finished the first welcome cup and were well into the second when Conor arrived. Bearing his infant daughter, Ciara, in his arms, with Aoife at his side, he took his place at the board and Dearg refilled the cúach and handed it to him. Conor lofted the cup, took a long drink, and then passed it to Aoife, who sipped politely and then moved it along to Fergal.

As the cup circled the little group, so, too, did the talk around the board as both Conor and Fergal explained what had taken place—sometimes talking over one another in their eagerness to relate all that had happened. They told of Lord Lenos's surprise appearance and their visit to the Aessídhe on Eilean Ceó; they described the Hatti smiths and the discovery of the strange new metal, the silvery haranbar, and how they had tested the strong iron. They spoke at length of Lord Lenos's offer and how, once they realised his intent to make weapons to wield against the Tylwyth Teg, they had refused the offer. Lastly, they described summoning Rhiannon, and warning her and Gwyddno of the impending threat to their people.

After hearing all that was said, Aoife asked, 'What will happen now?'

Conor glanced at Donal, sitting at his left hand, and said, 'Sooner ask Donal See-Far. I have no idea. We offered to help them, to be sure. We also asked the House of Llŷr to join with us in forming an alliance to fight the Scálda. But, in the end, Lady Rhiannon thought it best to return to Ynys Afallon and put the matter before King Morfran. They can do nothing without his assent.'

'What you propose is for the good of everyone,' said Aoife. 'Morfran must see that.'

'I'll not be holding my breath waiting for that to happen,' said Fergal, reaching for the cup. 'Morfran will be difficult to persuade. He wants nothing to do with us.'

Aoife, cradling the infant to her breast, said, 'I do fear for those people. This strong iron could be the ruin of that fair race. And if they go, much that is beautiful and magical in Eirlandia will go, too. All the world will be the worse for it.'

'Then we must make sure that never happens,' Conor said. He raised his hand and stroked the hair on his daughter's tiny head. 'For Ciara, and for all our children now and yet unborn, we must do all we can to help the faéry.'

The thought of a world without the faéry settled as a cloud of gloom over the group. The annihilation of the source of much of the beauty and wonder from which they derived so much pleasure and inspiration was not to be contemplated. Aoife was first to leave the board and Médon departed a few moments later, leaving only Donal, Fergal, and Conor alone with their thoughts—but not for long: Dearg, the hearth master, burst into the hall to announce that a rider had come with a message for Lord Conor. 'Bring him in,' Conor said, 'and fetch food and drink. We will see him here.'

'He is gone again, lord. It seems he has others to see and could not stop. He said the message comes from Rónán, who wishes to inform you that the Ard Airechtas will be held here at Tara.'

'Here!' exclaimed Fergal. 'They're coming here? Why?'

Dearg shrugged. 'He didn't say.'

'What *did* he say?' asked Conor.

'Only that a summons has gone out to Vainche and many other lords who might have an interest in attending such a gathering.'

'And they're all to come here? How many?'

'He didn't say.'

Conor thanked his hearth master and then turned back to the board, shaking his head slowly as the news sank in. 'So now, the brehons are coming here—'

'And Vainche,' said Fergal. 'And the other lords as well.'

'We'll have a job of work to do to make everything ready,' said Donal. 'Lughnasadh is not so long away.'

They fell to discussing all the necessary preparations and how everything should be ordered to receive the high druids and lords. Later, when Conor told Aoife the news, she said, 'Aye, it will mean a deal of work to feed and house them all. But it is only right and fitting. After all, a judgement as important as this should be held here in full sight of everyone—not hidden away in some dank old druid grove where no one ever goes. To have it here is a subtle acknowledgement of Tara's past and future. All Eirlandia will see how treachery is repaid and all will know the judgement was fair and just.'

'It seems you and Rónán are of the same mind,' Conor said. 'Though a fella could wish more of our building works were finished. There is still so much to do.'

'Ach, then why are you dallying here?' She gave him a push to send him on his way. 'On your way and do some work!' Conor rose from the edge of the raised pallet where she reclined with the infant Ciara sound asleep. He paused at the door to their bower and Aoife blew him a kiss as he stepped out.

In the yard once more, Conor saw Médon, Calbhan, and Aedd coming from the stable, leading three of the new Brigantes horses down to the plain to test the extent of their training. 'I heard there was a messenger . . . ,' called Médon, as Conor strode to meet them. He took one look at the expression on Conor's face and said, 'What did I miss?'

23

Over the next weeks, preparing for the Ard Airechtas became the preoccupation of most everyone at Tara. With much of the settlement still in various stages of construction, and the settlement's first harvest to be gathered in, there was nearly everything to be done. The farmers worked the flocks and fields, the carpenters pressed on with the urgent building work, the women made ale and cheese and prepared food to store against the coming demand, and the warriors—when they were not riding the borders and scouting the surrounding territories for Scálda incursions—took on chores Donal found for them, lending a hand wherever a hand was needed. Almost every conversation turned into a discussion of how best to feed and house the high-ranking druids, lords, and kings and their advisors who were expected to attend this once-in-a-lifetime gathering.

Dearg took on the task of making certain the food and drink would be ready, Fergal kept the warriors dutifully occupied, and that left Conor to ponder how and where to house everyone. The lord of Tara was most often seen in the company of his ail-duinn, Donal, as the two inspected the building work to see which of the new structures could be readied soon enough to receive their eminent guests.

As the days dwindled down to Lughnasadh, Tara's busy pace doubled, and then doubled again: pigs, sheep, and cattle were slaughtered and carcasses dressed and hung; the sweet heather ale that had been brewed was put in casks and tuns, and the fermented honey mead poured into jars and sealed; mounds of reeds and rushes for rooftops and floor coverings were cut and trundled up from surrounding marshes and riverbanks; seasoned firewood was split and stacked, and fire rings prepared; new bowers were erected and sleeping pallets fashioned; fleeces and linens were washed and aired; additional boards and benches were set up in the hall and the long boards hard scrubbed with lough sand; all this, and more, occupied the various work parties from first light to last. If this was not enough, the harvest labour in the fields continued unabated as ripe grain was cut and the sheaves were stacked to dry for threshing and winnowing. Warriors, when they were not busy with other chores, roamed the surrounding woods and forests for game to stock the larders.

Then, four days before Lughnasadh, one of the scouts watching the northeastern borders came pounding into the yard to announce that druids had been sighted and were on their way. Conor dispatched an escort and then hurried to his bower to make ready to receive them. He stood fidgeting with a fold of his cloak while Aoife's nimble fingers renewed the braid of his hair. 'We have done all we can to prepare,' Aoife told him. 'The lords and brehons must take us as they find us.'

'I suppose,' Conor agreed with a sigh.

Aoife finished braiding his hair and gave him an affectionate pat to let him know he was ready. 'We will hope for the best,' she advised, deftly attending to her own braid. 'Anyway, it does no one any good to be all sulky and broody about it.'

'Sulky and broody, am I?' Conor spun around, caught her about the waist, and pulled her to him. 'I will have you know that I am the most pleasant and sunny fella you would ever hope to meet.'

'The most boastful, to be sure.'

Conor tightened his embrace and gave her a kiss. 'There,' he said when they broke for air, 'now you have something to boast about, too.'

Aoife laughed and pushed him away; she snatched up the sleeping Ciara and, bundling the infant into a fold of her cloak, said, 'Let us go and welcome our first arrivals.'

As soon as they were sighted, Fergal had sent a body of warriors to escort them—an antique courtesy practiced but rarely anymore, and then only for the most distinguished, valued, or esteemed guests. Songs and tales of elder times told how a tribe showed its respect for special visitors by going out to meet them while they were still far off, and then bringing them into the ráth or settlement.

The brehons appeared to appreciate this traditional courtesy and, surrounded by their armed bodyguard, arrived like the lords they were: lords of law and lore, members of a noble caste whose least utterance was to be obeyed. There were already a fair number of people assembled in the yard and most of these had never seen a brehon other than, perhaps, Rónán, but every last tribesman knew with a certainty bordering on dread that these men held the fate of Eirlandia and all its people in their hands.

There were nine of them: five long-bearded men of august age, and one of these very advanced in years; two women of middling age; and two younger druid lords, and one of these was Rónán, who led the delegation into the yard. All wore cloaks and long mantles dyed in the rich greens of field and forest, or the subtle greys of sky and stormy seas, and each carried a large cloth satchel embroidered with intricate spirals and knotwork; their brócs were well-made, tall, and laced high. The men wore wide belts of fine leather tanned and tooled and, some of them, studded with silver stars or shells; the women wore red girdles with long trailing tails and tiny silver bells on the tasselled ends. Each carried a long rowan staff topped with caps of silver or gold in the shape of wings, or horns, or the head of an animal. Accompanying the high-ranking druids were several ovates and a filidh or two to act as servants, and these came leading pack ponies laden with bags of provisions.

At first sight of Conor, Rónán slid down from his mount and strode across the yard to address his brother. To embrace him might have given the appearance of favouritism and thereby violated brehon practice requiring them to remain impartial in the hearing of cases and the application of the law. Nevertheless, he greeted Conor and Aoife warmly and, leaning close, said, 'Good news, Conor! Eoghan, our chief brehon, will conduct the Airechtas. Not only that, several of the highest-ranking ollamhs and filidh in all Eirlandia are here as well. The judgement of a king does not happen very often, so many were eager to view such a rare event.'

Then, mindful that his superiors were watching, Rónán straightened and, adopting a solemn air, proceeded to introduce his superiors to the Lord of Tara. He led Conor to where the druids had dismounted and now stood waiting to be formally welcomed. They stopped before a hunched and wizened figure and, with a gesture of reverence, Rónán announced in a voice loud enough for all the onlookers to hear, 'Lord Conor, it is my privilege to present to you Eoghan, our wise head and chief of the brehons in Eirlandia. He will be leading the Ard Airechtas through to its conclusion.'

Rónán gave a bow of deference to the old man, who turned a keen, eagle-like gaze on Conor and said, 'I have long followed your winding and wayward path, Lord Conor, and pleased as I am to meet you in the flesh at last, I must say you are not at all what I expected.'

Conor, uncertain how to take this, merely smiled and said, 'Most learned Eoghan, you honour us with your presence. Trust that my people and I will do all we can to make your sojourn here comfortable and productive.'

The old man released Conor's gaze and looked around as if taking in his surroundings for the first time. 'It has been many years since I was last here. I was an ollamh and advisor to King Amargin in those days. There was a great Oenach here. Lords from every tribe came. It lasted a month and an entire herd of cattle were slaughtered.' He took in the new hall and the ramshackle assemblage of temporary dwellings that still claimed the greater portion of the yard. 'That was a long time ago.'

'Then you will have noticed that we've made a few changes,' Conor replied. 'I hope you'll approve.'

'A king must do what is necessary for the welfare of his people whether I approve or not,' Eoghan replied.

'I am not a king,' Conor told him. 'One day, perhaps, but that day has not yet come.'

'I don't see that it matters overmuch,' sniffed the druid chief, then, fixing Conor once more with a keen dark eye, asked, 'How are you in yourself?'

Conor spread his hands and replied, 'I am as you see me.'

The old brehon merely nodded. 'I'm not at all sure what it is that I am seeing,' he said. Unaccountably, Conor felt his face begin to warm and tingle and Rónán, seeing his brother momentarily discomfited, stepped in. 'There are others waiting to meet you, Conor. If our wise head will allow me—'

Eoghan waved them away and then moved on to greet Aoife, Donal, and others of the welcoming party. Noticing his alarmed look, Rónán gave Conor a pat on the back and an encouraging nod and smile as if to say, *Well done.*

Next came brehons Brádoch, Eithne—the senior of the two female druids—and Bráonán in turn. These three, Rónán explained, would serve as principal aides to Eoghan and would be supported by the remaining brehons: Orlagh, Targes, Nolán, and Durien. All four were suitably austere and spare in their greeting. Only Orlagh, the other banfaíth, allowed the barest hint of a smile, and that was reserved for Aoife and tiny Ciara.

Rónán steered Conor through greeting the ollamhs and several of the filidh he knew well. They all maintained a polite but definite distance, which might have been construed as unfriendliness if Rónán had not explained as soon as they were finished. 'From the moment they entered the yard, they will be wary of having their impartiality compromised by any sentiment—kindly as it may be,' he told Conor as they walked to the hall.

'Meaning?'

'They fear their liking for you will cloud their judgement.'

'They like my Conor?' wondered Aoife, taking her place at Conor's side. 'Ach so, they hide it very well.'

'But they know nothing about me,' Conor said, 'for all we've only just set eyes on one another.'

Rónán chuckled. 'Never underestimate them. They know more about you than you imagine.'

The party moved into the hall to share the welcome cup—a short, rather subdued affair, owing to the age and travel fatigue of the guests. The ritual observed, the brehons were shown to their lodgings and the residents of Tara returned to their manifold chores in readying the settlement for the gathering. Later in the day, Lord Laegaire of the Laigini and three advisors arrived and were greeted in similar fashion. By the time Conor finally drew off his siarc and breecs, he declared himself exhausted by all the meeting and greeting. 'And Lughnasadh is still three days away!' he complained as he collapsed into bed.

'Shh!' hushed Aoife, cradling her infant. 'You'll be waking Ciara with your moaning and then no one will get any sleep.'

Conor admitted she was probably right, settled back, and soon drifted off, caressing his daughter's downy head.

24

The morning sun had scarce quartered the sky before the last arrivals reached Tara for the high council. First to be received and welcomed was the Concani king, Lord Toráin; he was accompanied by his battlechief and two advisors. A little later, Lord Aengus of the Cauci made his appearance; in his party were five advisors—three of them warriors who had been present at the Mag Cró defeat.

Last to arrive was Lord Vainche. Not satisfied with travelling in the company of an advisor or two like his brother kings, he entered Mag Coinnem in regal pomp with a full complement of supporters and servants. In a show of power and as a personal affront and humiliation for Conor, he led Lord Liam and a small Darini contingent as well. Like a conquering hero, with flags and banners flying and ranks of mounted warriors and a bevy of advisors, the Brigantes king set up camp on the plain, pitching tents, lighting fires, and erecting picket lines. He did not deign to join his brother kings up on Tara Hill, but remained aloof, inviting those he considered his client kings to attend him in his camp, where they would be entertained and given food and drink and gifts to reinforce their fealty.

The next day, Vainche proceeded to host a Lughnasadh feast and entertain any who would come to a lavish meal and celebration down on the plain. Sounds of revelry could be heard from the camp—gales of laughter and lusty loud singing—all the way to the top of the hill and far into the night.

As dawn broke on Lughnasadh morning, the druids assembled to observe a rite to mark the day. There would be no festival at Tara—no feast, no races, no contests of strength and skill, no dancing; the Ard Airechtas had assumed that place. Instead, the druids made a simple obeisance to the day. As the first rays of sun streamed forth, the banfaíth Eithne kindled fire in a golden bowl using shredded birch bark and a piece of crystal fashioned for the task. Then, taking three stems of harvested grain, she tied them together with three leaves from the stems, and fed this bundle into the flames while a filidh played the harp and Banfaíth Orlagh sang a song to Danu and her daughters. When that concluded, Nolán, a brehon of high rank, took up a loaf of bread—freshly baked and marked with the sun sign—and made a sunwise circle three times around the golden bowl of flames. Elevating the round loaf to the new-risen sun, he chanted an invocation to Lugh, god of warriors, craftsmen, and druids, to sain and bless the year ahead for the protection and prosperity of all who would share in the harvest. Another song was sung and the observance concluded. The little crowd of watchers dispersed and began preparations for the momentous day ahead.

The boards had been removed from the hall and set up in the yard, and here the lords and their advisors assembled to break fast. While they were eating, Lord Vainche came thundering into the yard. Having galloped up from the plain, he and his retinue reined to a halt only a few paces from the board, scattering the serving boys and girls tending the tables, and disrupting everyone else. Arrayed in royal finery with his hair neatly braided and moustache trimmed, his golden torc burnished bright and gold bracelets on both arms, his cloak and siarc and breecs immaculate, he sat for a moment enjoying the splash his arrival had made. Then, laughing, he climbed down from his horse and strode to the nearest board and took up a cup, drained it, and slammed it down. Gioll, his hulking battlechief, swaggered with the others in his retinue to the board and insinuated themselves in among the diners.

Fergal, standing with Conor and Donal at the door to the hall, gave a snort of derision. 'Smug as a swine in swill—look at him. Lord of Lughnasadh in the flesh! Everybody bow down and kiss his feet. Ha! And here I was thinking he would run away like the craven coward he truly is.'

Although newly shaved, his hair brushed and braided, his cloak clean and neatly folded, Conor wore his ordinary breecs and siarc, and his well-worn belt and brócs. The Ard Airechtas was no place to be flaunting the impressive garments given him by the faéry—lest anyone accuse him of trying to rise above himself. Conor took one look at the preening, pretentious Vainche fawning over the druids and, his crimson birthmark itching, turned disgusted from the spectacle. As the stable master and his boys came running to lead the horses away, Conor stepped into the hall to see that all had been made ready.

He paused a moment just inside the doorway to allow his eyes to adjust to the dim light within, then entered to find that everything had been rearranged to accommodate the council. Every available bench, chair, and stool the settlement possessed, with a fair few wool bags included, had been moved into the hall and arranged in a large circle around the central hearth, cold now save for the slowly cooling embers of last night's fire. The rest of the hall was empty to allow more room for all the participants.

Conor was still standing there when the first of the gathering's participants entered the hall. Five of the brehons and several of the ollamhs moved to the nine chairs grouped together on one side of the hearth, followed by a few of the filidh and ovates, who took up places standing behind them. Rónán came next, leading lords Aengus, Laegaire, and Toráin, whom he directed to wool sacks on the right side of the hearth. Lord Morann and Ruadh, his battlechief, took places beside them; of the three already there, only Laegaire acknowledged their presence. Aengus, a frown fixed firmly on his broad, battle-scarred face, stared straight ahead, giving every impression of a man dragged there against his will.

Chief Brehon Eoghan was next to arrive; he entered the hall with his long staff in one hand and his oversized sparán in the other. Trailing him were Eithne and Orlagh; Eithne took her place at the druid chief's right hand, with Brádoch seated on his left. As soon as they were settled, Eoghan passed his staff to Orlagh, who took her place behind his chair surrounded by the higher-ranking ollamhs and filidh. The ovates filled in among them where they could find a space.

Each lord was allowed two advisors—one to sit at his right hand and one to stand behind his chair—and Conor chose Fergal and Donal to attend him. Fergal and Conor occupied one of the overstuffed wool sacks to one side of the hearth opposite the brehons, and Donal stood behind and between them at the ready. Médon and others of the fianna who had been in the battle at Mag Cró hovered at the door outside, staying nearby in case any word came their way, or should their witness be required.

It was not until everyone had taken their places that Vainche made his entrance. He and his battlechief Gioll strolled to a bench in the front row among the other lords, leaving Liam and Eamon to take the last two places on the bench beside them. Liam did not look at Conor, but kept his gaze on the druids clustered loosely around their chief.

When all were settled, Rónán, in recognition of the fact that he had brought the case to the attention of the brehons, rose from his place and, taking his staff, thumped it on the floor three times, each crack resounding throughout the hall. One of the ollamhs stepped forward and proceeded to relate a long and seemingly exhaustive history of previous proceedings and judgements from various cases in times past, thereby reminding everyone present of the authority wielded by the brehons. Even renowned kings bowed before the judgement of a druid, as the recitation amply demonstrated. When he finished, another ollamh rose and, in a song, invoked the spirit of justice and righteousness to prevail throughout the proceedings.

When these rites had been observed, then Rónán took his place at the hearth and, raising the long length of rowan above his head, called on everyone within the sound of his voice to abide by simple rules of order. 'The staff in my hand signifies the consent of the brehons. No one who is not a brehon will speak unless holding this staff. The person speaking must be allowed his say without interruption and all others will maintain respectful silence unless called upon to speak. If anyone here cannot abide by these decrees, then that person should leave now.' He passed his gaze around the ring of chairs and those standing in attendance; when no one quit the hall, he said, 'Let all within the sound of my voice know that the Ard Airechtas of Eirlandia is begun.'

He turned to Eoghan and presented the staff to the brehon chief, who took it in his right hand and stood. 'You have been summoned to hear a complaint of most grievous substance and far-reaching implications—one that demands our full and faithful consideration. In order to rightly discern the truth of this matter it will be necessary to revisit certain past events. When we have done that, we will determine whether an offence of any kind took place. Only then will we see clearly if a judgement is required and, if so, what that judgement should be.'

Returning the staff to Rónán, he took his seat. Rónán turned to the lords and said, 'Who is it that invokes the judgement of Eirlandia in this matter? Rise and be recognised.'

188 ❖ *Stephen R. Lawhead*

The question met with silence and hung unanswered in the air. Fergal shifted in his chair and gave Conor a nudge and a look as if to say, *He means you, brother.*

Conor rose from his place on the wool sack, and Rónán extended the rowan staff. 'Conor mac Ardan,' he intoned, 'take the staff and state your complaint.'

Gripping the staff, Conor collected his thoughts and took his place before the hearth. Every eye was on him as he cleared his throat and began. 'Word came to us here at Tara that Scálda ships had made landfall on Auteini lands in the north. I raised the fianna and rode to lend support to the defenders. At Mag Cró we found them already hard pressed and joined in the fighting.' He paused to choose his words and then proceeded to describe the two failed attacks and how the warleaders agreed on a plan to break through the enemy chariots.

'We formed the battle line—three separate wings. Fergal led one, Vainche another, and Toráin and the other lords were to hold the centre. At the agreed signal, the centre was to break off the attack and feign a retreat to draw the enemy chariots into giving chase. The two side wings—the fianna on the right, Vainche and the Brigantes and Darini on the left—were to sweep around the outside and then strike at the chariot line from the rear.' Conor paused, remembering the struggle to stay alive that day.

'What happened then?' asked Rónán, his voice low, gentle.

Conor lifted his head. 'What happened? Every lord and warrior within the sound of my voice knows what happened next,' Conor spat. 'We rode out. The signal was given. The centre collapsed. The Scálda gave chase—as we knew they would. Fergal and the fianna made the turn and swept in from the right . . . but instead of Vainche and his battle group, we were met by a host of enemy chariots.'

'And the looked-for attack from the right?' asked Rónán.

'It never came,' replied Conor softly. He turned his eyes to Vainche and shook his head. 'The attack never came because Vainche had deserted the field and left the fight, taking his warriors with him. He abandoned his swordbrothers in the midst of battle and rode away.'

Conor moved around the hearth ring to stand directly before Vainche, who refused to meet his gaze. 'Thirty-two men died that day. Settlements burned. And I want to know why!' demanded Conor. 'Why all the lies and deceit? Why the treachery? Was it only in service to your insufferable vanity?

Was it jealousy? Ambition?' Standing over Vainche, Conor shouted, 'Why? This is your chance to help us understand. Why did you do it?'

Vainche, rigid with hatred, remained silent and stared straight ahead with cold fire in his eyes.

Having spoken his mind, Conor passed the staff to Rónán and returned to his place on the wool sack beside Fergal, who gave him a nudge of approval. Rónán then turned to the chief brehon, who climbed slowly onto his stiff legs and stood for a moment with a hand pressed to his forehead.

Then, in a voice that seemed to come from beneath the hard-beaten floor of the hall, he said, 'The crime of treason has been invoked—namely, that Lord Vainche, having allied his forces with those of the amassed Dé Danann defenders, withdrew the warriors of his battle group during battle. This battle group—which included the Darini warband under the leadership of Liam mac Ardan—was unexpectedly withdrawn while successfully engaged in a counterattack. This action, it is claimed, not only led to the failure of the counterattack and the needless deaths of thirty-two Dé Danann warriors, it ultimately resulted in the loss of the lands and settlements belonging to the Auteini.'

He allowed the enormity of the crime to sink in, then continued, 'In fairness, I must point out that warriors die in battle and that is a cruel fact of war. How many of the deaths at Mag Cró might have resulted directly from this treacherous action we cannot know. Therefore, lamentable though it may be, we cannot reckon those deaths in the matter before us. Even so, it will be understood that deceiving and forsaking warriors who have placed their trust in a warleader is a grave and appalling offence. To do so while engaged in battle is the breadth and height of treason. This, then, is the crime we have been asked to assess and, if cause is found and proved, this is the crime we will judge.'

25

Turning slowly around, scanning the crowded hall, Rónán called out, 'An accusation of treason has been made. For this allegation to be judged, brehon law requires at least two witnesses. Is there one among those who fought that day who can speak to this charge?'

The lords glanced around at one another to ascertain which among them would be the one to cast the Brigantes king to his fate. But, before any of them could rise and be recognised before the brehons, Vainche was on his feet and moving to the hearth at the centre of the ring. Rónán regarded him with cool indifference. 'You will have your chance to speak,' Rónán told him. 'Now is not the time.'

At this, the Brigantes king drew himself up and said, 'Grievous charges have been laid against me, and I am come here willingly today to defend my honour and that of my people. To that end, I respectfully ask this august assembly to consider the character and actions of the one who has made these scurrilous claims which I am now compelled to answer. You have heard what Conor mac Ardan had to say—and he wove a most convincing tale to be sure. Yet, I will tell you that this same man has perpetrated a crime against me that is itself answerable and must be taken into account.'

'What is he doing?' muttered Fergal.

'Listen!' hissed Donal.

Rónán started to insist that he wait his turn, but the chief brehon waved aside the objection, saying, 'There are those among us who are able to keep two ideas in their head at the same time. We will allow it.' To Vainche, he said, 'I would like to know how the truth of this matter has been distorted. Please satisfy an old man's curiosity.'

Rónán passed the rowan staff to the king, and stepped aside. Lord Vainche thanked Eoghan for allowing him to clear up the misunderstanding that had brought them here. He then began by acknowledging the seriousness of the crime, and expressed his belief and trust in the wise brehons to give the matter a fair and just hearing once they had learned the true facts.

He took a few slow paces before the hearth, as if to compose his thoughts; then, grasping the staff in both hands, Vainche looked to the seated lords and, in a voice of utmost innocence tinged with sadness, he said, 'One day not long ago, I was about the business of ruling my people with the fair and considerate hand they have come to expect of my kingship. On that day, like any other, I rode out with a few of my men to the hunting runs for which the Brigantes are rightly renowned. While I was away, Conor arrived at Aintrén with a warband and forced his way into my fortress.

'In order to avoid a skirmish and bloodshed, my queen—at great risk to her person—made bold to challenge him. She was humiliated in the presence of the tribe and her pleas for peace ignored. Conor would not relent. He was angry. Enraged. He had come for a fight and since I was not there to engage him, he took out his anger and frustration on my queen and property. He stole horses from my herd, depriving my warriors of the animals on which they depend for the defence of our lands.'

Shaking his head slowly, as if labouring under a painful memory, Vainche appealed to the lords seated on the wool sacks. 'But rather than stoke the fires of hatred and animosity this deluded man obviously feels toward me, I chose to suffer the hurt in silence.' He looked around, appealing for sympathy. 'If this was all that man did, it would be enough to bring him before the Airechtas, but he went further. Having gained entrance to the ráth and dishonoured the queen, he then proceeded to try to poison her good opinion of me and destroy the natural harmony and affection between a king and his people. How did he do this? He did it by delivering a highly inaccurate account of a recent battle and lying about what took place.' Vainche glanced at Conor and shook his head as if unable to fathom the depths of his adversary's depravity. 'Not only did he lie about what took place on the battlefield, he lied about his part in what can only be described as a disastrous and shameful defeat—a defeat for which Conor mac Ardan is largely responsible.'

This last claim caused a flutter of confusion in the hall and brought Conor to his feet. His birthmark burning, he strained forward and was pulled back by Fergal, who quickly drew him back to his seat.

'With these lies,' Vainche concluded, 'this lowborn cheat and liar not only deceived my queen and people, but persuaded some of my warriors to join him. He despoiled my herd, gutted my warband, and tried to turn the tribe against me.'

Rónán, arms crossed over his chest, stood grimly looking on. Seeing that the Brigantes lord had finished, he looked to Eoghan, who, after a moment's discussion with Eithne and Brádoch, said, 'We have heard your complaint of theft of horses and the unlawful enticement of warriors away from their rightful lord. Is there someone present who can speak to this contention?'

The brehon looked around the assembled lords and advisors, and Conor, too, turned to see who might speak up for him. When no one volunteered, the call went out to those waiting outside for anyone who might be able to tell what happened on the day of Conor's raid on Aintrén.

It was Médon who answered the call. He pushed through those standing and stepped into the space around the hearth. There was a murmur of voices and a shuffling of feet, and Médon put out a hand to receive the rowan staff.

Rónán stepped before him. 'Were you at Aintrén the day of Conor's alleged raid?' Médon nodded. Rónán passed the staff to him and said, 'Then tell us what you heard and saw.'

'I rode with Conor and Fergal to Aintrén to get the horses we were promised. Since Lord Vainche was not there when we arrived, we spoke to the queen instead. She gave us the horses and we left. As we were riding away, members of the Brigantes warband came running after us. They said they wanted to come with us and join the fianna. Conor agreed and we rode back to Tara.' He concluded with a shrug. 'That's all.'

A quiet commotion coursed through the hall. Eoghan cast a stern glance around and rose from his chair. Folding his hands before him, he said, 'You say you rode to Aintrén with Conor and Fergal.'

'Aye, we did that.'

'Three warleaders. And how many warriors accompanied you?'

'None,' replied Médon. 'It was only us three alone.'

A patter of nervous laughter greeted this statement, relieving some of the tension that had gripped the room since Vainche's attack on Conor. The chief brehon held up his hand for silence. 'Lord Vainche has declared that his stronghold was stormed and that horses and members of the Brigantes warband were stolen or otherwise removed.' He fixed Médon with a stern, uncompromising stare. 'Are we to believe there were only *three* of you to storm the Aintrén fortress and force your way inside?'

'Only the three of us,' insisted Médon, 'but we didn't *force* our way inside—there was no need. The gates were open when we got there.'

'You say you spoke with the queen,' continued Eoghan, 'and asked for the horses and that she gave them to you. Did you use force or threaten her in any way to obtain these horses?'

Médon shook his head. 'Nay, lord. None of that. The queen gave them to us because that was what was owed.'

'Owed?' said the chief druid. 'In what way were these horses *owed* to Conor?'

Médon briefly explained about how the northern lords had called Conor to account for stealing Tara, but that the judgement of the airechtas had gone against them, and that as a result Conor was awarded five horses from each of the kings who had taken part.

Eoghan turned to Rónán and said, 'You were the brehon in charge of this airechtas, I believe.'

'I was,' answered Rónán. 'Lord Cahir of the Coriondi contacted me and I made my way to the council, where I took charge of the airechtas in question. I can verify that this man's account is accurate. I will also remind the brehons of the determination that was made which allowed Conor to lay claim to Tara Hill and its surrounding lands.'

Eoghan confirmed the ruling and resumed the questioning. 'You are telling us that the Brigantes fortress lay open to your entrance and that the horses were given willingly by Queen Sceana in payment of the honour debt awarded to Lord Conor by the airechtas of the northern lords. Correct?'

Médon nodded. 'That is it, exactly.'

'Now then, moving on quickly—what can you tell us about the warriors Vainche claims were taken from his warband that day?'

'Aye, that did happen.'

'How many warriors were taken?'

'Two.'

Again, there were chuckles from the ranks of onlookers.

'Two warriors?' Eoghan repeated. 'Only two?'

'Aye, only two. And they weren't *taken*. They quit the Brigantes warband and came to us because they were ashamed of how they had been made to serve a cowardly lord. They said they wanted to join the fianna to make amends.'

'Amends, you say. What reason did they give for wanting to do that?'

'Because of what happened up on Mag Cró,' replied Médon simply. 'That's what they said.' He cast a glance over his shoulder at the crowd behind him and added, 'I expect they are here in the hall somewhere—you can ask them.'

'Since that would seem to be the most expedient way of moving this inquiry along, we will do just that.' Eoghan raised a hand and signalled to Rónán, who called for the two Brigantes warriors to come forward and make themselves known to the brehons.

From the back of the hall near the doorway, there came a small stir and the two warriors pushed their way to the hearth. Looking uncertain and distinctly uncomfortable to be the objects of brehon scrutiny, they moved to stand beside Médon. At Rónán's command, they identified themselves as Comgall and Mongan, former members of the Brigantes warband.

'Did you abandon your lord and swordbrothers to join Conor's fianna?' asked Eoghan. Both nodded. 'And did Conor compel you in any way?'

'Nay, lord,' said Comgall. Mongan shook his head.

'Perhaps he offered you something in exchange for your service and loyalty,' suggested Brádoch from his chair. 'Gold, perhaps? Or, a higher position in his fianna?'

'Nay, lord,' replied Comgall firmly. 'He never did.' The warrior glanced at his brother beside him. 'It was all our own idea. We didn't even know if he would have us after what had happened at Mag Cró.' He glanced at Mongan, who added, 'But we had to try.'

Chief Brehon Eoghan dismissed the two warriors and returned to Médon. 'Now then, if I understand you correctly, warrior, the order of events would suggest that because of what happened on the northern battlefield of Mag Cró, Conor went to Aintrén intent on confronting Lord Vainche and avenging this grievance. Would I be right in thinking this?'

'Nay, lord, nothing like that,' replied Médon, glancing across to Vainche. 'It is in my mind that Lord Conor went to Aintrén not for revenge, but to collect the honour debt which Vainche refused to pay.'

'The five horses awarded to Conor by the northern airechtas.' The chief bard looked to the lords and said, 'Who among you were present at this northern council hosted by Corgan Eridani? Stand up so that we can see you.'

At first no one stood, but then, slowly, Toráin rose to his feet. He nudged Aengus beside him, who also stood; after some hesitation, Liam joined them. Eoghan accepted this tally and asked, 'And did any of you pay what was owed to Conor? If you did, raise your hands, please.'

One by one, the standing lords raised their hands.

'All of you paid? Finally, I will ask how this debt was discharged. Did you take the horses yourselves and deliver them to Conor? This would have been expected in the circumstances.' At the wagging of heads, the chief druid said, 'No? You did *not* deliver the animals. How then was payment made?'

Eoghan pointed to Aengus, who muttered, 'We gave grain and cattle instead, and Conor's men came to collect it. That was the agreement.'

'Conor's men collected grain and livestock in settlement of the honour debt,' intoned Eoghan. 'Just as he collected the agreed-upon horses from Vainche.' He turned to his fellow brehons. 'I think we have heard enough to make a decision.'

The brehons huddled together, conferred briefly, and, after a word or two, Brehon Brádoch announced, 'There is no point in belabouring the matter any further. We find Lord Vainche's claim of horse theft misrepresented and false. No further action or comment will be entertained by this council.'

The chief druid confirmed the decision and, returning to his place, announced, 'The accusations brought against Lord Conor are considered baseless and without merit and will be forgotten by everyone here. Now then, before proceeding any further, we will pause for a short while to refresh ourselves.' He raised his hands to the assembly and said, 'You will be summoned when the Airechtas resumes.'

26

Tara's hall was filled to overflowing and spilling out into the yard when the Ard Airechtas continued just after midday—the ranks swelled by curious onlookers who had snuck in and now stood packed together like salted herring in a box. Eoghan, recognising the enormous interest in the proceedings, allowed them to stay so long as they remained quiet.

When the last of the brehons had resumed their chairs near the hearth, Rónán, holding the rowan staff, announced that they would now consider the crime of treason that had been raised in regard to actions performed in a battle with the Scálda in the Auteini territory at the place called Mag Cró. 'This council has heard the claim,' said Rónán, 'that Lord Vainche removed his warband in the midst of battle—a deed that ultimately resulted in the loss of life and lands.' He looked around the room. 'I will now call on Lord Vainche to answer this accusation.' He turned to where the frowning monarch sat hunched and fretful. 'Lord Vainche, will you rise?'

With a show of laboured reluctance, Vainche climbed to his feet; the former swagger of an affronted nobleman was gone and in its place the demeanour of a cruelly abused victim.

Grasping the staff offered by Rónán as if it was a branch offered to a drowning man, he launched into his account:

'Word came to me that enemy ships had made landfall in the north and were ravaging our brave Dé Danann tribes in that region. Not a moment was to be wasted, so I raised the Brigantes warband at once and rode north—as any right-thinking warleader would do. Lending blades and blood to the defence of those ill-protected lands was my only thought and my sole consuming desire.

'I will not try the patience of this assembly with an account of the many hardships and injuries we endured in the fierce battles that followed, but suffice to say that the Brigantes shouldered the duties of leadership, and under my command and that of my battlechief, our forces—combined with those of the lords here'—he made a deferential gesture toward the kings seated nearby—'our forces were able to turn back this vicious enemy incursion. In short, we secured what I had every reason to believe would be a decisive victory.'

Vainche paused to look around as if expecting praise and admiration for the selfless bravery shown on the battlefield. Eoghan, unmoved, said, 'The Brigantes joined forces to help fight this latest incursion. Perhaps now you could tell us what happened during the battle in question.' He gestured for him to continue.

Vainche drew a breath and swallowed hard, as if gathering strength and will to face an unpleasant task. 'As I was about to say, the Brigantes along with the considerable aid of our client tribe, the Darini—as well as Laigini, Cauci, and Concani—were able to secure the Auteini lands, subdue the enemy, and repel the Scálda invaders. No sooner had we done so, than an unrecognised warband led by Conor mac Ardan arrived on the battlefield. Why he and his men thought to involve themselves at this late time I cannot presume to guess—though I suspect it was an attempt to worm his way into an unearned repute among the lords.'

He glanced across at Conor with a regretful, pitying look—as if it pained him to have to speak about such shameful behaviour. Turning back, he finished, saying, 'Conor arrived and immediately attempted to assert himself as warleader—and this though he had yet to strike a single blow against the enemy. Naturally, this concerned me, but seeing that my warband had borne the brunt of battle and were much fatigued from the numerous attacks we had endured, I made the decision to remove my men from the field and allow fresh warriors to take their place.' He shook his head sadly. 'This innocent action has, I fear, been grossly misinterpreted and this alone is the reason I am summoned to be here today.'

'Stinking lies,' muttered Fergal. 'The man is beyond all shame.'

Eoghan, in consultation with the other druids, said, 'I see that Brehon Eithne has a question she would like to ask.'

Rising to her feet, Eithne stood and in a somewhat tremulous voice said, 'You maintain that your warband had secured the battle and that you relinquished your place in order to allow the fianna of Tara to take part. Is this something warleaders generally do when engaged in battle?'

Vainche looked down at his feet and shook his head. 'Not generally, no.'

'Then why did you do it?' asked Eithne.

Again, with an air of great reluctance, Vainche replied, 'The truth, regrettable as it may be, is that this *self-elevated* lord and I have had many unhappy dealings in the past. I feared yet another troubling confrontation, so to avoid any needless conflict—much less injury or bloodshed—I did what was best for my men.' He glanced around the room and added, 'Looking to the welfare of my people is always my foremost concern—as anyone who knows me will tell you. Obviously, if I had known my motives would be twisted into a noose to hang me, I would never have given him the chance.'

Brehon Eithne indicated that she had nothing further to ask, and sat down. Eoghan rose and took her place; he paced a moment in front of his chair, deep in thought. Every eye in the hall followed, watching the old man, who appeared to be marshalling the combined wisdom of his age and long experience to unleash a withering storm of reckoning. Yet, when he spoke his tone was that of a gentle grandfather coaxing a wayward child. 'If I understand it, Lord Vainche, your claim is that Conor mac Ardan arrived at the place of battle after the fighting was largely concluded and that he proceeded to make such a threatening intrusion that you departed rather than risk an unnecessary and potentially harmful confrontation. Is that your contention?'

Somewhat warily, Vainche nodded. 'It is.'

Eoghan paced some more and then raised his voice to the crowd looking on. 'It is Lord Vainche's assertion that the Brigantes warband under his command bore the weight of the battle at Mag Cró and, with the aid of other tribes, secured the defeat of the enemy. Further, he claims that the battle was in the main concluded when Conor and his fianna arrived and, recognising their presence as a potent source of conflict, he took the very sensible precaution of withdrawing from the battlefield lest trouble between their two warbands lead to violence and injury. It is Lord Vainche's belief that this action has been misrepresented in the complaint against him.'

The aged druid paused to gaze around the ring of chairs and ranks of silent onlookers. 'This is the claim before us. Who can speak to the veracity of this claim?'

A strained silence met Eoghan's question. The onlookers looked to the lords, and the lords looked to one another, but no one made bold to answer.

Vainche, his face darkening with anger and frustration, glanced around at Liam, urging him to speak. Liam gazed down, refusing to be drawn.

The old brehon passed his gaze around the ring of noblemen and asked again if any would speak to verify Lord Vainche's version of the events of that fateful day. When no one rose to confirm Vainche's claims, he said, 'Since no one is prepared to verify Vainche's account, is there someone here who can disprove it?' The brehon looked to the lords on their wool sacks. 'Perhaps one of you would tell us your version of events as you saw them.'

Those lords who had suffered loss and injury through Vainche's betrayal rose as one and clamoured to be heard. But one voice was louder than the others. Eoghan pointed at him and Rónán stepped forward, handed him the rowan staff, and said, 'What is your name, friend?'

'I am Toráin mac Torbha, Lord of the Concani,' he declared, his voice firm despite the nervous fidgeting of his hands. 'I was there on the battlefield that day—both before the battle and after.'

'Tell the brehons what you know,' Rónán invited. 'And if you could avoid speculation, that would be much appreciated.'

'There was no fighting when I arrived,' said Toráin. 'The Dé Danann warhost was still forming up at the northeastern end of Mag Cró. Lord Aengus and his warband were already there, and Lord Laegaire and the Laigini warriors.'

'I notice you did not mention Lord Vainche just now. Was he there also?'

Toráin shook his head. 'He arrived later—that is, sometime after me.'

'It has been suggested that you and the lords you mention were waiting for the Brigantes to arrive before engaging the Scálda in battle. Is this so?'

'Aye, we were all of us waiting for Vainche.'

'Why would you be doing that? You came to engage the enemy, why did you wait?'

'Lord Vainche had sent word that he was coming and that we were to wait for him to arrive.'

'I see,' replied Eoghan, stroking his beard. 'Is that the usual way you engage the enemy?'

'Nay, but we thought it would be no bad thing to have the aid of another warband or two in this battle. The Scálda numbers were greater than we expected. So we agreed to wait.'

'You waited for the Brigantes warband and when they finally arrived the battle commenced, is that right?'

'Aye,' replied Toráin. 'We formed the battle line and made a foray, but it failed because the Scálda war carts are very fast and difficult to attack on horseback. We had not faced them before and had no choice but to retreat.'

'This first attack failed,' Eoghan repeated. 'What did you do then? Tell us everything you can remember.'

'Ach, well, we broke off the attack as I say, and returned to our battle camp. That was when Lord Conor and the fianna arrived. They came to join the warhost and that was a great relief, I can tell you. So, then we made another foray, but that failed, too. The war carts—the chariots they use— are just too fast, and there were too many of them.' Toráin shook his head at the memory. 'We broke off the attack and retreated to make a better plan. It was in Conor's mind to outflank the Scálda chariot line, get in behind them, and take them from the rear. So, that is what we did.'

'In other words, you launched a third attack,' said Eoghan with an encouraging nod. 'How did you fare this time?'

'We made the charge, as I say, and the Scálda met us in their war carts as we expected. Lord Aengus and myself, and Laegaire and Morann—we took the centre of the line, and Conor and the fianna took the right flank. Vainche and Liam formed up on the left flank as we had agreed. As soon as the enemy committed to the fight, those of us in the centre made a feint to draw the Scálda to follow. This was to allow the two outer flanks to get around behind the Scálda line, see. Then they would fight to the centre and split the Scálda attack from behind.'

'And were these two separate flanks able to get around behind the enemy chariot line?' asked the chief druid. 'Did the battle plan succeed?'

Toráin glanced at Vainche, then lowered his gaze and gave a slight shake of his head. 'Nay, lord. The attack did not succeed.'

One of the elder druids, Nolán, leaned forward in his chair and said, 'As this is the heart of the matter before us, I would like to request confirmation.' Eoghan nodded, allowing the question. Nolán half turned to address the lords. 'Who among the chieftains on the field that day can confirm the truth of Lord Toráin's assertion?'

Morann, whose lands were overrun, was first to verify Toráin's account.

'The right flank did their part—that is, Conor and the fianna engaged the enemy as planned. But the Brigantes and Darini—that is, the left flank—quit the field. The attack collapsed, leaving the fianna alone to work in behind the enemy. This they did, but they could not break through the Scálda chariot line on their own. And the dog-eaters were quick to turn against them.'

'You say that the left flank—that is, the warriors under Lord Vainche's command—failed to fulfil their part of the battle plan as previously agreed and it is your opinion that this is why the plan failed,' said Nolán, carefully rehearsing the gist of Morann's account.

Morann nodded, and Eoghan turned once more to Toráin and asked if he also thought the failure of the attack was owed to Vainche abandoning the fight.

'I *know* right well it was,' said Toráin, his voice taking on grit for the first time. 'The Brigantes deserted us. It's as simple as that. If not for Conor's courage and battle wit, we all would be lining a bench in the Hag Queen's hall.'

'Yet, here you are. You survived.'

'We survived—thanks to Conor,' declared Toráin, 'and no thanks to Vainche.' The young lord cast a dark look across to Vainche, who sat motionless, staring straight ahead.

The brehons, who had their heads together in quiet discussion, finished their debate and Eoghan asked, 'Is there another question for Lord Toráin?'

Brehon Brádoch rose to his feet and, in a slightly tremulous voice, asked, 'I am curious to understand how it was you knew that Lord Vainche and his battle group deserted you during the fight. Someone in the midst of battle cannot always discern what may be happening elsewhere. Perhaps the Brigantes warband was prevented in some way from fulfilling their part of the plan. That could have happened, could it not?'

'Aye,' agreed the young lord, 'that *could* have happened, I suppose. But it's not what happened that day.'

'How do you know? This is what I'm asking.'

'I know because when we finally fought free of the dog-eaters, Vainche and his battle group were gone.'

'Gone? Gone where?'

'I don't know. All I do know is that they were not on the battlefield. And I know this because Conor sent some of his men to look for them and find out what happened, and they could not find Lord Vainche or any of his warriors anywhere. I'm thinking they turned tail and rode for home.'

'They might have been killed,' suggested Brádoch. 'You said many men were killed. Could that have happened?'

'Aye,' allowed Toráin, his brow creasing at the notion, 'but since Vainche and his battlechief are sitting right here today, I think it's safe to say that's *not* what happened.'

This also drew laughter from the onlookers, and even the brehons smiled. Brádoch merely shrugged and said, 'My purpose was to point out that strange things can happen in the course of battle, and even those most intimately concerned cannot always know for certain what is taking place or why.'

Eoghan paced around a little more, then addressed the druids. 'Brádoch has raised a point worth considering. Does anyone else have a question or observation?' No one came forward, so the old druid turned to those ranged behind Conor. 'Who among you is able to confirm or deny the claims made by Lord Toráin just now? Perhaps someone who rode with Lord Vainche on that day?' He scanned the ranks of warriors, lords, battlechiefs, and advisors. 'Lord Liam, you rode with Vainche—maybe you could tell us what happened.'

Liam, looking shaken and contrite, shook his head and silently looked away. Eamon saw his lord refuse the staff, hesitated as if weighing the matter in his mind, then stood and held out his hand to Rónán, who said, 'Were you among those who rode with Vainche at Mag Cró?'

Grasping the staff, Eamon replied, 'As battlechief of the Darini warband, I was at the forefront of the fight that day.'

'Tell us what you know.'

'It is as Lord Toráin has said—all of it. Just as he said. Two forays failed. On the third foray, the battle line formed up and the Darini and Brigantes and some others took our place on the left wing according to the plan we'd made and agreed. The signal was given to ride out and the charge began. Our battle group looked to Vainche to give *us* the command. . . .' He faltered, drew a shuddery breath, and, his knuckles white on the staff, said, 'But that command was never given.'

Eoghan, at his place before the druids, stopped pacing and regarded Liam with his keen dark eye. 'Why is that?' he asked. 'Why was the agreed command never given?'

'Why? That is what I have been asking myself ever since.' Eamon lowered his head and in a sorrowful tone continued, 'In truth, I cannot say, because I don't know the why of it. All I know is that we sat there waiting for Vainche's command as we watched our swordbrothers ride into battle.'

'You waited,' said Eoghan. 'What happened then?'

'The next thing I knew, here was Vainche and Gioll telling everyone we were quitting the battle and riding for home. And that is what we did.'

'This must have caused you some distress—seeing the Dé Danann warhost riding into battle without you. Did either Vainche or Gioll offer a reason for this curious behaviour?'

Eamon, gazing at the floor, made no answer, so the druid chief asked the question again. Eamon raised his head and, tears glistening on his cheeks, he said, 'They never did.' He dabbed at his eyes with the back of one hand. 'I raised a complaint. I said it wasn't right—as any of the Darini warband will tell you—but Vainche . . . Vainche refused to listen.

'It was my swordbrothers out there! Counting on us! Fighting without us! Vainche left the field and left them to their fate. If there was treachery anywhere, it was then and there. And I tell you the truth, I heartily regret my part in it.' He turned his sorrowful gaze on the Brigantes king. 'Sooner cut off my right hand than ever allow myself to follow that man into battle again. Call him a king? In my eyes, he is not fit to shovel muck from the stables.'

'Liar!' shouted Vainche, his voice a thunderclap in the hushed hall. He leapt to his feet and started forward. 'He lies! Tell them the truth!'

Rónán spun on his heel, putting himself between Vainche and Eamon. 'Sit down, Lord Vainche. You will have your say, but Eamon holds the rowan staff, and it is his place to speak.'

'I will not sit in silence and suffer these lies,' Vainche shouted, spittle flying from his lips. He thrust a finger at Conor and the fianna ranked behind him. 'They have had more than enough time to dream up a tale for others to tell against me. I will not hear it.'

Lord Aengus, sitting next to Vainche, grasped the outraged king by the arm, whispered something to him, and pulled him back to the bench. Liam, now decidedly pale and ill at ease, turned his face away. When Vainche was seated again, Rónán asked Eamon if he had anything further to add to his account.

'There is one other thing I would say if you will allow it, brehon lords,' said Eamon. 'Most people here will know that Conor was exiled from our tribe and made outcast owing to a plan set in motion by Lord Cahir's druid Mádoc. This was an attempt to obtain information on the designs and movements of the Scálda. I know for a fact that Conor never did the crime for which he was exiled. That was just part of the ruse that Mádoc devised. Conor was blameless. So far as I know he has never betrayed Eirlandia in any way.'

Eamon handed back the rowan staff and returned to his place at the bench. Liam leapt to his feet and started around the hearth ring. Conor rose and put out a hand to his brother as he passed, but Liam snarled, 'Do not touch me!' Swiping the offered hand aside, he shoved past Conor and stormed from the hall.

Conor, birthmark tingling, watched his brother shove through the crowd. 'Leave him be,' whispered Donal, bending over his shoulder. 'He made his decision.'

Eoghan paused to allow the hall to quiet once more, then said, 'It is my opinion that we now have a better understanding of what happened that day at Mag Cró. I would like to know how many standing beneath this roof agree with what has been said. Therefore, I will ask for a cast of stones.' The druid chief motioned to two of the filidh, who stepped forward to join him at the hearth. One bard carried a bowl, and the other an empty leather bag. 'Every man who was on the battlefield that day will come forward to cast a stone into the bag—a black stone if you agree that Vainche is guilty of the charge against him, or a white stone if you disagree and think him innocent.'

With a gesture toward the filidh, Eoghan returned to his chair and sat down as the lords and warriors stepped forward to select a pebble from the bowl and drop it into the bag. Conor was the last to cast a stone into the bag and when he had resumed his seat, Eoghan nodded to Eithne, who rose and stepped to the filidh holding the bowl; she took it into her hands, raised it, and tipped the remaining stones into the hearth. Then, showing that the bowl was empty, she gestured to the filidh with the bag, who proceeded to pour out the contents of the bag into the bowl. This done, she took the bag and turned it inside out to show everyone that it was now completely empty.

Then, taking the bowl, she looked into it, stirred it with a crooked finger, and then carried it to Eoghan. He, too, looked into the bowl, stirred it with his finger, and then directed her to announce the result.

'The casting of the stones has revealed that the black stones outnumber the white.'

'No!' shouted Vainche. 'Count them! I demand you count them!'

Without a word, Eithne moved to the outraged lord and extended the bowl to him. Vainche peered into it and saw only two white stones shining like lone stars in the night sky.

Snatching the bowl from between her hands, Vainche stirred the contents with his finger, gave out a strangled cry of frustrated rage. He hurled the bowl into the fire pit, scattering stones across the floor.

27

The sun went down on the brehon's contemplations. As the sky took fire in the west, Rónán emerged from the hall to say that the Ard Airechtas was concluded for the day, and that they would resume their deliberations in the morning. Meanwhile, the people of the settlement had got on with their chores: food and drink were prepared, children were bathed and animals fed, clothes were washed and dried. In the lower fields, the harvest continued: grain was cut, the sheaves bunched and stacked to dry; turnips, carrots, cabbage, and apples were picked and prepared for storage; honey and honeycomb were gathered—the honey put up in jars, the wax set aside to be made into candles.

Upon leaving the hall, Liam had gone to his bower and refused to speak to anyone except Eamon. Nor was he to be seen later that night at the board with the other lords. Vainche and Gioll had returned to the Brigantes camp on the Council Plain. Brehon Brádoch suggested the precaution of sending a small contingent of the fianna to place a perimeter watch around the camp lest the lord or his battlechief be tempted to sneak away in the night. Fergal agreed with the precaution, and sent Galart and Aedd along with seven of the fianna to maintain a vigil through the night.

Then, as the moon rose through a cloud-tattered sky, Galart returned to Tara with an unexpected visitor—a late arrival to the gathering: a lady and two attendants, a young woman and a warrior. He escorted her to Conor and Aoife's bower and ushered her inside, where Aoife had just finished feeding Ciara and laid her down for the night.

'I am sorry to disturb you at your rest,' said Galart. 'But I didn't know what else to do.'

At the door to the bower, the lady pulled back the fold of the mantle she had been wearing as a hood.

'Lady Sceana!' said Conor, rising from the edge of the bed where he was sitting.

He hardly recognised the Brigantes queen. She was dressed in drab clothing with nothing to show her royal rank save the thin gold torc at her throat. Her long, auburn hair was cut brutally short and there was the ugly mark of a purple bruise on her cheek below her eye, and one on the side of her neck.

'I would gladly have waited until tomorrow,' she said, 'but Galart and his men saw us arriving and brought us here.'

'Come in, come in.' Aoife pulled her into the bower. The small single-room dwelling was hardly big enough for three with a sleeping baby, but Aoife moved things around to accommodate their visitor and offered her one of the two stools in the room. 'You will be hungry and tired from your journey. Let me get you something to eat.'

'Do not trouble yourselves,' said Sceana. 'My maiden and I will go to the Brigantes camp and take something there. I just wanted you to know that I am here and stand ready to bear witness to the deceit and treachery of . . .' Here she faltered, and then said, '. . . of my husband, Lord Vainche.'

'You cannot be going down to that camp,' said Conor. 'Not tonight. You will stay here at Tara. I'll have a place in the women's house prepared for you.'

'And we'll have food brought there for you,' said Aoife. 'Come sit down, and rest a moment while we make arrangements.'

'Is anyone with you?' Conor said. Sceana nodded. 'I'll speak to them.'

Conor stepped out, exchanged a word with Galart and the queen's escort, and sent them away on separate errands. Returning to the bower, he found Sceana and Aoife sitting together, and Aoife gripping the queen's hands in her own. 'I cannot imagine what you must think of me,' Sceana was saying. 'Coming here like this . . . but I could not stay away. How could I remain at Aintrén while the brehons determined the fate of my people? In truth, I had to come to see justice done.'

Conor assured her that the brehons had the matter well in hand. He explained what had taken place that day during the Airechtas—including the witness of Toráin and Eamon. 'They are to deliver their judgement in the morning,' he concluded.

The Brigantes queen lowered her head and put her face in her hands. 'I have been a stupid, foolish woman—and I have no one to blame but myself.' Despite Aoife's assurance that there was no need to explain, Sceana seemed determined to make them understand; she went on to explain how, following the death of her husband, Lord Brecan, she was lonely, and woefully unprepared to be leading a tribe as large and demanding as the Brigantes. 'Whatever else Brecan was, he was at least a king who knew his people and how to rule,' she told them. 'He took care of everything. When he was killed, I was lost.' She looked pleadingly to Conor. 'You know this. You were there. And more than that, my people were lost. It is an unfortunate truth, but a woman cannot be both king and queen to her people. I was weak and confused, I admit it, and Vainche appeared and made it seem that in trusting him, all the unpleasantness and strife would go away and everything would be just as it was. He charmed me, wooed me, and made airy promises. Foolish woman that I was, I made a rash judgement, and one that I have not stopped regretting since the moment he ascended to the Brigantes throne.'

Sceana lowered her head and a shudder quivered through her. But when she continued, her voice was firm and merciless. 'The throne was all he wanted—and even that was not enough. He never had a single thought about the welfare of the tribe. His desires, his appetites, his fancies always came first. He cared nothing for the people who depended on him to care for them. He put my people at risk and squandered our wealth, our security, the goodwill of our neighbours—and all to feed his ravenous vanity and greed. Though it shames me to say it, I stood by and watched him rain ruin down upon our tribe. Our people were made to suffer and I did little to prevent it.' She sighed. 'I know I must bear responsibility for that.'

'He deceived you as he deceived everyone who trusted him,' Conor told her.

'I knew, Conor. Deep down, I knew. But I told myself that now he was king, Vainche would rise to the high position expected of him. He would be the ruler we needed him to be. He let me believe that.' Sceana bent her head. 'But that, too, was a lie.'

Aoife squeezed her hands in sympathy.

Leaning close, Conor inspected the bruise on her cheek and said, 'Did Vainche do that?'

The queen nodded. She put up a hand and fingered her short hair.

'That, too?' asked Aoife.

Sceana nodded. 'He blamed me for allowing Conor to take the horses. He threatened to kill me if I ever crossed him again.'

'And yet you came here,' Aoife said. 'That took courage.'

'Let him do his worst to me. I don't care anymore. I came here for justice for our people.'

Their voices disturbed the sleeping baby, and the infant woke with a cry. Sceana looked at the little swaddled bundle on the pallet. 'Is that . . . ?'

Aoife retrieved the child and held her close. 'This is Ciara.'

The queen reached out and cupped a hand to the infant's pink cheek. Tears came to her eyes. She pushed them away and rose from the stool. 'I'm sorry. . . . I—'

'Here,' said Aoife, handing the baby to Conor. She put a hand on the queen's shoulder. 'You're tired. I'll take you to the women's house and see you settled so you can rest. We'll talk some more tomorrow.'

The two stepped to the door and Aoife cast a glance at Conor, whose crimson birthmark seemed to take on a fiery glow that reflected the anger burning in his heart.

Morfran

I never expected to be king. My brother Gwydion was destined for the throne, not me. I loved my brother, supported his kingship, gave him my best counsel whenever he asked—and sometimes without his asking. I sustained my ráth and the people within my care according to his wishes and dictates. But when the Scálda killed him, the throne and torc of kingship passed to me, and now it is for me to lead and direct the Tylwyth Teg in this worlds-realm.

I have long been of the opinion that the time has come for the faéry to leave Ynys Afallon and make the journey to Tír Tairngire. We are not as we were. Once the faéry folk were supreme among the firstborn of creation. Alone among the Great Mother's sons and daughters, the faéry were all her pride. That was long ago in an age past remembering. The mortals, crude in manner, plunder their way through their short, wretched lives, upsetting the ordered balance, threatening our existence in this worlds-realm. If the faéry are to have a future at all, that future lies in the Land of Promise—of this, I was convinced. Indeed, I believe it still.

But others among us disagreed. And though I did not hear in their arguments anything to cause me to change my mind, I listened. It is strange how words are like seeds. Conor's words of warning were the seeds that sprouted within me, took root, and bore the fruit of peace and renewal. Those few words yielded so much.

If the Scálda defeat us, Conor said, *the Tylwyth Teg will be next.*

Though I was angry with Rhiannon for going against my wishes to meet with him, her report of that forbidden meeting rang true. Conor's warning that the Aes-sídhe had developed a weapon to wield against us caught my full attention. And the fact that Conor turned down Lord Lenos's proposition to supply the Dé Danann with weapons of strong iron rather than allow them to be used against us moved me deeply. Conor had a difficult choice put before him and though it meant a loss to himself, he chose to protect us. That was the decision of an honourable man—a man to be trusted.

This realisation, along with Conor's warning, began to work in me. I summoned my council of elders and advisors to my palace at Tarren Awelon and there had Rhiannon and Gwyddno tell what they had learned from Conor. Some of these had met Conor when he and his friends sojourned among us when Gwydion was king.

Becoming entangled in the affairs of mortals, as distasteful as that was to me, seemed an inevitability I could no longer avoid. And though I had vowed before my people never to involve them in human dealings again, it occurred to me that I might ameliorate the dilemma somewhat by going to the Aes-sídhe and seeking the aid of Lord Lenos. In exchange for his help, I would uphold the peace that my Lord Gwydion had proposed—the same he had been about to pledge when he was captured and killed by the Scálda. It seemed to me that together we might aid the Dé Danann and avoid becoming further ensnared in mortal concerns. Moreover, if we succeeded we would be rid of the repulsive Scálda.

I proposed this very thing to my council and they agreed to support the plan. Accordingly, I have chosen a delegation—Rhiannon and Gwyddno among them—to go to the Aes-sídhe and argue for their aid in exchange for peace. This was my brother's dream, not mine. But I will do it in memory of Gwydion, and should anything come of it, I will count it his victory, not my own—assuming I can even persuade the contrary Lord Lenos to speak to me at all.

Ha! A bold and likely futile assumption, that. No friendly word has passed between us for far longer than I can remember. And my memory's reach is long indeed.

28

'Every betrayal is a mockery of honour and a desecration of belief,' began Chief Brehon Eoghan. Rising from his chair, he clutched his druid staff in his right hand and moved to the centre of the ring next to the hearth where a small fire burned. 'But betrayal in battle is the most potent form of disloyalty, for it destroys trust, destroys faith, destroys hope, and all too often results in death for many—death of kinsman and brother, friend and ally, and any who had placed their confidence in the betrayer.

'Those so affected by the betrayal naturally demand to understand the reason for the act. As Lord Conor has reminded us so eloquently, those who were made to suffer demand an answer. They want to know *why*. Why was this cruelty visited upon them?'

The Ard Airechtas had reconvened as soon as everyone had broken fast and assembled in the hall. This time, the crowd of observers was tightly packed as grain in a sack. The circle around the hearth had been made smaller to allow more people in, but people crammed the doorway, straining for a look at what was happening inside. In among the spectators were the wives, mothers, and families of the slain warriors of the fianna. Conor had seen to it that they should be included, so that they could see and hear all that took place. Aoife, with Queen Sceana at her side, stood behind Conor's chair—much to Vainche's chagrin and displeasure. He scowled at his wife and mouthed murderous threats, but she refused to look in his direction and kept her attention on the brehon chief as he stood before the gathering.

The chief brehon moved to the hearth and stood leaning on his staff. He raised his head and looked around the overcrowded hall. Lifting his voice, he said, 'In brehon law we find that the cause of certain crimes is of little importance in determining the ruling or judgement to be applied. Treachery in battle is one such crime. For, whether from cowardice, hatred, malice, or spite, the consequences flowing from that evil act are much the same. And those consequences can be and, alas, most often are catastrophic—not only for those on the battlefield, but for those whose lives and livelihoods depended on the warriors who were so wickedly deceived. We know from ancient tales that whole tribes and races have been destroyed by simple acts of betrayal—as the suffering of the Auteini even now attests.'

The chief brehon took a half step to the side and, planting himself directly before Vainche, gripped his staff in both hands and said, 'Vainche mac Simach, stand up on your feet and receive the judgement of the brehons.'

The Brigantes king made no immediate response, but was prodded to his feet by Aengus and Liam on either side of him. Gioll, his battlechief, stood gripping the back of his lord's chair, his bloodless hands clenched like claws.

The brehon chief held out a hand and was given a folded cloth by one of his ovates. He shook out the cloth to reveal a hood, which he drew over his head, and, raising his staff before him, he intoned in slow, ominous tones, 'It is the judgement of the brehons that you are guilty of the crime for which you stand accused. You did lead men into battle at Mag Cró and did agree to support the efforts of others fighting to repel an enemy incursion. Having pledged your support, you did not honour that pledge and instead removed the promised aid by deserting the field in the midst of that battle, thereby subjecting the Dé Danann warhost to increased hazard, peril, and death.

'The penalty for this crime cannot redress the injury caused,' Eoghan continued, pacing before the hearth. 'For what remedy exists that can restore faith, can redeem hope, or heal trust once it has been broken? What reward can compensate for the horror, the desperation, the fear and agony of those whose death resulted from the cruel and wicked act? What compensation can be given for a life once it is extinguished?'

The wise head of the brehons allowed the questions to go unanswered as he paced around the circle a little more, then said, 'Though no material compensation can ever be equal to the loss, yet reparation will be made. In established law the honour price due for the unlawful death of a warrior is equal to the price of five sét in silver or gold.'

He looked to Liam and Aengus, sitting on either side of the Brigantes lord. 'The brehons have determined that you who supported Lord Vainche, while not wholly blameless, did so out of misplaced loyalty. In short, you trusted an unworthy overlord. You were not the first to pledge fealty to a master of deception and lies, nor will you be the last. You must live with the guilt of that decision and suffer whatever consequences your involvement with Lord Vainche and his schemes may bring in future dealings with your brother kings of other tribes. Further, to reclaim your honour, you are required to reconcile and redeem yourselves to any and all other lords who may have cause to hold grievance against you because of your actions on that day. This is the judgement of the brehons.'

Lord Aengus lowered his head in meek acceptance of the decision.

Turning to Liam, the chief brehon regarded the shaken, chagrined king and said, 'Regarding your part in the crime, the judgement of the brehons is that you are guilty of complicity in the betrayal of the Dé Danann war-host. In recompense, you will pay to the tribe five sét for the life of each slain warrior.' He paused and looked to Liam for an answer.

'I will pay,' said Liam, his voice small and uncertain.

'Moreover,' continued Eoghan, 'it is the judgement of the brehons that you had opportunity to oppose Vainche's decision on the battlefield, but chose instead to follow him in abandoning the fight. Therefore, a more stringent punishment is required.'

Liam visibly cringed as the brehon chief drew himself up to deliver the brehons' ruling.

'For failing to challenge Vainche's treason, you will relinquish all claims to the lordship of your people until the debt of honour is discharged. Failure to pay in a timely manner will result in the permanent loss of your kingship and the forfeit of lands and cattle. Do you understand?'

Liam, owning his fault at last, received his punishment without objection or complaint.

Turning from the convicted men, Eoghan said, 'As for you, Lord Vainche, the honour price for a malicious death is double the price for an unlawful death. Therefore, the brehons of Eirlandia have determined that you shall be required to pay the price equal to that of *ten* sét to the families of each of those warriors whose lives were lost during the battle at Mag Cró.'

'Outrageous!' spluttered Vainche. 'It is too much!'

But Eoghan was not finished. 'That is the compensation to be paid to the survivors of the victims of your crime. I ask you now how you intend to pay?'

Vainche, seething, spat, 'Pay! I . . . cannot pay. I will not! It is too much.'

Eoghan, frowning mightily, stared at the Brigantes king. 'Then you will forfeit all lands and—'

'*I* will pay!'

Every head turned to where Sceana stood with Aoife. The Brigantes queen, green eyes narrowed to angry slits, gazed upon her disgraced husband and, in a clear, hard voice, declared, 'Though it cost the whole of my realm, I will pay the honour price to the families of those warriors whose lives were forfeit to Lord Vainche's treason. I alone will redeem the honour of my tribe.'

Vainche swallowed hard and, unable to endure the ferocity of her gaze and the shame of his failure, turned his face away.

'As Queen of the Brigantes, I declare my marriage to that man'—she raised a hand and pointed at Vainche—'repudiated and dissolved.' She touched the bruise on her cheek. 'From this moment, that man is no longer husband to me and will no longer reside at Aintrén or receive a welcome there. I know him not.'

The chief brehon looked to Banfáith Eithne, who, after a quick word with Orlagh, simply nodded her approval of the dissolution. Satisfied, Eoghan inclined his head to the queen and said, 'It shall be as you say.'

Eoghan paused and regarded Vainche with a solemn countenance before continuing. 'It is the view of this council that no recompense is sufficient to restore or redeem what has been lost and broken by this heinous breach of faith. Therefore, punishment will be added to the judgement.'

Raising his staff, he held it crosswise above his head and, in a hard, unyielding tone, declared, 'Hear me, Vainche mac Simach. By committing the crime of treason in battle you have forfeited your noble rank and are no longer worthy to be called lord or king. Moreover, we find the just punishment for your crimes will be to share the fate of those you betrayed.

'As you abandoned the tuath in battle, so the tuath now abandon you. I, Eoghan, Chief Brehon of Eirlandia, have spoken.'

At these words, a visible shudder passed through the Brigantes lord's body and he seemed to sag inwardly upon himself. He groaned and swayed on his feet. Both Liam and Aengus reached out to hold him upright as three ollamhs stepped into the circle and came to where the convicted man stood. Without a word, the senior ollamh put his hands to Vainche's throat, took hold of the king's fine golden torc, spread wide the ends, and removed it from around his neck. He carried the torc to the brehon Brádoch, who received it into his care.

One of the ollamhs took Eoghan's rowan staff and the other went to the hearth and, with a little pair of tongs, removed a still-warm coal from the ashes of the previous fire. He carried the ember to Eoghan, and the old druid extended both hands, placing the palms together. He held them like this and closed his eyes; his lips moved silently for a moment. Then, opening his eyes, he parted his hands and the ollamh dropped the spent coal into the brehon's open palm.

Closing his eyes once more, the brehon spoke a single word—a word in a language that awakened in Conor a distant memory. For a fleeting instant, he was a gawky lad standing spellbound and barefoot in the dust watching the first druid he had ever seen pronounce a curse upon his beleaguered tribe . . . and there was his da, Ardan, kneeling in the road, begging for the curse to be lifted.

Brehon Eoghan repeated the word and the half-dead coal began to glow, taking on a ruddy blush once more. He spoke the word a third time and a wisp of flame sprouted from the glowing ember. He then glanced over his shoulder at his attending ollamhs who approached and extended the palms of their hands toward the ember. Conor watched in fascination and became aware of a low, thrumming sound; he looked around and realised it was coming from the two ollamhs. The uncanny drone grew in timbre and volume as more voices were added to the weird chorus, and soon all the ollamhs and filidh had the palms of their hands extended. The eerie sound swelled until it seemed to fill the entire hall.

The glowing ember lifted from Eoghan's outstretched palm. Supported on waves of sound, it floated in the air, spinning slowly at first, and then faster and faster until there came a crack and a flash of fire; the single tiny flame flared to robust life.

The live coal hung suspended, burning brightly, illuminating the astonished faces of everyone present. But the flame did not last long. As brightly as it flared, it quickly faded and the coal became a glowing ember once more. The ollamh with the tongs reached out and plucked the ember from the air and presented it to Eoghan, who gave a nod of approval and indicated that it should be given to Brádoch, who took the tongs and crossed to where Vainche stood, forlorn and bereft, like a man balanced on a cold sea cliff contemplating the deadly plunge before him.

With one swift movement, Brádoch pressed the smouldering ember against Vainche's forehead and held it there. The former lord gave an agonised yelp and fell back onto the bench, pressing his hands to his head. He sat there, rocking back and forth, moaning in pain and humiliation. No more a king or nobleman, he was now nothing but an object of pity: wretched, miserable, and pathetic.

'By this stain you have been marked as a sign of the stain on your soul that your falsehearted betrayal has earned you. Your name will be satirised by bards throughout Eirlandia. As the loss of life and destruction your crime has caused cannot be undone, neither shall this satire be removed. It will endure as long as memory endures.'

'Outrageous!' shouted Vainche, leaping to his feet. 'Lies! All lies!' Shaking off the hands of the bards, he started forward as if he would stride from the hall. 'I will not . . .'

His voice seized and his display of anger instantly altered to an expression of alarm. His jaw continued to work, but no words came out. His hands fluttered to his throat and his fingers tore at the soft flesh there. The high colour drained from his face and he tottered forward on his toes one step, and another, before crashing to his knees. Then, clutching his chest, he fell facedown beside the hearth and lay there unmoving.

Gioll, standing behind the disgraced king, watched in dull horror as the man his blind loyalty had aided and encouraged throughout his contemptible career received his well-earned punishment. But the chief brehon was not finished. Eoghan commanded the battlechief to step forward and said, 'As you have benefitted in your lord's gains at the expense of others, so you will share in his losses. I have no doubt your unthinking support was a weapon he wielded and often called upon. We will not deprive him of it now. Therefore, you will join your lord.'

At a gesture from the chief brehon, four filidh moved out from behind the circle of chairs and crossed to where the battlechief stood. The four put hands on Gioll and thrust him forward to receive the searing imprint of the burning coal on his forehead. Gioll gave out a startled, strangled cry and shook off their hold. He bolted for the door of the hall, thrusting his way through the throng, shoving people out of the way. He made it only a few running paces before he, too, was stricken by the strange malady that had afflicted his master. He gave out a whimper and slumped to the floor, never to rise again.

Brehon Brádoch, still holding the flaming ember, moved to the hearth and calmly dropped it into the fire. He turned to Eoghan and declared, 'The judgement is complete.'

29

The low, heavy sky threatened rain, but in the west streaks of clear blue could be seen splashing through the grey. The Ard Airechtas was concluded and the lords—shocked and amazed by the strange power commanded by the brehons—watched in stunned silence as the bodies of Vainche and Gioll were carried from the hall. Wrapped in their cloaks, the two would be taken by the ovates and ollamhs to a hidden location in a nearby wood and buried in unmarked graves.

No sooner had the grim procession passed from sight than the lords began preparing to depart. 'Look at them,' said Conor as he and Donal watched as the horses were brought out and the kings and their advisors made their hasty farewells to one another. 'Running away as fast as they can lest the taint of Vainche's shame cling to them.'

'Don't judge them too harshly,' Donal said. 'Vainche deceived them, too—just as he deceived everyone he ever met. And they suffered for it, too.'

Absorbed in the leave-taking, they did not hear Aoife and Queen Sceana approach until the two appeared beside them. 'Are you for leaving, too?' asked Conor.

'Soon, but not yet,' replied the queen. 'I am tired and the Brigantes are camped down on the plain. I will rest there tonight, and return to Aintrén tomorrow. There is so much to be done in the days ahead.'

'Trust that we will help you in any way we can,' promised Aoife. 'You have only to ask.'

Sceana pressed her hand. 'You have already helped me and my people more than you know. It is more than I deserve, and I am grateful.' She lowered her head modestly. With a quick glance at Aoife, the queen leaned forward and kissed Conor lightly on the cheek, then put her hand to the place. 'You have ever been my true friend. Thank you.' She reached out and pressed Donal's hand. 'Thank you both.'

When she had gone, Aoife and Conor and Donal were joined by Rónán, who announced that the brehons would be leaving soon. 'The day will hold fair enough, I think. If we go now we can be back in Clethar Ciall by tomorrow evening,' he told them.

'So soon?' asked Conor. 'Could you not stay just another day?'

Rónán hesitated. 'If we had reason to stay, perhaps. Why? What is in your mind?'

'Well, it is Lughnasadh, after all,' Conor replied. 'We have the druids with us and cause for celebration. Is that reason enough?' He saw Rónán wavering and added, 'We could observe the rite at dawn tomorrow.'

'At dawn tomorrow,' replied Rónán, nodding in agreement. 'I'll speak to Eoghan and the others. We might find them agreeable.'

'Little Ciara's soon hungry,' Aoife said when Rónán had gone. 'I'll feed her and you see to reordering your hall. If there's to be a celebration, there's that much to be done.'

'I'll be taking care of that,' replied Donal. 'Go, both of you—go and see your daughter.'

Conor spent a happy few moments playing with Ciara, tossing her in the air and kissing her little pink feet and blowing soft breath on her smiling face. He thought her much grown since he had last seen her. With each passing day, she seemed a little fuller, rounder, more settled, more herself. 'You are every bit as beautiful as your mother,' whispered Conor into her tiny ear. 'My treasure.'

The infant gurgled at the sound of Conor's voice, then let out an almighty wail. Aoife undertook to feed the baby while they talked about the brehons' judgement and the changes it would bring for the region and for all Eirlandia. Ciara fell asleep while they talked and a rare moment of peace and contentment claimed that little corner of the ráth. Conor basked in the happy feeling and had just stretched himself on the bed when voices sounded in the yard beyond the bower.

'It sounds like the lords are leaving,' he said, sitting up again. 'I expect I should go see them away.'

'Must you?' said Aoife. 'Stay. Rest a little. Let Fergal see them off.'

Conor looked at his wife and nursing child and hesitated. But the voices grew louder and were joined by shouts from farther off, followed by the scurry of feet outside. An instant later there came a rap on the flimsy door-frame that shook the entire bower. Conor rose and pulled back the door cloth to see Maol's anxious face. 'Fergal is raising the warband,' he said. 'There's a Scálda raiding party.'

Casting a last glance at Aoife and the sleeping baby, he stepped outside. 'How far away are they?'

'In the forest east of Mag Rí. It looks like they're coming this way.'

'How many?'

'A few raiders only. Maybe more. They are too far away to tell,' replied Maol, wiping sweat from his face. 'Caol is down there. He'll bring word soon enough.'

Conor started for the hall. Maol fell into step beside him. 'Go find Donal and Médon,' Conor ordered. 'Tell them to meet me at the watch post above Mag Rí.'

Maol darted away on the run and Conor hurried to the eastern side of the hilltop and joined Fergal at the rocky outcrop they used as a lookout. A quick look revealed nothing moving on the plain below, nor could he see any movement in the dense woodlands that followed the curve of the river from the east to the north. 'Scálda raiders, is it?' asked Conor. 'Seen any sign of them?'

'Not yet,' replied Fergal.

Together they scanned the dark wood beyond the plain and then Fergal stabbed out a finger. 'There!'

Out from the woodland to the northeast, two riders emerged and sped across the plain at a fast gallop. 'That'll be Caol, I'm thinking,' said Fergal. 'Aye, and from the haste they're making they've seen something to put speed into their flight.'

The two riders reached the base of Tara Hill and started up the difficult eastern track to the top, dismounting halfway up and proceeding on foot when the path became too steep and rocky. As they neared the top, Caol, who was leading the way, caught sight of the observers and gave a wave. Putting his hand to his mouth, he shouted, 'Scálda!'

The words were hardly out of his mouth when a second cry sounded behind them. Conor and the others turned to see Galart on his horse, charging across the yard. He and Nuadh and Comgall had been riding the western borders out beyond Tara Plain. 'They're here!' he shouted, throwing himself from his mount. 'The whole filthy Scálda warhost is here!'

30

Conor ran to the western watch post with Fergal right behind. Donal and Maol were there, and Donal, rock-still, gripping his charmed spear tight in his right hand, gazed out across Mag Teamhair. Conor recognised the rigid, almost otherworldly stillness. Donal was seeing something no one else could see.

Fergal opened his mouth to speak. 'Wha—'

Conor quickly waved him to silence. They watched. Waiting.

A few tense moments slipped by and then Donal exhaled heavily. His broad shoulders slumped and his grip on his spear relaxed. He glanced at those gathered around him and rubbed a hand over his face.

Conor put his hand on Donal's shoulder and said, 'How many did you see?'

'Too many to count.'

'Do you have any idea at all?' said Fergal.

'They're spread out through the trees.' Donal swept the blade of his spear over the wide expanse of the plain. 'They'll soon be *everywhere.*'

'Raise the alarm,' ordered Conor, and Maol raced away. Turning to Médon, Conor said, 'Tell the other lords to summon their warriors. Send a warning to the Auteini settlement on Mag Rí, and another to the Brigantes camped on Mag Coinnem. When you've done that, send someone to take word to the farms round about.' Conor took him by the shoulder and gave him a push to get him moving. 'Go!'

'I see them!' cried Donal as Médon raced away. A thin, dark line of horse-drawn chariots emerged from the dark wall of trees at the far northwest end of the plain. This first line was soon joined by another a little farther to the west, and then another. Slowly, silently, like the tendrils of a monstrous, grasping plant, or the tributaries of a river, the enemy war carts rolled out of the woodland and onto the gently sloping grassland.

Conor stood and watched the advance of the enemy and knew that he was seeing something he had not seen in Eirlandia for a generation: more than a summer raid, it was a total Scálda invasion. Not ships this time, but chariots.

Across the yard, the frantic clanging of the iron bar on its post outside the hall sounded a jangling alarm—a chiming clang that did not begin to alert the ráth to the enormity of the threat arrayed against them.

The first of the fianna arrived a few moments later, armed and ready for whatever would be required of them. These were swiftly followed by the greater portion of Tara's resident population—the lords of the Airechtas among them—all hurrying to the rim of the hill. The sight of the Scálda host amassing on the plain below stopped the warm hearts beating in their breasts and stole the words from their mouths. Chariots in wave after wave rolled out from the far woodland, carving ruts in the grassy plain.

Rónán threaded his way through the press of people to where Conor and the fianna stood; he took a long, unflinching look, and said, 'We must rally the tribes.'

'If I leave now,' said Fergal, 'I can maybe outride—'

'You're needed here,' Conor countered. 'Someone else can ride.'

'Let me through!' called Lord Aengus, shoving himself forward. 'I've got to raise my warband. I'll warn everyone along the way.'

'I'm going, too,' cried Lord Toráin, pushing in behind him. 'I'll raise the warband and return before dawn. You have my word.'

Liam appeared next to him. 'No, you stay and help here—both of you. I'll go. Eamon will go with me. The two of us will have a better chance of getting through. Once we're free of any pursuit, we'll sound the alarm and send men to raise *all* the tribes.'

Conor regarded his brother, weighing the decision; Liam seized on the slight hesitation. 'Hear me, Conor,' he said, 'I know there is no way to re-store the trust we once had. No doubt you think I should join Vainche in his shroud and it may be you are right. I was wrong to side with Vainche against my own blood kin, wrong to participate in that shameful betrayal at Mag Cró. I blame no one but myself. The fault is mine and I own it.'

'This is not the time—' began Conor.

'It is the perfect time,' insisted Liam. Looking to Rónán, he said, 'This may be the *only* time. Neither of you will ever know the guilt and regret I have endured since that dreadful day. If I'm ever to reclaim some small portion of your trust and redeem the honour I've squandered and abused, it will be through a service like this.'

Conor could see that, however he felt about his brother, the decision made sense. Liam was a formidable fighter, and if anyone could find a way to get a message through the Scálda-infested forest to the kings and warbands of the neighbouring tribes, he was their best hope. 'Let it be as you say,' Conor relented.

Liam reached out and gripped his brother's arm in the warrior's salute. 'You'll not be regretting this,' he said. He turned away abruptly. 'My horse!' he shouted. 'And Eamon's, too! Now!'

Conor, seeing Dearg nearby, called, 'Prepare fresh water skins and bó-saill for their sparáns. Hurry!'

Rónán, arms crossed over his chest, stood gazing in grave concentration at the slowly assembling enemy host. Suddenly, he jerked himself upright and turned around. 'Eoghan!' he cried. 'Eoghan! Where are you?'

'I'm here!' The old druid emerged from among the press of people lining the rim of the hill and Rónán hurried to meet him; the two stood together, their heads almost touching as they conferred. A long moment passed and then the druid chief turned and stumped away. Rónán returned to where Conor and the others waited.

'We can help,' said Rónán. 'Eoghan has gone to speak to the brehons and ollamhs. We may be able to aid Liam's errand and perhaps give us a little more time.'

'Go on,' said Conor.

'Banfaíth Eithne has long delved into weather lore and had some experience in that realm. Judging from the sky, we may be able to do something.'

'Weather,' said Fergal, his tone flat, skeptical. But into his mind flashed a memory of another battle where weather had made all the difference. That any defenders had survived the Tara massacre at all was owing to the thunderstorm that night.

'Do it,' Conor told him. 'But do it quickly.'

As Rónán disappeared through the anxious crowd, Aoife and Queen Sceana moved to Conor's side. Aoife turned fearful eyes on the growing ranks of Scálda spreading in a dark flood across the grassy expanse. 'It is even worse than I thought.' She reached for the queen's hand and the two stood together, supporting one another, their hands entwined.

'Your warning came just in time,' Sceana told him. 'We heard something moving in the wood. It seemed the very ground was trembling. Then your man sounded the alarm and we fled the camp. Everyone is here.'

'How many warriors are with you?' asked Conor.

'Seventeen,' replied the queen. 'We have no battlechief or warleader now. They are yours to command.'

Conor saw Médon coming toward him and called to him. 'Are Liam and Eamon ready to ride?'

'They are just about to leave,' Médon reported. 'Liam wants to speak to you before they go.'

'I'll see them off,' Conor told him. 'You go speak to the Brigantes. Tell them their queen has placed them under our command. Make sure they are well armed and add them to the fianna.'

Médon dashed away, and Conor hurried to the stable where Liam and Eamon were just about to take their mounts.

'I'll go to the Eridani first,' Liam said as Conor came running up. 'Eamon will go to the Coriondi. They're closest.' He gestured behind him to where Eamon held the halters of their horses—each with a shield on a strap and a spear holder carrying two spears. 'We'll go by the northern track across Mag Teamhair. We'll have a better chance to outrun them and we can lose any pursuit in the forest.'

'Wait but a little,' Conor said. 'Rónán and the druids are making a spell to help you.'

'No time,' replied Liam. 'If we're going to have any chance to get through, it must be now.'

'It may already be too late for charging the ranks like that,' Conor told him. 'They are thick on the ground down there.'

'I'm willing to try,' said Liam.

'You've never lacked courage,' Conor replied. 'But let's wait and see what the druids can do. If they succeed, then you two will have a better chance to get away.'

Aoife called from across the yard, near where the druids had gathered. 'Conor, they're starting!'

The ovates, filidh, and ollamhs had formed a circle around the three elder brehons—Eoghan, Nolán, and Brádoch; they, in turn, stood with their heads covered and their rowan staffs upraised and the three tips touching at a point directly over the kneeling figure of the banfaíth Eithne.

'What are they trying to do?' asked Sceana as, slowly, the outer circle of druids began moving. Arms linked, one slow step at a time, they moved in a sunwise circle, making a low, throaty humming sound as they went.

'I guess we'll find out soon enough,' answered Conor. Leaving them to watch, he moved on to where Liam and Eamon were waiting at the rim of the hill, holding the reins of their mounts and increasingly impatient to be gone.

'This is taking too long,' Liam complained. He gazed down upon the long double rank of war carts already assembled in a wide half circle some little distance from the base of the hill; more were spreading onto Mag Rí to the north. 'We have to go now while we still have a chance.'

'Give it a little more time,' urged Conor. 'The brehons know what they're doing.'

'There *is* no more time!' snapped Liam. 'The attack could come at any moment, and there's nothing to prevent it.' He glanced around. 'You don't even have any walls up here, Conor! Were you even thinking at all?'

'Keep your voice down, brother, and listen,' said Conor tersely. 'We have the biggest warband raised in Eirlandia for seven generations at least. And if you and Eamon get through the enemy chariot ranks and raise the tribes, we will have the largest host anyone alive has ever seen.'

'*If*,' muttered Liam. He looked to Eamon, who cast a doubtful eye to the threatening sky.

'We could wait a little,' said Eamon.

Leading the horses, the three made their way to the watch post located at what Tara's inhabitants considered the back of the hill; it overlooked an area of boggy lowland to the north and eastward to Mag Rí. The trail was steeper and made several switchbacks before it reached the foot of the hill. On the plain below, the Scálda chariots appeared to have halted their advance and were now forming a long double rank across the plain and around the base of the hill to the west. The enemy would soon encircle the entire hill. 'They're putting a ring around Tara,' observed Eamon. 'They mean for no one to escape.'

'Look!' said Liam. 'What's that? Something's happening.'

He pointed to the northeastern slope of the hillside where, curiously, the first searching fingers of fog had appeared and were feeling their way down the steep incline of the hill. Like the morning mist that often forms over a bog or lough, the wraithlike tendrils slithered and slid down toward the base of the hill, where they gathered, and thickened and flowed on. And out across the plain, along the line of the river, the fog began seeping out from among the trees, filling up the low places, thickening into an ever-growing wall—building, banking, blanketing the slope and flowing on, running in rivers toward the base of the hill in rippling rivulets that pooled, deepened, and spread—now reaching to the tops of the chariot wheels of the nearer ranks, flowing on, lapping the flanks of the horses, engulfing the footmen. Meanwhile, the fog continued cascading down Tara's steep slopes like the surge of a waterfall, like an avalanche, burying the ground in a deluge of obscuring mist.

Out on the plain, they could hear voices raised as enemy warriors tried to calm horses that were agitated by the peculiar inundation. Soon the entire plain was steeped in fog above man height—a barrier as dense and impenetrable to sight as any timber wall. To the ranks of fianna assembled on the top of Tara Hill, the surrounding plains looked flat and white and smooth as a deep snowfall in winter. Of the besieging enemy there was neither sight nor sound. The cloaking fog concealed all.

'The druids have done it,' said Fergal, rushing up just then. 'Rónán tells me it won't last forever. You should go.'

'It's now or never, brother,' Liam said, squinting his eyes to make out the torturous path leading down the rocky slope. 'You decide.'

With a last glance at the milky moon-washed expanse below, Conor said, 'Go—and Danu give you wings.'

Liam gave a curt nod, gathered up the reins, and mounted; Eamon swung up onto his horse and turned his mount, and the two riders disappeared over the edge of the hill and were gone.

31

A dull, dirty sun faded in a darkening sky. And with the evening came the distraught Auteini settlers, who had braved the perils of both the enemy and the druid fog to reach the precarious safety of Tara Hill. 'We had to leave everything,' said Morann. 'The stock, the tools, the grain stores . . .' He made a gesture of helplessness. 'Trying to avoid the dog-eaters was hard enough and the fog didn't make things any easier.'

'But you got here safely,' said Donal. 'No one was left behind?'

'No one,' confirmed the Auteini lord. 'The farmers and herdsmen were already with us—because of Lughnasadh, we were coming up here in the morning anyway. Otherwise . . .' He let the thought go unsaid.

'Never mind, you're here now and we need you. Take your warband to Fergal,' Conor told him. 'Donal will see to your folk.'

Leaving Morann and Donal to organize the newcomers, Conor went to collect his faéry weapons, find Aoife, and maybe get something to eat. If there was to be a battle at daybreak, he wanted everyone to have a little something in their stomachs. Who knew when they would have a chance to eat again?

Tara's inhabitants had not been idle. All through the night, Donal and Dearg hustled from place to place and task to task, assigning various du-ties: assigning folk to feed and water the horses, and slaughter a few of the sheep and cattle that happened to be on the hill, others to prepare the hall to receive the wounded.

The yard outside the hall had become the locus of activity. Aoife and Sceana had arranged the women and children into groups: the elders among them for baking, or cooking, others for preparing food; the children for tending the fires, and procuring supplies. Three huge pots of stew were bubbling on the embers, apples had been quartered, and cheese had been cut into chunks the size of walnuts to more easily feed hungry people in a hurry. Tara's womenfolk were also busy preparing the hall to receive wounded warriors: they had pallets of rushes, skins, and fleeces readied, and baskets of unspun wool and bindings for wounds, and pots of willow bark and yarrow leaves steeped in ale and mashed into a paste for medicines.

Nor was this all. Those women who had knowledge of weapons—wives of warriors, mostly—were working with a group of craftsmen and the older farmers and boys and all were hard at work preparing replacement weapons for the battle line: sharpening spears and stropping swords until they gleamed with lethal light. Others were renewing any loose or frayed grips or bindings on swords and spears, and repairing and tightening shield straps. Some of them had armed themselves and donned the fighting gear of the fianna. When battle began, they would take their place on the line alongside their men.

Conor paused on his way to the hall and stood taking in the activity; he felt a surge of pride lift his spirits. Death might well come for them all today, but if it did, it would not find them hiding in a hole or cowering under their cloaks waiting for the end. Death, when it came, would find them defiant.

As he stood watching, he saw Aoife emerge from the hall intent on some errand; he hurried to catch her. 'What's happening down on the plain?' asked Aoife as he fell into step beside her. 'Any word?' She had little Ciara wrapped tight in a blanket and strapped to her back.

'No change. The Scálda are assembled and awaiting the command to attack. That could come at any moment. I thought it would have started by now, but they seem inclined to wait.'

'Why?' asked Sceana. 'What is preventing them?'

'In truth, I wish I knew. But they won't wait forever. There will be an attack today. And when they come, they will come in force.'

Aoife understood the unspoken implications of her husband's reply. 'Whenever it comes, we'll be ready,' she told him. 'Do not spare a thought about that.'

Her courage touched him; Conor looked at his wife and daughter and felt as though his heart would fall out of his chest. He put his hand on little Ciara's sleeping head and rested it there for a moment, before moving on to the hall to take up his weapons: Pelydr, the lightning-quick spear engraved with saining charms of flight and power; Eirian, the ever-sharp sword; and Pared, the shield that could resist any blow. Sliding the sword through his belt, he slung the shield onto his back and took up his spear, feeling its lively weight fill his hand. Just holding the spear and feeling the shield on his arm made Conor feel better about the coming battle. Sustained by this hope and the activity he saw around him, he paused to take a bit of bread and beef before returning to the battle line, where he found Fergal pacing along the rim of the hill, taut with impatience.

'I'm thinking Evil Eye means to lay siege to Tara,' he said, stepping close to Conor and speaking low so the warriors nearby would not overhear. 'He is daring us to come down and fight him on the plain.'

'Aye,' agreed Conor. 'On the plain—where his chariots can overpower us and crush us.'

'I hear you, brother,' replied Fergal. 'But even without chariots, the dog-eaters can climb the hill and overwhelm us by force of numbers.' He flung out a hand to the innumerable encampments scattered across the plain. 'There must be fifty of them for every one of us—maybe more!'

'Is it that you think I do not know this?' Conor countered. 'I have been thinking of nothing else.'

'Well?'

'We stay put. If Evil Eye wants us, he must come up here and get us.'

Fergal flung a hand out toward the plain. 'Don't think he won't, brother. Don't think he won't.'

They settled back to watch and wait. The sun edged ever higher, slowly burning away the last rags of the night's mist and revealing the enemy warhost amassed upon the plain. To most of Tara's inhabitants, who had never seen a chariot before, the sight was shocking—a chilling reminder of the overwhelming power marshalled against them. From the Royal Plain in the north to the Council Plain in the south, the leather-clad enemy stood ready to attack. With rank on rank of chariots, outflung wings of horsemen, and battle groups of footmen, Balor Berugderc, he of the Evil Eye, had committed the entire Scálda warhost to this battle.

As the last of the mist cleared, Rónán came with a message from the brehons. 'Eoghan would speak to you.' Before Conor could ask why the chief brehon wanted to see him, Rónán moved off again, saying, 'Follow me—and bring your men.'

'How many?' Conor called after him.

'All of them!'

With a last glance down onto the enemy ranks amassed below, Conor started away. 'You heard him,' he said to Fergal. 'Bring everyone.'

Fergal and Médon each brought their battle groups and followed Rónán to the council ring, where the druids had gathered around the big cauldron they had used for the druid fog the night before. The discussion ended as Conor reached the outer ring of ditches, and the brehons, ollamhs, and filidh turned to receive the warriors.

As soon as the fianna had assembled, Brehon Eoghan raised his staff and called out in a loud voice, 'Hear, Eirlandia, the voice of a True Bard!'

Others, working nearby, heard the cry, and a sizeable crowd pressed in behind the fianna.

'In the age before iron was given to the Dé Danann, there was a king by the name of Artuin mac Datho. Through many battles he defeated the giants and wild beasts that ruled this island realm. Seeing that he never lost a fight that he entered, the great goddess Danu took a liking to him, and one day came to him with a warning. "Goemagog, Lord of the Aggarb and Anbul, is coming to fight you today. He has formed himself a weapon of power such as you have never seen—a hammer of fire that cannot be quenched except in the blood of a champion. The king of the giants means to extinguish the fiery hammer in your blood, my friend."

'Dismayed as he was to hear this, King Artuin stoked his courage and said, "Let him come, that oversized sack of bones, and if fear does not turn his bowels to water, let him try to defeat me. I have faced all the other giants, I will face him."

'"Brave words, Artuin, but words alone will not save you today. That is why I have come. I bring a gift to help you in the fight." At this, the great goddess called for her attendants, who appeared, with a cart drawn by a brindled ox. In the cart was a large jar made of pure white stone.

'Danu commanded that the jar be brought to her and she told Artuin to put off his clothes and stand before her. He did so. The goddess put her hand into the jar and withdrew it covered in a strange liquid of radiant blue. Stepping near, she placed her hand on Artuin's chest, leaving the mark of her palm over his heart. "By this mark of woad," she said, "Goemagog will know that you are mine and that I go before you in this fight. He will strive and he will battle and he will do all manner of hurt against you. But my sign will protect you and the raging adversary will not prevail." This Danu vowed to Artuin.

'The great king looked down at his naked torso and said, "If such as this can protect me from harm in battle, then paint me with signs against every evil so all will know that Danu the Wise is my powerful protector."

'The goddess commended Artuin for his wisdom and did as he wished. Again and again, she dipped her hand into the jar and brought out the bright blue woad and marked the king's flesh with signs of power and protection. Lord Artuin then went out and answered the wicked giant's demand for battle and though many blows were struck that would have shattered lesser men, the king bore up. Protected by the blue woad, he suffered no injury; while the giant Goemagog gradually began to tire and, as the sun went down on their combat, the monstrous enemy exhausted his strength.

'Unable to lift his fiery hammer above his head, much less swing it, the giant sat down on the ground. Artuin, who had endured much through that long day of strife, was not slow to seize his opportunity. Quick as a cat on a rat, the king drew back his sword and delivered a blow that carved the giant's vile soul from his odious body. The immense carcass slumped against the hillside and Artuin leapt upon it. He hacked off the giant's arms and threw them to the north and south; the giant's legs he cut off and threw to the east and west. But Goemagog's head he left where the giant had fallen.

'In time, the hideous great head was covered with earth and grass grew over it and, the fairest of hills, it became known as Tara of the Kings. Out of gratitude for Danu's aid in his time of need, Lord Artuin decreed that all his people henceforth would honour the Good Goddess as their queen. And that is how we became the Dé Danann.'

Lowering his staff, the chief brehon then turned and put his hand to the cauldron and said, 'Today, we face an enemy in much the same way as Artuin faced the giant. So, it is only right that we put on the protection that Danu provided.' He smiled and asked, 'Who will be first?'

All eyes turned to Conor as he stepped up to the cauldron, stripping off his siarc as he came. Eoghan nodded to Rónán, who dipped his hand into the big pot and withdrew it dripping with blue paint. Then, pressing his hand against Conor's chest, he left a bright blue print of his palm over his brother's heart. Next, he drew a series of jagged lightning bolts along the ribs of Conor's left side and more of the same on the right. 'My face, too,' Conor told him. 'But not too much—I want Evil Eye to know who it is that defeats him this day.'

Rónán smiled and, dipping his fingers once more, drew four parallel lines down the clean side of Conor's face from forehead to chin, but leaving Conor's distinctive birthmark unpainted so no one would mistake him for anyone else. Satisfied, Conor returned to his place and took up his charmed spear and shield once more.

'I'll be having that,' Fergal shouted. He had already removed his siarc and now stepped before Rónán to receive the handprint of the goddess over his heart. He pointed to his right upper chest and Rónán drew the swooping swirl of a spiral, and then a line down either side of his torso. Fergal gave out a battle cry and, taking up his weapons, pushed his way through the press and returned to the rim of the hill to reestablish the battle line.

'Who will be next?' called Rónán. He might have saved his breath. The fianna were already shedding cloaks and siarcs and jostling one another forward in their eagerness to receive the woad. Médon, Galart, and Calbhan pushed their way to the front and received their blue prints and swirls and bands.

Such was the demand that an empty ale vat was set up and ovates filled it with a sharp-smelling liquid while two filidh crumbled dried lumps of pale blue stuff into the vat, stirring the mixture to make more paint. Siarcs were discarded and left in a pile beside the woad pots. The brothers mac Morna went further. Stripping off all their clothes, they demanded to be painted from head to foot in stripes and prints, spirals and zigzag lines.

Their bold gesture was taken up by others, who, in the manner of their Dé Danann forefathers, entered battle naked save for the emboldening blue signs painted on their bodies. One of the ollamhs produced a bag of fine red clay and proceeded to make a thin paste, which he applied to the heads of the warriors who unbound their hair and demanded to have it raked into spikes and spines and thorny crests.

'This is how warriors went into battle in a previous age and time,' observed Conor with approval. 'It is fitting that today we will face the enemy as the heroes of old.'

Aoife was there beside him. 'And if it is fitting for the men, it is fitting for their women.' She took her place in the line and, baring her shoulder, received the blue handprint above her left breast, and a line down either cheek. Sceana likewise received the mark of the goddess, and many of the other women as well.

Resuming her place with Conor, Aoife raised her hand to his disfigured cheek and said, 'This is right and good, my lord. There will never be another day like this. So, go and win us the victory and free us from the Scálda curse.'

Conor took her hand and kissed the palm. 'What flesh and blood and spirit can do, I will do,' he said.

'And I will do no less.' She kissed him then, and Conor took up his weapons once more and joined Fergal on the battle line.

One by one, and in groups of two or three, the fianna reassembled on the hilltop. Fifty-eight warriors, forty-two women, seventeen druids—all of them wearing the blue of battle and supported by sixty of Tara's residents—gazed down upon the Scálda-infested plain of Mag Rí, the Royal Plain. From somewhere among the warriors on the battle line there came the slow rhythmic beat of a spear shaft against a shield rim. This sound echoed down the line as another and then two more, and then ten more, took up the beat. Soon the hilltop resounded with the loud clattering, rattling, ear-numbing clash of Dé Danann weapons.

Conor felt the ruby stain on his cheek tingle and warm to the thumping pulse as the battle rage roused within him. He put back his head and shouted, 'Scálda!'

The cry was instantly taken up by others and the shout became a roar, echoing from the hilltop and down onto Mag Rí, where it appeared to have an almost immediate effect. From the plain below came the piercing blast of a battle horn. A thousand Scálda throats gave out a tremendous war cry and the Battle of Tara commenced.

32

The foremost rank of chariots ringing Tara Hill moved out and those behind parted, opening a way for Scálda footmen to advance. They reached the base of the hill and broke into two branches. Arrayed in the full Scálda armour: chest plates of hardened leather, some with shoulder plates; iron skullcaps or pointed helmets sprouting horsetail plumes; round, iron-rimmed shields—some small as a cask lid, others large as a cartwheel; and long, slender-shafted iron spears. At some unseen signal the enemy leapt forward and began scrambling up the long slope, shrieking as they came.

An answering clatter of weapons echoed across the hilltop as down the line Dé Danann shields were swung into place, spears taken up, swords readied. Conor took up his place immediately behind the front rank, ready to leap to the defence of any warrior in difficulty. Planting his shield before him, he lowered Pelydr and loosed a battle cry, 'For life! For Tara! For Eirlandia!'

The fianna, well-schooled in their craft, instinctively tightened the line. Crouched low behind their shields, they levelled their spears and readied themselves for the onslaught.

The enemy pounded up the hillside. Howling like the Hag Queen's hounds, the first wave hurled themselves upon the fianna. The crack of shield against shield resounded across the hilltop. Blades flashed and slashed and the battled commenced.

Conor, Pelydr at the ready, kept his eyes moving along the battle line, alert to any warrior in difficulty. The sound of the clash—screaming Scálda, the grating crash of shield on shield, the metallic ring of blade on blade, shouts of encouragement and cries of warning, screams of the wounded—rent the air, numbing the senses.

Conor caught a flash of frantic movement beside him as Fergal sprang forward; a warrior in the fore rank took a tremendous blow on his shield and staggered back a step. Before the Scálda could strike again, Fergal was there. With a rapid series of jabs, he held off the attacker and allowed the warrior to get his feet back under him and rejoin the line.

Then it was Conor's turn to aid a warrior who was struggling to hold his own against two Scálda assailants—one armed with a battle-axe, and the other with a stubby, shield-piercing spear. Lowering Pelydr, Conor rushed to the line and thrust the charmed blade under the lower edge of the beset warrior's shield. The blow caught one of the attackers on the shin above the ankle and slid off, slicing deep as it passed. The battle-axe disappeared, leaving only the short spear for Conor's man to parry.

Conor stepped back and took a swift look down along the line to see if he was needed elsewhere. He saw Médon, standing in the centre of the line, where the attack was heaviest, lunge forward and, with two quick jabs, force two assailants to retreat a few steps, allowing the defenders to regain their footing. All along the battle line, he saw the same situation: the defenders were hard pressed, but holding their own. At least, there were no Dé Danann wounded on the ground.

The attack, though forceful, was short-lived.

Just as the battle was settling into a rhythmic exchange of blows, with the Scálda shoving forward and the defenders pushing back, a battle horn sounded from somewhere down below—distant, but clear and insistent, three sharp blasts that blared across the plain. On the third blast, the Scálda abandoned the assault. They fell back and streamed down the hill, melting into the forces below.

The Scálda had lost a score or more; their bodies remained where they had fallen, untended by their swordmates. The defenders, however, had suffered only minor injuries in the attack. Médon raised a victory shout and Fergal called for the warband to tighten the line and remain vigilant. He then hurried to where Conor was watching the enemy retreat. 'What was that?' he said. 'A test only?'

'Aye, I'm thinking Balor was wanting to discover the true size of our warband and the strength of our defences. It may be that Evil Eye has learned some small respect for this hill of ours. I expect the next attack will be with exceeding force.'

'Let him come,' said Fergal. 'He will find it no easier to conquer than last time.'

'Brave words, brother.'

'Do you doubt it?'

Conor took his time answering. 'Do I doubt our warband's courage? Or their skill? I do not. I know these men and they are the best in all Eirlandia.'

'Aye,' agreed Fergal firmly. 'We have made them that and no mistake.' He looked into Conor's clouded face. 'But?'

Conor gestured to the expanse of Mag Teamhair and the teeming enemy warhost gathered there. 'Balor has brought his entire warhost and means to take Tara and claim the sacred centre of our island realm for his own.' He turned once more to regard the ranks of chariots and horsemen below. 'If Tara falls, I do believe the rest of Eirlandia will fall, too. And the Dé Danann race will be but a memory soon forgotten.'

Fergal regarded Conor closely. He knew his old friend well enough to know that he rarely gave vent to such grim pronouncements—even if he harboured them. To hear him talk so when awaiting an imminent attack sent a cold finger of fear along Fergal's spine and he turned his face away. 'Ach, well, not if *we* have anything to say about it.'

Conor heard the subtle admonition in his friend's tone and smiled. 'Tell the fianna to look to their weapons. Replace any damaged blades or shields. We have a moment's respite now that may not come again later.'

They heard quick footsteps behind them and Donal came running up. 'That horn,' he said, excitement lighting his dark eyes. 'Did you hear it?'

'Ach, aye,' replied Fergal. 'We heard it. Why do you ask?'

'Don't you see? We can use it.'

'Use it how?' said Conor. 'We don't have a battle horn.'

'I haven't heard one since . . . I can't remember when,' said Fergal.

'But the Scálda use them,' shouted Donal and raced away again. 'That's the whole point!'

'What he's on about?' wondered Fergal. 'Have you ever known the Scálda to use a horn in battle?'

'Not in any fight I've ever fought.' Conor scanned the rows of chariots and dark knots of Scálda footmen and added, 'Then again, this is a battle like no other.'

They both fell silent for a time and stood scanning the plain, trying to discern the movements of the enemy to guess what would happen next. They saw chariots wheeling this way and that, a clutch of mounted warriors trotting off toward the Council Plain, and others on foot moving into position. What they saw gave them to know that never in all their years of warring had either of them seen so many Scálda in one place.

'There must be a thousand,' murmured Conor at last.

'More maybe,' said Fergal.

'And how many fianna?'

'Fifty-eight fianna,' replied Fergal, 'and I reckon maybe half again as many folk at arms.'

'You know what this means?'

'Ach, well,' sighed Fergal, 'it means we must content ourselves with only a dozen or so dog-eaters each.' He glanced at Conor and smiled. 'Hardly worth getting out of bed of a morning.'

Out from among the chariots, the Scálda ran, quickly forming three branches—one for each of the surrounding plains, the largest branch anchoring the centre with a flank on either side. The central branch moved out, advancing to the foot of the hill, their leather armour dull in the sun, their blade edges bright.

Conor took in the sight and called all the defenders on the hilltop to gather to him. When all were assembled, he called out in a loud voice, saying, 'Balor Berugderc, Lord of the Fomórai, King of the Scálda, has decided that today will be the last day of the Dé Danann in this worldsrealm. He has chosen to attack us here because he knows that Tara Hill was once the sacred centre of Eirlandia. The enemy believes that if he can defeat us here, then Eirlandia will fall to his hand, and the long invasion of our favoured island will at last be complete.

'So, today we fight, not for ourselves alone, but for the sovereignty of our lands and the survival of our race—but not *only* our race. For, if we fall, then other realms and races will fall in turn—the faéry will also be driven down into the darkness of oblivion, never to rise again.

'Now, the world may not heed our passing, nor remember the battles we fought and hardships we endured to survive against a cruel and merciless foe.

But, if the Tylwyth Teg and the Aes-sídhe and the faéry tribes in the Land of the Everliving are lost, then much of what we have loved and fought so hard to preserve will disappear and all creation will feel the loss—for the greater part of what we know of beauty and wonder in this worlds-realm will have been extinguished.

'Today we will face our great enemy in battle once again. But today we have the chance to lift the scourge that has laid waste to our homeland for far too many years. Here, on the Hill of Tara, we make our last stand. If we live then we will live here. If not, then we will remain here dead. We will not be moved.

'But take heart, my brothers and sisters, and know that we are not alone. For, though we may be few, we are joined in battle by the spirits of all Dé Danann warriors who have gone before us and gave their lives to drive this hateful enemy from our lands. Therefore, let each and every one of us bind courage to our hearts and souls, and we will triumph!'

Silence settled over the hilltop then—the silence of men and women who were, as Conor had said, binding courage to their hearts and souls. The fianna turned once more to the battle line, and those in the rearward ranks—the women, farmers, and craftsmen who had taken up arms or were maintaining the stocks of weapons—scattered to take up their places.

The Scálda battle horn sounded out across the plain below—a single long, rising blast. The enemy gave out a throaty growl and started up the hill once more. In two howling, bone-trembling waves they came. And they came fast.

To drown out the hateful sound, the fianna raised their own voices, calling on Badb, the Blood-lusting Queen of the Halls of Darkness and Death, to guide their blades and welcome eager guests to her gruesome banquet. The warriors shouted crude insults and wild challenges and mad exaltations to the sun-washed sky as the enemy horde thundered ever nearer. Tara's besieged defenders banged the ringed and riveted spear shafts against the sturdy rims of their shields, and the resulting clangour resounded across Tara and everyone knew the battle had at last begun in earnest.

'Crom Cruach is hungry, brothers!' Conor shouted, resuming his position behind the line, ready to provide support where needed. 'He wants fresh meat for his feast.'

The first wave of attackers to reach the hilltop hurled themselves at the defenders' shield wall. The resulting crash sent a sympathetic tremor through Conor's frame and he could have sworn the ground trembled beneath his feet. His crimson birthmark pricked and burned with a smouldering heat, and Pelydr took life in his hands. The defending line buckled but held, and the fianna went to work—stabbing, jabbing, slashing—and soon their keen-edged blades ran red. Shrieking their hateful battle cry, the Scálda swarmed, lashing out at any flesh present-ing itself to view. The metallic clash of blade on blade, shield rim, and helmet quenched all other sound, and even dimmed the cries of the wounded and dying.

Conor ranged swiftly to and fro behind the battle line, darting and diving to deliver a thrust here, a swift stab there, a slash, a jab— supporting a struggling or outnumbered defender. Fergal did the same, as did Médon, and it soon became apparent that the advantage of the hilltop was slowly countering the enemy's superior numbers: there was simply not enough room on the crown of the hill for the enemy to exert their dominance. Any Scálda not in the front rank could not drive past the crush at the fighting line. Prevented by their own warriors from engag-ing, the largest portion of the enemy battle group was effectively removed from the fight. So long as the fianna held the hilltop and kept the line tight, they could stand.

A faéry blade or two would be useful just now, he thought. *If only Gwydion was still alive.*

The battle frenzy quickly exhausted itself, and the Scálda fell back, leaving behind two score of their own dead and wounded. Seeing the foe retreat, the defenders sent up a shout of triumph. Conor pushed forward to see the enemy running down the hill; but, as they fled, the second wave was charging up to take their place and a third was moving out from among the chariot ranks, ready to make the ascent up the hill.

In this, Conor grasped the shape of the enemy's battle plan: like the sea pounding on the rocky shore, Balor would send wave after wave to wear down the defenders' resistance and, ultimately, break it. Balor's forces were virtually unlimited; he could lose scores, hundreds. He would attack again and again, without pause, without rest, sending surge after surge of fresh warriors until the fianna were simply too exhausted to lift blade or shield. There were simply too many Scálda. Sooner or later, the numbers would tell. In the end, the beleaguered defenders would succumb to fatigue or wounds. The slaughter would be complete. The last Dé Danann would fall and the Scálda would take Tara.

Pushing the thought aside, Conor called to Médon to take his place and ran to confer with Rónán and the druids.

'Can you do anything, brother?' he asked when he had explained Balor's likely strategy. 'A storm might help,' he suggested. 'The wind and rain saved us the night of the massacre. It could help us again.'

'We thought of that, and the ollamhs and filidh are at work as we speak. But it takes time. Just now we have a better idea,' Rónán replied. 'Donal told us about the battle horn and we have a remedy.'

'Do it,' Conor said. 'Don't wait. Do it now!' With that, Conor raced back to the marge of the hill, where the fianna were bracing for the second assault.

As before, the enemy's chief tactic was to hurl themselves at the shield wall and break through a weak place, or force a gap they could exploit.

'Shoulder to shoulder!' cried Fergal, shouting to be heard above the rising tumult. 'Tighten the line!'

Conor resumed his place and, scanning the fianna ranged before him, saw one warrior bravely striving against two sword-wielding assailants—one of which had snagged his spear and was trying to wrest it away while one of the others slashed away at the outmanned defender. Leaping to the warrior's aid, Conor charged in, Pelydr straight and level and eager in his hand. A swift thrust of the charmed blade sent one of the attackers reeling backward; another quick jab and the second Scálda swordsman scrambled for safer footing elsewhere. The freed warrior shouted his thanks, and Conor saw that it was Aedd.

Conor turned back to the fight and an instant later a breach opened a few paces to the left. One of the fianna had taken a blow from a Scálda shield boss full in the face and had dropped to his knees. With a whoop of triumph, the Scálda leapt through the gap, hacking at the defenceless warrior as he passed.

Conor dove for the spot and met the Scálda brute as he clambered to his feet. Right behind him a second attacker bashed his way through the slender gap to join the first. Conor had time to shout a warning that the shield wall was breached, and then he had his hands full as the two helmeted Scálda bore down on him in a frenzy of slashing blades.

Conor went to work.

Crouching low behind his charmed shield, Conor launched himself at the nearest assailant. Bulling forward, he slammed Pared into the onrushing foe. Shield met shield and the crash staggered the attacker and sent him reeling. As he fell back, Conor pivoted to the second assailant, sweeping Pelydr in a lethal arc. The shaft of the charmed spear connected with the iron rim of the Scálda shield with a shattering crack; the shield flew sideways, allowing Conor to slide the blade into the attacker's side. The spearhead met hard leather. Conor threw his weight into the blow and felt the blade pierce the armour. The warrior stumbled back, dropped his spear, and fell.

Conor swung around and caught the first attacker as he regained his feet and drove in again. Throwing Pared before him, Conor slammed into his assailant again, and again. Unbalanced, the Scálda's heavy shield flew wide, and Conor drove Pelydr's sleek head into the centre of the black-armoured chest. The blow threw the Scálda off his feet. He squirmed and thrashed, trying to rise, and then slumped and relaxed his grip on life.

Spinning on his heel, Conor shouted to the downed defender, 'Are you wounded? Can you fight?'

The warrior clambered unsteadily to his feet. He was bleeding from a cut to his forehead, and a dark bruise was already forming on the side of his head. 'Only a scrape,' he called back. 'I can fight.' He took up his weapons and lurched to the line.

Fergal, raw-voiced, his face blue and fierce, was shouting encouragement to the fianna, praising their stamina and valour. The Dé Danann's stalwart defence seemed to anger the Scálda all the more. In the grip of their battle frenzy, they threw themselves upon the shield line time and time again.

Above the battle din, Conor heard someone call his name and cast a quick glance over his shoulder. He saw Donal, Rónán, and two filidh hurrying toward the battle line; the druids, having stripped off their outer robes, wore only their mantles, which they had gathered to their knees and belted, and in their hands they clutched slender curved objects. Behind them, some little distance away, the ollamhs and filidh had formed a semicircle and linked arms.

'This will only work once' were the first words out of Rónán's mouth. 'If it works at all.' At Conor's questioning glance, he added, 'The deception, I mean.'

Conor looked doubtfully at the three objects in the druids' hands: each held a ram's horn such as shepherds sometimes used. 'Do it!' Conor shouted as he turned to counter another surge. 'We're about to lose the line! Do it now!'

Raising his hand above his head, Donal turned to the druids. He gave out a shout and the druids raised the ram's horns to their lips. Donal dropped his hands and Conor saw the druids' cheeks puff out as they blew into their improvised battle horns.

The resulting sound emitted from the instruments was much as Conor would have expected—a thin wavering bleat that hardly penetrated as far as the battle line. If anyone heard it at all, they gave no sign.

At the sound, the ollamhs and filidh who stood looking on raised their hands, and a low sonorous chant snaked through the air. Suddenly, the weak, wavery bleat became the brilliant, high-pitched, ear-shattering blast of an enormous bronze battle carnyx.

The sound splintered the air, shimmering with a metallic clarion call. Rónán and the druids sounded their ram's horns, and three times the carnyx sounded. It lasted only an instant, but that was enough. Like dogs trained to their handler's whistle, the Scálda fell back in retreat. The rearward enemy ranks turned and bolted down the hill, leaving those at the battle line exposed; these did not wait, but abandoned the attack and fled after them. The shrill cry of the horn was still resounding across the plain as the last of the attackers fled the fight.

The fianna, seeing the enemy quit the field, raised a throaty cheer and shouted abuse and derision at those who, only moments before, had been on the verge of overwhelming Tara's overstrained defence.

Conor watched the last of Balor's warhost fleeing for the plain and then hurried to congratulate Rónán, Donal, and the druids and thank them for their good service. 'It worked!' cried Conor, thumping Donal soundly on the back by way of commendation. 'You did it!'

'We've gained a breathing space is all,' Donal told him. 'The dog-eaters will attack again.'

'They will, aye. And we'll be ready.' Conor saw the sudden change in Donal's expression; his dark eyes took on a faraway look that Conor had seen before. 'What is it, brother? What are you seeing?'

Donal's reply was slow in coming. His features relaxed and he looked at Conor. 'Somone's coming,' he said at last.

'Friend or foe?' asked Conor.

'I don't know.' Donal closed his eyes and shook his head. The vision was gone. 'It was like nothing I've ever seen before.'

33

'How soon?' asked Conor, craning his neck around to look back across the hilltop—beyond the hall, past the Lia Fáil, past the Tomb of the Kings—toward the little-used eastern approach. 'I don't see—'

'They're already here!' Donal started off on the run.

'Who?' shouted Conor. When Donal failed to answer, Conor called to Médon and told him that he was leaving the line, then raced after Donal and caught up with him as he reached the broken pillar of the Lia Fáil. 'Brother, wait! Who is it? Who have you seen?'

'I thought . . . ,' said Donal, dark eyes scouring the area: warriors clustered on the rim of the hill . . . smiths repairing weapons, women bearing baskets and bundles of food . . . 'I was that sure . . .' Disappointed, he turned to Conor. 'I thought they had arrived.'

'You were not wrong, my friend.' The disembodied voice came from somewhere beyond the Pillar Stone.

It was a voice Conor knew and recognised. He turned toward the sound. 'Can it be?'

He caught a movement out of the corner of his eye—a subtle shifting of the light, a wrinkle in the air—and a slender figure took shape and solidity before his eyes. Dressed in bright-burnished armour decorated with sprays of stars and crescent moons, and a high-crested helmet with a veil of interlocking gold rings, the strange figure raised its gloved hands and removed its helmet.

'Rhiannon!' cried Conor, running to greet her.

A second bronze-clad warrior solidified in the air beside Rhiannon and likewise removed a veiled helmet. 'Our journey here took longer than I anticipated,' he explained. 'I am sorry we could not come sooner.'

'On my sword, I never thought to see you again at all,' said Conor. 'Welcome, Lord Morfran.'

'We had hoped to join you before the enemy arrived in force.' The faéry king looked toward the besieged hill. 'At least, before the battle commenced.' Striding forward, he stood before Conor and gripped his arm in the warrior's embrace. 'Even so, I trust we are not too late to be of some aid to you now.'

'Whatever happens,' said Donal, joining them just then, 'we will remember you came to help when help was sorely needed.'

The faéry greeted Donal, and Rhiannon said, 'Truly, our delay was of necessity.' She slid the slim blade in her hand into a sword belt at her side. 'Although we were more than willing to come alone, Morfran argued that any support we provided would be that much more potent if we brought friends.'

Morfran's stern features arranged themselves into a rueful smile. 'This, too, took more time and effort than I imagined.'

'Friends, you say?' said Donal, glancing around quickly. 'Who is with you?'

Morfran half turned and, with a wave of his hand, summoned three more warriors encased head to foot in battle gear that appeared as if it might have been carved from stone. With odd angles and many joints, it shone with the dull lustre of slate cut, perhaps, from the roots of a mountain; the helmets, gloves, and leggings were adorned with jagged ridges, and the surface of the each item was chased with symbols and charms. In their gloved hands they each carried a silvery sword of a kind Conor had seen before: strong iron. The warrior removed the stone-coloured headpiece to reveal the long, narrow face of the Kerionid king.

'Lenos!' exclaimed Conor. 'I never thought to see you again, either.'

'It is time we repaid the debt we owe a friend.' The faéry king gestured to the two with him, who removed their helmets to reveal his advisors, Armadal and Sealbach. 'I regret we did not come sooner, but I trust our blades will more than make up for the delay.'

Conor looked from Lenos to Morfran. 'How?' was all he could think to say.

'A tale for another time,' replied Morfran. 'But suffice to say, Rhiannon supplied the voice of reason.'

'I merely reminded my lord of the sacrifices you and your people have made on our behalf, and how you have proved your friendship through suffering and blood,' replied Rhiannon. 'Morfran and Lenos did the rest.'

Conor glanced behind Lenos across the hilltop. 'And are there more of you?'

'No,' replied Lenos. 'Only these you see before you.'

Morfran saw the look on Conor's face and guessed its meaning. 'Do not be disheartened, my friend. Our ways in battle are not yours.'

'We are here to aid you,' explained Lenos, 'and to that end, we have brought you a gift.' He gestured to Armadal, who released a strap holding a bundle slung upon his back. He knelt and unrolled the soft leather and there were seven new swords made of strong iron.

'These are for you and your men,' Lenos said. Stooping, he withdrew a long, thin blade from the pile and held it across his palms and presented it to Conor. 'I would there were more, but what we have, we give you to use as you see fit.'

'Is this the haranbar you told us about?' asked Donal, taking up one of the blades. He slashed the air a few times to try its balance. 'Lucky the fella who has one of these. We'll soon put them to the test.'

'And you will be more than pleased when you see the way these blades perform,' Lenos told him. 'The best blades of the Scálda are no match for these.'

They then had to decide how best to employ the faéry and quickly came up with a plan and, while Donal and the faéry considered it further, Conor hurried to speak to Fergal and Médon, who were keeping watch at the battle line.

'Only five?' said Fergal when Conor had explained the plan. 'Do you *want* to die today? If that is your heart's desire, this crackbrained idea of yours should succeed right well.'

'Five warriors is all I need,' Conor told him. 'There are five faéry—one for each Dé Danann.'

'The faéry are here?' said Médon. 'And they agreed with this? You're certain?'

'Aye, they did,' Conor insisted. 'Lenos and Morfran both. They know we must do something to stem the Scálda tide—and that soon, otherwise

Tara will be overrun. If not the next attack, then the one after. We dare not wait.'

Médon looked to Fergal. 'It's true. We cannot hold this line much longer. The Scálda were this close to breaking us last time.'

'You're with him in this?' Fergal said, his voice rising in disbelief. He looked around to where the faéry stood watching.

'Well?' said Conor impatiently. 'If you have a better idea, I'm eager to hear it. But we have to do *something*, and do it quick.'

'We won't survive the day,' Médon declared flatly. 'That is the sorry truth.'

Fergal wiped the sweat from his face and spat on the ground at his feet. 'I don't like it.'

'The chance of success is a narrow thing at best. I know that, brother. But unless I hear a better plan—'

'Aye, so you said. When will you go?'

'Now. Before the Scálda mount another assault.' Conor went on to explain that it would take a little time to work their way around behind the Scálda encampment on the plain. 'Once we're in position, we'll strike.'

'And then?' wondered Médon.

Conor flashed a sudden grin. 'And then we'll see if this monster has a head.'

34

'I wear this loathsome gear,' said Conor, 'but my true garment is my woad.' Holding out his arms, he turned around in a slow circle. 'How do I look?'

Donal surveyed Conor and the four behind him with a critical eye. 'Close enough, I reckon—so long as no one looks too close.'

'The truth, brother. Will we pass?'

'Ach, well, it won't do to press it overmuch, but keep moving and you should evade the hasty glance.' He nodded firmly. 'Anyway, if the faéry do their job, you won't be needing any of this. Then again, you need all the help you can get. It'll do.'

Although it made Conor's stomach squirm he had donned Scálda armour removed from dead enemy combatants on the field. The dusky leather breastplate and leggings, the horsetail helmet, and heavy round shield might disguise him well enough. Unwilling to leave his charmed shield behind, Conor also slung Pared onto his back as well. Galart, Aedd, Calbhan, and Diarmaid—the four chosen to accompany Conor—had retrieved their own battle gear and now all five stood dressed in the rough guise of a Scálda raiding party. Their weapons, however, were of the more superior kind supplied by the faéry. These they daubed with mud to reduce their innate brilliance.

Aoife, having learned of the faéries' arrival and Conor's plan, came to bid her husband farewell. Got up in Scálda armour, he hardly looked himself. His strange appearance made parting even more difficult than she imagined it would be, and she could not suppress a gasp when she saw him. Conor heard her sharp intake of breath and, stepping close, took her hand.

'If there was another way, I would take it,' he told her, keeping his voice low. 'I do this for you, for Ciara, for everything we cherish and hold dear. This is the only way I know.'

The low, guttural rumble of thunder, like the grumble of a slowly awakening god, sounded across the hilltop. Instinctively, both Conor and Aoife glanced up. The sky, bright and cloudless only moments before, now lowered with dark, angry clouds. Lightning scattered shadows in all directions and the resulting thunder trembled the ground beneath their feet. From the yard outside the hall there arose a strange, ululating wail as Rónán, Eoghan, and all the higher-ranking druids strode purposefully to the edge of the hill. They planted themselves at the end of the battle line and there they stood: heads thrown back, hands raised high, a low droning chant issuing from somewhere deep in their chests. With a scathing curse in the secret language of the Dark Tongue, they conjured a storm to break upon the heads of the enemy. The force of their voices, combined and united in a single, unending note, sent a chill through the bowels of everyone who heard it.

Aoife put a hand to Conor's chin and turned his head to look at her. 'I will always trust you, my heart,' she said, unable to keep the quaver of emotion from her voice. She leaned in, kissed him quickly, and released him, saying, 'Go and do what you have to do to save us.'

With a last embrace, Conor led his four chosen fianna to the eastern side of the hill, where the faéry were ready and waiting. Aoife watched them troop off and caught sight of Princess Rhiannon, almost radiant in her peerless armour, reaching out and putting a hand on Conor's arm. The sight of the two of them together sent a sudden pang of jealous longing through her. She averted her eyes abruptly, pushed the unworthy thought from her, and made her way back to the hall to help with the wounded warriors.

Conor paired each of the fianna with one of the faéry, matching them as seemed best to him. When he was happy with the arrangement, he addressed his little band. 'What we're about to do we do not only for the survival of both our races today, but for the survival of Eirlandia, Albion, and Cymru tomorrow.'

Reaching out, he put a hand on Médon's shoulder and gathered the fianna with his eyes. 'My friends . . . my good and faithful friends, I expect nothing less than the courage I have seen in you and know you all to possess. Call on that courage now and, whatever may befall us today, let us acquit ourselves with honour in the midst of our enemies.'

Grim-faced, the fianna and faéry voiced their assent. Turning to Rhiannon, Conor gave a nod, and the faéry princess raised her hand palm outward and addressed the fianna, saying, 'You and your lord have taken on the appearance of the enemy so that you may pass among the foe unobserved and, with every hope, unhindered. But you should know that the Tylwyth Teg have long possessed this quality and raised it to an art through our mystical skills. I will now touch each of you with a charm of concealment and you will be paired with one of the fair folk so that the charm will retain its potency long enough to allow us to penetrate the enemy line. After that, we must all rely on our skill at arms. May Danu lend strength to our arms, courage to our hearts, and cunning to our minds.'

Morfran took over and quickly ordered the warriors into Conor's selected pairs and said, 'Prepare yourselves to receive the enchantment of our people, a gift to you from those for whom you fight today. Open your hearts and minds and believe in the righteousness of our cause, and remember— you fight not only for the life of your people today, but also for the continued light of your people in this worlds-realm for ages to come.'

So saying, he took his place among the warriors, and Rhiannon, stepping before each pair of warriors in turn, traced a strange sign in the air and, with a light touch to each forehead, spoke the words of the concealment charm in the tongue of her people. One by one, the warriors faded from view. Lastly, she made the charm for Conor and herself, and put her hand to his belt. The charm took force and Conor could once again see his men—though it was as if he saw them through a film of mist; around each pair a vague, watery nimbus shimmered.

Satisfied that the faéry magic was working, Conor gave the signal to move out and they started down the hillside. Each of the faéry would hold tight to a defender's belt and in this way remain in constant contact to enable the charm to work as long as possible. Crouching low, and keeping to the natural ditches and gulleys carved into the rocky slope, the raiders made a somewhat laboured, awkward descent of Tara Hill's steep eastern side. They had almost reached Mag Rí when the storm broke. The air gusted with a sudden blast of icy wind, and rain began to pelt down in big, hard drops. Within moments, the hilltop was awash in driving rain and

Tara was surrounded by a dense curtain of water. Thunder boomed and lightning flared; rain lashed the upper slopes, fierce and cold, turning to a sharp, stinging hail.

Upon reaching the foot of the hill, the little raiding party flitted across the plain and ran for the surrounding wood. Once well into the shelter of the trees, they began working their way around the perimeter of Mag Rí toward Mag Teamhair, picking their way through the close-grown thickets of elder and bramble and stands of hazel and birch, thankful that the storm masked the sound and movement of their passing. Even so, it was tense work and tedious. As he navigated their path, Conor turned in his thoughts to the coming confrontation and how he might make best use of his brief advantage and avoid the numerous dangers before him. He did not allow himself to consider whether he would survive the fight; instead, he desired, above all else, merely to locate Balor Berugderc and get in close enough to strike. That was his sole aim and desire, and if he could accomplish that, he would trust Pelydr do the rest.

Eventually, the charmed company reached a position Conor judged well behind the enemy encampment. Allowing the others to rest a moment, Conor and Rhiannon went on ahead to spy out the field and determine exactly how the enemy was positioned and what obstacles they would encounter upon leaving the shelter of the wood. The trees and brushy undergrowth thinned as the two crept nearer the open plain, and they began to hear battle sounds on the distant hilltop. Nearer still, the sound of the clash grew louder until the cover of the woodland gave way to a view of Tara Plain spreading before them with the hill looming in the near distance beyond. Closer, they could now see what they could observe only dimly from the hilltop: scores of small camps clustered around crude tent-like shelters scattered from one end of the plain to the other and spilling over onto Mag Coinnem.

Beyond these camps, innumerable ranks of horses on picket lines and empty chariots waited to be called into action. Farther on, past the horse pickets and war carts, stood the Scálda warhost, spreading across the plain and swarming up the slopes of Tara Hill, where storm clouds roiled and churned—strange and lurid and threatening. Rain fell in sheets, wreathing the hilltop in a veritable curtain of water, sluicing down the slopes, and channelling into rivulets and runnels, saturating the ground and making the footing treacherous for combatants at the sharp end of the fighting as well as for those attempting to climb the increasingly slippery paths. The storm, as much as the crush along the battle line at the top, prevented the main body of the enemy attack force from advancing and overwhelming the defences.

Conor scanned the Plain of Tara, marking how the Scálda chariots were arranged, looking for anything that might indicate where Balor had established his command post. He spied a sizeable buildup of men and horses in the centre of the plain surrounded by what appeared to be supply wagons. 'If I was Balor, that's where I'd be,' Conor whispered. 'We'll try there first.'

The two crept back into the cover of the wood and returned to where the others were waiting. 'Fergal and the fianna are holding their own up there,' Conor reported, rubbing his cheek with the smooth shaft of his spear. 'The druids' storm has stalled the fighting up there for now, so we have a small space to work. Stay close together and however tempting it might be, do not strike out at the enemy unless you are attacked. It is crowded on the plain, and getting close to Balor will be difficult enough without drawing unnecessary attention to ourselves.' Conor glanced into every face to make sure his instructions were understood. 'Remember, Balor is the only foe we seek. Find him, and the battle is ours.'

The charmed company moved to the edge of the wood and paused briefly to look out onto the scattered Scálda encampments and survey the wider battlefield. Conor did not allow the sight of the enemy hordes to overawe his men. Swinging his shield into place, he pointed with his spear and declared, 'Somewhere out there Balor Evil Eye awaits the doom that he has earned ten thousand times over. We won't keep him waiting any longer.'

35

Conor drew a breath and, with Rhiannon right beside him, stepped cautiously out onto the verge of the Tara Plain. He signalled the others to follow and moved on quickly. Veiled by the faéry charm of concealment, they headed for the nearest Scálda camp in the centre of the plain. Silent as fog and invisible as air, they crossed the lumpy, uneven ground—chewed and broken by the passing of many horses, chariots, and feet—and reached the first of the outlying enemy camps.

Little more than a shabby scrap of a tent and a fire ring, the camp was deserted; every last Scálda warrior was somewhere among the battle groups massed out on the plain and around the hill. Lines of empty chariots had been drawn up behind the enemy warhost with a corridor of sorts separating the war carts from the Scálda horde. Along this passageway, footmen and riders and chariots came and went in constant motion. Conor, with Rhiannon's slim hand gripping his belt and her footsteps following his own, proceeded directly to the ranks of waiting chariots where he paused again to survey the battleground. Some little distance to the northwest, he caught sight of a dense knot of enemy warriors clustered around a slightly raised mound.

'Just there,' he whispered, indicating the slight elevation and surrounding Scálda throng as the four fianna and their faéry escorts gathered around him. 'If Evil Eye is out there, I'm thinking *that* is where he'll be found.'

'Reaching him won't be easy,' Lenos pointed out. 'So many bodies close about.'

'We'll have to work quickly—get in fast before they know we're there,' suggested Galart.

'Will the charm hold long enough for us to get there?' wondered Aedd. Rhiannon looked doubtful. 'I cannot say.'

'It doesn't matter,' said Conor. 'We are disguised enough to pass among them if we just keep moving. Rhiannon and I will lead the way. Stay close and stay alert.'

Out from among the empty vehicles and into the wide grassy corridor they ran, dodging the horsemen and war carts passing along the strip. All the while, Conor kept his eye on the mound in the near distance, trying to discern what was happening there; as they drew closer, he became ever more convinced that Balor was there directing the battle. So tightly packed were those around the elevated vantage point, however, that getting in close enough to strike soon became an ordeal requiring steady nerve and nimble footwork as they stole ever closer to the mound Conor had identified.

Halfway across the gap, and Conor was sweating in his ungainly, ill-fitting armour. Owing to the continual rush of chariots and men, the passage was proving more fraught than he imagined and it was taking all his stealth and skill to avoid colliding with one or the other as they raced back and forth behind the lines. From time to time, he heard Rhiannon breathe a word of warning or encouragement as they moved over the uneven ground in an awkward stop-and-go lockstep to avoid a racing chariot or a troop of hustling Scálda.

The mound lay just ahead, and Conor was searching for a way through the thronging enemy when Diarmaid gave out a strangled shout. He spun around to see his crew strung out some way behind him—and Aedd and Sealbach standing directly in the path of an onrushing chariot. Diarmaid shouted again and the two dived out of the way, rolling aside a hair's breadth from the pounding hooves and wheels.

Aedd lost his grip on his spear as he fell, and the long shaft was kicked by one of the horses and flipped up into the harness, where it caught. The animal stumbled. The chariot slewed sharply sideways, tipped, and spilled the occupants onto the ground. The terrified horses continued to run, dragging the overturned cart into the ranks of enemy footmen. Within a heartbeat, Scálda were scattering in every direction as the runaway cart and horses ploughed into the throng of swarming bodies.

Instantly, half the Scálda host was caught up in the collision and the other half was thrown into confusion. The cursing and shouting drew the attention of the Scálda on the mound. One of the Scálda chieftains barked a command and several warriors leapt to obey; pushing through the mob, they ran to take control of a situation that was quickly descending into chaos.

As more warriors on the mound turned their attention to the commotion in the ranks around them, Conor saw his chance.

With Rhiannon at his back, he dove unseen into the rapidly thinning host. Darting through gaps, halting, feinting to one side and then the other, and, when he could not avoid it, shoving an unwary warrior out of the way with his shield, Conor advanced. The fianna and their faéry escorts followed in his wake, employing all their cunning to avoid colliding with the foe. They reached the mound—a crude hillock made of earth and turves hastily hacked from the ground and piled into a great lumpen dune to allow Balor an elevated view of the Scálda battle groups scattered across the plain. Conor started up the side of the earthen knoll, but Rhiannon pulled him back. 'Conor,' she whispered with harsh urgency, 'your legs!'

He looked down and saw that the watery aura that had so far surrounded him was fading: first his legs and then his entire lower half were taking on substance. Magic spent, the concealing charm had done its work; it was finished. The much-distracted enemy failed to notice this bizarre transformation, however; Conor did not wait to be discovered. Raising Pelydr, he said, 'Let me go.'

Rhiannon, still clinging to his belt, refused. 'I'm staying with you.'

'Let me go, Rhiannon. This is my fight!'

'Take him, Conor,' she said, releasing her hold. 'End it!'

Conor sprang forward. The enemy parted and there stood Balor Berugderc, Lord of the Fomórai, King of the Scálda—looking much the same as the day Conor first saw him: the matted hanks of thick black hair, the livid scar that cleft his face from chin to brow and left him with a malevolent stare and twisted his mouth into a vicious snarl. The one-eyed king wore the long siarc of heavy leather studded with tiny triangular iron plates and he carried a two-handed iron sword with a grip of braided silver. An oversized chair made of ox bones and covered in horsehide had been set up atop the mound—a battle throne from which to command his troops. Leaning against the throne was a large, round oaken shield with an iron rim, bearing the image of a coiled serpent. Standing next to Balor was one of his commanders, a thick-bodied brute with a tangled mane of thick black hair and a braided beard. At their feet, a black pot sat on a smudgy fire giving off aromatic fumes of darkly pungent incense.

Six flying steps took Conor to the foot of the mound. The fianna and faéry, visible now, trailed behind and strove to keep up. Away on Tara Hill, thunder crashed, booming out across the plain. The rain and hail drenched the upper heights, impeding the assault and driving the stragglers down the increasingly slippery slope. For Conor, however, that tumult became a blur and distant thrum—like that of surf tumbling rocks on a beach. He saw only Balor—standing beside his chair, waving his sword back and forth as he shouted commands to his battlechiefs ranged below the mound.

Throwing aside his ungainly Scálda shield, Conor swung Pared into position, lowered Pelydr, and charged. Balor, his attention still occupied with the battle elsewhere, did not see Conor closing on him, but the Scálda battlechief beside him did. The enemy chief shouted a warning and, raising his sword, stepped into Conor's path. Pelydr's charmed blade easily penetrated the Scálda's thick leather chestplate, burying its head deep in his side. The chieftain gasped and fell back, releasing his sword. He clutched at the spear as he fell and took the charmed weapon with him. Conor released the shaft and drew the blade Eirian from his belt.

With a savage growl, Balor yanked the spear free and squared off. He raised his heavy iron sword and swung once, twice, and a third time in quick succession, trying to drive Conor back down the side of the mound. Conor parried the first blow, ducked the second, and lunged as Balor's third swipe went wide. With a neat upward flick, Eirian caught the Scálda lord's right arm on the outward stroke and the razor-sharp blade opened a livid gash. Balor jerked away, swinging hard on the backstroke. The strike was clumsy and ill-timed; Conor easily evaded it and let Pared take the hit. The charmed shield shivered under the force of the blow, but did not dent or crack.

Conor sprang back fast. Balor, blood streaming down his arm, gathered himself, and drove in again hard. Conor planted his feet and prepared to meet his assailant blow for blow and thrust for thrust. The faéry sword seemed to take life in his grasp, quivering in its eagerness to strike.

Conor let the charmed blade have its way.

Again and again, Conor swung and Eirian sang, dealing out a dizzying series of savage strokes. Pressed hard, the Scálda war king deflected each and every one with the battle-honed skill of a seasoned warrior. But Conor's fevered onslaught began to exact a toll: Balor's iron sword was slowly bending, the edge growing scored, notched. Soft Scálda iron was no match for the otherworldly strength of the faéry blade.

Enraged, seething, his eyes ablaze with hatred, Balor was forced to give ground. Sweat streamed down his face and neck; his hair was wet and plastered to his head; blood coursed down his arm. Wiping his hand on his leather tunic, he snatched up his shield from beside his ox-bone throne, fitted it to his arm, and began beating on the shield rim while shouting in his loathsome tongue. Roaring, raging, spittle flying from his fleshy lips, the Scálda king jeered and taunted, defying Conor to come for him.

Conor, too, stepped back, and began pulling on the straps fastening his Scálda armour. Suddenly, Rhiannon was there; her deft fingers worked the laces, and the hard leather carapace fell away. Piece by piece, Conor threw off the repulsive enemy battle gear, shedding the thick chest plate, the leggings, and the pointed, horsetail helmet. Half naked, he stood before his great adversary as a true blue-painted Dé Danann warrior.

'You are free, Conor,' said Rhiannon, stepping away. 'Finish it!'

Planting his feet wide apart, Conor cried a challenge: 'Come to me, Evil Eye! Meet the doom you have earned ten thousand times!'

Balor put back his huge, shaggy head and loosed a deafening roar. He gathered himself and charged, throwing his serpent shield before him. Conor braced himself for the impact, then made a subtle half turn as Balor closed on him. Balor's shield met Pared at an angle and slid off, leaving him momentarily unprotected. Conor saw the opening and struck out. The charmed blade bit effortlessly into a crease in the Scálda king's iron-studded leather even as Conor spun away. Balor cried out—more in anger than pain. Off-footed and unbalanced, the Scálda king rocked back on his heels. He swung his sword in wild desperation, but Conor was already out of reach.

Growling, snarling yellow teeth clamped in a grimace of monstrous fury, the Fomórai lord lumbered toward him, cursing in his abhorrent tongue as he came. The instant Conor was certain Balor had committed to the charge, he dropped his sword, leapt to his right, spun, and grabbed the shaft of Pelydr. The spear, still embedded in the Scálda chieftain's armour, stood at a slight upward angle, and Conor gave it a hefty yank and pulled the trapped blade free. Spinning around, he slammed the butt of the spear into Balor's serpent shield with all his strength; the oak splintered and cracked from top to bottom. Balor staggered and almost went down.

Before Balor could recover, Conor thumped him again in the same place, and then again. Each knock rang with a clear, resounding note as splinters and chunks of oak spun away. After the fourth hammering, Conor could see daylight through the crack.

Balor, foaming with rage and frustration, lashed out. With wild, scything sweeps of his ragged iron blade, he bulled forward, bellowing as he came. Conor was forced back a step, and then another. With a mighty cry, Balor swung his cracked shield. The edge hooked Conor's shield, pulling it aside just enough to allow the Scálda king to slash at Conor's throat.

Conor reeled backward and the snaggled blade raked his upper chest. Stinging pain blazed through him, bringing tears to his eyes. The acrid scent of blood filled his nostrils and he tasted the sharp, coppery taste of blood on his tongue. Beads of bright crimson welled from the cut and oozed down Conor's naked torso, blending with the blue woad tattoo.

Crouching low, Conor gathered himself and leapt, launching himself full stretch at his assailant, throwing Pared before him. The collision caused chunks of broken oak to fall from the serpent shield. The Scálda king staggered back on his heels, but did not go down.

From somewhere in the distance came the unmistakable blare of a battle carnyx, its flat, metallic call floating out across the plain. There were sounds of the clash, too, from the foot of the mound, where the faéry and fianna, their strong iron blades scarlet and streaming, toiled to secure the perimeter of the mound and, if not able to help Conor, then at least prevent any aid from reaching Balor or taking Conor from behind.

Balor, reeling from the clash, steadied himself, gave out a groan, and attacked with a flurry of wild, desperate blows. Conor easily avoided some of these and parried others, but Balor bulled ahead, slashing with his sword, again and again and again, forcing Conor back and back.

Labouring now, his breath coming in rasping gulps and gasps, Balor swung his wrecked shield like a bludgeon, trying to knock Conor off his feet. Seeing his enemy's strength ebbing away, Conor gave ground. The two circled one another, each wary, watching for an advantage to exploit. They passed the ox-bone throne and Conor happened to step in the little fire ring next to the chair. His foot struck the iron smudge pot; the pot rolled beneath his foot and Conor stumbled, losing his spear as he fell. He slammed to the ground, throwing up a cloud of smoke and sparks and hot ash.

Balor was on him in a heartbeat.

Rolling on his back, Conor attempted to fend off the attack. Slashing this way and that, the Scálda king tried to beat down Conor's defences with a sustained burst of brutal, hacking blows. Time and again, Conor saw Balor's arm rise and the iron sword sweep down upon him; and each time Pared absorbed a blow that would have ruined a normal shield.

Conor, without a weapon now, saw the snarl on the brute's scar-twisted face, that perpetual sneer, the pitiless hatred firing the dark depths of that single baleful eye. He also saw that a sickly pallor had seeped into Balor's swarthy face as the Scálda king plied his jagged sword.

As Conor tightened his grip on his shield strap and tensed beneath the hammering blows, he felt someone take hold of his arm. The hilt of his sword Eirian was thrust into his hand, and Rhiannon's voice sounded in his ear. 'Finish it!'

Conor gripped the faéry blade and felt an uncanny calm settle upon him. The inflamed birthmark on Conor's cheek—a self-contained blaze until now—suddenly flared with a ferocious heat that seemed to envelop his entire being. Reaching down within himself, calling on his last reserve of strength, Conor raised Pared and, as Balor continued to batter away at him, Conor steadied himself and awaited his chance to strike.

That chance came when the battle horn sounded again, closer now, emanating from the far northern edge of the Tara Plain. From somewhere below, Galart gave out an almighty shout. 'Dé Danann!' he cried. 'The Dé Danann are coming!'

Balor looked toward the sound and gnashed his teeth in rage as a great, formless mass appeared, streaming in from the direction of Mag Rí. The battle horn sounded again and Balor lunged, throwing his ruined serpent shield before him. Conor saw the gaping hole in the shield and, without a flicker of hesitation, shoved Eirian through the breach, driving the razor-sharp blade into the Scálda king's exposed shoulder. The cut was vicious and deep into the muscle. Wounded, winded, Balor Berugderc threw back his head and bellowed his pain and frustration to the heavens.

'Call on her, Evil Eye!' Conor cried. 'Call on the Hag Queen! She is waiting for you!'

Balor answered with a bestial snarl of rage, hefted up his sword and let fly. The iron missile slammed into the charmed shield with a shock that Conor felt in his bones. But Pared held firm and the misshapen blade skidded away. Balor spun around, searching for a weapon. He spied Conor's spear on the ground a few paces away and went for it. He took two steps, slipped on the blood-slick ground, and stumbled to his knees, releasing his broken shield as he fell.

Conor flew to the attack.

Drawing back his arm, he delivered a stroke he had practiced a thousand times: a swift downward sweep of his fully extended arm. The unerring blow struck the Scálda king's exposed neck just below the skull even as Balor grasped the errant spear and half turned to rise.

The faéry blade sliced effortlessly through flesh and bone, carving the Scálda king's head from his shoulders and carrying his evil, shrunken soul into the next world. The headless torso hung suspended between rising and falling . . . and then crumpled into a lifeless heap.

Conor, his breath coming in great, gawping draughts, stood over the bleeding corpse of his great enemy. He felt none of the wild exultation he imagined he might feel in this moment. He felt neither remorse nor relief. If anything, he felt only the sweat on his back and the pulsing sting of the wound to his upper chest. Nothing more.

Suddenly, Rhiannon was there beside him. He felt her first, and then heard her voice. 'The victory is yours, my friend,' she said. 'It is over.' She retrieved Pelydr and handed the spear to him, then turned and shouted to Lenos and Morfran and the others at the foot of the mound. 'Balor is dead!' she called. 'Balor Evil Eye is defeated!'

Conor, his heart still racing, stared in disbelief, refusing to accept what his own senses were telling him. Balor Berugderc, the brutal scourge of his people, was dead—at long, long last . . . dead.

With his foot, Conor rolled the corpse and, taking up Evil Eye's crooked sword, plunged it into the unmoving chest—forcing the bent blade down, working it through the armoured tunic and layers of flesh and muscle and bone into the dead king's black heart. He plucked Balor's head from the ground and hoisted it by the hair to eye level and gazed at the viciously ugly features, now frozen forever in a grimace of agony and hate.

Then, taking the severed head in both hands, Conor raised it, and jammed it hard onto the hilt of Balor's upright sword. There was resistance at first, the severed veins and flesh of the windpipe and tongue, and the bones of the jaws and skull had to be broken and pierced. Again and again, Conor pounded the raw neck against the hilt, bashing through the meat and bone and gristle until at last the thing stuck: a grisly standard, a grotesque trophy for all the world to see.

The dreadful display produced an instant effect. Those nearest the mound witnessed their king's head perched on his sword and cringed at the sight. An unnatural silence spread out from the top of the mound, coursing through the Scálda ranks as word of Balor's death sped through the scattered enemy battle groups.

The carnyx blared again. Peering through watery eyes, Conor looked out across the plain toward the sound and glimpsed a mounted warband emerging from around the far shoulder of Tara Hill: a hundred or more Dé Danann warriors galloping to the fight. As the first of these pounded onto the plain, they were followed by another warband riding in hard right behind them.

The sudden appearance of these fresh mounted fighters plunged the now-leaderless enemy into instant disarray. The alarm already kindled by Balor's death ignited and flared. Like a grassfire driven before the gale of its own making, fear spread through the enemy ranks, and those nearest the fighting edge began falling away. Within moments, it seemed as if the entire plain was on the move in every direction at once. The mounted Dé Danann—led by Liam with Eamon at his side—charged onto the battlefield and a tremendous cry went up. The new arrivals laid into the Scálda invaders, and chariots, riders, and footmen began quitting the plain, racing for the shelter of the wood.

Conor took in the sight and waved his sword. He drew breath to call out to his brother and instead doubled over and vomited; his empty stomach dry-heaved and filled his mouth with sour bile, which he spat onto the ground. Wiping his mouth on his bare arm, he straightened and started down the side of the mound. He took a single step and halted, suddenly woozy. He felt as if his bones were made of stone and his limbs useless lumps of wood. It took every scrap of stamina to simply remain upright. His vision dimmed and black spots swarmed before his eyes, and the pain he had so far ignored broke fresh upon him. He looked down and saw that he was also bleeding from a deep cut to his upper thigh. How he had come by that he did not know, nor did he feel it at the time. But now, having seen it, he was aware of a throbbing fire radiating out from the gash.

Morfran, Galart, and Calbhan appeared atop the mound and hurried to him. 'Conor is injured,' Rhiannon told them. Morfran moved in close, concern etched upon his face. 'Why not sit down and let us have a look at your wounds?' he asked. He and Galart made to ease him down onto the grass.

'It's nothing.' Conor made a swipe at the blood oozing down his chest. 'A scratch is all.'

'We cannot stay here any longer,' called Lenos from the foot of the mound where he stood with Armadal and Sealbach. 'The Scálda may regroup.'

'He's right,' said Galart. 'We must go. One of Balor's battlechiefs will surely come to claim the throne.'

Conor turned on him. 'Let them!' he spat. 'They'll see their mighty king as he is.'

At a gesture, Galart and Calbhan hurried to Balor's corpse, took up the headless body, and dragged it to the chair. They arranged the lifeless lump of torso and limbs into a sitting position, and planted the iron sword at his right hand. Here, they left him: the Scálda king sprawled dead upon his ox-bone throne, his gaping head on his own battered sword, staring out at a land he would never rule, the notorious Evil Eye empty, vacant, blind.

Aoife

The blade that cut my Conor was poisoned. They brought him back to Tara out of his head, raving, one foot already in the grave and the other slipping down fast. Fresh from the battle, Galart, Aedd, Calbhan, and the faéry king Morfran carried him up from the plain and laid him on the board in the teeming hall among the other wounded and dying. Our fine hall was a turmoil of pain and anguish that day: men screaming, wives weeping, druids and women rushing here and there to help where they could. The noise . . . the stink . . . the throbbing fear that claws at the heart and chills the soul—these I'll remember always.

While Liam and the other lords with their lately come warhost drove the routed Scálda from the plain and pursued them into the forests round about, Banfaíth Orlagh, most skilled healer among the brehons, joined Rhiannon and together—head-to-head, working as one—the two hovered over Conor's wounds, searching their formidable knowledge for a cure. After a time, I became aware that Fergal and Donal, sweating and bloody from the field, stood with me at the foot of the board, helpless, their faces ashen, watching as Conor's life ebbed from him. Now and again, one of them would try to comfort me—though anyone could see they needed consolation every bit as much as I did.

Morfran sent an urgent appeal to Tír nan Óg for faéry physicians, who shortly arrived—do not ask me how—bringing their skills and rare medicines, and for more days than I like to recall, my best beloved hovered between this worlds-realm and the next. The druids and faéry worked together to heal Conor and all the other wounded among us, and under their most strenuous efforts, the Lord of Tara and his stricken people began slowly to recover.

Eirlandia herself was not so fortunate.

I expect the bards will make no end of stories about Balor Evil Eye's last battle and the valiant defence of Tara. These tales will be revered by many and, perhaps, even treasured through ages to come as the day our proud Dé Danann race stood tall in triumph. Right and fitting as that may be, the stories will fall far short of the mark. The bards will touch but lightly on the gore and stench, the waste and despair and heartbreak of that day and all the days that followed. And none will think to mention the crippling hardship that so swiftly snuffed the golden glow of our glorious victory.

Was there relief? Aye, we wept with relief. And joy—so full our battered souls could not contain the half of it. But it was sweetest joy mingled with a full measure of bitter grief. And even that was fleeting. Our joy at the defeat of the Scálda lasted but a day. The sorrow is with us still.

And if anyone imagined that our torment ended with Balor Evil Eye's death and the downfall of our great enemy on Tara Plain, that illusion faded with the first flush of victory. In truth, our last and hardest travail had only just begun.

The Scálda fled, as I say. Liam, through sheer effort of will, rallied the tribes. They say he cheated death a dozen times that day, and I do not doubt it. Somehow, evading the wiles and weapons of the Scálda, he broke through the enemy lines and, with stalwart Eamon by his side, reached Corgan of the Eridani. Fast riders raced with word to Cahir and the Coriondi, Torna and the Volunti, the Ulaid, Robogdi, and Concani, too—and all of them flew like avenging eagles to Tara's aid, keen to secure the victory and finish the rout that Conor and the fianna had started.

Without their lord and chieftain, the Scálda scattered—like leaves before a tempest gale they flew. They could not flee fast enough. Liam and the lords harried the retreating enemy warhost relentlessly and without cease, never giving them a chance to rest or breathe. Those Scálda nearest the coast ran to the sea and to the waiting Black Ships that had carried them north; others fled south in the hope of crossing the mountains and reaching safety in the stolen territories beyond the deadlands; others simply flailed about, scattering destruction in their wake.

But the pursuit was dogged, absolute, and unyielding. The desire to rid Eirlandia of the Scálda was vicious strong in every Dé Danann whose blood still ran quick and hot in the vein.

In our victory rapture, some voiced the hope that the scouring would be concluded in a day, or a week at most. But that hope, like many another, was born to disappointment. Indeed, winter was hard upon us before a few wounded, bedraggled troops of the Dé Danann warhost returned with word that the harrowing of the south had finally begun and would likely last the winter. Aye, and a hard, hard winter it was, too. What the hateful chariots did not churn up, the evil-minded enemy burned: crops, orchards, settlements. The fields around Tara which had become the ground of battle lay fallow that year; though we worked long and hard to put them right, we could not plough them. The retreating Scálda killed the cattle and ruined the wells and wreaked every manner of destruction they could devise in every settlement that lay in their path on their flight to the sea or to the south. They poisoned pools and streams out of spite. I do believe the retreat was more devastating than the assault.

Folk made homeless when the wicked Scálda passed through and set fire to their farms came seeking refuge at Tara though we had little enough aid to give. Food ran short, dangerously so. Toward the end we lived on scavengings and whatever the hunters could bring in; but a buck or pig, a few birds snared, or a creel of fish from the lough or stream does not feed an entire tribe. And though we had stored what we could and others brought what they had saved or pulled from the flames, hunger became the unwanted guest at every meal. Parents grew gaunt and their young ones wasted away before our eyes.

Weakened by hunger and cold, or by the wounds they received from battle, many perished. We shared what we had and watched kinsmen and loved ones pass away. And now I say it: little Ciara died that winter. Food grew scarce. Everyone was hungry. I starved. We all did. My milk dried up and that precious tiny life could take no other nourishment. My baby, my child, grew sickly and died one night when fever took her. I held her in my arms as she breathed her last and saw the light of life go out of her eyes.

The bitter agony of it is raw even now. Two seasons have passed, and I ache with my baby's absence. I still feel her warm infant body in my empty arms, and each new day dawns afresh with the knowing that she is not here. She will never be here.

Winter waned. Imbolc came and so did Eamon, dear Eamon—sent ahead of the returning warhost with the news that the enemy was at long last banished from our shores. The chariots were broken on the rocks, or mired in bogs, or otherwise lost and abandoned. The Scálda had been rooted out, like rabid badgers they had been pulled from their strong-holds and settlements and either put down or disarmed and made captive. The Scálda remnant—the widows and children, the old men and women, the sick and injured—had been rounded up and herded onto the Black Ships and sent away. Their detestable fortresses, farms, and settlements had been put to the torch, their cattle, grain, and supplies confiscated to be portioned out and distributed to our own needy folk—though many, I reckon, would choke on the stuff if they knew where the gatherers had got it.

Only then did we count our victory complete.

One bleak, rain-rinsed day not long after, a delegation of nobles and battlechiefs arrived at Tara Hill with a petition sent by the conquering lords requesting that Conor honour their request and take the high king's throne. He has agreed. So now, at Lughnasadh, Rónán and Chief Brehon Eoghan will come to perform the necessary rites to deliver the Sword of Sovereignty into Conor's hand. No man alive deserves it more than my Conor, and that is the honest truth.

With the spring comes new hope. As soon as weather allowed, the farmers returned to the land to begin rebuilding their farms. Somehow—I know not how—the fields were planted, lambs and piglets were born, and the yearned-for peace bloomed with the flowers on Tara Plain where the blood of warriors had lately flowed. Slowly, slowly, warmth has settled over the island and slowly, slowly, the torment of the long Scálda night-mare is yielding to the thought that we might make of Eirlandia a better place than it has ever been before—a land where the druids are esteemed and respected for their wisdom and learning, and where the faéry can flourish in their own way without fear of mortals, where kings rule in friendship. We were always a people with a past; now we are also a people with a future.

Bards tell of a realm untouched by hardship, grief, or woe, and of a good beyond every imagining. The Kingdom of All Tomorrows they call it. I may be wrong, but I like to think my little Ciara has found her way to that place and is waiting for me there.

36

'Will it be finished in time?' called Conor across the yard as he stood, leaning on Pelydr. The polished blade of the faéry spear gleamed like a shaft of fire in the noonday sun of a cold, bright day. Rónán, tall and straight in his grey druid robe, stood with Conla, the master builder, and his assistant as they discussed the work yet to be done. Nearby, workmen led horses pulling turf-laden wagons up the hill and into the yard. At Conor's call, Rónán glanced over his shoulder, saw his brother, and, with a nod and a half smile, waved him over to join them.

'Well?' said Conor again when proper greetings had been exchanged. 'Will it be finished in time?'

'And is this not the very thing we are talking about?' said Rónán. 'We have every expectation that work will be finished in time. The funeral ceremony will take place as planned . . .' His voice trailed off and he flicked a look at the builder, who was frowning.

'If?' said Conor. 'Was I about hearing an *if* forming on your tongue, brother?'

'Ach, well, the tomb will be finished *if* the carving can be completed for the entrance,' said Rónán, nodding to Conla.

'Aye, as soon as the carvers finish the pillar stone, we'll see it planted,' added Conla. 'The last of the turves are going up top now and that'll be finished by nightfall tomorrow latest.'

'And there's limewash to be applied,' Rónán said.

'There's that, so there is,' agreed Conla.

Leaving them to their discussion, Conor continued on to where the stone carvers had set up beneath a simple shelter behind the cookhouse. Nothing more than a roof of thatch atop four slender pine poles, the work-space housed three carvers, hard at work; the incessant tap, tap, tapping of their mallets could be heard from across the yard. At the Lord of Tara's ap-pearance, all three downed tools and stood. 'Don't let me stop you,' Conor told them. 'I'm only here to see if you require anything to speed your work to its completion.'

Credne, the craftsman overseeing the carving, shook stone dust from his leather apron and gestured toward the stone beside him, 'Nearly done, lord, as you see,' he replied. 'There is only touching up left to do.'

'Touching up?' wondered Conor.

'Aye, we're just chasing the patterns with the fine point now,' explained the carver. 'See here . . .'

He motioned Conor to the massive stone standing upright in a wooden cradle: tall as a man and twice as wide, and smooth as a river pebble, the flat, honey-coloured surface had been grooved with a dizzying series of swirling maze patterns connected with such cunning there was no way to tell where one ended and the next began. On the narrower sides, a line of ogham script had been carved bearing the name of the king in whose reign the stone had been erected, and under whose inspection it now stood.

Conor stood admiring the work as Credne ran his fingers over the grooves, feeling for places left to chase and smooth. 'What do you think?'

'I think it is . . .' Conor hesitated, choosing the right word and settling on '. . . magnificent.' He turned a wide, satisfied grin to the other two carv-ers, who were watching his reaction with somewhat nervous interest. He moved on to the second stone: a smaller, oblong rock that would sit directly at the entrance to the tomb. This one was patterned with circles, sun disks, water symbols, and interlocking spirals indicating the eternal cycle of birth, death, and rebirth.

As the chief carver had done, Conor reached out and traced the patterned grooves, feeling the strength and permanence of the worked surface. 'Well done, everyone,' he declared, pressing his palm flat against the stone. 'Well done.' Turning once more to the chief carver: 'Now then, Samhain is soon upon us. What help will you need to put these stones in place?'

Credne stroked his jaw with the end of the mallet for a moment and said, 'Ach, well, I expect we'll be needing about as many fellas as it took to haul the stones up here the first time.'

'So, most of the fianna, then,' said Conor. 'Consider it done.'

'And some horses would not be standing idle the while,' added the master carver.

'The fianna and as many horses as you need. Anything else?'

'Just the holes, then.' At Conor's raised eyebrow, Credne quickly explained, 'For the planting of the stones, you know.'

'Ach, of course. Leave it with me. Is that all?' Upon receiving assurance that digging and lining the foundation pits would speed the work to completion, Conor commended the carvers to their work and went to find Dearg or Donal, who could assemble a work crew to ready the foundations for the erection of the commemoration stones—going well out of his way to pass the tomb site one more time and examine yet again the state of the work as construction entered its final stage.

Three years in the planning, gathering, digging, and raising, the new tomb atop Tara Hill was to be the culmination of Conor's inauguration as high king: topping a nearby hill, a grand construction comprised of an enormous hollow mound with seven large chambers separated one from another by slabs of stone and linked by a central passageway. The entrance to the tomb was carefully oriented to the east so that sun rising on the first day of spring would shine through the doorway and illuminate the tomb and chambers within. Tall as a standing man, each chamber contained dozens of shelves, nooks, and alcoves built into the fabric of the walls, and the structure had been roofed with massive slabs of cut stone. Then, as the third year came to a close, earth dug from the riverbanks round about had been carted up the hill and the entire structure laboriously covered with dirt, tamped, smoothed, and turfed with fresh green grass. Inside the tomb would be placed the sun-bleached bones of all those who had died defending Eirlandia as well as those who had perished through the tribulation of suffering that followed.

Conor paused to watch the workers haul up the last loads of turf used to create the smoothly rounded artificial hill that rose like a green half-moon from the hilltop. It was an impressive structure and, not for the first time, Conor's heart swelled with pride. For, in the graceful mound of stone and turf, he saw a suitably majestic tribute to the unquenchable valor of the

Dé Danann in their staunch defiance of the Scálda invasion begun nearly twenty years ago. *We fought the battles thrust upon us,* thought Conor. *We did not always win, but we did not give up. We did not surrender, and in the end we prevailed.* There was honour in that.

One of the labourers saw Conor and put down his turves, causing the others to stop as well. Realising his presence was creating an unnecessary interruption, Conor lifted his hand in a wave of acknowledgement and continued on his way.

Four days later, the sun rose on a raw and rainy morning, and Conor fretted that the evening's ceremony would be a dull, wet affair. 'We'll just build the fire that much higher,' Aoife told him. 'Worry instead that we will run out of mead.' At Conor's stricken expression, she laughed and said, 'Worry about that and you'll worry in vain, my heart. If the mead vat runs dry we will drink ale instead. Never fear.'

During the day, the bones of the deceased—washed, anointed, and carefully bundled in shrouds made from their own siarcs and cloaks—had been transported to the tomb and arranged in a double row to form a long aisle leading to the central pillar stone, which had been erected in front of the tomb the day before.

As the sun dipped below the horizon in the west, the drizzle ceased and the wind fell away, leaving a rapidly clearing sky decked with a scattering of orange and crimson clouds, and the first evening stars took light. An ovate sounded a long, low, blaring note on the carnyx, summoning Tara's folk and visitors—lords Cahir, Toráin, Corgan, Aengus, Torna, and Liam, and other noblemen and warriors—to follow the rain-damp path to the tomb. Once there, they assembled along either side of the avenue of bone shrouds and stood in solemn witness as Rónán supervised the interment. One by one, ovates carried the shrouded bundles to the waiting hands of three ollamhs, who distributed them among the various chambers inside the tomb. Added to the remains of the defenders were the bones of those who had perished in the aftermath of the war. The smallest of these bundles were the bones of infants and children who could not endure the privations of the following winter and had not survived. Last to be entombed was the bone shroud belonging to little Ciara.

The tiny bundle disappeared into the low square of darkness that was the tomb's doorway, and Aoife stifled a cry and buried her face in Conor's

274 * Stephen R. Lawhead

sleeve; he put a comforting arm around her shoulder and pulled her close. The moment passed. Aoife straightened, dabbed at her eyes, and then smoothed her hands over the bump of her belly that had just begun to show.

When the last bundle had been entombed, the ollamh and ovates formed a line in front of the mound and turned to face the crowd. Rónán took his place before the pillar stone and, in a loud voice, cried, 'People of Tara! Now is the propitious time! It is the time-between-times when the veil between this world and the next grows thin, when spirits may freely pass between realms without hindrance.'

One ovate appeared with an oaken bucket, and another bearing a branch of holly. Raising a fold of his cloak, Rónán covered his head and, taking the holly, dipped it into the bucket containing water in which mistletoe had been boiled and steeped for thirty days and nights. To the crowd of onlookers, he said, 'With this water, I sain this tomb. It shall forever be sacred to the memory of those interred within.'

Turning to the tall pillar stone, Rónán shook the dripping holly branch at the stone, scattering drops of holy water over it. This he did three times and then moved on to the smaller, oblong stone established at the entrance to the tomb, where he dipped the holly sprig again, and shook it three times. Wetting the branch a final time, he shook sacred water on the post and lintels of the tomb's low doorway. Then, putting aside the holly and bucket, Rónán removed the fold of cloth and, raising his hands shoulder high with palms outward, he called in a loud voice that would echo and reverberate across Tara Hill and down through the years:

'In the dying of the day, the night is born, and night's last embers are extinguished in the flames of a new morning. So it is for these, our friends of heart and hearth, who closed their eyes on this world and woke in a world warmed by a different sun. That the Dé Danann triumphed in the Scálda War, they will surely know. Aye, from their high place they will look upon us and they will see an Eirlandia much changed because of their sacrifice and that of so many others who, like themselves, perished in the long struggle to wrest the land of our birth from the cruel oppression of the invader. And I tell you that though they may not share in the victory they helped to win, they will rejoice in it and they will be glad.

'From this day to the end of days, let all who come after celebrate their memory with food and drink and laughter, and with stories and songs of their valor, remembering also the work of their hands, the dear ones they held close to their hearts, the children they bore and raised, their grievous mistakes and righteous judgements, their sorrows and the small things of life that gave them joy. Though they no longer walk the Land of the Living, they will be remembered by those of us who knew them because it was for us that they lived, and it was for us that they died.

'In the same way, we will remember those who have fallen to hunger, whose bodies were weakened by want, whose injuries could not be healed. Also, we will remember those who perished through illness or age because it was their time—they are part of this story, too. May all of these who were known to us in life, remain alive forever in our hearts.

'One day, each of us here will find a resting place in this great tomb. Here we will lie with our brothers and sisters, our mothers and fathers, our neighbours and friends. As we mourn today, so we will be mourned in the day of our passing by those who loved us. We do not know when that day will arrive, so in the time that is left to us, may we who mark this day live lives worthy of remembrance.'

* * *

When the ceremony had ended, everyone moved on to the hall and yard to celebrate Samhain with ale and cakes; roast pork and venison; bread sweetened with walnuts, dried berries, and honey; and cups, bowls, jars, and horns full of rich, heady mead. But Conor still lingered within the sacred precinct of the new tomb, watching as evening deepened around him and peace settled over the hills and plains.

He saw a dull, flickering reflection on the pillar stone and a moment later, Fergal and Donal were there beside him. 'They are asking for you,' Donal announced.

'They don't want you to miss the feast,' added Fergal, 'and the mead horn has already passed you by—twice.'

'It is a fine thing, is it not?' said Conor, gazing at the gentle curve of the mound against the darkening sky.

'It is that,' said Donal. 'A fine and handsome thing.'

Fergal clapped him on the back. 'You have done well, brother, building this. Your father would be proud of you.'

'I didn't do this for him, or for me,' Conor said, 'but for *all* of us— that we should be remembered—as Rónán has said.' Extending his hand toward the monument, now lit by the glow of torchlight, he added, 'When Tara's hall is dust, and Eirlandia herself but a distant memory, this tomb and these stones will remain to remind the world that the Dé Danann passed this way.'

EPILOGUE

From the
Eirlandia Poetica

OF PATRICK, AT TARA

Patrick, best beloved of Ireland, decided to spend Lughnasadh on Tara Hill, also called Cnoc na Teamhair, to bless that hill and dedicate it to the Lord of Hosts. So, on the eve of the celebration, Patrick, along with his priests and attendants, three princes and their servants, arrived to begin chanting psalms and blessings. But as the servants set about making camp in the shadow of the Tomb of the Kings, the sainted one became much troubled.

'There is little rest in this earth,' declared Patrick. 'This hill and its plains have been awash too much with the blood of warriors, the gore of invaders, and ichor from offerings made to the old gods of Ireland.'

'What shall we do?' asked his priests. 'If prayer and psalm cannot shift these old ones, then what can be done?'

'I'm thinking we must listen to them,' replied Patrick in all mildness.

'Forbid it, lord! We will never appease or honour these false deities,' answered the priests and princes. 'Better that all should die and vanish from this island than that we should ever slip back into that deadly ignorance and suffocating darkness.'

'I tell you most truly, brothers, there will be no silencing these restless spirits until they have had their say,' declared Patrick, Pillar of God. 'Therefore, all of you bear witness to what you shall now hear from my lips, and mark that I shall make no blasphemy, nor profane the name of the True God which we and all peoples who live in light worship:

'Whose name is Love
And whose path is Love
And whose passing on the path
'Brings light to all in darkness,
Brings peace to all in strife,
Brings life to all who will receive it,
'Sight to the blind,
Healing to the lame,
Hearing to the deaf, and
Speech to the dumb.

'Amen.'

So saying, Patrick pulled his cloak over his face and lowered his head. When he spoke, he spoke with many voices not his own, voices from the past. 'Hear first,' he said, 'the voice of your True Father, he who created this much-favoured land:'

OF THE TRUE GOD, THE GOD WHO IS ONE,
THE CREATOR OF IRELAND AND
ALL THE REALMS AND WORLDS WE KNOW

'I alone formed you;
I raised you from the sea;
I spread grass upon the rocks
So that cattle and sheep may live on it,
And you on them.
You knew me in that time, as I knew you.
'Nameless, I was, yet you called on me.

Blind, you were, yet you felt me.
Hearts wanting nothing, being filled,
We slept alongside one another,
Even as in the morning we awoke separately.
'I loved you from that time.

While you lived I called you mine,
And when you died I brought you into

The Land of Promise where warm, sweet waters flow,
And where mead and wine are plenty.
All who dwell there are stately and beautiful,
Thought without sin, desire without lust,
Love without care, world without end.
'And on the day that you left me,

I yearned for you as a new bride yearns for her
Husband who leaves her in the day.
You left for another, and I longed for you.
I stood waiting at Tara, Sacred Hill, watching patiently
For you to come back to me, with my eyes fixed
On the distant fields and forests, searching for you,
Preparing for that glad day of your return.'

When he had said this, Patrick came to himself once more and looked around as one awakening from sleep. As night was fast upon them, the attendants built a fire and made camp. While the servants cooked a meal, Patrick again pulled his cloak over his face and began to speak. He said, 'Hear the voice of one beyond memory:'

OF THE FORGOTTEN GOD OF IRELAND, THE FEARED GOD

'Children of Noah, Cessair, and Partholón! Far-travelled! Flood exiles! You took me with you from my hilltop in the east, carried me with you to escape the rains, and then set me upon Tara.

'You did not want a loving god, and I was not one to you. You wanted a god of security, a god of order against the chaos of the world as it was then. I commanded sacrifice and you gave it to me willingly. I said: "This man's death will appease me, for he is my enemy and also yours." You listened and you obeyed. You killed him and gave me his blood as a sign.

'I said: "This land is mine, keep it pure, keep everyone away who does not speak my name. Put all foreigners to death lest they tempt you to other gods."

'I said: "Give me priests so that you may be more obedient to me."

'I said: "Let my priests rule over you."

'I said: "Give me blood. Give me obedience. Give me fear."

'And you did all these things—above all, fear. You learned to fear me so well. You feared me unto the death of your enemies, feared unto the death of your neighbours, feared unto the death of your wives. Then, you looked at your children and said to yourselves, "This one wears my face, but is not as I am. I fear and he does not. I watch my steps in public, and she is careless. I sit quietly in the hall, and they laugh with their friends. These children of ours care little for the god we brought from the east. I fear their fearlessness and their arrogance."

'And so you killed your children, although I did not ask it of you. Fear replaced me and you forgot my name, and now the island has all but forgotten yours, and your fear shall follow the last of you into the tomb.'

* * *

Even as this last voice finished, another began:

OF THE FIRST FAIR GOD OF CESSAIR, THE FAIREST OF BOTH GODS

'I lay beneath Tara Hill, a lover awaiting the beloved.
My hair is the matted peat, my eyelids are the daisies.
A pile of stones pillows my head, the grass my bedsheet.
Two crows are my eyes—with open beaks they caw loudly.
Hobgoblins dance a jig at my temple, round and around.
When young women seek me at night, I woo them.
When a lord approaches through the woods, I flee him.
Though he begs my embrace, I wag my head and turn away.
Come to seek your fortune inside me, I will not open.
I am an egg uncracked, a sealed cask, a tale untold.
Hunters ride past and I spin them around,
I send them home hungry and wanting.
But lay with me without demand or expectation, and
I shall give young dreams to the old,
And old dreams to the young.
I will lure with honey the groom from his bride,
I shall touch soft harp-strings and finger little bells.
Let any who will sleep unbroken with me,

One night or ten thousand.
Let them awake to wondrous sights,
Or not at all.'

OF THE SECOND FAIR GOD OF NEMEDIANS,
WHO IS FAIRER THAN THE FIRST

'Switch the babies, and stop the mother's milk.
Bewitch the rafters and harden the cheese.
Throw darts at the cows to make them kick out.
Sell young pretty maidens to rich old lords, and
Lock them up in high towers of pearl.
Visit the old men in their hills of wood,
Lay grass on their eyes, and moss at their ears.

'Come, my children, pull my arms around you,
Let us dance a merry dance through the woods.
Lead them a goosewild chase through the forest
Let the soles of their shoes be worn right through,
And the skin of their feet cut to crimson ribbons.
We will dance in the day and in the night,
Today and all the todays of tomorrow.'

Patrick was silent a long while after this. He sat before the fire with his priests and princes around him, and just when they thought he must have fallen asleep, he said, 'The gods of the Tuatha Dé Danann speak on Tara. Hear me, the All-Mother, I, too, have something to say:'

OF THE GODS OF THE TUATHA DÉ DANANN

DANU, THE ALL-MOTHER, SPEAKS:
'In the evil day, I will raise up a king at Tara
A king from a line of kings,
An outcast, a rejected heir,
Unclean by my decree, but made righteous
By my command.

'He will set his foot upon the stone
He will set his face to the East
And a black tide will ebb at his outstretched arm.

'My king will be called "The Death of the Formoire,"
And he will cast my spear at the face of Balor,
Evil-Eyed One, and shatter his visage.
'My beloved children shall walk beneath the shield
And banner of Conor mac Ardan,
And they will be called golden as the dawn
And fierce as the night-dark storm.

'They shall robe themselves in twilight,
Taking flight on the freshening wind,
Dancing on the waves.'

BADB THE CARRION GODDESS OF WAR
AND QUEEN OF THE SHADOW WORLD, SPEAKS:
'See, the crows flock from every sky to darken the
Earth of Tara. From their eyes a fall of
Blood, like rain scattered from the gods of the crowded
Skies. But no thing will grow.
The cauldron of plenty shall be broken.
A black field will spread out to the glory of
Nothing and no one, but my own,
On Tara.

'See, the clouds turn in the sky, the
Earth reels, clothed in the
Blood of futile hands. The empty
Skies look down upon a field of
Broken spears and shivered shields, with
Nothing left to answer,
On Tara.

'See, the destruction of the
Earth, a price paid in

Blood. The lorn
Skies weep over the lost. Let
Nothing stand
On Tara.

'See, the
Earth's
Blood.
Skies
Broken for
Nothing,
On Tara.
'See blood,
Broken Tara.
'See, Tara.'

CROM, THE GOD WHO SITS IN DARKNESS, SPEAKS:
'Tell me:
How long are victors victorious?
Summer will one day be without blossom.
And then cattle shall not give milk,
Nor eat at the green slopes of fair Tara.

'Women will walk without modesty,
Men without honour will stand
Their godless feet on Tara
And, kingless, will conquer.

'The woods will not give lumber,
The sea will not give fish,
The ground shall be used up,
And dust fill the farmer's hands.

'False judgements of old men will be bought,
False precedents of law-speakers will be set,
Every man will be a betrayer and speak no truth.
Every son will be a pillager.

'In that time Ireland will be unmade,
And I shall depart, and all valour with me.
Dark, my name; darker still my destination.
We shall sleep in the hills
Until woken.'

The night drew on and many of the priests and attendants wrapped themselves in their cloaks and fell asleep. Those few stalwart companions who remained awake heard him speak again, in a voice that sounded as if it came a great distance from across the sea:

OF THE GODLESS MILESIANS
WHO HOLD THEMSELVES EQUAL TO THE GODS

'We broke the stones at Tara because we were troubled by the dark memories they held. Wandering for so long, we brought no gods with us—the unblessed peoples, we came to a land that was built by the gods for themselves.

'Yet those who dwelt here did not honour the land they had found. Nor did they honour themselves, or prize their own worth. They had fallen far, knowing nothing of their past and not caring for their future, they remained prideful of their ignorance.

'Beautiful of face and straight of back, they devised arts that will long outlive their time, yet the people do not prosper on the land. Dignity without heart, life without passion, breath without air, they are passing. They are as ghosts. Witness them, as they make their final parade:

'White shields borne in light hands,
Traced with moonlit silver design;
Blue swords encrusted with stars,
And tall horns yawning overhead.

'A glorious assembly, a night-river on the march,
Pounding soft drums and sounding low bells.
Their silver spears rise as a forest among them,
Pale-faced and fair peoples of the grey night.

'Battalions scatter before this sight,
Like a well-honed sword they pierce the foe.
In carried starlight they march to combat,
A relentless avenging host!

'Sons of queens and kings are one and all;
Each, of noble birth, wear golden-yellow locks
And torcs of silver and gold.
A hero's feat has each one performed
No wonder that their renown be wide.

'Smooth and comely of body,
Bright, blue-starred eyes,
Pure, white crystalline teeth,
High noble foreheads,
And thin, wine-red lips.

'They are as skilled at man-slaying as singing,
Melodious in the ale-house,
They compose long ballads,
Masterly epics of their wars.

'Each trill is a war cry,
Every plucked note is a crushing blow . . .
Yet their song will end,
For they have forgotten Tara.'

AGAIN, OF PATRICK, AT TARA

When Patrick had spoken all these things, he slept. Some while later, as the sun was coming up, he took his cloak from over his face, and his attendants brought him food and drink to break his fast. The priests and princes gathered around to hear what he had to say, for they were still greatly puzzled and not a little concerned by what they had heard during that long, strange night. Patrick sipped his ale and ate his barley cake until he felt his strength returning. When he finished, he stood and took up his priestly staff, and turned to gaze upon the Tomb of the Kings.

'Witness,' he cried, 'that though I have spoken with tongues not my own, yet I have uttered no untrue thing. So shall we build our church in this land. And as we make those holy places, let the names of the gods be remembered hereafter as an ogham script on a stone is remembered— merely a sign that a fellow traveller passed this way before, but has long since moved on.

'Their path is not our path and even if we have joined it for a time, it must divide again. Those who moved along that road did not know how to get to where we shall all arrive at, but we pray that one day their wandering will finally cease and they will find peace.

'May it be that all who walk in darkness see a far-off light on a distant hill. Let them approach that gleaming city and be welcomed by those happy folk living there. And in that fair place, may those weary travellers eat and drink and find the rest and contentment that they never did find all the days they wandered.

'And in that moment, may they know that they are home and find peace everlasting in the Kingdom of All Tomorrows.

'*In nomine Patris et Filii et Spiritus Sancti.*

'*Amen.*'